MW00882920

God Bless!

OATH
KEEPER

by

Daryl E.J. Simmons

Copyright © 2016, 2022 by Daryl E.J. Simmons

All rights reserved. This book or any portion thereof may not be reproduced, distributed, or transmitted by any means, including photocopying, recording, or other electronic or mechanical methods, without the prior written permission of the publisher except for the case brief quotations embodied in critical reviews and certain other noncommercial uses permitted by copyright law. For permission requests, write to the author at the address below.

Thinkery Group, LLC
5265 W. Rogers BLVD, STE A #123
Skiatook, OK 74070

Printed in the United States of America

Second Edition, 2022; First Edition, 2016

ISBN: 978-1537687407

Cover images taken from the public domain. Layout, and design Copyright 2016 by Daryl E.J. Simmons

Second edition edited by Heather Nuttall Westover
First edition edited by A.E. Mayes

Author photograph by Project46 Media.

The story and all names, characters, and incidents portrayed therein are fictitious. No identification with actual persons, places, buildings, programs, or products is intended or should be inferred. Any similarity or resemblance between the contents of this story and any locations, events, objects, or persons - living or dead - is purely coincidental.

This story is a work of fiction created purely for the purpose of entertainment. It is entirely contrived by the author's imagination, with absolutely no involvement of the United States Government, its officers, offices, or subsidiaries. In accordance with the Information Security Oversight Office, Executive Order 13292, 13526, 13556, 13587, *ad nauseam*, as well as any and all applicable Department of Defense directives and instructions, no privileged or classified material is contained herein, nor was used in the creation of this story. This story is not authorized or endorsed by the United States Government, any of its branches, divisions, or subsidiaries. Any similarity between any portion of this story and any real government activities, offices, or programs is purely coincidental, and not based on any forethought, foresight, or foreknowledge the author may or may not possess.

DEDICATION

First, foremost, and always: I thank Jesus Christ my Savior, who carried me through the valley of the shadow of death. Several times.

This book - every word, every letter - is dedicated to the brave men and women, past and present, who serve our country in uniform: my brothers and sisters in the military and law enforcement. We are the one-half of one percent. Nobody who hasn't been where we have can truly understand what it feels like to sacrifice your time, your livelihood, your family, or the promise of a future in order to secure the blessings of Liberty for millions of strangers. Remember that the promise we made had a purpose. Stay strong for each other. We are the real Americans.

My heartfelt thanks and love to my wife - who still stands by my side and tries to understand me long after everyone else quits.

I would be remiss if I did not take this time to thank my various writing teachers over the years. Or blame them, depending on how this whole thing turns out. To Leeman Loftis, my 8th grade English teacher, whose simple words to me decades ago - "Remember: writers write…" - still echo in my ears every time I sit at a keyboard. To Amy Pezzelle, whose confidence in me as a writer gave me the boldness to undertake this endeavor. To Laura Stevens, who cut me absolutely no slack. Thank you all.

To A.E. Mayes for your friendship and mentorship. And to Heather Nuttall Westover for your attention.

And finally, my most sincere thanks to every one of my readers. This work is not for my vanity. It is for your entertainment. I hope that I have written something that you will read on purpose.

PROLOGUE

THAT NIGHT'S JOHN was a regular, and he always paid extra for his privacy. For her share of five thousand dollars cash Krystal was always happy to oblige.

The bed frame knocked against the wall repeatedly in their softly lit upstairs room. Krystal squealed and moaned in her husky, dark voice as an older white man panted atop her. Back when this old cowboy was her age the idea of a white gentleman from a proper Louisiana family engaged in the mattress rodeo with a black woman was taboo all by itself - never mind the particulars in play this evening, such as the difference in their ages, his marital status, or how he had her handcuffed to the headboard. This was the kind of action a respectable, Southern gentleman just could not get from a proper, ladylike wife. Sometimes a man like this needed angry sex. Dirty sex. The kind that excited young adults and raised scandal in polite society.

The mixed duo continued their bawdy brawl, unaware of the walker as he carefully placed the ball of his foot first, then transferred the weight slowly and pulled himself down the hallway like a jungle cat stalking his prey. The couple's screams and pants were so loud that neither noticed when the door into the room - directly behind them - silently opened. There was no reflective surface, no mirror or picture to fall off the wall above the head of the bed, to divert their attention and reveal a man dressed in airbrushed camouflage fatigues when he slid into the room like a shadow and silently re-closed the door.

The shadow carefully wedged his soft, well-broken, tan right boot against the bottom of the door. It would hold tight against any potential interruptions. Not that there was anyone else around to intrude upon tonight's business. He had already made sure of that before he crept into the house. It was just a habit, as natural to him as it was to hold his firearm in close at the low ready position to minimize his profile while transiting a doorway.

His eyes dart purposefully from the couple to the window, then the couple, the closet, the couple again, the bathroom door, then once more the couple as he shouldered a carbine with a home-machined suppressor at the bed. For tonight's work he chose a Kel-Tec Sub2000. It was plenty of gun for close-in work, packed discreetly into his backpack during transit, and used the same 9mm magazines as the Glock 17 holstered on his leg. Utility breeds efficiency, the old adage went. Without warning, the green shadow double-tapped the carnal Oreo before him. Both rounds struck the white-haired man from behind in a half second. Twin pops sounded in the room. Unlike the movies, in the real world suppressed gunfire was not truly silent. The older man screamed in pain as the paired shots ripped into the flesh just to the left of the spine and below the shoulder blade. Arterial blood burst from the older man's aorta and spurted from the double wound in his pasty back in crimson plumes.

The whore screamed as her gentleman caller fell into the bed next to her, bleeding profusely. Wordlessly, the shooter delivered a lengthy barrage into his target, perforating the man's torso with dozens of projectiles. Crimson explosions erupted from the dying man's body with each shot fired, accompanied by a staccato sound like an old-fashioned typewriter as the carbine rapidly cycled. The bed's white, striped sheets were redecorated with a dark red confetti pattern. Krystal's mocha skin was streaked with splattered gore.

The gunfire stopped for a moment, but Krystal's screams continued. The killer stood at the door with his gun held in front of his masked face. He ejected the Kel-Tec's 33-round magazine, swapped it for a new one, and stuffed the spent accessory back into place on his hip. A textbook tactical reload. Then, he reached into a hook-and-loop pocket on his green/grey/tan shirt jacket with his gloved left hand, pulled out a folded piece of paper, and casually tossed it. The crisp white square spun through the air and tumbled lazily like a leaf until it landed on the floor next to the bed in an expanding pool of blood. The sticky red puddle grew as it was fed from the target like a hot spring. The old man's blood seeped into the paper, transforming it from snow white into scarlet.

For just a moment the killer stayed next to the

door. He took careful aim once more, unaffected by the hysterical whore screaming on the bed in front of him, and slowly fired three more rounds, all into the back of the old man's head. Each impact punched through the skull from behind, spraying a bright mixture of blood, bone, brain matter, and feathers all over the bedding, head rails and wall.

Krystal's horror spiraled into shock. Her screams died down to an unending, unintelligible whine cried into the now-spotted pillow under her face. Ass up, clothed in nothing but lingerie pulled around her middle, she struggled against her handcuffs in a futile effort. But she was trapped. Completely defenseless. Tears blinded her eyes and burned the pillow, but they did nothing to obscure a lifetime of regrets and bad decisions that flashed before her mind.

Satisfied with his own handiwork, the killer hesitated in thought mid-turn toward the door. During the pause he retrieved the dead man's pants - draped across the back of a chair beside the door - and procured the John's wallet, car keys and a money clip stuffed with green bills. He threw the door open again, quickly scanned for any response, then briskly exited the room.

Choking back another tear, Krystal sniffed. She craned her head, twisted her neck. "Hey!" she called out. Nobody responded. "Hey! Help! Somebody help me. Please!" Her screams were met with nothing but empty silence. "Hey! Somebody get me the hell outta here! Hey!" Krystal's fear transformed into rage. "Hey, motherf-!" She yanked angrily against her bonds, which still held her tight to the bed. "Get me out of here!" Her attention returned once more to the bleeding corpse lying next to her on the bed. Her voice found a new level of urgency. "Get! Me! Out! Of! HEEEERE!"

Amid the clanging of stainless steel against cast iron, Krystal heard the soft crunch of gravel outside, compressed under the assassin's boots as he walked. She looked through the window past the dead John and saw glowing red taillights exit the Chambre Rouge's gravel drive from the rear parking lot. Krystal let loose another protracted scream, but the red taillights just faded and disappeared into the night.

CHAPTER 1

"IN CONCLUSION," Special Agent Daniel Wakefield's eyes scanned the room as he ended his brief, "the evidence clearly indicates that Abdullah al-Masud is part of a network of Sunni business owners who also operate as a front for money laundering operations in support of Islamist cells both here in the US as well as abroad. We think al-Masud is funneling money from overseas to fund future acts of terrorism or subversion here in the States." His attention returned to the oldest, and most senior, man in the briefing room. "Pending your questions, sir, that concludes my brief."

The older man's disheveled hair, herringbone sport coat and beyond-ironing collar stood in stark contrast with Danny's crisp, clean appearance. Of course, seniority had its privileges, and the Jesuit educated department head had long ago earned the right to a little dated eccentricity with regards to personal appearance. His mouth, rounded a bit by age, worked as if chewing on his thoughts as though they were a bite of steak. "When I gave you this case two weeks ago, it was to investigate a report from a fraud analyst at Bank of New York that indicated al-Masud had some sort of cash-only revenue line that he was trying to hide, possibly for tax evasion purposes."

"Yes sir," Danny answered.

"And he claims he's just passing dowries between families. That this whole thing is a big misunderstanding," the man - Dr. Jonas Wiley, head of the Analysis Division at the United States Secret Service Headquarters in Washington, D.C. - continued.

"Yes, sir. His story is that he uses revenue from his ghost accounts as a *hawala* for other Sunni families."

The *hawala* was a staple of Arabic society dating back centuries. Ancient Beduin traders used the transfer houses when they moved goods from one city to the next. It relieved them of the liability of carrying currency. Everyone in the intelligence community - certainly everyone in the Secret Service Analysis Division - was presumably well versed in the tradition. Wakefield looked around the room and decided that in some of his colleagues' case, he would not bet on it.

Seated next to Wiley, Nick Brown piped in. "These other families… I presume they used the al-Masud *hawala* for things like *mahr* and such?"

Brown never passed up on an opportunity to look smarter than he really was. Back in his day he had been an enlisted cryptologist. Now he was a retired Navy man complete with his stained Chief Petty Officer's coffee mug and beer belly. For all his faults - and Danny knew them to be many - Brown was at least marginally savvy to Arabic customs and culture. Not as much as Danny was, and certainly not even close to the most familiar in the office. But perpetual conflict in the Middle East required Nick - whose office nickname was Nick the Dick - to be familiar with the culture. He knew as well as Danny, Jonas, and the real heavy hitters in their niched community, that Muslim tradition included a practice known as *mahr*, or the "bride price." The sums of these dowries could range from hundreds to thousands of dollars, depending on the families involved.

Danny nodded in assent. Though he did not personally care for Nick, he forced himself daily to put those feelings aside and keep things professional in the workplace. "Yes. al-Masud's *hawala* allegedly handles everything from *mahr* to tuition payments for kids going to college here in the States."

"Doesn't '*masud*' mean '*lucky*' in Arabic?" Nick continued.

"Yes."

Nick chuckled. "'*Lucky's Bank.*' Something that corny sounding just might be legitimate."

"But you disagree." That from Wiley again. Jonas raised an eyebrow in challenge. "Lay it on me."

Danny reached back onto the speaking dais to his left and keyed a few commands into the lectern's computer. The first of his additional slides, hidden within his main presentation, appeared on the 96-inch screen behind him. An animated map zoomed outward from New York City and followed lines to various Middle Eastern, European, and North

African nations in full high definition. "al-Masud is Sunni, and the couriers and cash that we have been able to trace all lead us back to originators in Yemen, Syria, Saudi Arabia and at least one final payee in South Carolina, all of whom are either themselves known terrorists or directly linked to terrorism."

"How did you trace the money?" Nick again. *This*, Danny thought, *is where he starts actively trying to poke holes in my case.* It was nothing personal. Everyone in the intelligence community learned along the way that an assessment that could not withstand scrutiny was a worthless theory. Danny stood calmly next to the podium while Nick continued his question. "Last time I checked, the Treasury Department doesn't have the ability to identify people dropping off money at a hookah shop in Aden."

A former intel bubba should know better. "We don't," he conceded. "While I was in Buffalo checking this out, I got the names of some of his clients. I bounced them past my contacts at the NSA and JSOC. Some came back dirty."

Nick rubbed his hands across his face as if to physically muffle a comment before speaking. He took in a breath, looked down at his yellow notepad, and drummed a syncopated rhythm with his pen as he spoke. "The last time I checked," he preached in mounting frustration, "your badge said, 'Department of Homeland Security.' This is the Secret Service, Wakefield. Not the Marine Corps."

"Aren't we supposed to use every resource?" Danny cut him off. "Provide thorough, fused analysis? Foster interdepartmental cooperation?"

"You're supposed to maintain focus," Nick countered. This was not the first time he and

Wakefield had breached this particular topic. "Building relationships is all well and good, but solve problems internally. And stay on the mission. You were supposed to verify or rule out a charge of alleged tax evasion. You're not in the terrorist-hunting business anymore."

Danny's jaw set. A quick glance showed Wiley was still chewing on the information just placed before him. He digested the 15-minute brief like a three-course lunch. Jonas was the department head, and the fact that he had not shot Danny down yet was significant. It showed he felt Danny's theory held at least some merit. Then again, so did the fact that Jonas had let Nick give Danny this tongue-lashing in front of the rest of the division.

"Well," Jonas quipped after a moment, "at least you didn't shoot anyone this trip." Danny stood blankly, as still as a statue but without actually adopting the formal position of Attention. Months ago, an investigation into a money laundering operation by a drug cartel in Miami had gone horribly wrong. The climax, as far as most people were concerned, occurred when Wakefield was forced to shoot a 23-year-old Columbian cocaine runner who also happened to be the cartel leader's nephew. "I saw you wrote a full report on this. Is all of your data in it?"

"Yes, sir. Well, obviously not my contacts' identifiers." It was a common practice for investigators to withhold their sources. In fact, it was almost unheard of for a federal agent to divulge the identifying information of a contact, source, informant, or other such individual. And on the rare occasion that said individual was a member of the

Intelligence Community - complete with special accesses, privileges, tools and assignments - it was usually best to just pretend the contact did not exist.

"Right," Jonas nodded. A lifetime of federal service ago, Dr. Jonas Wiley, Ph.D. in International Relations and Director of Analysis for the United States Secret Service, had been Jonas Wiley, Captain, United States Naval Intelligence. He knew the way things worked better than anyone Danny Wakefield had ever met or probably ever would. "Okay, I dig it. Send everything on this to Fort Bragg, and copy DIA here in town. Let the guys at JSOC play with it for a while and see what they come up with."

In the modern age, the Secret Service held twin bosses. The Treasury Department provided tasking on all money crimes that fell within federal jurisdiction. But since fiscal year 2002 and the federal government's response to the 9/11 terrorist attacks, their ultimate overlord was the nebulous Department of Homeland Security - which, while responsible for counterterrorism Stateside, was notoriously bureaucratic and much less effective at stopping terrorist activity than the Department of Defense. Especially when that activity crossed national boundaries. Passing this case off to the Defense Intelligence Agency was Jonas' way of designating the situation as a terrorist threat while simultaneously acknowledging Brown's point about proper lane management and departmental priorities. If the all-wise powers-that-be chose to pursue al-Masud and his affiliates, that task would now fall into the capable hands of the Unites States Joint Special Operations Command.

"Sir," Daniel began to protest, "I've already done

most of the legwork on this one -"

"Lateral the ball," Jonas ordered. His mind was made up. Now, like a quarterback who had worked his team into scoring position, Wakefield was forced to hand this well-developed case off to someone else and watch them get all of the credit for finishing it.

"Yes, sir."

"Before you send that out, though," Jonas continued, "I need to see you offline in my office." Daniel nodded obediently. Wiley looked at the rest of the Special Agents, Agents, and Analysts sitting around the conference room's semi-square arrangement. "Anything else? No? Break." Dr. Wiley rapped his knuckles twice on the table as he stood, an archaic gesture carried over from academia which everyone else had learned meant they were dismissed.

Danny had not even turned fully back to the speaker's podium to log out of the computer before he heard Nick's voice calling across the conference room, purposefully loud enough for the rest of the department to hear. "Don't forget your Anger Management session at eleven, Wakefield…" Danny sighed, closed his eyes, and spread his fingers like an eagle's talons to simultaneously strike the Control, Alt and Delete buttons on the computer's keyboard.

*   *   *

Summer fell on the Louisiana bayou like a hot wet blanket, and while her coworkers insisted that no insect repellant known to man could keep all of the Louisiana bayou's mosquitoes away, Special Agent Sandra Elbee had sworn when she left the FBI Field Office in New Orleans that she would put that claim to the test.

As she strode across the muddy grass in her waterproof hiking boots, she pushed away her concerns about bug spray, bites, or hives and focused on the crime scene before her. Fourteen months at the New Orleans office had been fairly bland, with the usual mix of felony cases, most of which centered around narcotics. Elbee loved to work on narcotics cases. They were a particular area of fascination for her dating all the way back to her undergraduate days and carried with her when she left her native New Jersey. She had seen plenty of illicit drug use around her when she grew up, and now the investigation and prosecution of narcotics manufacturers, smugglers, dealers, and users fueled her career at the FBI.

Drugs were Special Agent Elbee's business and business was good. When modern Americans thought of New Orleans their minds were usually occupied by images of Mardi Gras and Hurricane Katrina. Most Americans forgot that the Big Easy was also one of the largest seaports in the world. Port of New Orleans handled the transshipment of millions of tons of cargo each year. Products from all over the world were offloaded in those muddy, brackish waters and funneled up the Mississippi or over land to consumers all across this great nation. Most of Elbee's working hours were spent trying to make sure those boats did not also deliver Colombian nose candy or heroine to the world's largest narcotics market.

When her boss handed Sandra the case file for a murder at a swamp brothel, she jumped in with open expectations. The Chambre Rouge was just outside of New Orleans proper. It had taken her longer to stop at her townhouse and change into field clothes than to actually drive to the little patch of swampland between Lake Verret and Duck Lake. But something about the buzz within the army of technicians and cadre of local law enforcement agents funneling into and out of the decrepit old two-story house was different than most of the narcotics cases she had worked, even the ones which had involved fatalities.

When she was three steps from the brothel's porch, just one quarter of the remaining distance from her car to the Chambre Rouge's entrance, a well-rounded Caucasian man in his early fifties abruptly broke off from whatever conversation he had been holding next to the front door, locked onto her and zeroed in at a surprisingly brisk wallow. The wooden porch creaked beneath his feet and his brown-on-tan uniform strained to contain his girth. He stopped on the bottom step, directly in Elbee's path.

"Obadiah Beahen," he announced with hands placed squarely on his cracked leather duty belt. "Sheriff," he clarified. Just in case Elbee could not read the word stenciled on every piece of clothing the portly man wore. He drew a loud, wet breath in through his porcine mouth. "You the agent from New Orleans ah asked for?"

"How'd you guess?" Elbee mocked. The blonde flashed a humorless smile and pointed up past her sunglasses. "It's the hat, isn't it?" Compared to Sheriff Beahen's penchant for departmental labeling, a navy-blue ball cap with FBI stenciled in four-inch white letters was just downright subtle. Sheriff Beahen could have taken the snarky remark worse. As bad as his day had apparently been, he barely managed an annoyed expression. Elbee adopted a more serious, professional tone, "Special Agent Sandra Elbee. My superiors told me you have a homicide." At such close proximity to the butterball, she could not point at the door directly without slapping the Sheriff's portly form. She could smell him basting in the swamp's summer heat but fought to maintain her professional composure. "Care to show me inside?"

Beahen's jowls jiggled as he nodded. He turned and waived her to follow him through the front door. Technicians moved out of his way, more out of an apparent concern for their own safety than from professional courtesy. "Lil' Darlin'," Beahen shook his head as he sauntered into the house of ill repute, "ah've seen some kill'ns, but ah ain't never seen nuthin' quite lahk this."

Sandra had seen the inside of more meth houses than whore houses in her time with the FBI. The rest of the house, while generally run down, was fairly normal looking. The fixtures, furniture, and everything else in it was older, for sure, but fairly clean. As she walked from the front door to the upstairs room where activity seemed to be centered, the normality of it all caught her a little off guard. The Chambre Rouge looked more like a set piece from "The Best Little Whorehouse in Texas" than some dark den of iniquity.

"So," she asked as she followed Sheriff Beahen up the stairs, "I assume this is a drug related homicide?"

The house's quaintness disappeared abruptly when Elbee entered the room at the end of the upstairs hallway. She imagined it had started off untold years ago as some little girl's bedroom. The way the walls angled in halfway up to match the pitch of the roof outside made this a perfect room for someone not yet fully grown. The oversized window on the far wall could have once housed a window seat or provided a view of the bayou to inspire a young imagination. Its location at the end of the upstairs hall was the perfect place to tuck a young one away for a quiet evening's sleep.

If the room's usual usage these days had not completely robbed it of its picturesque innocence then last night's gruesome deeds certainly had. The naked, dead man who laid in the bed looked wrinkled from age more than from the loss of the blood which soaked through the sheets, pooled and congealing on the floor.

Elbee's face wrinkled at the macabre sight. "This doesn't look like it was drug related."

"The only drug at work in this room last night was Viagra." Elbee tracked the female voice back to a dark haired, fair skinned technician in a navy FBI polo shirt and khakis standing nearby. "*Rigor mortis* set in before the vic's ED meds wore off." Sandra fought the reflex to allow her eyes to glance back at whatever part of the victim the technician was pointing at with her pen. The comment about erectile dysfunction painted enough of a picture for Elbee's imagination. "Hope they at least close the bottom half of the casket."

Elbee was all business. "Hudson? Give me the scoop."

Agent Amanda Hudson, the senior forensic technician on the scene, rattled off facts like a weatherman detailing a forecast. "Witness confirms the vic was caught mid-coitus. Multiple GSW's to the torso and cranium. Hemorrhaging would have killed him," Hudson traced a circle midair above the corpse's chest with the distal end of her pen, then pointed to the head "but the shooter tapped him in the CNS anyway for good measure."

Elbee focused on the triple hole pattern on the man's head. "Clean marksmanship," she noted. "Tight spread. All into the parietal bone. Small holes. Pistol caliber, maybe? Nine-millimeter?"

Hudson nodded. "Very good, ma'am. Now, guess what these are," she pointed back to the torso.

Sandra examined the mess that was once a human chest and belly. Now, it looked more like a package of hamburger that had been ripped open and spilled across a kitchen countertop. Her instincts called an answer to mind, but the answer was that obvious, the forensic tech would not have issued the challenge. "Twenty gauge?" she guessed.

Hudson smiled and her doe-like brown eyes flashed. "That, ma'am, is why you pay me." The technician pointed to the floor. "So far, we've recovered about three dozen spent nine-millimeter casings. That's it." Sandra's look of utter disbelief prompted Amanda to produce a serialized plastic bag. Inside the sealed evidence bag, held up for Sandra's inspection, was what looked like bloody flecks of golden pepper or rocky sand. "Frangible projectile. It's made of copper and tin. No jacket, no core. Shatters on impact. Causes massive tissue trauma with reduced penetration."

Elbee's lips puckered unconsciously in thought. "So, we have one or more shooters who break in and gun him down while he's bumping uglies with, I presume a prostitute, whom I also presume is our witness..?"

"The girl," Beahen interjected, "will be talking with mah people shortly."

"We're going to need access to this girl," Elbee announced.

"Woman, really," Beahen corrected. "She's in 'er twenties. A local some of mah people know."

"We need access," Elbee pressed.

"We can ask -"

"Don't stonewall me, Sheriff," Elbee glared over her should back to the portly man. "I don't care whose family she is, or who in the Parish she's been servicing. She's a material witness to a federal murder investigation. You'll give her to me immediately. And if you or any of your people try to hold out on me or mine, your office will be slapped with a jurisdictional grievance, charges of obstruction, and at least one drunken village idiot who swears to the local media that you're the prostitute's father. And not in that order."

A matronly chuckle sounded from the hallway, accompanied by a saucy, muffled voice singing the words, "Now, wouldn't that be somethin'?" Elbee walked to the door and was surprised to see a strong looking African American woman in her forties. She still cut a mean figure and her face bore some of the signs of when she was younger, but her beauty now felt like it came from the confidence and grace she exuded rather than glamorous makeup or tawdry clothing. She walked with an irrepressible dignity that seemed strangely out of place at such a horrid crime scene. She wore no uniform, displayed no badge and carried no gun; but the Parish deputies let her walk freely through the house. Even so, she stopped short of the doorway and displayed a concerted effort to keep the room - and its gory contents - out of her direct line of sight.

Elbee raised an interrogative eyebrow. "And you are?"

The other woman gently placed her right hand on her chest, held her left hand out slightly, and slowly bowed. "Cherre," she answered in a smooth Creole accent, "the real question isn't who I am. It's who he is." Without the madame acknowledging that the room even existed, Sandra knew that she meant the dead man. "And that, li'l darlin', is why the good Sheriff called you down to our li'l corner of heaven."

"You've known the vic?"

The older woman nodded sadly, but it was Sheriff Beahen whose voice answered. "Why, don't you know anything, lil' girl? That's Duke Evans! As in, Senator Duke Evans."

CHAPTER 2

GIVEN THE VICTIM'S IDENTIY, it came as no surprise to Elbee when her superiors scheduled an ad hoc briefing on her case for the day after they dropped it on her lap without any forewarning or information to prepare her for the scene. What was unusual, however, was the pair of agents from the Secret Service seated at the table in the third floor conference room when Sandra began her summary.

Both agents were white males. One was markedly older, easily gleaned by his hound dog face and wraparound hair. He was clad in a dark grey suit, white shirt and a cheap tie, sporting alternating yellow and gray stripes. The other looked to be about Sandra's age, with steel blue eyes set in an otherwise unremarkable face but drawn out by his navy-blue suit. Like his boss, he wore the white dress shirt that just screamed government employment - Sandra's blue blouse being the only exception in the room. But the younger agent's bold red tie drew Sandra's eyes to another spot of red on his lapel: a small, circular, metal pin. Sandra could not read the pin from across the room but knew from experience that it read HONORABLE DISCHARGE in small, gold letters around its edge. She had seen more than one veteran wearing such a pin during her time at the Bureau.

"The forensics team is still working on some of the details," she explained after a quick rehash of the facts surrounding Senator Evan's grizzly murder, "including most of the lab work - blood toxicology and such. Given the bloody nature of the murder, it's the clean parts of this scene that stand out."

"Go on," Jack Thompson, Deputy Station Chief elicited from the seat at the head of the conference table.

"Well, sir," Elbee pushed a button on her remote to advance the slide displayed upon the sixty-inch briefing monitor mounted to the wall behind her. The image showed a fully defined, high resolution photo of the crime scene *in toto* taken by Hudson. Sandra used the remote's built in laser pointer to draw a circle around a cluster of evidence tags near the image's right-hand side. "We have three dozen spent casings. All nine-millimeter. At least two different types of ammunition were used, but they seem to have been fired from the same position. Not one casing has even a partial print."

"Multiple shots all fired from the same position points to a single shooter," Thompson concluded. "So, he cleaned his bullets before he loaded them?"

Sandra nodded. "Traces on the casings themselves suggest the shooter wiped them with some form of acetone before or while he loaded the gun to get rid of his fingerprints. Also, there were no stray shots. The shots grouped around center mass," she traced another crimson circle around Evans' torso, "appear to have all utilized frangible ammunition. Hudson's team have yet to recover a single projectile intact. Not from the body or the room. And they don't believe they will. In addition to reduced penetration in target, because frangible rounds disintegrate there is no cohesive ballistic signature left from the gun's barrel. The only collateral damage found at the scene came when the head shots penetrated the Senator's cranium. Those rounds went through the pillow, punched out the wall behind the bed and buried themselves in the front lawn. Three nine mil slugs were recovered from the mud by a tech with a metal detector." Sandra advanced her slide show again, presetting an image of three nearly-pristine projectiles.

"Well, at least we might be able to tie those back to the gun. If we can ever get a suspect." Thompson's serious expression devolved into an open frown. "The bullets look that clean after all of that? Tell me those aren't armor piercing rounds."

The side-to-side movement of Elbee's head was almost apologetic. "Yes, sir. Steel core, fully jacketed, nine-millimeter projectiles. Designed specifically to penetrate light armor. The senator could've been wearing an Army helmet and he'd still be just as dead."

"Someone really hated this guy," Thompson offered.

"What about the note?" asked the older Secret Service agent from the next seat over.

"The note," Sandra advanced her slide show to an image of the bloodstained paper at the scene, side-by-side with another photo which revealed the page's face when the FBI forensics team unfolded it back at their lab. "It was completely saturated by Senator Evans' blood, but we've been able to make out what it says pretty easily." Elbee cued her slide with a click, and the words on the image were artificially highlighted.

'Those unworthy of the public trust have lost the consent of the governed.'

Elbee gave her audience a moment to digest this particular piece of data. After that moment, she drilled her point home. "Serial killers leave notes to taunt law enforcement. Our concern right now is that we are dealing with the start of a spree. And while we have very little to go on at this point, if our murderer is willing to target one government official then there's nothing to stop him from trying to kill another."

Thanks to her studies in criminology and psychology, Sandra knew that notes were the calling cards of serial killers. Psychopaths of this particular flavor tended to see themselves as above - or certainly outside the scope of - traditional social conventions like laws. The notes left behind by serial killers were often left as a personal challenge to law enforcement... a sort of dare for the cops to catch them. If they could.

"Is there anything peculiar about the note itself that might lead us back to the killer?" Thompson asked.

"No, sir," Elbee shook her head. "Common font, printed on paper with commonly available commercial ink for a fairly popular model from a

Hewlett-Packard printer you can buy pretty cheaply just about anywhere."

"This is a real problem," Thompson announced, "and precisely why we're bringing in some extra help on this one." The Deputy Chief gestured to his left. "The Secret Service is lending us a hand with the case."

"Was Senator Evans a presidential contender?" asked Agent Underwood, one of the FBI officers attending the brief and seated far enough to Thompson's right to denote her junior status within the Bureau.

"Not that we are aware of, no," the older Secret Service officer answered. "But, like almost half of Congress, he was up for re-election in this year's mid-term. I'm Elias Johnson from the field office here in New Orleans." As Elias introduced himself, Elbee noted that he slurred New Orleans into *N'Walins*. He must have been here for a while, she thought. *I've been here more than a year and I don't talk like a local.* "This," Elias arched his left thumb to the younger agent sitting beside him, "is Special Agent Wakefield. He specializes in this sort of thing."

That remark caught Elbee's attention. "I thought the Secret Service mostly investigated money fraud and threats to banks," she challenged.

"We do," Johnson answered, "but Danny has a lot of experience outside of our traditional mission set."

"Elbee," Thompson directed, "Wakefield will liaise with you on this case."

Sandra's eyes shot back to her boss. "Sir," she started, "I really don't think -"

"I really don't care," he cut her off. "If you're right

about this case, our killer is a significant threat. We're all one big, happy Department of Homeland Security, and you will play nice with the Secret Service until this case is put to bed."

"Yes, sir," Elbee breathed.

"Anything else?" Deputy Chief Thompson invited.

"Not at this time," Sandra replied. "If that's all, I've got to get back to forensics to see if they've turned up anything else."

Thompson cast Johnson a quizzical look, who answered with a dismissive head shake. Nobody else in the room spoke. "Very well. Dismissed." The handful of briefing attendants stood from the table to leave, and the FBI Deputy Chief turned once more to Sandra, flashing a humorless smile. "And Elbee: don't forget to take Wakefield with you. He's your new partner."

Sandra stormed down the hallway, daring Danny to keep up. He stayed one step behind her and to her right, toward the middle of the third-floor corridor. The duet paused long enough for Sandra to pass her badge over a small, dark, rectangular panel mounted on the wall next to a locked door. After she punched a short series of numbers into the accompanying keypad, Danny heard the familiar click of an electromagnetic lock cycling, and the door was opened.

Inside the door lay an open bay filled with blue-grey cubicles, each populated with an agent who busied him-or-herself with the tasks and tools of their shared trade. Danny had seen this scene countless times before. He had long equated these types of offices with government employment. His own department back in D.C. was built around the same type of setup, as had been his previous station. He remembered a joint intelligence center he saw back in the Corps whose cubicle walls were an archaic, faded maroon...

"Welcome to our humble abode," Sandra called back to him over her shoulder as she strode across the bay. Danny matched her pace, ignoring the half-hidden glances he knew were cast toward him by several of the agents. Though he shared many things with these people, he was a stranger to their hive. Until he took the time to integrate into their subculture and social hierarchy, he knew that he would continue to be an outsider in their minds. And Special Agent Daniel Wakefield had no intention of staying here long enough to fit in.

Sandra ducked into one of the cubicles toward the perimeter of the cluster. She unlocked the half-sized file cabinet stuffed under the right-hand side of her desk, produced a small purse and a pre-holstered Sig P-230, then slammed the drawer shut again and locked it.

"You keep your service pistol in your desk?" Daniel asked with a raised eyebrow.

"Of course." She snapped her head. Her shoulder length, blonde hair whipped around. Her finger was pointed at the cabinet's lock. "It's secure. Where else would I keep it?"

Danny could not imagine walking around as a federal agent without his gun. Especially if he was on duty. A word of professional advice leapt to mind, but he pushed it back down. Instead of offering what could be considered criticism, he took a half step to the left to clear Elbee's path back to the door. "I take it the forensics guys aren't in this building?"

Sandra started back to the hallway. "The lab's being remodeled," she confirmed. "We had to lease a space a few minutes away until it's done."

Wakefield's left hand casually slid into his suit pant pocket. "I'll drive."

"That won't be necessary," Sandra patted her purse.

"Not necessary," Danny conceded, "but my car is covered on my travel orders, so it'll save you the gas." It was true. Standard travel procedure for federal employees included a rental car and allowance for incidental expenses like fuel, in addition to a *per diem* paid on top of their normal salary. By taking Wakefield's rental car, the pair's excursion was fully funded by taxpayer money rather than their own salaries.

Sandra nodded in assent. The one universal skill shared by all government employees regardless of branch, department, mission or pay grade was the ability to milk government funds at every turn.

*   *   *

So, Danny noted to himself as they crossed the parking lot, *that's her 'incredulous' face.*

"How in the hell," Sandra asked, "did you score this thing for your rental car?"

Danny smiled as he remotely unlocked a brand new, bright yellow Chevy Camero. The muscle car obediently *chirp*'ed. "One of the advantages of a late flight," he explained. "My boss told me to take the first thing smoking out of D.C. last night, which was the twenty-hundred out of Baltimore." The agents climbed into the car, which Danny had backed into its parking spot. It started with a throaty growl that prompted Sandra to pucker her lips just a bit. "Didn't get to the rental car counter until almost midnight," Danny continued. He slowly pulled out of his spot and smoothly maneuvered to the parking lot's exit. "By that time, all of the cars everyone usually picks are always taken. No compacts. No mid-size sedans. Not even a small sport utility. It was pretty much this or a fifteen-passenger van."

Sandra shook her head in mock disgust. "And," she finished for him, "since you're using a government reservation, the rental agency had to upgrade you for free." She closed her eyes as the instantly cold air conditioner blew the Louisiana heat off her silky face and throat. She caressed her deep seat with her left hand. "It's even got leather," she purred.

Danny perked up a bit. "You're into cars?"

Sandra sobered. "We sometimes travel," she explained, "but never out of state. So, it's usually either in my car or a Suburban from the Bureau's motor pool."

"Ah," Danny nodded. When government employees used their personally owned vehicles - or POV, another of the ubiquitous government acronyms - for official business, they were reimbursed a few cents per mile. It was, in some situations, a far cheaper option for the government than buying large fleets of vehicles or renting a vehicle for every trip undertaken by every employee. "So," he inquired absently, "what's your POV?"

"It's a right out the lot," Sandra directed as if she

had not heard the personal question. "Then a left at the light."

Danny followed her instructions as they drove across town to the FBI's temporary forensics lab. After a few minutes of taking in all of the sights that the Big Easy had to offer, he decided to breach what he suspected would be a sensitive subject. He thought about approaching the topic cleverly, but what little time he had spent around Elbee told him instinctively that she was more of a no-nonsense kind of gal. So he tried the direct approach. "So," he breathed out, "when are you going to tell me about the hooker?"

"The lab's up here on the right," Sandra pointed, keeping her gaze directed through the front windshield. "Tell you what, exactly, about what hooker?"

"C'mon," Danny cajoled as they waited for the light before them to change from red. "Senator Evans, aged sixty seven, is found," he pointed a finger into midair, "dead," another finger rose, "at a house in the middle of nowhere," a third finger, "that was not his own," the next finger ticked, "naked," Danny thrust his thumb up to complete the set, "and harder than Chinese algebra, and you're going to tell me that there was no hooker in that room with him when he was shot?"

"That wasn't in the brief," Sandra dodged.

"Exactly," Danny's tone was accusatory. "And nobody else bothered to ask, either. Which is kind of odd, because titillating little details like that are usually all the rave during an investigation. Especially a murder. Especially with a high-profile vic. Which means one of two things is going on: Either everyone you work with is a complete idiot, or your people already know everything and aren't discussing her outside of the Bureau. I do assume it's a *her*, anyway. Not that I'm one to judge," he added as an aside. "It takes all kinds. But if it wasn't a 'her' then that would help explain the Bureau's secrecy on the matter." The light before them switched to green and Danny proceeded. "Anyway, despite all of my previous dealings with the FBI - which universally point to the first conclusion, by the way - I'm betting the latter is the case today."

"If you're so sure," she countered, "then why didn't you bring it up during the brief?"

Danny made a dismissive face. "Because I didn't want to waste everyone else's time getting into a measuring contest. Some people need to show others how smart they are. So they ask know-it-all questions in front of as many witnesses as possible in order to make themselves look better than they are. Me? I knew I'd have time afterward to address it. No need to Bogart the brief."

"Bogart?"

"As in Humfrey. But in this context it means to intrude on someone else's party."

The way Elbee's eyes remained fixed forward, Danny guessed that she was biting back some choice words. "How'd you know that we'd have time afterward? Did you know that you were getting assigned as my partner?"

Danny knew that any attempt to hide or soften the truth would only serve to insult them both. "Before I got on the plan here." He waited a beat as she processed that information. "I'm guessing nobody told you in advance. Look, Elbee, it's your ball. You call the shots. I'm just here for passes and rebounds."

"I hate sports metaphors," she offered through clenched teeth. "Fine," she caved, "there was a prostitute. The Madame of the house, Ophelia Flowers, pointed me toward her - but only under conditions of complete anonymity regarding the investigation. The Bureau considers her a Confidential Informant."

Danny was better versed in running human sources than he suspected this blonde would ever be. "Okay, she's a CI," he drilled. "I can dig it. So, what did she say?"

"Nothing."

"Bullshit," Danny spat. "If she gave you nothing, you wouldn't protect her. You'd've said something in the brief like, 'After a brief interview with the whore, we concluded she was a nonviable source and dismissed her usefulness as either a witness or a suspect'." Danny pulled into a convenient spot, put the car into Park, but left the engine running. "Solving this case pretty much lets you write your own ticket for the rest of your career, so ruling out someone who was obviously one of the last people to see the victim - somebody who usually is one of the first suspects - means she's given you a suspect. One you're not telling me about."

Sandra shook her head. "She didn't give us a suspect."

"Or, maybe she did," Danny countered, "and you don't realize it yet. Either that, or you don't want to share." He breathed a long breath out of his nose. "Look," he continued, more calmly, "interagency cooperation only works if we all play the same game with the same pieces." He waved his hands in a dismissive gesture. "Otherwise, I'm just here for the cajun food."

There was a pause. Then Sandra surrendered. "Madame Flowers - yes, I know that's not her real name, but it is the one she uses - only agreed to give me the girl if I agreed to two conditions: anonymous trauma counseling and complete anonymity."

"Please tell me that Ms. Flowers said this from inside an interrogation room while you were holding her feet over the fire. I mean, there have to have been a whole boatload of charges you could use against her as leverage."

Special Agent Elbee shook her head in frustration. "Flowers is untouchable. She's too well connected with local officials. Hell," she hissed, "the Sheriff and his people acted like she was in charge at the crime scene."

Danny had seen this sort of situation before, though it was less common Stateside than it was in other countries. People were people, no matter where you went or where you found them. Most people had vices. Some folks' guilty pleasures were as innocent as a weakness for a certain ice cream, other folks had more despicable tastes. Danny preferred to take the edge off of a hard day with a drink or two, but he never let it get out of control. Nevertheless, he knew that when people in power relied upon unsavory persons to satisfy their sordid appetites, those people who provided their clients with the goods or services gained a certain amount of *wastah* - an Arabic word that loosely translated as political power people can see. Street cred, as the young folks said.

Wakefield nodded. "Fine." Then again. "Fine, keep your source confidential. I can respect that.

Really, I can." As he met her eyes, Sandra could see his sincerity. "But I need to know everything she said."

"She's less than a witness," Sandra explained. "She was handcuffed on her front, facing the bed, with her back to both the senator and the room when the shooting started. She saw some of the rounds hit Evans, but never got a look at the shooter. Never saw him come in. Never saw him leave."

Wakefield mulled over this new information. "How'd she get out of the handcuffs?"

Sandra's anger took on a new level of righteousness. "She laid there in that bed, next to a dead guy, with his blood splattered on her and soaking up the sheets, for hours, screaming and crying. Hours, Wakefield. Until finally, hoarse, exhausted, and totally screwed up in the head, she heard the madame come in at her usual time - around noon."

Danny's suspicion and frustration became surprisingly sympathetic. "And Madame Flowers, seeing her girl in a jam, got her out, cleaned her up and tucked her away somewhere the police couldn't run her through the wringer."

"Exactly," Sandra ended. Then she challenged, "What? No joke about the whorehouse having spare handcuff keys?"

Danny pursed his lips and shook his head. "No. You're right. Your witness is just another victim, Elbee. And I don't mock victims." He sniffed, then turned off the Camero's engine. "Okay, so I try not to make fun of them. I try really hard. Sometimes. And today's a good day. But, maybe some other time." Danny resumed his business manner. "Anyway," he bobbed his head toward the medical lab, "let's say you introduce me to your forensics team?"

*   *   *

"Alright, Hudson, what have we learned?"

"In total, we recovered exactly three dozen nine-millimeter shell casings from four different manufacturers," the technician rattled off as she handed Elbee a printed copy of her report. "Unequal distribution among the case markings. At least one of the manufacturers carries the type of rounds that were used to shoot the Senator in the back of the head."

"Steel core nine mils?" Wakefield wondered aloud. "Who the hell hated him that much?"

"Our shooter definitely likes obscure ammo," Hudson nodded.

"And he likes to spend for it, too." Danny's comment provoked Elbee's eyebrow. "The military uses steel core projectiles to pierce light armor," he explained. "A lot of teams downrange get them now because of the proliferation of body armor amongst the bad guys."

"Some cops use them, too," Hudson added.

"Yeah. Anyway, that's all good and well when Uncle Sam is springing for the bullets, but these aren't the cheap rounds your Uncle Jim buys at the Shop-N-Save."

"Who's Uncle Jim?" Sandra's brow furrowed.

"I have an uncle named Jim," Hudson seemed a little too enthusiastic as she offered that little personal tidbit.

"Everybody has an Uncle Jim."

"I don't," Elbee pointed.

"Anyway," Wakefield steered, "my point is, you

usually have to special order this stuff. I do, anyway. Especially the pistol calibers." He caught his new partner's stare. "What? Don't judge. When I shoot a guy, he stays dead."

Hudson saw where his line of logic led and shook her head in dismissal. "There are, like, a dozen places online that we've found that stock them, and none of them will give out customer data without a warrant or subpoena."

"I'll talk to a judge," Elbee offered, "but don't get your hopes up. That's a pretty broad net to cast without more specifics."

Danny's head bobbled. "Right. Sorry, Hudson. What else?"

The forensics technician brightened a bit. "Oh, it's no bother. We're all just thinking out loud, right? Oh, and you can call me Amanda."

"And then?" Elbee pushed.

"Oh, right. Um. Blood splatter patterns on the walls indicate the victim was still coupled when he was peppered in the back, then fell forward onto the bed. He was pronate for the head shots. All three of those rounds exited the Senator's face, travelled through the bedding, and went out the wall near floor level. We recovered all three from the mud in the front yard. A reverse trajectory from the exit path indicates the shooter finished the job not more than a meter away."

"He was standing over him," Danny noted. "Point blank range."

"Exactly."

"That's consistent with -" Wakefield thought that Sandra was about to say the witness' statement, but quickly caught herself, "- with what we were thinking. But the question still remains as to why." Elbee chimed. "The Senator was shot all to hell. There was no way he was gonna survive all of the other gunshots. So why bother with the head shots?"

"I'm totally switching to frangible ammo," Danny became a little too excited as he pointed to one of the photos, "cuz that's totally sick." Elbee's glare sobered him. "Sorry. Continue."

"But that's my point," she continued. "These other rounds - the frangible ones - they aren't cheap, either. Which means our shooter went to great expense and care to make sure not to penetrate his victim. So, why go to even more expense and care to over-penetrate on the last three shots?" She waited a beat to see if anyone else had any ideas. "I think the shooter is trying to tell us something."

"He left a note for that," Danny pointed.

"Something else."

"Could it be something to do with how the Senator was found?" Hudson offered. "I mean, he was mid-coitus when he was shot. There seems to be a theme of penetration here." Danny caught the brunette's doe eyes as they darted in his direction involuntarily, then back again, then downward. He refrained from making any *double entendres* involving penetration.

"I don't think so," Elbee slowly aired her doubts. Her eyes were on the crime scene photos, but her mind seemed to look past them. "Wakefield, you're a shooter."

"Yep."

"Obviously, a shooter uses frangible rounds to reduce collateral damage," she continued.

"Right. And to remove the ballistic signature of the gun used."

"But we got ballistics from the other bullets," Hudson offered. "Clean markings from two, mostly good from the third - which seems to have struck a rock in the mud."

"What if we were meant to find those bullets?" Elbee challenged.

"You think our shooter wants us on his trail?"

"Some killers want to be caught, Wakefield," Elbee reminded him. "They leave notes, witnesses, clues. Sometimes they taunt the police directly. It's a game with them. It's the classic pattern for a serial killer."

"But we've only got one victim," Hudson countered. "And the marks on the mud bullets don't match anything we've found so far in the Bureau's databases. That gun's never been used in a crime before."

Danny snickered. "Yeah, well, it has now."

Elbee shook her head. "Then this might just be his first. Maybe that's what he's telling us. What else do you have?"

Hudson continued. "The cases may be mismatched, but the trace residue from inside them indicates the same type of powder was used in all of the bullets fired on scene, which suggests our killer manufactured his own ammunition."

"It's called reloading," Danny offered.

"Thank you, Wakefield. We know what it is called."

"Sorry, Elbee. You two just struck me as, you know, the indoors type."

"I love the indoors," the previously pale skin on Hudson's cheeks started to blush.

"Back it up for a second," Wakefield held up a

hand. "You can tell the difference between different powder types from a spent casing after it's been fired?"

"Oh, yeah," Amanda beamed. "From the microdots." Danny's face clearly conveyed that he had no idea what she meant. "Microdots. Microscopic inert material mixed into the gunpowder."

"Smokeless powder," he corrected.

"Right. Sorry. Anyway, federal law requires all manufacturers to mix in specific microdots when they produce explosives. They're in everything from fireworks to C-4. Each batch of microdots is manufactured with a unique set of markings, and the manufacturers have to record which microdots are used in what batch of explosives and turn that information in with the ATF."

"And since we're all one great big Homeland Security family," Wakefield continued, "we have direct access to the database with that information without any pesky warrant nonsense."

"Exactly," Hudson smiled. "So, whenever we find any explosives residue, we look for microdots and match them to the manufacturer. I can tell you the date, and sometimes the time, that the powder was made."

"Can you tell me who bought it?" Elbee asked.

"Well, that can be tricky," Hudson frowned. "You see, the original manufacturer might keep detailed enough records to tell us what distributor bought the product, but those batches can cross lines among multiple purchasers, so the chain-of-custody becomes a bit sketchy. And that's just the distributor level. We'd likely lose track of what actual retail vendor bought the powder from them. And there's no way to tell which live customer walked out of a store with it."

"Then how is this helpful?" Sandra insisted.

"It's a signature," Amanda pointed. "Despite the disparate manufacturers of the casings, all the ammunition used at this scene used the same powder, so it was presumably made by the same person. If we find more spent casings at another scene, we can compare the residue to see if it, too, came from our suspect."

"It's a little shaky," Danny rubbed his jaw. "I mean, this'll only work as long as our guy uses the same powder. If he runs out, then he'll have to get more and we'll be back to square one."

"Don't forget the part where we can only follow this lead if he strikes again - which is what we're trying to prevent. And if he runs out," Sandra offered, "then it'll be because we've failed. Then we'll definitely have more victims."

"And there are a lot of reloaders out there," Wakefield pointed. "Guys just sitting in their garages with time to kill on a Saturday afternoon. Somebody else out there has to be using powder made from the same batch. Only they're not killing folks."

"I admit it's not exactly a fingerprint," Hudson frowned, "but it's all we've got right now. I'm sorry."

"It's still circumstantial at best," Elbee agreed. "We'll never be able to use it for a warrant, let alone a conviction. Anything else?"

"Uh, Evans' toxicology all came back fairly normal. There was medication used to treat erectile dysfunction in his system. No surprise there, given the rumors about the senator's recreational activities and where - and how - we found him. But no narcotics, alcohol or other toxins. We'd like to keep the body as long as possible to continue our examination…"

"But Mrs. Evans wants it for the memorial," Sandra finished. "Thompson has been breathing down my neck pushing for the release." She drummed her fingers on the table. "Are we likely to get anything else out of the corpse?"

"At this time, it's impossible to be certain," Hudson shook her head. "If we knew what to look for maybe."

"If you haven't already, be sure to run up a full imagery workup. MRI, CT, x-ray, the works. And pull some extra tissue samples just in case. Discreetly. If we lose the fight with the senator's wife and have to give back the body, I don't wanna have to exhume his corpse just to look for more clues."

"I'll make sure we have a full radiographic file as a backup just in case."

"What about the scene itself?" Danny asked.

Amanda's shoulders dropped in disappointed resignation. "The yard is a waste. Between the grass obscuring the tracks and the local cops who trampled all over the place, that muddy mess is useless to us. We did find a set of treads that correlated to the senator's car in the gravel driveway. The tracks turn north and lead away from the house, but we lost all trace of them on the paved road after a few yards. That pretty much sums up our preliminary findings."

"Thanks, Hudson," Elbee closed. "Keep us informed as updates pop."

*　　　*　　　*

"I don't see as how you've got a choice," Danny pushed.

Special Agent Elbee propped her arm up on the Camero's passenger door. "I know," she fumed.

"Don't pout, Elbee," he teased. "Look, I respect the fact that you've got sources. But forensics is a bust. If we're gonna catch a break on this, the best place to look is your witness."

"I already debriefed her, Wakefield," Sandra protested. "She's got nothing - except for the obvious emotional trauma from what happened to her."

Danny steered the sports car into a gas station. He had plenty of fuel. He just needed to stop the car to make his point. "She gave you nothing," he corrected his new partner. "That's not the same as having nothing. You have to know that."

"You're not the only one on Earth who ever learned how to interrogate people," she snapped back.

"I played baseball in high school," he countered, "that doesn't mean I'm ready to open for the Yankees."

"I hate sports metaphors."

"But you get my point?"

Sandra worked her jaw, then pulled her phone out of her pocket. "Fine. I'll arrange a meeting. Just promise me you'll be tactful, Wakefield."

Danny held his fingers up in the okay sign. "Sensitive. Got it."

"I mean it."

"Got it."

*   *   *

"Seriously, Wakefield, don't push her too hard." Elbee marched down a hallway in a subsidized apartment building. "She's been through a lot. Even before the other night."

"Roger."

"I did an extensive interview with her," Sandra continued as she guided him around a corner. "People have been taking advantage of her since before she was old enough to drive."

"Understood."

"She's had a hard life. She's made some bad choices," she held up a finger in warning. "No cracks. Play nice in there or I'm ending it."

"As you wish."

Elbee knocked on a cheap wooden door that identified apartment 306 in fake brass numbers. The top screw had come out of the last digit, causing it to hang upside down and become the number 9. "And let's keep it brief, okay?"

"You bet'cha."

Scratches sounded from the door as the locks cycled. Danny counted *one* as a dead bolt slid across its receiver, and *two* as another one from within the doorknob freed its hold. A crack opened between the door and frame. A cheap metal chain dangled, while somebody held the door open just wide enough for a single eye to peer at them. "What'chu want?" a man's voice demanded

"We're here to see Krystal," Sandra answered.

"Ain't no Krystal here."

"I'm sorry. You don't understand, my name is Sandra Elbee. I know she's here. She's expecting me."

"Burn out, fool," the voice dismissed her as the crack grew more narrow.

Wakefield's foot caught the bottom of the door before it shut and pinned the portal open. "Open the door, Homey-oh," Danny smiled. "We're not asking."

"Push on, poh-poh," the doorman protested, but his repeated efforts to push the door shut only allowed the agent's foot to gain more purchase until it pulled the chain tight. Wakefield heaved back, then threw his shoulder straight into the door at its closest point to the chain.

The door held. But the cheap little screws that anchored the chain into the wall were ripped out of the doorframe. The edge of the door slammed into Homey-oh's forehead. Danny pushed his way past the rebounding doorman and walked into the apartment like he owned the place.

"Wakefield," Sandra protested, "what the Hell are you doing?"

"A'ight, fool," Homey-oh recovered his balance and stepped up to Danny. The street thug threw his unbuttoned outer shirt open to reveal a chiseled physique and the handle of a stainless steel nine-millimeter pistol tucked into the front of his waistband. His face was barely an inch from the agent's, "you done fu-" Whatever threat he was about to utter was cut short when Wakefield's left hand seized the earring in the thug's right ear. With the wannabe tough-guy's face twisted in pain, Danny relieved him of his handgun with his right hand while his left steered Homey-oh into a more agreeable position.

"Don't be an idiot," Wakefield warned the younger black man. "There're no cameras here to impress. Now, where's Krystal?"

"Owowowow! Leggo of my ear, man!"

The young man writhed as his earlobe was stretched well beyond its usual proportions. "Krystal," Danny repeated.

"I dunno, man! You're rippin' my ear off, man!"

"No," Danny calmly corrected, "I'm tearing your earlobe open. *This* is what it feels like when I rip your ear off…" He switched his grip from the young man's earring to the cartilage of the ear itself and began to twist. "Feel the difference? It's kinda like a burning sensation, as opposed to a stabbing pain."

"Tyrone!" a woman's voice sounded from the small apartment's bedroom door.

"Krystal," Elbee interjected, "I'm so sorry-"

"Let go of Tyrone!"

"Listen to me, Tyrone," Wakefield warned, "I'm gonna let you go. You're gonna sit down on the sofa over there with your hands where I can see them. And you're gonna shut up. Or I'm gonna feed you this stainless-steel sissy pistol I just lifted from you. One bullet at a time. You feel me?"

"Yeahyeahyeah, man. Whatever." True to his word, Danny released the young man's ear. Tyrone felt the nearby couch was the perfect place to keep up his end of the bargain. He checked his throbbing ear for blood or missing tissue.

"Sorry about that, Krystal," Danny offered as he ejected the cheap Taurus' magazine and caught it in his off hand, then transitioned the mag so that he held it with his right pinky finger. "But I'm sure you understand that federal agents don't like to be obstructed by thugs with loaded handguns." He racked the pistol's slide back to the rear and caught the shiny round that it ejected into his left palm in a well-practiced maneuver.

"He's just tryin' to protect me," Krystal explained.

"And he's doing a bang-up job of it."

"Wakefield!"

"What?" he pocketed his new gun's ammo. "That's a compliment, right? Or is it some sort of new street term for 'clumsy?'"

"I thought we was done talkin'," Krystal rolled her eyes at Sandra.

"I'm sorry, Krystal," Elbee soothed, "but we just wanted to check up on you. Like I told you on the phone earlier."

"I told you. I'm fine. Leave me alone."

"Krystal," Danny inquired, "I'd be willing to bet that Special Agent Elbee here found you this nice place to stay, didn't she? Probably put the rent on the Bureau's credit card? Just to make sure you were taken care of. And in a place where nobody would think to look." He shrugged. "That was real thoughtful of her and everything, and I don't know about you, but I'm pretty sure that if the taxpayers are paying your bills, that kinda puts us in a sort of relationship."

"So what'chu want?" Krystal rocked her head.

"Now that you've had a while to think," Elbee calmly explained, "we were hoping that maybe you've remembered something from the other night. Something that you didn't share with me before."

"I don' wanna think 'bout it!"

"Krystal, please," the blonde agent implored, "this is important."

"Uh-uh," Krystal shook her head. "Nut'n."

"I'm sure you understand that anything at all would be helpful," Sandra consoled.

"I told you," Krystal's voice shook as events played themselves out again in her mind, "dude came in while we was bumpin'. I had my back to the whole thing. I didn't see nut'n."

"How'd you know it was a dude?" Wakefield

asked.

"What'chu mean?"

"You said the dude came in," he repeated. "How do you know it wasn't a chick that shot Evans?"

Krystal stood in stunned silence for a moment. The only thing that moved was her eyes, which fidgeted like a squirrel on meth. "Well," she stammered, "I mean, it had to be a dude, right?"

"You saw something." It was not a question. Danny could see it in her dancing brown irises.

"No."

"Yep," his gaze bore into the back of her brain. "As a matter of fact, you're seeing it again right now." His voice softened to a near whisper. "It's there in your eyes. You don't want to see it, but you can't help it." Wakefield kept his eyes locked with hers while he tucked his newly procured pistol into his belt. His service pistol, a Sig P-230 just like Elbee's, was still safely tucked into its shoulder holster under his sport coat. "It's burned into your brain. I know it is. You don't forget something like that. Nobody does. I don't care how hard you are." Danny's voice was hypnotic. "I know. Because I see it, too. Every one of them. Every night. You see it right now, don't you? Tell me what you saw, Krystal."

Krystal's pupils jittered. She could not blink for a million dollars. Her body stood motionless in the cheap little apartment, but her mind was back in the Chambre Rouge. "I turned around," she whispered. "When Duke…" Her choked words came slowly. "I turned my head to see. After the first shot. Looked behind myself."

Elbee stood in total silence, but Wakefield kept his voice gentle as he guided Krystal through her horrid memory. "You saw him," he assured her softly, "you saw the shooter. Tell me what you saw."

"He weren't no man," Krystal stammered. Tears pooled up in her wide eyes. "I know it sounds crazy. That's why I didn't say nut'n earlier. But he was a shadow. He was gray, but green. And black." She shuddered. "I don't know how he got in there, but he was there. He just appeared. Like a monster."

"Tell me about his face," Wakefield directed with his hypnotic voice.

Krystal's eyes looked up within the memory. "It was black and green," she said. "I couldn't make it out."

"His hair?"

"His hair was like moss or sumt'in," Krystal snapped. "I know how it sounds, but it's like he was made outta moss. You know? Like some kinda monster up 'n walked outta tha swamp. You know?"

"I do know." Danny did not know how much longer he could hold her before the stress from her traumatic memory broke Krystal completely. "Then what?" He had to try to get more information out of her.

"Nut'n," she stepped back and started to back down the hallway behind her. "Dude shot him again. Kept shootin' him 'til he was done and left."

"Thank you, Krystal," Wakefield nodded. "That was very helpful." He turned back toward the door.

"We appreciate your time," Sandra forced an extra dose of assurance into her voice. "I'm sorry we had to put you through this again. It's very brave of you." She produced a business card from inside her suit jacket. "If you need anything, please don't hesitate to call."

"Hey yo!" Tyrone hopped up from the couch. "Whadda 'bout my nine? How's a broth'a s'posed to stay safe 'round here wid'out a Gat?"

Halfway out the door, Wakefield stopped and turned back to the young man. "How old are you, Tyrone?"

"Twenty-two, officer," Tyrone held his chin up defiantly.

"Any felonies on your record?" Danny challenged.

"I ain't done nut'n, man."

Wakefield scrutinized the homeboy for a second. "Of course you're clean," he said sarcastically as he produced the shiny pistol from his waistband. "And you know why I believe you? Because I have no probable cause not to. That's why." He locked the slide back and handed the gun back to Tyrone grip first. "And because you know that if you're a felon, merely touching that firearm would earn you an automatic ticket to jail." He waited, dared Tyrone to do or say anything. But the younger man did not blink. He just grabbed the pistol. At that, Danny turned back to the door.

"Yo, homes," Tyrone called, "what about the clip? An' my bullets?"

"It's called a 'magazine.' Not a 'clip.' And you can come out to the FBI office to pick them up," Danny sardonically replied from the hallway. He turned back to Elbee, who was frowning at him from within the apartment. "See, Elbee?" Danny made a giant okay sign with his fingers and smiled at his partner. "Sen-si-tive."

CHAPTER 3

"IT'S WEDNESDAY, eleven o'clock Eastern and the big story today: If you haven't heard already, Senator Duke Evans was killed this weekend."

"You know, Lonnie," the radio cohost chimed in, "I don't want to come across as advocating murder or anything, but this might be good news for America in the long run."

"That's terrible," Lonnie Chase chastised. Kyp had been his partner on-air for nearly a decade, and the two personalities often came to conflict on Lonnie's show. They were open and comfortable with that fact. Both men knew it was just such banter that drew a significant portion of their audience, even though sometimes their so-called arguments were widely suspected to be scripted shtick. "And really, Kyp, let's be honest. If you have to begin a remark with the phrase, 'I don't want to sound like I'm advocating murder, but...' then whatever point you're trying to make is just awful. Whatever you have to say after that 'but' is just wrong. That's a pretty big 'but.' And you'd have to be a horrible person to use it."

"Look, Lonnie," Kyp explained, "here we have a sixty-seven-year-old Democrat who's been in the Senate for three decades."

"He did serve a long time," Kyp's boss conceded.

"And what good did it do?" Kyp challenged. "He voted for the stimulus three times, voted for government run health care… He was on the Senate Armed Services Committee but voted to gut the Defense Department's budget! He was a tired old Socialist who belonged in a retirement home, not in Congress."

"Just because we want him to stop mismanaging our country doesn't mean we should want him dead," Lonnie scolded. "I've said it before, and I'll say it until my dying breath: Yes, we want a revolution - but no, we don't want bloodshed! Good God, man! What we need is a peaceful revolution. To take our country back - not with hate, but with love, compassion, and common freaking sense."

"Well, obviously," Kyp caved, "peaceful revolution would be preferable."

"Not just 'preferable!' Necessary!"

"Okay, Lonnie," his cohost pled, "but, do we even know how he died?"

Cue Factcheck Fred, the producer and junior cast member on the Lonnie Chase Program. "They haven't released the details. All they are saying at this time is that the Senator died this past weekend and they are treating the case as a homicide."

"Who said that?" Lonnie quizzed. "Who is 'they?'"

"That would be Senator Evans' office."

"So, there is an investigation?" Lonnie pressed.

"One would assume so. Yes."

"They shouldn't waste their time," Kyp offered. "I mean, unless they're looking for a guy to pin a medal on -"

"Stop it," Lonnie cut him off. "Just stop. That's horrible. We do not want violence." Over the last decade, Lonnie had built a multimedia empire out of a light-hearted show that was half stand-up comedy, half news analysis, and anyone who had listened to him more than twice could have predicted what was to follow his long pause. Lonnie sighed heavily, breathily into his microphone. With an audible effort to push on past the emotions welling up in his voice, he continued. "It's time for a quick break. Our sponsor for this segment of the Lonnie Chase Program is Goldstein Financial Group…"

"Well," Sandra surrendered as she clicked her mouse. The program streaming on her desktop muted. "There goes our media blackout."

"It was never gonna last," Danny offered. "You knew that."

"The press is having a field day with this," she grumbled.

"Have your Public Affairs Officer put in for hardship pay," he teased, "'cause it's gonna get worse." Danny rubbed his chin thoughtfully, recalling yesterday's trip to the lab and their interview with Krystal. "Okay, so there's nothing new or earth shattering from forensics."

"And, like I said, the witness is worthless."

"Oh, I wouldn't say that" Danny opined.

"She gave us nothing. No name. No description.

Nothing."

"She told us he was wearing a ghillie suit," he corrected.

"Hair like moss," she recalled. "A suit like that could let him approach the house undetected."

"Not that there was anyone watching out for him. But, yeah."

"He was definitely prepared for this."

"Over-prepared," Danny noted. "I don't suppose the FBI has any previous offenders or unsolved cases that line up with this one?"

Sandra shook her head. "I already ran down that line. If our killer has struck before, it was a totally different M.O."

Both agents knew that criminals tended to establish patterns in their behaviors - a *modus operandi*. Danny expected that a killer with such a brutal signature would stand out. Even the FBI should have noticed if someone had seen something familiar, though. But there was nothing, so Elbee and Wakefield sat at her desk in her cubicle at the field office trying to create solutions to the problem. Sandra combed through Hudson's reports and her own notes - including those from her interview with the prostitute. Danny examined photos from the scene. He kept returning to two particular photos: the wide shot of the bedroom and the street view of the Chambre Rouge.

"Where's the Senator's car?" Wakefield asked.

Sandra shook her head. When an agent hit a roadblock, it was perfectly normal to start fishing for new leads, new avenues of inquiry. Usually, this new angle of approach was precisely what was necessary to break the case wide open again and ultimately solve it.

Sometimes, though, it led the investigator down a rabbit hole - a bottomless and ultimately meaningless line of inquiry. Or it could turn into another brick wall.

"Sheriff Beahen interviewed Mrs. Evans," Sandra flipped to another report and handed it to Danny. Elbee was already familiar with the report's contents. "She took the Mercedes to her bridge club, leaving the senator with the Beamer. She gave the Sheriff the particulars." Wakefield confirmed. A black BMW 535i was listed in his report, including license plate and vehicle identification numbers, as missing. "An APB has been issued. Until it turns up, the car's a dead end."

Danny pursed his lips. The All Points Bulletin would alert all law enforcement agencies to the fact that the FBI wanted that specific car. If everybody did their job, any vehicle that closely resembled Duke Evans' BMW would be scrutinized by any cop that saw it. It was the best they could do. Danny was not as hopeful as Elbee seemed to be that the APB would yield any results. "You told me Krystal told you Senator Evans was a regular." He chewed on his imagination for a moment. "Any chance that Mrs. Evans found out about her husband's indiscretions and acted predictably?"

Elbee drummed her fingers on her desk. "The Sheriff doesn't think she's a suspect," she announced.

Wakefield's look became devious. "In a typical murder investigation, the victim's significant other is always one of the first suspects."

"Is there anything about this that seems typical?" she challenged.

"Fair point. But procedure is procedure and it's

there for a reason. Part of that reason is because it tends to work. Personally, I like to use it for cover - you know, 'Don't blame me, I'm just doing my job.' But another big part is that it gives you something to fall back on when you've got nothing else."

"I'm not a rookie," Elbee grew defensive. "What's your point?"

"My point is this: you're gonna take the advice of some idiot sheriff on a case this important?"

But Sandra had no better ideas. She needed to do something, anything, to break this case open. So, Sandra stuffed the reports back into a brown file folder and stood from her desk. "Alright," she agreed. She grabbed her purse and jacket, "but we're not taking your car."

"Free gas," Danny reminded. "And leather."

Sandra led the way out of the office. "There is no way I'm pulling up to a dead senator's house in a yellow hot rod," she resolved.

*   *   *

The Patriot sat inside his pop-up camper and worked along, aided more by the lamp that shone over his shoulder than what sunlight filtered through the window's cheap curtains. He had to keep the curtains closed to prevent potential passersby or curious eyes from seeing his work.

Even after careful preparations, the killer had to work quickly in the hours that immediately followed the hit at the whorehouse. Senator Evans' wallet contained a few hundred dollars in cash, for which the killer could always find a use. He ditched the rich guy's credit cards one by one out the BMW's window as he drove away from the brothel and through the bayou during the darkened early morning. Plastic was traceable. Even if he used the check card somewhere - he knew Evans had plenty of money in the bank - there was too high a chance that he might be caught on some store's surveillance camera.

He had to stay anonymous. Forgettable. A blurred face in the shifting crowd. So long as he was free to move, he was free to act. Free to continue his mission. Anonymity made him invisible. It let him blend into the world around him and strike at his targets from the shadows. That is what he was good at: striking at wicked people from the shadows that inevitably filled their dark, secretive little worlds.

He tried to be a good husband, a lifetime ago. He loved his wife, but he was always gone. She never knew when he would go, or where. And she never knew when - or if - he would even come back. It was hard, but they did the best they could. They tried to be stronger than the world that tried to tear them apart. Sometimes the couple won. But in the end, fate was a sore loser.

He pulled the lever on the reloading press bolted to the workbench that used to be a table. Another nine-millimeter projectile was pressed firmly at a prescribed depth into a brass casing, which in turn had already been loaded with a precise amount of smokeless powder. Exactly like the other rounds in every way. They were uniform in length to the micrometer. Their weight was exactly the same. Each round held the same load right down to the smallest fraction of a grain of powder so that each bullet performed exactly like the others. With ammunition - just like with soldiers - consistency was the root of precision. To perform at his best, he needed his ammo to be consistent. Uniform. Anonymous. Proven.

The senator's car was far from anonymous. A nice luxury car like that drew attention, and this hunter knew that every cop and snitch in Louisiana was going to be looking for it as soon as the authorities discovered Senator Evans' body. Whoever got caught holding that Beamer was going to spend a long time bouncing between an uncomfortable jail cell and an even more uncomfortable interrogation room. There was no chop shop or salvage yard into which he could safely dispose of it. The BMW was just too hot. His first order of business after killing the lecherous pig was to check the car for anything of value or utility, then drive it down a back road, turn off onto a dirt trail, and follow that until the car fell into a mangrove and sunk up to the axles. Then, just for good measure, he doused the interior with lighter fluid from his pack, stuffed a rag down the fuel intake, and lit it up. The sun had not even broken the horizon before he had stuffed his gear back into his backpack, humped his kit back to the main road, and navigated his way back to where he had previously stashed his truck.

If everything worked as it should, he had some time to lie low. A day of rest and resupply back here at the camper also gave him time to think. Time to plan. Time to monitor people's response to his handiwork. And time to get himself - and his gear - ready. And clean. Frangible rounds like the ones he used last night tended to leave a bit of residue on his suppressor's baffles.

Picking his next target was no simple matter. There were plenty of options, but each individual presented unique challenges. Circumstances associated with location, logistics, timing, and the target's impact to his ultimate goal all had to be addressed. Any one of a long list of variables could play a factor in determining how and when his targets needed to be neutralized. He learned long ago that in order to be truly effective, he had to tailor his tactics to fit his target. Make the how and when fit the who and where, as the lesson went. That was how a man played the Find, Fix, and Finish game if he wanted to win.

And he had to stay random. Cluster kills led to patterns. Patterns got a guy caught - or at least gave his intended targets the chance to anticipate his movements. *I come like a thief in the night.*

The campground he stayed at, funded by Senator Evans' cash, provided plenty of electricity for his trailer. In addition to the lamp, a small refrigerator ran in the corner and a radio played softly on a shelf at the front over the small, folding rack where he sometimes rested with a light nap. He never really slept. Not anymore. Not in what felt like forever. It had been years since his dreams and memories - and before then, his work - allowed him a full night's rest. Years since he had last sunk comfortably into a soft bed for six or more hours' uninterrupted sleep. Time felt funny these days. Sometimes he was here, but then he'd take a step and he was back in the mountains. Sometimes when he cruised down the street, he would turn a corner and find himself driving down some avenue in some godforsaken desert town just waiting for the next roadside blast to rock his truck. He knew he came back from the war, but he was not sure he left all of the war behind him. And the place he came back to did not feel like America. Everything was off. The country felt wrong. It was like someone had come into his house while he was out and moved everything an inch. Too many things had changed for him to ever truly settle in and be the same man again.

A gloved hand caught the manufactured bullet as it was extracted from the reloading press. He carefully wiped it with a rag soaked in nail polish remover, then placed it into the tray to his right. The one that contained the bullet's identical predecessors. Then he plucked another casing from the tray on his left, set it in the reloader, and pulled the lever again. He repeated the process, long familiar to him, with less than half of his attention. Topping off his ammunition reserves would take hours. Part of his brain could relax during that time. It was almost like sleep. He could take a mental nap. Tension slowly eased out of his legs and other parts of his body. The rest of his imagination was focused on his next task. Who? Where?

A voice on the radio announced the news - headlines that he knew were mostly untrue. Most of the stories the sheeple heard from the media were lies. Some of the lies came from honest errors or gaps in the information, but a lot of the lies were purposeful misinformation. The majority of Americans listened to propaganda and brainwashing. They blindly followed instructions and sensations, clueless about how the world around them truly worked or looked.

The Patriot no longer saw himself as just another American. Unlike the majority of folks who composed the mindless mass that he hid within and moved among, he was a fighter - a dog who clothed himself in sheep's wool to more easily hunt the wolves. He was a Patriot with nothing left to stop him from doing what must be done for the good of his country. Not the country as it had become. No. He fought to bring back the country he and his brothers spent a lifetime sacrificing to protect. That was the America for which he fought. They had all lost so much. In the Patriot's mind, it was high time to start taking things back.

Of course, Sunday night's hit was the big story. Everything else in the news cycle would revolve around Senator Evans' death for a while. And the follow up story inspired not only a glance at the map taped to the wall in front of him, but also an idea for his next step.

*   *   *

The black Chevy Suburban was synonymous with government service. Years ago it might have served as a low profile vehicle, but its overuse in official business over time transformed it into the stereotypical vehicle of the United States federal government.

In the passenger seat, Danny was just thankful that this particular Suburban smelled clean. Cleanish, anyway. In theory, the guys in motor pool were supposed to keep all of a unit's vehicles clear of debris, washed, and running. Sometimes, though, you were lucky that the car or truck you just checked out possessed any two of those three characteristics.

Elbee pulled the truck through a wrought iron gate at a respectfully slow pace, which also prevented any of the media hounds outside the fence from following her up the long driveway to the large plantation-style home at its far end. Willows and cypress trees provided shade up the full length of the driveway, which terminated in a loop. Sandra stopped the Suburban midway through the circle, at the closest point to Widow Evans' door.

"I'll do the talking," Elbee directed as she shut off the government vehicle.

Wakefield jumped out of the truck and recovered his jacket from the back seat. "It was my idea."

"It's my case," Elbee reminded him. "And my state."

"If it's your state," he baited, "then why haven't you taken me somewhere to get some proper Louisiana cooking?"

"I wouldn't want to mess up your travel claim by buying you dinner," Sandra mocked.

Danny fluffed and straightened his suit jacket as they walked up the steps to the Evans home, freeing the fabric that sometimes bunched around his shoulder holster. "I'm not asking you to buy," he corrected, "just point. I've spent most of my adult life traveling. I like to make it a point to eat local food as much as possible when I'm on a trip. Just give me the address of a place I can sample the local wares."

"And just what 'local wares' were you hoping to 'sample,' Special Agent Wakefield?" Elbee asked in a measured, accusatory monotone.

Both agents wore sunglasses, which prevented either from fully reading the other's expression, but Danny knew that her meaning implied something besides food. Maybe she thought he wanted to revisit the Chambre Rouge as a patron, rather than an investigator? Or did she think he was soliciting her for a hook up with an easy friend? Danny snickered. The way Elbee kept her head locked straight forward was just one of the many cues that told him she disapproved of anything that was not strictly business.

"This crime happened within the context of a culture. To fully understand the crime," he explained, "I must fully understand the culture. And to truly understand a culture one must partake in its menu." Wakefield's sounded less like a guy looking for a snack and more like a college professor explaining a complex sociological theory. "Everything about a culture can be gleaned from its weapons or its desserts. How about some real, made-from-scratch peanut butter pralines?"

Sandra looked a little surprised to find Danny talking about food literally. Classic southern praline candy was a signature Louisiana dessert which was deceptively difficult to make. One of her pencil-thin eyebrows rose above her Ray Bans. "Are you asking me to make you some praline candy?"

"Why? Do you know how?"

"I don't really cook," Elbee announced with a mixture of indignity and pride, "not anything special, anyway." Her posture - head up, shoulders back, arms crossed - during that proclamation made it clear to Danny that Sandra was baiting him to say something about a woman needing culinary skills. He offered her little more than a non-committed grunt, more a breathed than spoken. "Don't you think it's more than just a little chauvinistic to just expect me to cook because I'm a woman?"

"Not at all," he reposted. "I expect you to be able to cook because you're human. I mean, you eat, right? So I assume that means you can do a little better for yourself than slap together a salad and call it good?"

"What's wrong with eating salad?"

"Salad's not food," Danny declared, "it's what food eats."

"A diet based on mostly fruits and vegetables is the basis of a healthy lifestyle. It's what our ancestors ate. And they had a much lower incidence of cancers, diabetes, and diet related illnesses."

"Tell that to a lion." He looked and her and shook his head. "You know, Elbee, I don't think I should eat your pralines. Even if you could make them. I mean, besides the part where you are doing it for me might stretch the bounds of professionalism. What I mean is, you're not actually from Louisiana. I need something from a native. Something authentic. Something real."

CHAPTER 4

"SPECIAL AGENTS Elbee and Wakefield to see you, Ma'am," the dark-skinned butler, James, announced as he escorted them into the Evans' parlor, which was decorated entirely in Louis XVI-style furniture and furnishings. Mrs. Evans was already seated behind her ornate desk at the far end of the room from the French door Elbee and Wakefield entered. Wakefield knew Mrs. Evans to be a nearly seventy, but her fair skin and subtly dyed blonde hair gave her the appearance of a woman at least fifteen years younger. The gray skirt suit she wore flattered her trim figure. Only the red rings around her eyes - telltale marks of the tears she kept hidden for private moments - betrayed her age. An elegant triple strand of pearls hung around the widow's thin neck in tasteful contrast to her black silk blouse.

Sitting in one of the seats before the desk was a man whose white hair and goatee, paired with his thick glasses, painted him in Wakefield's mind as Colonel Sanders' stunt double. He matched the southern fried chicken king's girth, but nearly ruined the illusion by wearing a three-piece suit that was light grey, rather than stark white. *Probably what the Colonel would wear if he was in mourning,* Danny remarked inwardly without the slightest break in his professional bearing.

"Thank you, James." Mrs. Evans accepted the agents with a slight and prim nod, which also served as James' signal of dismissal. "Agents," she continued with her hands clasped properly upon the desk, "this is my attorney and advisor, Ernest P. Littleford, the third."

The fact that a pair of wealthy southern white folks were sitting in a parlor decorated in antiquated fashion inside a plantation house while being served by a black butler gave the whole scene a not-too-subtle antebellum feeling. And a lawyer named Ernest was, in Wakefield's estimation, a bit of an oxymoron.

"Mrs. Evans," Elbee began in a voice that was confident, but tender, "I am sorry to disturb you, but if it's not too much trouble, we would like to ask you a few questions about your husband's death."

"Certainly, dear," Mrs. Evans replied. "That is just what Mr. Littleford and I were discussing."

"Thank you, Ma'am." The agents walked the handful of steps across the parlor. At Mrs. Evans' gesture, Elbee took the remaining seat from the pair in front of the desk. Like all of the furniture in this room, it featured ornately scrolled woodwork and bone white cushions. Wakefield settled onto the small love seat nestled against one of the cool blue walls.

Sandra's tone remained respectful and compassionate. "I know you have already discussed a lot of this with the local police, but there are a number of details we need to clarify."

Mrs. Evans' hard face, Danny could tell, had once been that of an absolute knockout. A few years younger than her late husband, she had aged with grace and dignity. Her skin was still smooth and her blonde hair had silvered gently, but her cool blue eyes remained vibrant. She was still filled with the energy of life. Had Danny met her at a country club, he imagined, he would have found her quite attractive despite the fact that she was technically old enough to be his mother. Well, maybe his mother's younger sister. And, after a drink or two, who knew what bad decisions the two of them might make...

But now, in the wake of her husband's murder, all of Mrs. Evans' grace and beauty was locked away. In its place was an armored veneer. Wakefield had seen it on more than one grieving family member. She wore that facade like a steel helmet to keep the world from hurting her any further. She was stone now, like a statue in a museum that looked as soft as silk but was actually made of solid marble.

"Mrs. Evans," Sandra asked, "We weren't here when the Sheriff's Department visited you, so I'm sorry if some of these questions seem redundant. We're just trying to be thorough."

"Anything, dear," the matron responded, "if it helps find my husband's killer."

Sandra skipped the rest of the customary warm up. "When did you first learn of your husband's death?"

"Murder." Mrs. Evans corrected sharply. "My husband was murdered."

"Indeed," Sandra allowed. "When did you first learn of your husband's murder?"

"Monday afternoon. When Sheriff Beahen came by the house to inform me."

Sandra nodded. "And you last saw Senator Evans Sunday?"

"That's right," Mrs. Evans affirmed. "I left the house around three thirty or so. My bridge club meets at four o'clock Sunday afternoons. Duke was still here when I left."

"But he wasn't here when you came home?" Elbee probed.

Wakefield could see a tear behind Mrs. Evans' steely facade. She hid it well. "No," her voice barely broke. "He told me before he left that he was going to his office in town, and that he would likely stay the night. He did that from time to time, so I didn't think anything of it. I did explain all of this to Sheriff Beahen," she pointed.

Elbee cleared her throat quietly. "Mrs. Evans, did Sheriff Beahen tell you where the Senator's body was found?"

Widow Evans' clenched jaw and wavering lip told Wakefield everything he needed to know. "Yes," she croaked. "He was found at - at that house."

"I'm sorry, Mrs. Evans," Elbee continued, "but I have to ask: Did you know about your husband's visits to that house?"

Chandra Lee Evans sneered. "Good God, no!" she spat. Quickly, she drew a breath and gathered her composure. "Don't get me wrong, dear," she continued more calmly - though far from happy. "I know better than anyone what some of my husband's colleagues do with their off time, and I admit that I've long had my suspicions as to my husband's fidelity." The widow's hands clenched tightly, still on her desk. "But, a whorehouse? Really!" She gasped at the thought. "And it just goes to show you, too. My husband was always a man of the people, but when decent folk get mixed up with, with, with those people..." Chandra Lee's eyes closed as her voice trailed off. "Well, there it is," she said at last. "It isn't right, but he should have known better."

Those people..? Wakefield thought. *As in, 'black people?' 'Lesser people?' Like your butler?* He felt that, by the looks of things, Elbee was doing a better job of enduring Widow Evans' racist overtones than he was. Danny wanted to slap the stupid out of the old swamp witch.

"Mrs. Evans," Elbee continued, "did your husband have any enemies?"

Chandra Lee scoffed. "Dearie, my husband spent a lifetime as a Senator. Of course he had enemies."

"Anyone who would want him dead?" Elbee pressed.

"Everyone he ever beat in an election. Anyone wanting to run for his seat." Chandra Lee chortled. "At least half the people we've had here at the house for dinner."

"Anyone specific? Someone he might have had a recent conflict with? Bad business deals?" Elbee fished.

Widow Evans furrowed her brow. "What are you talking about?"

"Our understanding," Mr. Littlejohn chimed in, "is that Senator Evans was shot in the back after an unfortunate decision to solicit a prostitute. Perhaps you should focus on shaking down pimps and questioning whores, rather than bothering my client while she's grieving. Hmm?"

"I'm surprised you stayed quiet so long," Wakefield remarked with false jocularity. His tone became cold and aggressive as his attention shifted. He fixed his penetrating gaze on the widow. "Senator Evans wasn't just popped once or twice in the back by some thug. He was shot more than thirty times, in the back, front and face. At close range. With military precision." He turned to the widow, whose face was a mask of horror. "I'm sorry, Ma'am. It looks like the Sheriff left that little detail out. Now, in the interest of catching your husband's killer while some of us are still young, let's try again: Do you know anyone in particular who might want to assassinate your husband?"

Wakefield's lack of tact prompted Elbee to grip the arms on her chair, wrenching the scrolled woodwork the way she wanted to wring her soon-to-be-ex-partner's neck.

"Assassinate?" Widow Evans gasped. Her mouth moved in stunned silence. Then, she finally managed, "Well, I never -"

"You might not," Wakefield interjected, "but I have a feeling you know folks who would."

"And just what is that supposed to mean?" Littleton demanded.

Wakefield answered the lawyer, but kept his eyes firmly set on the widow and his mouth set to rapid fire. "Before you married Duke Evans, you were Chandra Lee Devereaux. Daughter of shipping magnate Charles Devereaux. Before he passed, your father was a powerful businessman who built his empire the not-so-nice way. Rumor is that he was the kind of guy who probably knew how to reach professionals with certain — ah, *particular* - talents. Even if he managed to raise you completely in the dark about some of his less pleasant dealings, surely you aren't completely blind to how your brother, Wilford, runs the family fortune… Are you?"

"Don't answer any of that," Littlejohn barked.

Wakefield studied the widow's face carefully. He could tell she was thinking it over, mentally processing the idea that her husband was assassinated by a professional, rather than shot by some gangbanger as she had apparently believed. The way she looked down told him that she was remembering something - a person or people; some occurrence or events from her past. He knew by the way her eyes quickly darted back and forth that she was comparing those memories with the new information before her.

"No," she managed at last. "I don't know anything."

Danny turned back to the lawyer. "Are you going to cooperate with our investigation, or are you going to make us go get a Kentucky Fried Court Order before allowing us access to the Evans' financial records?" To her credit, Elbee sat in silence during Wakefield's inquiry and Littlejohn's harrumph. "I'll take that as a 'Yes, we'll cooperate.' Because nobody wants the embarrassment of obstruction charges."

Sandra produced a business card from her suit jacket pocket and placed it on the widow's desk pad. "We're sorry for the inconvenience," she offered, "and for your loss. Please feel free to contact me if you think of anything." At that, Elbee rose from her luxurious chair, cast Wakefield a meaningful glare, then showed herself out the door.

By the time Wakefield exited the house, Elbee was already climbing into the Suburban. She started the engine as he got in but did not wait for him to buckle his seatbelt before she pulled away.

"Somebody's in a rush," Danny quipped. "Did you think of something?"

"What the hell was that, Wakefield?" she demanded.

"What?"

"I thought I told you to let me do the talking."

"And I thought we were doing 'Good Cop, Bad Cop.'" With Wakefield's eyes hidden by his sunglasses, Elbee could not tell if he was teasing or if he was serious. "Look," he continued in a calming tone, "that was good in there. We don't not know who the killer is yet, but we just might be starting to get somewhere."

"The only place you're going is back to Washington, if you pull any crap like that again." Elbee fumed for a moment. Then, still annoyed, she asked, "What did we get out of that? Except maybe the opportunity to harass some poor old widow?"

Danny held his left index finger up. "First, we can now clearly eliminate her as a suspect."

"Really? How?"

Wakefield's tone became curious. "Really? You have to ask? You got a read off her, didn't you? She totally didn't kill her husband."

"That's what the Sheriff said," Elbee growled.

"Yes," he allowed, "but we sure as Hell can't take her word for it. She's hiding something, and up until a minute ago for all we knew it was that she was behind her husband's death."

"What do you mean?"

"The Sheriff didn't say anything about how that woman is physically incapable of murder. You saw her. Light frame. No callouses on the hands. Narrow hips. Gentle mannerisms. She's never done hard work or shot a gun before in her life."

Elbee shot him a quick look of disbelief. "Are you pretending to be a detective now?"

"I learned how to read people in the Corps," he defended. "Interrogation school. Don't feds get some of that?"

Elbee nodded. She had to admit, silently and to herself, that she had missed all of those details. "Narrow hips?" she countered. "She was sitting behind a desk."

"There was a picture of her and the Senator at some dog-and-pony show. Looked to be about six months old. Maybe a year. Her dress was rather, um, slinky."

Sandra scoffed. "You're a pig."

"Hey," Danny defended, "I'm a healthy, single, red-blooded American male and she's a rich woman. Smokin' hot too - except for the part where she's a racist bitch." He shook his head. "Pity. Still, I'll bet you a bagel that she tries to take her dead husband's seat in the Senate. Oh, and a cup of coffee that she's pulling a little trim on the side, too."

"I don't even want to know," Sandra dismissed. "And cops eat donuts, not bagels."

"Cops eat donuts. But you eat bagels," he corrected. "I saw the wrapper in your trash can. Besides, I've seen female cops who eat donuts," he offered, "and you don't look like one."

"Am I supposed to take that as a compliment," she asked venomously, "or file a sexual harassment complaint?"

"Donuts make cops overweight. Female cops faster than their male counterparts," he deflected innocently. "You're not fat."

"And you're still a pig," she noted. "Okay, fine. She's rich. Maybe she found out about her husband and paid someone to off him."

"Nope," Wakefield shut her down, but ticked another finger into the air. "She was genuinely shocked by the details of her husband's murder. You saw her face. If that was acting, then give her the friggin' Oscar. If she was responsible, she'd have been interested. Or even proud. Or she'd've gone into denial mode. Maybe feign ignorance. Which leads to number three," he matched the count on his hand to his words. "Sheriff Beahen is a lying bastard. He didn't tell her the truth about the senator's death, and then he lied to us in a report. At our earliest convenience, we definitely need to plant a boot in his ass."

"You think he's covering up more details? Maybe even involved?"

"Maybe," he mused. "You think he isn't?"

Elbee considered it for a moment. Danny could almost read her thoughts as she appeared to come to the conclusion that the idea had merit. Beahen and his men tried to cut her off before she could talk to Madame Flowers - who seemed to be unwilling to cooperate with his department. And he did lie, both to the widow and to her. "I think a little talk with our dear sheriff might be useful," she agreed.

CHAPTER 5

AFTER THE TERRORIST attacks on September 11, 2001, security around airports nationwide and around the world was significantly increased. In the bid to deny future terrorists of another potential weapon and a mass of victims every airport was infested with security cameras, scanners and an army from the Transportation Security Administration.

Every commercial airport anyway.

Linda Rogers, the Representative from California's 12th Congressional District, never flew on a commercial airplane. This privilege began long before her political career. Her considerable wealth did not originate from fiscal responsibility with her ample salary as a legislator, but as the daughter of fabulously wealthy parents. Of course, it also helped when she married the son of a spectacularly successful California vintner - and the sole heir to his family's considerable holdings - all those decades ago.

Generally, Rogers' position allowed her access to government aircraft. She had, over the years, grown accustomed to utilizing such planes for all manner of uses… not all of which were totally legitimate government business in the strictest sense. With the mid-term election season at hand, however, Linda needed to avoid any appearance of using the resources of her public office for private gain or electioneering. So, for the time being, she simply used her and Oliver's private Gulfstream G280 to ferry back and forth between Washington and San Francisco.

The Patriot knew about the Rogers' private plane. It was a common convenience for a family so wealthy, and Ms. Rogers' love of the limelight gave the media plenty of opportunities to observe her seemingly candid moments boarding and disembarking from the bird at public events. And while the congresswoman undoubtedly wanted the cameras focused on her own self as much as possible, elementary research of archived footage of Mrs. Rogers - clips that were, thanks to YouTube, freely and readily available - allowed virtually anyone to catch a glimpse of her jet's tail number.

Unfortunately, the Patriot did not know the exact timeline for Evans' memorial service. But the news anchors mentioned that it was going to be held at the National Cathedral in Washington, D.C. sometime in the next few days. He was sure it would turn into a highly publicized political circus completely irresistible to D.C. hacks and congressional celebutants like Rogers. He also assumed, based on what he knew about her character, that the Democrat *prima donna* would stay in San Francisco to campaign for re-election until the last possible minute.

So, he knew her current location, her future destination, her likely method of movement and found himself within a limited window of opportunity to act.

There were a number of private airfields in the bay area, but only a few could accommodate a bird like the Gulfstream G280. A quick search of press releases on the internet showed Rogers almost exclusively used what looked like Napa County Airport. The Patriot's pickup truck, complete with out of state plates and towing a camper, was a bit conspicuous in this town. Along the way to the airport, the Patriot left his truck in a paid parking lot and "borrowed" some local transportation that had been street parked a block away. It was midafternoon on a Thursday, so the Patriot figured the liberated vehicle's owner would likely be at work for at least a few more hours. At least, that was his most sincere hope. As much as they promoted welfare programs, he was not sure that Democrats actually knew anything about work.

And so, it came to be that the Patriot was able to conduct his reconnaissance of the Napa airfield on a red Honda CBR1000 with his stubby flathead screwdriver in its ignition and all of his mission essential gear stuffed into an innocuous backpack. The airport security cameras would be unlikely to pick up anything out of the ordinary… and even less likely that anything could be traced back to him. The risk of detection at this stage of his plan was fairly low. And after driving all the way across the American southwest in just a day and a half, he needed to get out of his truck for a bit.

The Patriot skirted by the airport's main entrance

and parking areas. He was not too worried about being seen. Riding the bike gave the Patriot an excuse to wear a full-face helmet and gloves, which masked his identity. Civilians designed security to be visible. Thus, it could act as a deterrent. So, he figured, the largest concentration of hurdles between himself and his objective was certain to be found via the most obvious approach. As his old mentor had taught him long ago, the direct route was always mined.

Like most airfields, Napa County was surrounded by a tall chain link fence topped with barbed wire. And, like most airfields, there was a road just outside of that fence that circumnavigated the property. Halfway around the airfield perimeter, the Patriot found an ideal entry point - a gap under the original fence made by washed out soil which had been haphazardly repaired with a strand of barbed wire stretched across its expanse. He shook his head in disgust and wondered if the grounds maintenance crew would have been deterred from crossing the Rio Grande in the dead of night by such shoddy workmanship. Then again, maybe that was the point. Maybe Jose the Groundskeeper's brother was Juan the Drug Mule.

He continued his orbit, just to be sure. One never knew when someone might absentmindedly leave a security gate open, or where one might find recent storm damage that would make his access even easier than the fence gap. Alas, the rest of the facilities appeared to be in fairly decent repair. There were no other glaringly obvious vulnerabilities on the perimeter to allow him unfettered access to the airfield.

Finding nothing along those lines, the Patriot

started his second lap around the airfield. Shortly before he reached the spot where he remembered the fence gap to be, he stashed the bike in a contracted maintenance parking lot. He hiked the rest of the way to the hole on foot. After some quick work with his pocket multitool, the Patriot was able to slide under the fence and - thanks to his nondescript jeans, safety boots, and black t-shirt - became just another superfluous groundskeeper as he walked across the grassy field. His facade was made all the more convincing by the safety helmet and reflective vest he produced from his backpack - which now covertly held his motorcycle gear.

The Patriot avoided contact with anyone else as much as he could without looking like someone who was actually sneaking around. As soon as he reached the first outer building on the airfield, he ducked under concealment, pulled a set of tightly folded, dark blue coveralls from his backpack and slipped them over his clothes. He also produced a few tools with carabiners looped through their handles and strung them along the back and sides of his pack to complete his disguise. He looked just like every other commercial maintainer on his way to some contracted job, and anyone who saw him was likely to assume he worked for someone else's team.

Coolly, the Patriot continued into the hangar. He still avoided direct contact with any of the legitimate workers. He might look the part, but he knew almost nothing about aircraft maintenance. His cover would not hold up to too much scrutiny by an actual tradesman. He worked his way around the metal cavern, bypassing the propeller driven planes and reading tail numbers of the larger ones.

There, his eyes locked onto a white passenger jet with twin engines. N72235. Same number as in the news clips. The private jet was near the far wall and immediately inside the massive hangar doors, which hung open to facilitate airflow, foot traffic and so the sunlight would help illuminate the work areas.

And under the right wing he spied a pair of mechanics and their rolling tool cabinet.

An innocent change in direction allowed the Patriot to shift his course and stop at another plane - this one a twin engine prop with red stripes along the otherwise bland, white fuselage. He tugged on the propeller blades and cowlings as he had seen crewmen and maintainers do before, pretending to check for some unspecific safety issue while he kept the Gulfstream and her maintenance crew in sight. The legitimate mechanics closed one of the Gulfstream's access panels and returned tools to the cabinet. Whatever they had been doing, they were nearly done.

The Patriot checked his watch. *Just past sixteen thirty.* He looked above the horizon outside the hangar doors. Clear and calm. Perhaps the Congresswoman planned to fly out this evening. This would explain the plane's easy location near the exit. This was where the mechanics would likely finish up the plane's last minute preflight maintenance. *Am I too late?*

One of the mechanics snatched up a clipboard from the deck while the other screwed the last panel into place. The former scribbled something, shot his partner a comment, listened to the response, then scribbled again. Both finished at about the same time, then the second guy tossed his tool into the cabinet's last open drawer. The one with the clipboard closed and locked the cabinet and slapped the clipboard onto its flat metal top. Then the duet walked away, pushing their cart and chatting about something or other. They passed within a few yards of the Patriot, but if they noticed his presence, they appeared to completely ignore him.

Rogers could be here any moment, complete with entourage and luggage. Then again, it could be hours before she boarded the plane. It could be another day. There was no way to tell how long the Patriot had before he was noticed, and he was sure to catch attention if he was hanging out of an engine when the owner wanted to take off.

On the other hand, he was maddeningly close to accomplishing his objective. And, if anyone ever discovered what he was about to do during the aftermath, the mechanics who just signed off on the plane would, in theory, take any heat that came down the pipe.

It was a matter of personal safety versus mission accomplishment. A point like this occurred during virtually every operation he had ever conducted in his entire career. A decision had to be made. Go or no go? The Patriot looked around quickly and saw nobody approaching, so he picked up his backpack and made for the Gulfstream as quickly as he could without drawing attention.

*   *   *

The laws of time always became blurry whenever he was on target. Seconds stretched. Hurried minutes turned into eternities. Yet it also felt to the Patriot like a half hour of his life had just evaporated while he blinked. He knew he was racing against a clock that could expire any second, but the Patriot had to be sure to leave no obvious sign of tampering. So, his work completed, he dogged the Gulfstream's service panel with purposeful speed, careful to leave the job cleanly done. His cordless screwdriver set each of the body panel's bolts securely, then he ran his hand around the seams and pushed to make sure the panel held tightly in place.

Satisfied, the Patriot dropped his tool into the outer compartment of his backpack, zipped the bag and disappeared into the labyrinth of planes within the hangar like a gigolo at a dance club. After a few minutes, he emerged from the other side of the crowd of aircraft. Another moment of observing the real maintainers' comings and goings led him to a service exit. It was designed and intended for authorized persons rather than the general public. The door was unguarded. It did not even require a badge or keycard to open from the inside.

The Patriot paused at the door long enough to spare a glance back into the main space of the hangar. He could just barely see the landing gear under the Gulfstream's left wing, unmoved from its parking spot. He unzipped his pack's outer pocket, reached in blindly, and withdrew a cheap wired ear bud, half of a pair, easily detected inside the bag by touch alone. The headset was the common earbud type everybody seemed to own these days. This particular pair was jacked into a walkie talkie, rather than a phone or MP3 player. The guts of the radio's mate made up the improvised transmitter for the device he installed in the G280. The Patriot left the receiver in the pocket as he zipped it, then slung his pack again and stuffed one of the earbuds into his right ear. He walked out of the service exit bouncing his head, pretending to listen to some imaginary hip-hop rhythm.

CHAPTER 6

THE DOOR TO the sheriff's office nearly flew off its hinges as it was thrown open. "Sheriff Beahen," Sandra growled as she blew through the portal like a storm, "you worthless sack of crap."

Obadiah Beahen sat comfortably at his desk, his mouth halfway into a chili cheese dog. Onions mounded on top of the fiery treat tickled his nose. The intercom built into his phone chirped. "Special Agent Elbee of the FBI to see you Sheriff," his assistant's voice mewled. The sheriff still had not figured out whether to abort or finish his bite as he hummed a muffled response.

Special Agent Wakefield crossed the threshold into the sheriff's office just a beat behind Elbee, then pulled short. "Oh, look! Pork rinds!" He plucked a large plastic bag filled with the fried confections off the top of a stack of file folders on the sheriff's desk.

"You don't mind if I help myself, do you?"

"We just got back from interviewing Mrs. Evans," Elbee stabbed. "It seems you left some things out from both of us about your visit earlier."

Sheriff Beahen placed his entree on a paper plate and snatched his fried pig skins back from Wakefield's hand. "If yer tryin' to play Good Cop/Bad Cop with me, boy, it ain't gonna work. Ah'm a cop. Ah know the game."

"Best watch out, Sheriff," Wakefield commented while he crunched the rind still in his mouth. "You are what you eat." Finally, Danny swallowed. "And I'm not Good Cop. Just a spectator who enjoys mocking inbred redneck idiots."

"Why did you lie in your report?" Elbee returned to the point.

"What on Earth do you mean?" Beahen protested.

"You didn't tell Widow Evans the truth about the Senator's death," Wakefield pressed. "About how he was shot."

"Well, ah may've spared a grievin' woman some of the more gruesome details -"

"You think that if she knew her husband was turned into swiss cheese she might've reacted differently?" Danny shot back while he crunched on a salty piece of fried pig skin. "Like, oh, I dunno, maybe by remembering something relevant to the case? I'm just throwing it out there."

"You're protecting her," Elbee accused. "My only question is why."

"Maybe you were hoping to console her in her moment of grief?" Danny insinuated. "Be her buttery shoulder to cry on, maybe?"

"That's outrageous!"

"Or were you playing nursemaid to a donor?" Danny continued. "You know what they say: Don't bite the tete that feeds you. Exactly how much did the Evans' contribute to your last campaign, Sheriff?"

"Well, ah never -"

"The only thing that matters, Beahen," Elbee interjected, "is that your office is wasting time instead of helping. Either you are the incompetent head of a bunch of bumbling buffoons, or you are intentionally interfering with a federal investigation. Which is it, Sheriff?"

"Look," the Sheriff threw his hands up in surrender, "ah've gotta live in this town. Long after yer gone ah'll be livin' he-ah. Sometimes you gotta just get along on the bayou."

"What a crock," Elbee spat.

"Look, Sheriff Butterball," Danny continued, "In case you haven't noticed, we ain't from around here. Me, personally, I'm really starting to hate this place. And my partner here looks like quite the woman scorned. She looks ready to burn this department to the ground just to see the glow. And I'm inclined to grab some marshmallows and enjoy the show. I don't give a flying flip. I'll be back in D.C. living my life. You'll be unemployed. Hell, she'll probably find an excuse to put you behind bars before she's done. How long you think you'll last in prison with all of those low lives you and your boys've locked up over the years?" Wakefield snickered. "You don't think you'll be pitching, do you? I bet before they shiv you, a few of the boys in the can have you screaming like a pig. Some of these bayou boys will rape your fat ass until your farts sound like this: *whoosh*..."

"Alright alright," Beahen flushed in a freshly sweaty pallor. The mental image of his likely future prompted the Sheriff to stow the rest of his uneaten food. "Now, y'all did'n he-ah this from me, but Duke Evans'd been goin' to the Chambre Rouge about once a month'r so for years. Decades, in fact."

"Really?" Elbee challenged him.

"Ah found out about the place ye-ahs ago while shakin' down a local pimp. When me an mah partner at the time kicked it in, there he was. Duke Evans. Lit'rally caught him wit his pants down. Trousers around his ankles an' ev'rthang. The senator offered us a stack o' cash to look the other way. We was good cops, but mah parter's little girl, Jenny, was just fix'n to go off to college."

"So, you took the senator's money," Elbee concluded.

"And let his favorite little *maison derrière* keep doing business," Wakefield added.

"S'not like they was hurtin' anyone, really," Sheriff Beahen argued. "An' after a while we made a deal wit Ms. Flowers that if any o' her Johns was up to sum'tin - drugs or the like - then she'd tell me about it and we'd bust 'em on down the road. Over the ye'ahs mah boys've made quite a few arrests thanks to her tippin' us off."

Sandra shook her head in disgust. "You can't just let somebody continually break the law for years because they're your informant, Sheriff."

"Li'l darlin,' surely you ain't that naive." Obadiah wiped his sausage fingers on a napkin. "Well, the'ah you have it. Now you know. Ah shielded all o' this from you cuz ah was protectin' a source. Now, Special Agent Elbee, if you'll kindly git outta mah office, ah've got thangs to do."

"You think I'm just gonna let this go?" Elbee's eyes were ablaze.

"Ah don't see how you've really got a choice in the matter, li'l darlin'." Beahen sat back in his oversized chair. "You see, as Sheriff, ah have the final say in all law enforcement operations within this parish. If you make a stink 'bout this, ah'll boot every federal agent right outta mah jurisdiction."

"You'd shut down a federal investigation into a senator's murder to protect a whorehouse?" Wakefield raised his eyebrow.

"Ah'm sure mah own people'd be able to handle it," Sheriff Beahen assured them. "An' ah'm also sure the guv'ner'd see things mah way. Just in case you was thinkin' 'bout goin' over mah head after you leave."

As much as the agents hated to admit it, Beahen had a point. While common sense outlined that national priorities superseded local authority, the fact remained that technically the sheriff of any county - or, in New Orleans' unique case, parish - was the chief law enforcement officer within that jurisdiction. He or she was the ultimate authority on who operated within their domain. And even though Wakefield and Elbee carried badges with eagles on them, they operated within Beahen's jurisdiction solely at his discretion. A jurisdictional measuring contest at this juncture would, more likely than not, end up as an embarrassing waste of everyone's time.

Danny blew out a breath. "He might be right, Elbee," he conceded. She shot him a look that made him glad her eyes were not lasers. "Then again," he pulled out his phone and tapped a few commands, "I found this anonymous tip that one of your deputies has been soliciting little teenaged girls online. Something about meeting a few of them for a late-night rendezvous. Oh my! Sometimes while he's on patrol… I sure hope someone with an untraceable email account doesn't send it off to two dozen or so different news outlets around the state." Danny let loose a melodramatic gasp. "That might be embarrassing." Wakefield pressed a button. His phone made a whoosh sound. "Uh oh." Sheriff Beahen's face turned red as the Secret Service agent continued. "And what is this? An audit of the department's finances and budget that indicates a bunch of money is missing from the general account? Land oh-goshin', Sheriff! You haven't been embezzling or misspending tax dollars for personal use, have you Obadiah? Isn't there a former sheriff sitting in jail in Missouri right now for that?" Whoosh. "Oh, now this is not good at all. Elbee, did you see this booking report? A black suspect in Beahen's jail who says four of our good sheriff's white officers beat him like Rodney King when he got stopped unarmed for loitering - in his own pal's front yard?" Wakefield smiled meaningfully at the sheriff with his finger hovered meaningfully over the big, green button. "There's no way that could bite you in your fat ass if it got national attention."

"You cocky li'l sonofabitch," Sheriff Beahen erupted out of his seat, but Wakefield just stood with his thumb poised over his phone's send button. "Alrightalrightalright," the portly police officer stewed, "you win. Ah'll cooperate." Danny's eyes widened expectantly, begging the sheriff to continue. "Mah men an' ah'll give you our full cooperation with yer continuing investigation. Includin' full access to all our resources."

"Thank you, Sheriff Beahen," Elbee smiled. "But we'll just take it from here. I think it's best for everyone if my people handle everything ourselves while your guys just stay the Hell out of my way. Your department should send anything pertinent to the FBI field office. And route any future leads up to us immediately. That way we can stay out of each other's hair. What do you think?"

"Certainly. Right away, ma'am." Sheriff Beahen glowered at the agents.

"Thanks for the pork rinds, Sheriff," Danny turned and walked out of the office. As he crossed the threshold to Beahen's still-opened door, his phone emitted another *whoosh*.

The Suburban's air conditioner struggled to cool the truck's cabin against the midday Louisiana heat. Special Agent Elbee finally addressed her partner. "Thanks for getting my back, Daniel. I'm sorry that I didn't trust you in there. For a second, I thought you were actually on his side."

It was the first time they spoke since they walked into Sheriff Beahen's office. Danny looked at her as she drove. "I've always got your back, Elbee," he assured her. "My dad was a cop, back in the day. I understand that sometimes when you're working a case you end up having to do things you might not want to. That's just the nature of the game. But there are two things you should never compromise."

"Oh, yeah? What's that?"

"Your partner and justice."

Sandra allowed herself a smile. "You'd've made a good cop, Daniel. You know that? The real deal."

"What do you mean, 'would have?'" he protested. "They didn't give me a badge and gun just so that I could look cool. I'm a federal agent who catches drug dealers, organized crime bosses, terrorists, money launderers…" Danny threw a thumb over his shoulder to indicate the police station disappearing behind them. "I put more real, hardcore criminals behind bars than any of those donut-eating traffic cops ever will." Danny held his chin up in pride. "I'm a freaking super-cop."

*　　　*　　　*

Linda Rogers struggled to keep her cool as she stormed toward her plane. The clomping from her Prada sling back shoes echoed with each heel strike against the smooth, cold concrete. She slapped her leather portfolio into her assistant's chest.

"You're an idiot, Nelson," she growled without wasting a single glance on the much younger man. "You know that, right?"

"I'm sorry, gram-"

Rogers' index finger darted into the young man's face with the speed and precision of an olympic fencer's foil. "Don't!" she barked, still refusing to turn her head toward the twenty something trying to keep up with her furious pace, "Ever. Call me that. I've told you before."

"Sorry," the man-child mewed, "uh, Ma'am."

Rogers' pace did not slow when she hit the G280's boarding ramp, but at least the carpeted staircase absorbed some of the sound from her sharp steps. Linda reached down and extricated her feet from the cream-colored shoes as she stepped through the hatch and onto her plane. She knew Nelson was her oldest daughter's firstborn son, but the last thing she wanted today was to be reminded that a dolt like him could somehow be related to her by blood.

"I asked you to do one simple thing, Nelson," Rogers continued. "So, how is it, exactly, that the bag with my black Armani ensemble got left back at the house?"

Nelson followed her to the rear of the plane, stopping along the way to stuff her portfolio and his attaché, both made by Louis Vuitton, into one of the overhead compartments. "I'm sorry," he emphasized. Again. He withdrew his phone from the breast pocket of his own tan Armani sport coat and handed the jacket to the muscular Latino male flight attendant. Nelson was pretty sure the lemmings who flew coach on public planes were too stupid to figure out that it was a myth that using a cell phone on a plane might cause interference with the flight instruments. He hurried to the seat across the aisle from the Congresswoman. "I must've left it in the anteroom when I was loading the Jag. The baggage handler got everything out of the trunk. I checked. It was totally empty."

"So, *what* precisely," Linda egged, "am I supposed to wear to the funeral tomorrow morning?"

"I'll pick you up something tonight while you're at dinner. Some of the shops in town will still be open."

Congresswoman Linda Rogers, House Minority Leader, and matron of her family dynasty, stared coldly at her grandson. "And with whom again, am I eating dinner this evening?"

Nelson withdrew his iPhone from his shirt

pocket. "Congresswoman…" he tapped the screen a few times, then brightened and looked her in the eye, "I mean, Senator Wolowitz."

Linda Rogers let out a sigh in utter disbelief. Dianne Wolowitz, her counterpart in the Senate, had been in the United States Congress longer than her grandson-turned-intern-turned-personal assistant had been alive, and the undergrad could not even remember in which Chamber she sat. Linda leaned back in her seat and held her hand over her face in surrender. The boy was hopeless. Her Pomeranian had more potential as an heir to Rogers' political empire than this sandy haired Cretan.

"Fine," she sighed. "You have a list of my sizes in that pocket brain of yours?"

Nelson tapped his phone again, scrolled with a finger, and then nodded. "Yes, Ma'am." He beamed enthusiastically, in obviously misplaced belief he could somehow assure her. "I'll make this right. You'll see."

"Just nothing Gucci," she tapped her armrest. "Remember: I am a very important person. The House Minority Leader does not want to look like a whore."

Nelson typed a note into his phone as the male flight attendant returned.

"*Señor*," the large Puerto Rican - a year or two older than Nelson - directed in a deep, Latin voice, "you'll need to put that away for takeoff."

Linda brightened a little at the steward's arrival. "Oh, Manuel, do be a dear and get a bottle breathing, would you?"

"*Sí, Madame*," Manuel smiled as the port engine started.

*   *   *

The Patriot was about two thirds of the way through the mechanics' parking lot when his ears, hands and legs started to tingle. It was the all-too-familiar feeling of his body dumping the adrenaline that had flooded his system while he worked. Working undercover seemed to make the sensation more intense. He oriented himself and coolly shifted directions toward where he had stashed the stolen motorcycle. A quick check of his watch showed it was well past seventeen thirty. The CBR's lawful owner would probably leave work soon - if he had not already. That meant the bike would likely be reported stolen any minute - if it had not been already. If they were on their game, the San Francisco Police Department should have an alert broadcast within an hour or so. He would have to ditch the Honda soon. Somewhere in town, away from the airport so as to keep anyone from linking the stolen bike to the Rogers' plane. He could walk or catch a cab back to the truck. He memorized the parking lot's address hours ago before he left.

A whistle rang in his right ear through the earbud. Even with the volume turned down, the sound was sharp. The Patriot waited for a moment, then turned over his right shoulder to see the Gulfstream taxi out of the hangar. Careful not to pull the earbud out, he crouched down between the last two cars at the end of the lot, slipped the backpack off, and placed it gently on the ground. He unzipped his coveralls, front and cuffs, and quickly peeled them off his frame.

The Patriot watched the G280 taxi across the

apron through the windshield of one of the cars next to him - an older Camry. Again, he opened his bag. Out came the helmet and a cheap disposable phone. In went the coveralls and the rest of his mechanic's disguise. His eyes remained locked onto the airplane. His adrenaline level spiked again.

Manuel, the flight attendant, knew a good gig when he saw it. His older brother Jorge was the groundskeeper back at the Rogers' mansion, but as little Manny came of age, he noticed the way some of the ladies in and around the Rogers house looked at him. He knew that behind his back the Rogers men all referred to any kind of grueling or smelly job as "Manuel labor." But as long as he worked hard, smiled all of the time, and wore the right swimsuit when he cleaned the family's pool and spa nobody asked about his or Jorge's immigration status.

"Manny," Ms. Rogers called as the plane taxied toward the runway, "I seem to be having some trouble with my seatbelt. Would you be a dear?" Cheerfully, the male flight attendant helped secure the Congresswoman's lap restraint. "Thank you, Manny," Linda smiled and winked slyly at him. Nelson pretended not to notice how his grandmother looked at the Latino helper.

"*De nada, Madame,*" Manuel flicked his eyebrow in a flirtatious flash.

By the time he was twenty-one, Manuel had bedded three generations of Rogers women - and about a dozen or so of the men's assortment of girlfriends, wives, and other gold digging *putas* that filtered in and out of the house. As scandalous as his behavior might have been, the exploits of the women within the Rogers family made Manuel look downright prudish. Now that Manny was twenty-three, Madame Congresswoman had hooked him up with the job at the airport. While he always worked her flights, the Rogers family were not the only clients for whom he flew. He only worked private flights, though. The ones where the passengers were usually rich enough to tip him more cash in a day than Jorge made in a week mowing the lawn and trimming topiaries.

Especially the *señoritas*. The younger rich girls who grew up within the dynasty tended to travel with their own whorish boyfriends - or playful girlfriends, for that matter - who could not resist the novelty of a mid-flight romp. Joining the Mile-High Club, they called it. Sometimes Manny got in on that action, other times he just had to know well enough to turn a blind eye and a deaf ear to whatever happened in the passenger cabin. Satisfying older women was easy though, and a regular part of his duties. Most of the grown-up gals got so little play back home that no matter what Manny did with them on the plane he looked like a stud. A lot of these silver foxes were straight up freaks too, he discovered. And Manny was a regular Rico Suave of the sky. He had been on both sides of spanking, pinching, and all manner of things going into places you'd need a doctor to find... all while cruising miles above the Earth. Manny was not just a member of the Mile High Club - as far as he knew, he was *el Presidente*. And the way Madame Rogers adjusted her hips while he buckled her seatbelt told him this would be another eventful cross-country flight.

The Patriot walked along the perimeter fence. His path kept him parallel to the G280s taxiway and toward the stashed motorcycle. He watched the plane turn onto the main runway. Heard the engines whine. Saw the plane pick up speed.

He palmed the disposable phone and kept his pace. The plane raced down a half mile of runway in a breath. The Patriot keyed a sequence, selected the numbers for two other disposable phones he had bought for cash at the same discount retailer, and sent them a group text. An hourglass icon appeared, prompting the user to wait while the progress bar filled the bottom of the phone's cheap screen. Finally, the bar was full, and a short message appeared on screen:

MESSAGE SENT

Gulfstream N72235 pointed its nose toward the clouds, lifted its wheels off the ground, and rose gracefully into the sky.

The Patriot blew out a long breath, put the phone back into his backpack, turned off his walkie talkie, and made for his stolen motorcycle. Along the way, he glanced at his watch. *Seventeen fifty-two hours.*

What if Paul Revere had to borrow somebody else's stallion to make his ride? the Patriot wondered. *Would they have tried him as a horse thief? Or are our sins annulled if we commit them while in the act of saving our nation?* The Patriot knew he should feel badly about stealing an innocent civilian's wheels. He could imagine their heartbreak upon finding their beloved bike gone. He also knew that they would probably never recover the beautiful machine... not by the time he was done disposing of it. But he did not feel bad - despite the fact that he knew he should. Not in the least. Because he had just used some vain shlum's street bike to make history.

And, like so many great and important deeds in history, his actions this afternoon would likely go unnoticed for a long time.

*   *   *

Jay Z's latest single punched its way into Nelson's ears while he ate his dinner. The early evening flight required things to be kept simple at mealtime. He made do with just an eight-ounce prime rib sprinkled with cracked pepper, accompanied by sides of baby potatoes and some steamed asparagus with butter. He was pretty sure the plate was not real chinaware, and the fork and knives were obviously stainless steel rather than actual silver. But what could one really expect from the plane's galley? At least the flight was smooth enough that his beer stayed in the stein - even if it was served in glass instead of Irish crystal.

Nelson had, at his grandmother's insistence, called up a digital copy of her platform, policies, and votes as soon as the plane reached cruising altitude and Manny the Nanny finally let go of the young man's electronic leash. Grams had ordered Nelson to compare his notes against the draft of her next speech and check for inconsistencies. Voters these days, she said, were starting to notice these sorts of things.

Fifteen minutes into the flight, Grammy had excused herself to the rear of the cabin complaining of indigestion and not returned. Manny went to check on her after he delivered Nelson's dinner. As soon as the coast was clear, Nelson switched his iPad over to music, videos, and games. Grammy would not approve, but in Nelson's opinion editing boring speeches was a job for interns. Well, interns who were not family, and therefore actually had to work. Not that the bums got paid either way.

I hope Manny gets back before I need another beer, he thought. He knew Grammy got these bouts of air sickness pretty regularly, and Manny was used to attending to the old gal. The rear of the Gulfstream's main cabin was closed off from the main section to provide convenience, privacy, and decorum, so Nelson did not have to hear his grandmother heaving and hurling into the toilet - or smell the aftermath. Just to be safe, he decided to keep the music turned up until she returned. If previous history was any indicator, Grams would be back on her feet in less than an hour.

*   *   *

Linda Rogers' jacket rested on a hanger in a small closet in the plane's rear compartment. She was bent over, leaning heavily on the vanity. She could see Manuel in the mirror as he stood behind her, versed in his duties.

The fact that Manny's ministrations required both of their pants to also hang in the closet, neatly, was probably unknown to Nelson. The House Minority Leader bit down on a rolled-up towel to muffle the sound of her squeals and moans. Much to her delight, Manny was delivering a powerful, merciless performance tonight.

Her head slammed involuntarily into the sink. *Did Manny just punch me?* Outraged, she thought Manny had finally gone too far. *Some lines just shouldn't be crossed.* Her needs were sometimes unusual, but Linda had given Manny strict orders to never do anything that might leave visible trauma. Especially to the face. Especially if she had a pending public appearance.

Madame Rogers pushed herself up from the vanity but was suddenly dizzy. Lightheaded. Weak kneed. She rose from the floor and levitated, then felt herself falling. *I'm going to slap that wetback man-whore*, she thought as she struggled for balance.

Nelson felt, more than heard, the loud bang. It came from somewhere behind him, just outside the plane. A split second later, it felt like the floor had fallen out from under him. His mind was instantly transported back to a roller coaster he rode last summer in Long Island. Nelson grabbed his chair's leather arm rests as he raised out of his seat. His iPad flew up and slammed into the cabin roof. "Oh my god," he shrieked, "we're crashing!"

CHAPTER 7

"TODAY ON THE Lonnie Chase Program," the famous voice announced to his morning audience, "I'd like to talk about Arizona Senator Jack McQueen, and how much he sucks. But first," the entertainer sighed heavily into his antique microphone, "our hearts go out to the friends and family of the late Congresswoman Linda Rogers, who - as I'm sure you've all heard by now - was killed last night when her plane crashed just west of the Rockies."

"Not that Rogers had any friends," Chase's sarcastic co-host chortled.

"What a horrible thing to say Kyp," Lonnie chastised. "This is a tragedy and a very serious matter."

"It is horrible," his cohost replied, "for the Democratic Party. That's three Democrats dead in a week. Now, don't get me wrong," he quickly added,

"Congresswoman Gibbons' car crash was a tragedy, and the Evans murder is a heinous criminal act but," his voice lightened noticeably, "Linda Rogers was a diehard, died-in-the-wool Socialist Progressive. And the world - certainly our country - is a better place with her dead."

"I can't believe you'd say that Kyp," the namesake host admonished.

"No, I mean it," the cohost held firm. "Besides, do we even know for sure that she's dead?"

Lonnie's voice grew stern, like a parent chastening their disobedient child. "She was on her plane when, according to the NTSB spokesperson, both engines caught fire. The plane plunged straight into the ground."

"But" the cohost took on a conspiratorial tone, "is falling out of the sky enough to kill a witch? I mean, we know that dropping a house on one will do the job. But what about falling from the sky while stuck inside said house? 'Cause, let's face it here, that woman was an animated skeleton. She had to be either a zombie or a witch or something."

Lonnie's tone was deadly serious. "Her burning plane Plunged. Into. The. Ground. From, like, thirty thousand feet. On fire."

"So, you're sure she's dead?" Kyp responded in a perfectly deadpan voice.

"You're absolutely horrible."

"*She* was absolutely horrible," Kyp did not budge. Instead, he ticked his points on his fingers, held up within view for paid subscribers to see via the studio's webcam. "While she was alive, she was easily one of the worst human beings alive on the planet today. Certainly, one of the many members of our own government that seem to be hell bent on destroying our once great nation. Voting to expand welfare. Gun control. Amnesty for illegal immigrants. She voted to raise the debt ceiling, like, twenty times-"

"Eighteen." That correction came courtesy of Factcheck Fred.

"Eighteen times! She's wildly pro-abortion..." Kyp's tirade continued for most of the rest of the first half hour of the popular morning news and entertainment show - which, listeners were reminded periodically, was sponsored by Goldstein Financial Group.

*   *   *

Danny was not surprised when Dr. Wiley called his cell Thursday night and ordered him back to Washington. He had suspected from the beginning that his trip to New Orleans would be short. This intuition compelled him to keep his bags packed back at his hotel room, only pulling out what he needed during the week and neatly repacking it when he was done. In Wakefield's opinion, the choice to field a Secret Service agent on a lone murder investigation was overkill, even if the victim was a sitting senator. A complete donkey cart chase, as he used to say back in the Corps.

The proverbial shoe fell, though, when Wiley quickly added that Wakefield needed to bring Special Agent Elbee with him. His new partner, as Father had phrased it. Danny did not like the sound of that at all. He had not yet gotten used to having Elbee as a wingman and quietly looked forward to the time when he could return to the professional bliss that was found in solo work. The news headlines he caught last night, however, made him suspect the reason behind this compulsory change in venue.

It was not that Danny was a misanthrope or anything. Working around other people back at the office was okay. Some of them, anyway. He and Derek had even become very good friends. But the whole partner thing, having another person in lock step with you every day, seemed so un-Secret Service-y. In Danny's experience, being in the service meant you either worked alone or as part of a team. This whole Dick and Jane deal made him feel a little too much like some archaic gumshoe walking some ancient beat in some city.

Wakefield kept all of his misgivings to himself as he and Elbee navigated the concourse at Hartsfield-Jackson International Airport. They were similarly packed, each with a garment bag folded in half and slung over one shoulder and a pulled rolling bag in the other hand. They were similarly dressed, too, in navy blue slacks and a white top - though his striped shirt did not exactly match her blouse. In his peripheral vision, Danny noticed that their rapid steps were synchronized, left and right feet struck the ground in near unison like they were marching.

"So, there were no direct flights?" Elbee asked as he steered them through the airport's center.

"Connecting through Atlanta gets us there quicker," he answered. "Cheaper, too. And you know how the travel office is. Always gotta pick the cheap flights. Ah, there we are."

"This is not our gate," Sandra challenged him.

"No," he answered, "this is lunch." Danny filed into the short line of folks waiting for their turn at the counter.

"It's eleven o'clock."

"And our connection doesn't board until 12:15."

"They'll probably serve something on the plane," Sandra pointed as she joined him in the food line.

"I'd rather eat this any day over whatever garbage they're gonna give us on the flight. Besides, this is the best part of flying through Atlanta."

Elbee looked up at the brightly lit sign above the service counter ahead of them. "You fly a lot?"

"Between this gig and my time in the Corps I racked up a boatload of miles," he smiled. "I use them to fly home for the holidays."

"Is that how you learned how to scam the best rental car?" she inquired, obviously in reference to the Camero he turned in back in New Orleans.

"*'Scam'* is such an ugly word," he deflected, "I prefer *'arrange for.'* And I also learned to pick flights based on what restaurants were at the airports you fly through."

"It's always about food with you, isn't it?" she accused.

"An army moves on its stomach."

"There are other places to eat around the corner," she offered. "Quieter places where we can sit down."

"But I like chicken," Danny emphasized. Something caught his eye as he waited his turn for the next cashier. A pair of casually dressed women stood with their backs to him. They were nearly finished with their order. An oversized suitcase rested next to one. The other, obviously decades older, trembled almost invisibly under an unseen weight. Danny noted that both the younger woman and the cashier fought to not stare at the pink headscarf wrapped around the woman's bald head. Before they finished their order, Danny took two long steps up to the counter and saddled in next to the ladies.

"Excuse me," he freed his left hand and placed it softly, but firmly, on the older woman's shoulder, "but their order is on me." The younger woman started to protest, but the older one just stared at Danny in bemused wonder. His hand stayed on her shoulder as he turned away from the cashier and looked knowingly into her tired eyes. "How's it going today, sweetheart?" His tone was almost flirtatious.

"Oh, I can't complain," the strange woman smiled.

"Yes, you can," Danny assured her. "Today, you of all people have the right to complain."

She gave him a curious look with her half-glazed eyes. "Are you a doctor?"

"No, ma'am. I'm a fed," he smiled and winked. "And you have my permission, as an official representative of the United States Government, to gripe about your health, doctors, or the price of gas." His over-the-top, officious tone elicited a snicker from the sickly old woman. "How do you feel?"

The older woman smiled back. Clearly, she knew what he was talking about. But she kept up the brave front she had obviously been practicing so much lately. "Oh, well, I'll be fine."

"Any cravings?" he asked.

The woman held a hand to her chest. Her t-shirt hung loosely on her frame. "You know, I've never really talked about it. I'm not hungry, but at the same time I really want some ice cream."

Danny turned to the counter. "Tack a hot fudge sundae onto her order." The cashier acknowledged.

"Oh, my. There's no need, really," the woman dismissed.

"It's my pleasure, dear," Danny smiled. "Besides," he adopted a heavy lisp, "a milkshake can be so much work. All of that sucking. It wears me out sometimes." It was a stupid thing to say. A dumb complaint in life. But it was delivered with all of the aplomb and timing of a professional comedian. The ridiculousness of his analysis made them both giggle. "Stay strong, okay? Get better."

"Bless you dear," the woman thanked him with watering eyes. Then she and her traveling companion walked away with their food.

A few minutes later, Danny and Sandra sat down and opened warm, white paper bags of their own. Wakefield opened his eyes from a quick prayer. Elbee stared at him with a puzzled look on her face.

"That was really nice Daniel" she commented.

"I always pray for my food," he opened a prepackaged container of ranch dressing, then another which contained spicy buffalo sauce.

"That's not what I meant," she countered. "Why did you do that? Buy that woman's lunch?"

"Isn't it obvious?" he asked as he dunked a fry into each of his sauces in turn. "The old lady had cancer."

"Lots of people have cancer," she pressed. "I mean, don't get me wrong, it was sweet and all, but… I mean, it seemed to me that there's more to it than just that."

Danny finished a buffalo-ranch dipped nugget, then wiped his fingers and soberly answered. "Fifteen hundred people die of cancer every day in this country. You saw her. Bald from radiation and chemotherapy. Tremors. Plus, her daughter hauling her stuff around in her own bag. Indicates fatigue. This airport's a hub, not a destination. They're on their way somewhere. Fast food, despite the fact that more than anything right now she probably just wants to sit down and rest. Tells me they're probably in a hurry to get there. Points to the idea that she thinks she may not have a lot of tomorrows left."

"Geez, Daniel," Sandra straightened at the cold calculation of his analysis, and how it contrasted with the warm sentiment she had just witnessed. "Don't you ever turn it off?"

"I can't. Not anymore. Not when I'm sober anyway. Years of training, and a lifetime of habits."

"Staying on like that all of the time must be exhausting," she concluded.

"Sometimes," Danny conceded. "But it tends to keep you alive." Without moving he was suddenly miles away. Like his mind had just transposed the world around him, traded it for another scene in a memory from long ago.

"You may be right," Sandra nodded, "but that doesn't answer my question. What made you want to do that for a stranger?"

"Here's a woman fighting for her life," Danny returned from a far-off corner of his memory, "the least thing I can do for her is recognize that bravery. That struggle. And cheer her on while she goes one more round in the ring against death itself."

"Have you ever lost someone, Daniel? To cancer?" Sandra asked as she stirred her coffee.

Wakefield wiped his fingers on a napkin and leaned forward a bit. "Yeah. Yeah, I did. My mom. A while back. Breast cancer."

"I'm sorry."

"It's not your fault. It's nobody's fault really. Just one of those things. Life happens." He drummed his fingertips together. "Mom was the greatest, you know? I grew up in Montana. Dad was a cop, Mom taught Third Grade. Made every game, kept pushing me in school. And she was tough too," he chuckled. "Damn near ripped my ear off when she caught me getting lippy with the neighbor one day."

"Wait - you mean, literally?"

"Yep. I thought for sure she had at least torn the cartilage. Closest thing I got to sympathy from Dad over the whole matter was him not whipping me, too. Anyway, my sophomore year of high school, Mom ends up in the hospital. Doc says they're doing everything they can, but Dad and I just stand there and watch her waste away right in front of our eyes."

"That must have been hard for you both."

"It was. Dad never was the same afterward. Grandpa and Grams kept taking me to Mass, but Dad never went to church again. Anyway, back to the point. Most folks see a cancer patient and they look the other way. They don't wanna think about it. They don't wanna talk about it. They don't wanna be reminded of their own mortality. Oh, sure, folks love to hear survival stories and some people give a little money to charities, but that's all just lip service. Me, when I see someone struggling with cancer, I see my Mom. I see a woman who won't stop fighting for her life, even after the doc says there's nothing left to do but make her comfortable. It takes real grit to soldier on when you know the fight's already lost. And I just think maybe the rest of us should do what we can to support someone in that position."

Wakefield returned to his cooling food. He sat back and re-awakened his tastebuds with another bite of buffalo-ranch chicken, then washed the savory morsel down with a long pull from his sweet tea. "So, what about you? Do your murder investigations give you many travel opportunities?"

Sandra probed her salad with her cheap plastic fork. "Truth be told, Daniel, I mostly do narcotics."

"Huh. And the FBI's cool with that?"

Sandra shot him a rueful grin. "You know what I mean, smart ass. I usually handle drug cases. And yes, sometimes they take me out of town. You know how it is: you go where the work takes you."

Wakefield wiped a bit of sauce off of his lip with a flimsy napkin that was barely up to the task. "Not that I don't think you're doing a bang-up job here Elbee, but why'd your supervisors give a high-profile homicide investigation to a narco cop?"

"I think Deputy Chief Thompson's grooming me," she replied. "It's not like that. For a promotion. But you know how hard it is to break out in this community. I'm eligible for a promotion in a few months, maybe a transfer to the Beltway. A case like this is a real boost to my resume. It's a great career opportunity."

"Wouldn't it also be a great career opportunity for one of the guys who usually work homicides?"

"They've got plenty to do."

"Not that it's any of my business," he offered nonchalantly, "but I've known gals who use their gender to advance their careers."

Sandra's blue eyes became pools of ice water. "Are you saying that I only got this case because I'm a woman?"

"Do you think that's why you got it?" he deflected. "I mean, it wouldn't be the first time. And a dude - or gal - has gotta look out for number one. I've seen tons of females who played the gender card to further their careers. We've all seen it. Happens all the time. Happened in the Corps. Happens in the Service. You can't tell me it doesn't happen in the Bureau."

"Whether I pee standing up or sitting down has nothing to do with my aptitude as an investigator or commitment to the mission, Daniel."

"It's not a question of aptitude, Elbee. It's about lane management. A team is a collection of individuals working toward a common objective. Everybody does their particular job to the best of their ability and gives their teammates the freedom to do their jobs in turn. Not everybody gets to carry the ball on every play."

"I told you I hate sports metaphors."

"Do you play music?"

"The piano," she nodded. "Since I was six."

"Alright, well I play the guitar, but it's the same thing, what I'm talking about here. You can't hit every key with just one finger any more than I can pluck every string. It doesn't matter if you're picking out *Happy Birthday* or laying down *All Along the Watchtower*. Each digit does their own thing so the others can do theirs."

"So you think a different agent would be more suited to this case?" she demanded. "Would do a better job? Or is there a problem with me personally?"

He shook his head. "This isn't about you, Elbee. You're fine. It's just..." Danny struggled to find a way to articulate his thoughts. "Look, you've been given a great opportunity with this one, okay? I'm not saying you haven't earned it. I'm just saying that you might be a little out of your element is all."

"How many serial killers does the Secret Service deal with?" she posed.

"More than you'd think," Danny answered. "But it's rarer in my division. Look, I'm just talking with my partner here, okay? Let's just wrap this one up so that we can both go back to what it is that we do. You can go back to doing drugs in the bayou," the way he phrased his comment elicited a begrudged snicker from his partner, "and I can go back to dodging Nick the Dick and playing my guitar back in D.C."

"You really don't like having a partner, do you?" she pointed. "Or is it that you don't like people in general?"

"Tell you what, Elbee," Danny fished another latticed French fry out of his bag. "If you do get transferred to the Beltway after we catch this mope, we can hang out. Yeah. Sure. Why not? Share a few drinks at Black Sam's every now and again. We could even start a band. You on the piano, me on guitar. No, I'm serious. We'll find a couple of other federal agents who play - a drummer and a singer or something - and start a little bar band. Call it Deep Cover or something special agent-y like that."

"Special agent-y?"

"What? That's not a word? It should be."

Sandra shook her head and laughed. Danny kept the conversation suitably lightened until well after they boarded their flight and enjoyed a companionable silence all the way back to Washington.

CHAPTER 8

JONAS WILEY sat behind his dark mahogany desk and tapped the cap of his fountain pen against the forest green velvet pad that protected his work area from scratches. "Alright son," he smiled, "it's time for another trip down the rabbit hole." The rabbit hole was a proverb taken from an old children's tale, used within the Intelligence Community when discussing issues that were deeply classified - just how deeply, even most people with clearances never fully appreciated.

But working in the Intelligence Community came with its downside, too. Along with the Top Secret clearance came the need to isolate work from the rest of your life. You could never share the details of your day when you came home. If you came home. And since most people identified themselves by their work, that meant cutting the people around you off from the very thing that those same people thought identified you. In the end, most people in the Intelligence Community found it simpler to sever relationships with so-called "normal" people and just stay down underground in the rabbit hole.

Working for the Secret Service only required a Secret-level clearance. Wakefield would have been downgraded years ago when he first signed on, but when he checked in at the Analysis Division Dr. Wiley - upon review of Danny's record - had prompted the Special Security Officer to renew Wakefield's Top-Secret clearance rather than let it expire. *It's easier to just do the Periodic Review*, his boss had told him two years ago, *just in case you decide you need it later for another gig.*

And now, Danny sat in front of that same boss's desk on a Friday afternoon long after everyone else in the building had already gone home to start their weekend. And the only piece of work Wakefield saw in his boss's office was a familiar, lone piece of paper laid out before him. The whole sheet, all but the bottom, seemed to be crammed with as many words as could fit. The last portion gave room for his printed name, social security number, signature, and date.

"You've signed an NDA before," Jonas reminded. "You know the drill."

"I think I signed an NDA about how many NDA's I've signed," Danny affirmed. A Non-Disclosure Agreement was an affidavit which a person signed any time their clearance was adjusted to include or preclude compartmentalized information. "I'm not due for Review until next year," he noted, "so what's the deal?"

"Like I said," Wiley did not blink, "you know the

drill. And that's all you get until you sign." The wizened old man took a deep breath, "But you need to know."

Ah, Danny nodded. *There's the rub.* Contrary to what many civilians thought, a Top Secret clearance was not an all-access pass to view every government secret. All data was compartmentalized, with different codenamed programs managing separate topics - Special Access Programs, or SAP, of Secret Compartmentalized Information.

If all government information was stored on books, having a Secret clearance was like learning about the library where all those hidden books were kept away from public view. Having a Top Secret clearance was like being given permission to actually go into the library. Compartmentalized codeword clearance gave you the opportunity to check out any book on that subject, and that subject only.

And Jonas was telling Danny that it was time to update his library card. Whatever this was about, it could not wait until Monday. It was something that the head of analysis could not have discussed when he called his rock star analyst on an open line. Something that he could not discuss until Danny signed the paperwork - until he committed his sacred honor to preserving the matter's integrity.

Wakefield surrendered, grabbed a pen from the nearby cup, and completed the form. "Now, what's going on?"

Wiley pointed to a static display set into one of the mahogany bookcases. Behind the cabinet's glass front his old dress blue uniform jacket hung, adorned with a respectable mixture of ribbons and medals. Four gold stripes marked the sleeve cuffs and shoulder boards. An officer's saber, polished like it was ready for a parade, leaned against the back left corner in its scabbard. "I've seen a lot in my day," he explained. "I've forgotten classified programs that the last two Presidents didn't even know existed in the first place."

Danny knew there was a point coming, but Jonas had not made it yet. "Lay it on me, boss."

"What I'm about to tell you, you ain't gonna like," the old Jesuit warned. "I know you well enough to know that. But we need to pull out an old resource."

Daniel Wakefield, Special Agent with the Secret Service and former Marine sniper-turned-intelligence operator, sat in respectful silence as his mentor told him a story. Jonas was right; Danny did not like what he heard. He felt betrayed, lied to. In the end, though, he accepted the dirty secret as an unpleasant, but not-too-surprising truth.

"Eventually, sir," he surmised after Jonas' explanation, "we're gonna have to share this with the Bureau."

"The FBI is the primary management authority on this one. I talked to Jack Thompson earlier. Your new partner is already up to speed."

Danny bit back a curse. He knew Elbee had been keeping information from him.

Doctor Wiley stabbed his finger down, pinning the Non-Disclosure Agreement to his desk. "This is not a prosecutorial tool," he warned. "This cannot ever see the inside of a courtroom. Not even for in camera review. This is a search aide only. Danny," Dr. Wiley reminded him. "Something to help guide your decisions. You and your partner build a case based on admissible evidence."

Wakefield caught his boss's meaning with perfect

clarity. "I guess I've got an RFI to submit, then." If Dr. Wiley was giving Danny this tool, the agent knew his boss expected him to use it immediately. That usually meant sending a Request For Information out into the classified ether in hopes that the faceless powers-that-be could throw you a proverbial bone.

Jonas shook his head. "It's already been taken care of, son. The ball is rolling. You just be ready to move. Somebody will give you a call with everything you need."

"Roger that, sir," Wakefield closed.

"Alright then," Wiley stood. "It's almost eighteen hundred on a Friday night. Everyone else is already gone, and I'm leaving too. Make yourself scarce."

"If you can manage the vault door, sir," Daniel stood as well, "I'll be headed out now." The Analysis Division was located inside a Specialized Compartmental Information Facility, and security protocol required the last person out of the office to batten down the massive vault door to the office. The process was not difficult, just time consuming. And the main entrance was literally a thick, reinforced metal door. The type used in bank vaults. Even on well-oiled hinges, it was heavy.

"Son," the older man smiled, "I've been managing the vault door since before you were born." Jonas chuckled to himself and grabbed a massive wooden pipe from a specialized holder on his desk. "Go," he winked mischievously at his protege, "and try not to instigate an interdepartmental grievance with that pretty little lady cop you brought back from Louisiana."

*   *   *

Elbee sat in the main space of the Analysis Division during Wakefield's briefing with the department head. *This is where everyone else would have worked*, she imagined, *if they had not apparently left already*. As was typical of many government offices, the cubicles had the neat, prim appearance and antiseptic smell that told Sandra their users' entire workday on a Friday consisted of coming to work, cleaning their desk area, and finally matriculating out by ones and twos starting around lunchtime.

Whoever that Jenkins guy is, she thought to herself as she scanned the room, *his desk is immaculate*. Jenkins' nameplate sat upon a desk that was completely free of pens, folders, or any other signs of daily use. There were no humorous little posters tacked to the soft walls. And while all the workstations were dusted - even Wakefield's, and he had been gone all week - Jenkins' cubicle was sterile enough for a doctor's office. In Sandra's estimation, only two types of office worker left a workstation so perfectly organized: the completely obsessive-compulsive type, and the type who spent all their time kissing up to the boss instead of doing any actual work.

Before Elbee could reach her final conclusion about this Jenkins fellow, Wakefield opened the door from his boss's office and beaconed her to leave with him. "What was that all about?" she asked.

"You heard about Linda Rogers' plane crash?" he asked.

"It was all over the news." Sandra's tone changed. "Let me guess: it wasn't quite as accidental as the news said?"

Danny blindly handed her a manilla file folder as

they cleared the vault door. "A copy of the NTSB's report," he identified.

The National Transportation Safety Board was known for few things. None of them were the speedy release of investigative reports or fast-paced analysis. Sandra skimmed the summary of findings as she followed Danny toward the exit. "Both engines... blast damage... originating from inside the cowling..." She looked up to see they were back in the elevator.

"Looks like somebody made a pair of homemade shape charges, put one on each engine near the manifold, then blew them both in midair," Wakefield reiterated.

"... and the plane just dropped out of the sky," Elbee closed.

"Killing everyone on board," Danny continued. "Gravity works."

Sandra did not miss a beat, even as she surrendered her visitor's badge to the security station at the front door. "Bomb equals murder," she announced as they exited the building, "they think it's our guy?"

"Might be."

"So, what's the next move?"

Danny sighed. *The next move is for you to freaking start trusting me with the details from 'your' case.* "The case has moved here to D.C. for the moment," he dodged. "Rogers was flying into the metro for Evans' memorial."

"Tomorrow morning at the National Cathedral," Elbee confirmed.

"We've been ordered to attend. They are concerned - justifiably, I'd say at the moment - about the potential security threat posed by a whackadoo out there killing members of congress. If he exists, he might see tomorrow's memorial as a target rich environment."

"Just for clarity," Elbee probed, "who is '*they*?'"

"You're a smart woman," Danny pointed, "who do you think?"

"Congress?" she guessed.

Wakefield nodded. "Who else would care about dead congressmen?" The Marine Corps had taught Danny a few helpful survival tactics. One of them was the ability to find humor in even the most serious and gruesome events. It was a coping mechanism common to combat veterans. *Laugh it off*, they reminded each other, *or it'll kill you*. "In light of this recent information, my boss is getting some pressure from above."

"Which is why my boss signed off on the travel orders for this little jaunt before I even heard of them."

The duo paused just outside of his red, 2-door Jeep Rubicon. To save time on the way in, they took his POV from Reagan National Airport, which he had left in long-term parking when he flew out Monday night. "Hey," Danny said defensively, "You found out when I did. I'm not holding out on you."

"Then why'd I have to wait outside of the office?" Elbee pointed. "If you're so transparent, why couldn't your partner come sit in on the conversation?"

"Whoa kettle," Wakefield responded. "So soon you forget about yourself trying to withhold your hooker witness from me."

Sandra blew a raspberry with her lips. "But you got to see her eventually. How long are you going to hold that over my head?"

Danny waited until they were both inside the Jeep and the doors were closed. "Father had to read me into one of your little programs," he said humorlessly. "PRIMER. Whaddaya know about that?"

"The secret firearms database," she confirmed. Sandra sat silently in her seat for a second. "I'm sorry, Daniel," she said at last, "but you know how it goes. I couldn't tell you before -"

"Yeah, I know," he grimaced. Wakefield had played the game long enough to understand the situation, even if he sometimes did not like it. Mission first. Need to know. God and country. But a voice from his past - one of his instructors from the Navy and Marine Corps Intelligence Training Center - echoed in the back of his mind. *In the Intel Community we lie, cheat, steal, deny and deceive... but not to each other.* A guy had to be able to trust his teammates. That went double for his partner. As far as fostering trust between departments went, this whole week had been one long exercise in frustration. "Let's take you back to the airport to pick up your car."

Sandra nodded. They left the airport in a hurry so as to not keep Wiley waiting a moment longer than was absolutely necessary. That meant skipping her check-in at the rental car agency. Sandra glanced at the Jeep's stereo to check the time. Her reservation indicated that she should have picked up her car hours ago. A smirk crawled across her face. "Think we're late enough for me to score a Mustang?"

*   *   *

The shortest route from the Department of Homeland Security Headquarters building to Reagan National Airport was to skirt around Alexandria and take the Key Bridge across the Potomac. In metro traffic going into a Friday night, Wakefield was glad the eight-mile trip took less than an hour and was relatively uneventful. After the fifth announcement that predictably described Beltway traffic as a miles-long parking lot thanks to an overturned semi on I-495's outer loop, Danny switched from local radio to the satellite band and let Elbee pick the station.

"Why do they call it rush hour?" Sandra fumed as Danny maneuvered his Jeep toward the rental car pickup entrance. "Nobody seems to be in a hurry to get anywhere."

"A great deal of these people are employees of our beloved federal government," Wakefield pointed. "When was the last time you saw a government employee in a hurry to do anything?"

"Since when did a federal worker stay after three o'clock on a Friday?" Sandra countered.

"*Touché*," Danny downshifted into second gear then threw her a mock salute. There were a thousand jokes about the work ethic - or, to be more accurate, lack thereof - displayed by government workers. One did not remain long in the nation's capital before one heard them all. It took even less time to discover the kernel of truth at the root of the dry humor. The radio signal disappeared as the Jeep passed into the bowels of the airport's massive concrete and steel parking garage. Danny stabbed the mute button. "Did you print your confirmation before we left?"

"Saved it on my phone."

Danny stopped at a kiosk. "I'll wait here until you

get loaded up."

Sandra showed her phone to the rental car attendant, who disappeared for a moment. When he came back with her car, Sandra was a little disappointed. She did not manage to score a free upgrade to a sports car like Danny did in New Orleans. The pint-sized Ford Focus reserved for her did, however, smell distinctly of cigarette smoke, so the embarrassed rental agent gave her a midsize at no additional charge and with his deepest apologies. Danny helped load Sandra's luggage into the dark grey Mazda 6's adequate trunk.

"Look," Danny offered as Sandra closed the trunk lid. "This case won't get easier unless we agree to work together."

"That's what we're doing, isn't it?" Elbee asked.

"No," he corrected, "right now we're not working *with* each other. We're working *around* one another. There's a difference. And that's not how partners treat each other." He breathed deeply. The air in the parking garage stank of exhaust fumes and musty concrete. "What do you say we make it up to each other?"

"What did you have in mind?" Sandra's tone was still neutral. Official. Suspicious.

"You're not from the area, so let me buy you a drink. Eight o'clock. That way you can get settled into your hotel, grab a bite, whatever." Danny pulled his cell phone from his pocket and thumbed the screen a few times. "There," he decreed, "I just texted you the address of this place I know."

"Look, Wakefield," Elbee sighed, "I appreciate the gesture, but I don't -"

"It's just a drink between colleagues. Alright? A

chance to restart this partnership on a better foot."

Sandra twirled the key to her rental car around her finger. "Fine," she surrendered. "One drink."

*   *   *

It was too risky for the Patriot to stay in San Francisco. It took him longer than he had wanted to find a quiet, out of the way pier from which to launch the stolen motorcycle into the drink, but as soon as that loose end was wrapped up, he was back in his truck and the bay area had disappeared from his rearview mirrors. Still, he drove and drove, stopping only for gas and short naps at rest stops as he crossed the expansive American interstate system.

Some people drove cross-country for recreation. Many navigated the webwork of roadways driving goods for a living. He, however, was on a crusade, and there were many targets left for him to zero out. *So many targets*, he thought, *but so little time.*

How many more had to die he simply could not say. He wondered if his campaign would even make a difference. No, it had to. He resolved to make things right, to protect his country from all threats. That oath had only one expiration date: the day of his death.

Was it God's fate for him to fight this fight alone? How long would it take before the people of America woke up? Fear might convince a few of the pigs ruining the country to change their ways, but the diehards would dig in, hold fast, and try to outlast him. *All they have to do to win is keep living. Keep themselves in power.* He could kill a hundred of them he knew, but all they had to do to win was take lonely old him out of the fight.

It did not even have to be a fed who took him out of the fight. Or a cop, or soldier, or anything like that, he realized. *I'm one car accident away from losing this war,* he thought. *One idiot drunk driver could take me out of the picture and damn this whole country.*

Just like the one who killed my wife and little girl, he fumed. *The one that damned me.*

His vision blurred at the thought of his lost loved ones. He blinked away the tears, steeled his heart and focused on the road ahead and his mission. The past cannot be changed. *Nobody can un-fire a bullet.* His mind went to work on his next step.

By now, he figured, even the clowns at the FBI have to have started to connect the dots. They'll probably have one or two agents working to solve this. He chewed on the thought with his mind while his mouth worked on a fresh bite of spicy beef jerky he picked up at his last gas stop.

A farmer could only lose so many birds out of the henhouse before he brought out the dog. It was time to step up his game. He had to hit harder and faster than his opponents could keep up. Change tactics, keep them guessing. Predictability would get him killed for sure.

The only way for a small group or lone individual to fight an opponent that was bigger than they were was to turn that enemy's daunting size against them. He was alone and they were bogged down by command structure and bureaucracy, so he could make decisions faster, travel lighter, and disappear. He could strike his targets at will, using any of a variety of tactics and classic guerrilla warfare techniques, whereas his presumed opponent had to be absolutely perfect one hundred percent of the time and operate within doctrinal guidelines and regulations in order to stop him.

A yellow sign on the side of the road advertised a roadside campground at the next exit. It was getting late. He had been driving for most of the last 52 hours. Time to pull off, set up camp, and get some quality rest, he decided. His destination - and his next target - were an easy drive up the road from here. He anticipated his objective would be stationary for at least a few hours tomorrow, and if everything went according to plan then his total time on target would only be a few seconds.

CHAPTER 9

SANDRA STEPPED into Black Sam's Microbrewery and scanned the open chamber for a familiar face. The pub was decked out with matching dark brown wooden floors, chairs, tables, and bar. The wainscoted walls' yellow-washed upper portions carried the abundant, warm glow cast by electric lights disguised as candle-powered lamps that hung from grainy wooden beams. The open room felt like it had been transplanted from the guts of one of the masted ships she just saw berthed outside on the waterfront. It had an obvious below decks, nautical feel - though it might have been just a little brighter than an actual sailing ship's innards. Some patrons sat in booths fashioned into the spaces between the "ship's" false framing. Others sat at the small tables scattered across the main floor.

A slow, southern rock song - which Sandra

imagined was the modern equivalent of an old pirate dirge - played in the bar's background. In the middle of it all, where Sandra imagined some real-life galleon probably kept its gallows, the deeply polished, robust bar was stocked with various glasses and adorned with bottles of every imaginable shape, color, content and origin. A lone, dark-skinned man smoothly moved through a routine of pour, smile, wipe, smile, pour. He was occasionally joined for a moment by one of a handful of waitresses who ferried drinks to remote patrons. Not far from the barman and the taps her partner sat with his back to the door. His black t-shirt and blue jeans were a far cry from the clothes she had seen him wear to work all week. Then again, she would never wear her knit summer dress to the office, either. Or this particular perfume. As he detected her gaze even with his back turned to her, Danny turned over his left shoulder and beckoned her to join him on the adjoining barstool.

"Home turf must be making you soft, Wakefield," she cajoled as she slid onto the stool's leather pad. "I thought you ex-Marines all sat with your back to a wall so you could see the exits."

Danny took a long pull from a tall stein until it was drained of its pale contents. "*Former* Marine," he corrected. "Four types of people in this world, Elbee: Marines, dead Marines, former Marines, and everybody else. Besides," he pointed subtly to the mirror panels behind the stocked bar shelves, "I can see the whole room in the reflection." Danny gestured to his left, summoning the barkeep - who in turn slung a frothy mug down the bar in the opposite direction. "Just like I can see that you're not wearing your gun." He smiled just a little. "Not under *that* dress."

Sandra placed her hands on her hips. "And what's wrong with my dress?" she challenged.

In Danny's eyes, Elbee's dress looked like little more than a longish, light blue t-shirt cinched around her waist by a belt. The thin, soft, lightweight jersey cotton - what there was of it - left a lot uncovered and very little to the imagination. He shook his head innocently. "Not a damn thing Elbee."

The dark bartender walked toward them confidently while Sandra watched the mug full of amber fluid slide across the smooth bar until a patron seven feet down its length abruptly caught it in his awaiting hand. "Hello, there, my dear," the bartender gifted Sandra with a brilliant smile that was equally dashing and roguish. "I'm Sam. What'll it be?"

"*Black* Sam?" Sandra challenged.

"Indeed, my dear," he winked. "Not the original, mind you. Named the bar after a famous pirate. And ladies' man, I might add." His eyebrows danced comically.

Sandra smiled at his over-the-top flirtation. Black Sam's million-dollar smile and ageless good looks - he could have been just shy of forty years old or more than sixty; she could not tell - reminded her of a soap opera rogue. "I'll have a beer."

"Just '*a*' beer?" Sam looked almost hurt. "My dear, we serve some of the best brew you'll taste anywhere, right here at Black Sam's. Whether it's our own microbrew or the best beers from around the world." He started to produce a placard, loaded with illustrations and descriptions of his wares, but then put it back under the bar. "Tell you what," he offered, "I think I've got just the thing for a lovely lady such as yourself." He turned to Danny, who made no attempt to hide the smile that showed just how much fun he was having at Sandra's expense. "You want a reload?" his eyes bounced down to Danny's empty glass.

"Let's switch it up," Danny pushed the tall glass away. "Build me a proper stout."

"Aye aye," Sam sauntered away.

"So," Danny turned fully toward his partner, "does that Marine crack mean you looked me up?"

Sandra nodded. "Seemed an appropriate move. I like to know who I'm working with."

"You could'a just asked," he offered.

"And you could have lied," she rebuffed. "Most people do."

… *But not to each other…* "Fair enough." Danny drummed a fast rhythm with his fingers on the bar for a second. "Alright, so you read the file. What's it say?"

Sam was back. He dropped a gravity pint of dark fluid topped with a creamy cap in front of Danny. "And for the lady," Sam's smooth voice toyed with Sandra's eardrums as he delivered an identically shaped glass with a less heady ale so golden as to nearly be orange. Danny hoisted his glass to Sandra, who matched his gesture in kind. Sam stood by as they both sampled their glasses.

Something sweet-smelling rolled over Sandra's tongue. She caught herself mid drink, then swallowed and regarded Sam with wide eyes. "That is good," she praised. "It's not bitter like most beers…"

"Honey ale," Sam announced. "Our own house brew, of course. Made with local honey from one of Maryland's finest and oldest beekeepers."

Danny still held his drink aloft after his first hit, which was much deeper than Sandra's. He stared into the dark, thick stout as if searching for the meaning of life itself. "Well done, Sam." Sam just smiled, then drifted further down the bar to cure his other patrons of their ills. "Grandpa Pat'd think he was back on the Emerald Isle." Danny put his drink back on the bar. "So," he returned his attention to her, "tell me about your new partner."

Sandra stole a second taste of her ale. "I just read your record," she replied. "Your DD-214 says you were a Staff Sergeant in the Marines. It lists a bunch of awards, says you were in Iraq and Afghanistan, and that you were trained as both a sniper and intelligence operator. That's different."

"Yep," Danny took another hit off his drink.

"After that, you joined the Secret Service. You've spent your whole time working the Treasury side - both here and previously in Denver. You have a B.A. in Intelligence Studies from some school I've never heard of," she lowered her drink, but kept the glass clutched in both hands, "and back in April, you killed a civilian in Miami - without receiving punitive action, I might add."

Danny returned what was left of his stout to the bar and twirled the glass in his hand. "Without *official reprimand*," he emphasized. "My punishment came in the form of having to see a shrink once a week for counseling. My direct supervisor - a guy we call Nick the Dick - came up with the idea just to get under my skin. He knows it's my own personal version of Hell." It was clear by the tone in his voice that a part of Wakefield would have preferred a suspension or pay cut. "Short version: a pair of bad guys drew down on me. Neither of them were civilians in the strictest definition. They were smugglers running dope outta

Cartagena for a Colombian drug cartel. Secret Service picked up the case from the money laundering side, which is why I was down there investigating. Both of them got shot. One didn't survive." He took another long pull from his stout, nearly draining the glass.

"And the other one?"

Danny placed his mostly empty glass on the bar. "He's sitting somewhere where he gets lots of time to rethink his life." To her credit, Sandra seemed to know enough about how things worked not to ask where exactly that somewhere was. She simply raised her glass again and savored the sweet honey ale. "Alright," Wakefield resumed, "so you've got the basic data. Now, tell me about me. As a person. What kinda guy am I?"

"You're a cocky former Marine," she reiterated.

"Nah," he blew air through his pursed lips, "that's just the data again. I'll let you in on a little secret there, Special Agent Elbee of the FBI." Danny adopted his most officious tone as he recited her title. Then he dropped the false reverie and used both hands to gesture as he explained. It was the first time tonight that Sandra saw him without a drink in hand. "There's different types of folks that join the military. Right? First, you've got the ones who need a job and can't get one somewhere else. Or they're lookin' for a free ride to college. That's the first type. They usually end up in the Army or the Air Force. Then there's the ones who've got something to prove. That's the second type. But every once in a while you find guys who are cracked in the head. They really, genuinely like shooting folks and blowing stuff up. It's their heroin. I mean certifiable nut jobs. Crazy guys who get their rocks off hurting and killing. These psychos almost always end up in the ground forces. They leave their multiple ex-wives behind for the rush of living on the front lines. Their lives are fueled by caffeine, hate, and tax-free re-enlistment bonuses. They try out for Special Forces and stay in for life. That's the third kind. But there's a fourth kind of soldier: the ones who do it for love. Not love of action, but love of their country. Love of their teammates. Love of our good ol' American way of life. They write a check for their lives made payable to Joe Taxpayer, who usually doesn't give a second thought or half a crap about some dude he's never met fighting someone he doesn't understand somewhere he doesn't know about. But that doesn't matter Elbee, 'cause that fourth kinda trooper - the real warrior - loves that idiot civilian just like he does everyone else in this country. And that's true-blue patriotism right there."

"Is that what you were?" Sandra asked over the top of her glass. "The patriotic warrior-type?"

"Ooo-rah," Wakefield quietly grunted. Then he scooped up his dark drink again and grew just a little more quiet. "At least, I was. Until I learned a hard truth."

"That serving your country wasn't as romantic as you thought?" she challenged.

"That civilians all suck," he corrected. "Simple truth is that the ones who don't outright hate the military generally just ignore us vets."

"Oh, that's not true! What about all the parades on Veterans Day and Memorial Day?"

"Some folks say '*thank you*' once or twice a year," he admitted, "but how many say 'you're hired' when a vet comes home? Compare that to the number of folks who expect a guy or gal who just put their life on hold for four, eight, or twenty years to be excited by the opportunity to go spend four more years at college - unemployed, maybe with a family to support - while their peers who didn't serve their country are rewarded by continuing to make buckets more money than that trooper has ever seen."

"I thought employers preferred vets."

"That's what the signs say," he nodded. "But the reality? All things being even remotely equal, the unemployment rate among vets is ten times higher than our civilian counterparts."

"You've got a job," she pointed. "A good one."

"I stayed with the government," he reminded her. "If I'd've gone civvy, I'd probably be sleeping in my Jeep under an overpass somewhere. Most interviewers just assume we're all trigger happy PTSD cases. Walking time bombs just waiting to go off. The percentages are highly skewed. And even the civvies that think they support us don't really understand. They can't. Not that it's their fault," he shrugged, "but it makes the romance kinda one-sided." He took another sip from his stout. "But still, they're mostly harmless, so it's alright I guess."

"That's a pretty cynical outlook."

"It's only jaded until it's true. Then it's just good predictive analysis."

"So why the Secret Service?" she probed. "And Treasury at that. Seems kinda dull for a guy like you."

"Action is overrated," he waved. "Getting shot at and blown up gets old. Fast. Trust me when I say there's nothing I'd like more than to stay tucked away somewhere out of sight and quietly burn the calendar until I'm eligible for retirement. Anyway, enough about me," Danny announced. "Your turn. What about you? Tell me about my new partner."

"I thought it was your turn to talk about me."

"But I don't know you," he admitted. "I mean, I have some theories about you, but nothing hard."

Elbee raised a curious eyebrow and lowered her half empty glass. "You mean you didn't look up my personnel file?"

"Nope."

"Why not?"

"Because I'd rather ask."

"What if I lie?" she teased.

Danny's eyes flashed. "Then I learn from those lies."

"How can you learn anything if I'm lying? You have no way of knowing the truth. Or if I'm telling it."

"I can tell."

Sandra's eyebrows rose in doubt. "You're not one of those guys who thinks you're some kind of human lie detector, are you?"

"Not exactly," he shrugged. "More like a truth detector. Sure, there's a kinda trick to telling if someone's lying. I guess it's part art, part science. But I just know a good truth when I hear it. The truth just sounds different from a lie. And I just stick to that."

"There's nothing to learn," she dismissed, apparently still dubious. "Nothing exciting compared to your history."

"Excitement's overrated," he replied. "Come on. You're a Special Agent. That means school."

"Monmouth University," she confirmed. "New Jersey."

"Degree in criminal justice?" he guessed.

Sandra nodded halfheartedly. "That was my

minor, actually. I majored in psychology. And I just finished my Master's thesis this spring at Tulane."

"You're working on your Ph.D while working at the Bureau?" Danny raised his glass. "Impressive."

"So," Sam's smooth voice called as he returned, "the lady is smart and beautiful." He had evidently caught the tail end of their exchange as he checked on his patrons. His smile was filled with promises Danny had seen him make to numerous women. "That puts her way out of your league, brother."

"We work together," Sandra explained.

"Well then," Sam winked at her, "that leaves you free to see other men." He suddenly grew just a little cautious. "Unless, you're not into guys."

"I am," she smiled.

"Not that I judge," Sam assured her.

"How 'bout a shot?" Danny interrupted.

"I've got something better than a shot," Elbee interjected.

"Oh, I don't know," Sam offered. "I bet the lady would love a Jolly Rancher." Sandra smiled, but declined. Sam walked away, his perpetually good spirits unhampered.

Danny was overflowing with curiosity. "What's better than a shot?"

"A suspect." Elbee produced her phone. "I found something on the internet that might be interesting." Her finger slid around the phone's screen, calling up a video which she played while holding the phone where Danny could see.

"... and I mean it," a bald white man barked into the camera. He wore a scowl that told Danny he was constantly angry and a goatee that looked like it belonged in a biker bar. "Look, a lot of folks 'er fed up. As far as I'm concerned, a couple'a dead congressmen ain't a tragedy. It's a good start." The angry man delivered his soliloquy standing in front of an American flag and behind a table adorned with a smorgasbord of handguns, a shotgun, an AR-15, a civilian clone of an AK-47, and sundry miscellaneous small arms. "I ain't cryin' none - not one blessed tear - for any'a these Commie sons o'bitches. An' I hope this weekend we get more..." Sandra cut off the video.

Danny read the video's header. "Jimmy Yates."

"Out of Dearborn, Michigan," Elbee continued. "Homeland Security says that area's a hot spot for domestic Right-wing terrorists just looking to strike out against government targets."

Wakefield had previously read the same annual terrorist report to which she referred. Everyone who had anything to do with law enforcement or the intelligence community did. Eventually, the media leaked it and a lot of Americans got pretty worked up over the assessment - which undeservingly identified many ordinary citizens and most veterans as domestic terrorists - potential or outright. "First off, that report was utter crap written by some idiot without a clue," he objected. "Taken at face value, that twit labelled me as a terrorist, just 'cause I own a gun. Secondly, I've seen some of this clown's videos. I wouldn't say I'm a fan, *per se*, but he's all talk. He may've done a stint as a logistics monkey in the Army, but he's no pipe hitter. From what I hear, the closest thing he ever saw to enemy action was hiding in a bunker during a mortar attack."

Elbee frowned. "Forensics has given us nothing. Neither has the senator's car. Or the review of the

Evans' financials that you strong-armed yourself into. According to FBI records, Yates is a licensed firearms dealer and has training and combat experience from the Army. He could be some ultra-right-wing zealot. Or he could be funneling guns and military training to a whole network of militiamen who want to overthrow the government. This is the closest thing we have to a lead in my investigation."

"Alright, alright," he held his left hand up in surrender. "I was wrong. I take it back. My partner has a suspect."

"We should question him."

"He's in Michigan," Danny shook his head. "We're supposed to be at the cathedral by oh-eight hundred."

"Not 'we,' as in you and me, Wakefield," Sandra chided. "'We' as in the Bureau."

"Right," Danny nodded. "You're gonna send in a couple of guys from the field office in Detroit to work him over and see if he's involved?" Elbee nodded. The idea of leveraging resources brought a fresh thought to his mind. "Hey Sam," Danny waved, "Can I get a shot with the next round? You want one, Elbee?"

"No, thank you." Sandra still had half a glass of honey ale. "Meanwhile, if we see Yates here in town tomorrow -"

"- then he's probably up to no good. And you've probably just bagged your nut job," Danny concluded for her.

"Case closed," Sandra cheerfully raised her glass in salute of her anticipated success. "I should probably take a day or two while I'm in town once this is over. See the sights. I've never been to the

Smithsonian." Sam delivered a fresh shot of an ounce of unidentified, jet black liquor. Danny downed the shot, slammed the glass on the bar, then chased it with a slow pull from his new ale. "Are you gonna be okay in the morning, Wakefield?" Sandra grew a little concerned.

"What? Me? Yeah. I'm good. Just a little jet lagged. Why? What time is it?" Danny flipped his left hand over to consult the black sport watch he wore face-down on his wrist. "Yeah, I should probably call it an early night, though. I'll head home after this round."

"You're not driving, are you?"

"Do I look stupid?" Danny chuckled. "Even if that was my plan, you don't think I'd be dumb enough to tell a cop I was planning on drinking and driving do you?" Sandra did not find the same level of humor in his joke as Danny did. "Relax Elbee. I took the Metro. I'll be fine. I'm a big boy you know."

"C'mon, Wakefield," Sandra placed what was left of her ale on the bar. "I'm taking you in."

"Swear to God, officer," Wakefield chuckled as he produced a plastic card from his hip pocket. "Metro card. This is D.C. Everybody rides."

"You think I'm gonna let my new partner stumble onto a subway drunk? The night before a big day? I'll drive you back to your place."

Danny slipped a few bills between what was left of his stout and the bar. "Great as always, Sam," he called to the far end of the bar, "but mom says I've gotta go home." Sam waved his goodnight, then busied himself polishing a glass and chatting up a pair of Asian girls in their twenties who were ordering their first round.

"Is it your time in the Marines or your Irish genes that helps you hold your liquor so well?" Sandra inquired as they walked down the hallway to Danny's apartment. "'Cause you hit it pretty hard tonight."

"Nonsense," Danny replied. "Just a little anesthetic to help counter the jet lag." He never stumbled, never stammered, did not even fumble as he plucked his key out of his jean pocket. Outwardly, he showed no indications of being intoxicated at all - beyond his more relaxed demeanor, anyway. But no amount of willpower or discipline could change Danny's blood chemistry. It would be hours before his body metabolized just the booze Elbee saw him drink. And there was no way for her to guess his total consumption for the evening. "And in answer to your question," he smiled broadly, "both."

"Alright. Well, I'll see you in the morning," Sandra nodded as she dismissed herself.

"Thanks for the ride, Elbee," Danny unlocked his door. "You know how to find your way?"

"I've got it, Daniel."

"Okay," he opened the door to his apartment, but remained in the hallway. "You sure you don't want a nightcap?"

"Gotta work tomorrow," she reminded him.

"And you have to drive tonight." Danny waited a beat longer, then turned toward his apartment. "G'night Elbee, stay safe."

There was not much to his apartment. His soft, brown, leather sectional occupied most of the living room area. From where he sat - almost in the center of the room, thanks to how the couch protruded from the wall - the kitchen was at his three o'clock. The only light on in the apartment at the moment came from a small half bath next to that. A storage closet next to that and an eat-in kitchen area at his four o'clock were equally neglected. A little walking space behind the couch led to master bedroom and its *en suite* bathroom at his nine o'clock. Further around the dial, a door led to the undersized second bedroom in which Danny stored his guns, ammo, and gear. The building's public hallway was on the other side of the long wall directly in front of him, against which his jet black Fender acoustic-electric guitar was parked.

The black six-string's cherry red, electric cousin sat on Danny's lap. This late on a Friday night there was little else to do than relax into his leather couch and let his fingers dance across the Stratocaster's steel strings. He strummed out a rhythm that he usually played on the acoustic guitar, but in his opinion, it sounded good on the electric, too. Headphones plugged into the amp allowed his neighbors to sleep peacefully while he worked a slow, sad song out of his system.

Sometimes sleep hated him. Sometimes he hated it back. It was the unfortunate byproduct of a lifetime of violence. Music was his outlet, his release from the stresses and strains of a demanding job, a hostile supervisor, worthless colleagues and a thankless public for whom he worked. Dr. Lola Fender was the only therapist he needed. She was a part of his life, as much as Dr. Jameson, the half-drained anesthesiologist on the coffee table next to Dr. Colt, his bronze-and-black, customized 1911. Between the three of them, one or the other always held the answer to life's problems.

Danny switched from finger playing to accentuated chords as his song picked up. Lots of vets felt the same way he did. Most, the way he figured. Every day, about twenty so guys just like him decided they just could not play anymore.

Whatever happened to the young man's heart?

he sang in his head.

It's swallowed by pain as he slowly fell apart...

A partially folded piece of paper on official letterhead now served as his coaster. *Upon review of your claim, the Department of Veterans Affairs has determined that there is insufficient evidence that your disability is service connected...* No. Of course. Danny's knee blew itself out during the war. It had nothing to do with any of his combat deployments, or the injuries he sustained overseas and were all documented in his medical record. The knee. The headaches. As far as the VA was concerned, that was all just a coincidence. *Thank you for your service...*

Danny hammered power chords into his instrument. Frustration poured through the amp and into his headphones. *At least I've got a job*, he sighed. A lot of his brothers were not so fortunate. In their place, how would Danny have fared? How did they cope with the constant fight against the government? The system. The public that could never understand. How did they deal with the daily struggle against the demons in their own minds?

CHAPTER 10

HALF AN HOUR into the formal memorial service, Danny's eyes scanned the room for the hundredth time. He swept the Washington National Cathedral's North Transept Balcony, looked for signs of trouble from his position on the chapel's Nave. Then he continued down to the main level - which was absolutely packed with members of both congressional houses, family members, and select celebrities all clad in black. Words buzzed in his earpiece. He ignored most of the radio traffic, listening only for key words or the voice of his partner, out of sight somewhere as she discreetly roamed through the building on a roving patrol that let her periodically recheck the ancillary chapels and other interior spaces within the cathedral's massive form.

D.C. Police had the perimeter fairly well-locked

down. The cathedral was the preferred venue for high profile services - presidential funerals and the like - so Capitol Police had a standing plan for how to secure the premises during such events. That operational plan was in full effect today. Uniformed officers manned barricades that blocked sidewalks and closed streets around the entire surrounding block. Access to the grounds was restricted to only those persons on the official roster of attendees and certain previously vetted members of the press.

At the foot of the same altar where Dr. Martin Luther King, Jr. preached his last sermon, two caskets - each draped with an American flag - sat in full view of the attendees and news cameras. The day had originally been arranged as Senator Evans' official service; Congresswoman Rogers' body had been quickly recovered from the wreckage of her plane and spirited to the capital to join her colleague's memorial. It made the event doubly tragic. Doubly dramatic. Four times as sensational.

Wakefield watched as Washington's Cardinal and Bishop joined other prominent church leaders, most of whom were celebrity pastors of megachurches from across the nation. Together they conducted what could only be described in Danny's mind as a tag-team ecumenical service filled with long speeches and stifled tears. Daniel Francis Wakefield, taking his middle name from his maternal grandfather, was raised Catholic until his mother's death. After she lost her bout with cancer, Danny's father never crossed the cathedral's doorstep. Grammy and Grandpa Frank kept taking Danny to Mass though.

Behind the all-star cast of clergymen, the High Alter and Majestics reached up to a series of intricate stained-glass windows as if its ornate sculptures were arms raised to heaven itself. Every inch of every surface from the floor tile to the vaulted arch was laid with painstaking care by craftsmen whose hands sought only to leave behind a legacy that reflected a love of something greater than themselves. Somehow, Danny thought as he took in the sight, the gathering before him cheapened that inspirational message for mankind.

Elbee's voice cracked over his earpiece. "Wakefield," she barked, "you've gotta see this."

Danny snapped out of his momentary reverie and discreetly keyed his mic. "What is it? What's your twenty?" Most organizations implemented a series of brevity codes to keep transmissions short. *Twenty* was the universal code for an operator's location.

"Meet me outside," she replied. "Out front. South entry stairs."

Danny wheeled to his left and made for the door beneath the South Rose Window. He was careful to maintain a cool composure and a casual pace so as not to distract or alarm any of the attendees. In a moment, he arrived at the heavy door, which was opened silently by a uniformed Capitol Policeman.

Outside, Elbee stood with her phone in hand. Danny's peripheral vision picked up a mounting flurry of activity among the press members camped out at the base of the Gothic cathedral's main staircase. He had more than half expected to see somebody - Yates maybe - sprawled out and bleeding on the church's marble steps.

"What's going on?" he asked again.

Elbee pocketed her smartphone. "A federal judge's car just exploded."

Danny's attention darted all around him, trying to key in on the all-too-familiar post-blast aftermath of a car bomb. Smoke. Screams. Sirens. "What? Where?"

"Olympia," Sandra answered.

Special Agent Wakefield felt a psychological gut punch. Olympia, Washington. Danny's mind raced as he made the connection. Their killer had indeed, struck a target in Washington - just as they had expected. Elbee and Wakefield were simply protecting the wrong Washington. "Where's Yates?"

"Dearborn," Elbee sighed. "Two agents from Detroit have been with him for the last two hours. The blast just occurred less than five minutes ago."

Wakefield shook his head and snickered - not in humor, but in disgust. "Nice," was all he could manage through a sneer.

"If Yates is our guy," Elbee pressed, "then he's got a network of partners. Louisiana, California, Washington..."

"Yates isn't our guy," Wakefield scoffed.

"Maybe he's the head of a group."

"Nope." The pieces started to fit together in Wakefield's head. "Who's the judge?"

"Judge Maria Gonzales Ramierez," Elbee answered. "Killed when her car exploded while pulling out of her driveway."

Wakefield did not recognize her, but he fielded a hunch. "Recently appointed?"

Elbee thumbed a quick search into her smartphone. "Uh, yeah. About a year ago. One of the president's first appointments. Why - oh, I see. Our killer likes Democrats."

A senator, a congresswoman, and now a federal judge. All killed in the same calendar week. All of whom belonged to the same political party. "No, Elbee," Wakefield contradicted, "I don't think he likes them at all. I'm pretty sure he hates them."

*   *   *

The memorial service that started out as a media show devolved into an absolute circus as news of Judge Ramierez's murder spread. Members of the press sought to scoop each other with ever-more-sensationalized commentary, while various and sundry congressional members jockeyed to deliver opportunistic sound bites. Elbee and Wakefield, convinced the National Cathedral was not a realistic target for their murderer, left the area as it deteriorated into a scene from the last days of Caligula.

"I swear," Danny commented as he drove away, "I really did see the girls from CNN and Fox break into a catfight."

Sandra rested her right elbow on the Suburban's passenger door, hand over her face. "Why did we think he was going to be here?" she criticized. "I'm deluding myself."

"Don't," he cut her off. "Don't do that. It was a workable theory based on what little information we had available. Don't beat yourself up over it."

"A federal judge is dead," she droned.

"And there was no way to anticipate that move," Danny assured her. "It's not your fault. You didn't kill her."

"You're just saying that to make me feel better."

"He rope-a-doped us," Danny continued. "It's a classic boxing move made famous by Muhammad

Ali."

"I hate sports metaphors."

"Then think of its equivalent from chess. It's pure and simple misdirection. You shoot left, left, left, and then you fake left and blast the guy with a right," Danny explained. "Your opponent's timing and reflexes are all geared for another left. He preconditions himself subconsciously, selling himself on the instinctive belief that another left is coming. And because of this expectation, he gets clobbered. The cathedral was a target rich environment. You made a perfectly good decision based on the best assessment we had, given what little information we had to go on." The truth of Wakefield's words did nothing to stop them from feeling just a little hollow. "He must've known we'd figure on him hitting it. So, he struck somewhere else."

"You don't think Yates is behind this?" she asked. It was a fair question.

"No. I don't." Danny turned off Massachusetts Avenue and onto Nebraska. He drove one of the Suburbans from DHS motor pool because using Elbee's rental car might have complicated getting into some areas that were more easily accessible with the Suburban's official plates and decals. Plus, if things had gotten tense at the Cathedral, the duty vehicle was stocked with a pair of carbines for response and a trauma kit for first aid, all discreetly stowed in the back. "What we're dealing with here is an asymmetric threat by one or more actors highly trained in a variety of tactics, weapons and explosives."

"So, a professional?"

"Yep," Danny resolved. "Maybe a few, but my gut makes me think it's just one guy. One with some skills in real tradecraft, too. Not some wannabe tough-guy like Yates. He's just a survival nut job with a crappy video channel." Wakefield maneuvered the utility vehicle past the weekend barricades at the Department of Homeland Security headquarters building.

Almost nobody who worked for the federal government - regardless of branch or department - worked on the weekends. Even most military buildings turn into ghost towns Friday afternoon. The handful of cars in the parking lot constituted heavy traffic for a Saturday, and two of those vehicles belonged to this duet. Nonetheless, Wakefield bypassed the main lot and parked the Suburban in the rear parking lot with the rest of the dark duty vehicles. Elbee continued her stream of thought as they exited the truck. "So, the question also becomes: 'Who hires a hit man to assassinate politicians?'"

"Might be less work to list the folks who wouldn't."

In a flash, the agents were upstairs unlocking the SCIF which, as was usual, had been closed for the weekend. Motion-activated lights flickered to life as Danny fired up his computer terminal. Sandra conscripted a chair from a nearby cubicle while he bounced a few feet to his left and punched a series of numbers on an off-white phone totally different from the standard, government-issued gray and blue Cisco phone right next to his monitor.

Whoever Danny had called, they answered quickly enough. "Oscar," Danny fumbled for a pen and paper, "this is Wakefield." A pause. "Well, you know how it is." Another pause. "Did you hear about the car bomb in Olympia?" Pause. "Yeah, well, I need to know if anyone has claimed responsibility. Or who's even talking about it. Right away." Another pause. "Yeah, I am."

Elbee sat in silence. She surmised that this Oscar fellow was some super-secret contact Wakefield had in some other government agency. Or another government's agency somewhere. *Secret Squirrels*, she had heard them called. Cagy people who lived in dark places, made paranoid by all of the secrets to which they had been exposed and which they protected. She tried to ascertain where Wakefield might have made his mysterious friend's acquaintance. Sandra's deductions conjured an image of Wakefield squinting, going blind staring voyeuristically at images beamed down from some ultra-secret satellite. The image just did not resolve itself in her mind with the fit Special Agent who sat a few feet away.

"Let's hope that's not the case," Wakefield said after a long pause. "Yes, yes… I know." Another pause. "Alright. Thanks. Out." He unceremoniously hung up the cream-colored handset, then turned slowly back to Elbee. "Well, it was worth a shot," he sighed. "Maybe we'll get something."

"Alright, Wakefield. What was that?"

Danny jerked his left thumb over his shoulder toward the light phone, now behind him. "That's a special secure line used by the National Security Agency," he explained. Sandra had never seen one before, but was not at all surprised to hear that the NSA - half-jokingly referred to in government circles as No Such Agency - had their own communication system. After all, one of the NSA's primary functions was to monitor, collect, and analyze all enemy communications and transmissions. And most people these days were convinced the Agency was tapped into all domestic transmissions, too. The federal government maintained at least one information network separate from the civilian world that she did know of, so it was not a huge leap of faith to accept the existence of another.

"I've got a buddy there," Wakefield continued. "A cryptologist I met a few years back. He's - well, uh… He's really plugged into the system," Danny struggled to explain in terms that would not violate national security. "Anyway, he's really good at this sort of thing. He might be able to give us some insight into who's doing this."

"And what, exactly, is 'this sort of thing'?"

"Think of him as a guy who listens to the ether to hear things before they're spoken." Danny could tell that his cryptic reply sailed over his partner's head. "Look at it this way: all electronic communications can be distilled down to digital data packets and electromagnetic emissions, right?" Sandra nodded. "Okay, well, Oscar listens to all of that like most folks listen to the car radio. All of it. At the same time. Most times it's just background noise, but every once in a while, you hear a song you were wanting to hear -"

"And you turn up the music because you like it." Elbee finished for him. "But you said he hears it before it's spoken."

"If you're in the forest and you don't hear a tree fall, what happened?" Danny challenged her.

"Nothing."

"You assume nothing," he pointed. "But what if somebody you never saw - some garden gnome or troll - saw the old, rotten tree split almost totally in half and silently plucked it up out of the ground and reduced it to dust before it fell?"

"That'd be nice, but why bother? Why not just let nature take its course?"

"What if he knew beforehand that the tree would fall on your head next week if he didn't act today?"

"Then I guess I'd be grateful," she answered. "But there's no such thing. There are no magical guardian sprites in the forest protecting hikers and bunny rabbits from falling trees."

"Maybe not," he conceded, "but there are cryptologists who monitor all transmissions. Some of them report about it. And a very select few individuals actually do anything. For everybody's sake that number has to be small. And Oscar is one of those few." Danny's point, though absurd, was valid. And Sandra knew it. While conspiracy theorists wailed about secret government programs and their nefarious agendas, she knew the truth was that the government spent time and money on programs that were truly designed with the best interests of the American people in mind. Now, whether those were the ends that people actually used them towards or if they were mismanaged and abused was the focus of much debate.

"So, you're saying that your friend Oscar at the NSA can detect a transmission and catch it in midair? How?"

"Isn't it obvious? Even in the digital age very little happens in real time. Email goes from your terminal to a router, through a server, across a line, gets beamed somewhere, then back down another line and all of that backwards. All Oscar has to do is intercept that email at any one of those steps. With a single keystroke he can make it disappear before it is ever delivered."

Sandra nodded in understanding. "And if nobody hears you, you didn't really talk."

"Exactly. Right now, Oscar is 'knocking on the sky,' as he would say. He's checking all resources for any mention of Judge Ramierez's murder."

"But everybody is already talking about it," Sandra pointed. "It's all over every channel."

"Yeah, but who talked about it first? Who knew before anyone else that Judge Ramierez was dead?"

"The guy who killed her."

"Maybe. It's an old adage in the intelligence community: You're not cool unless somebody knows you're cool. No matter how horrible an act is, there's usually somebody out there admitting to it. Bragging to his buddies about it."

Sandra nodded. "We see that a lot in law enforcement, too. No matter how good the evidence is, most convictions are actually centered around confessions. Either the suspect admits their actions to us, or they tell a friend who tells us, or something like that." Elbee's brow furrowed at a thought. "Why are we just now talking to your friend Oscar?"

"He's not my friend, exactly. Not in the strictest sense. He's a buddy. There's a difference. And the reason why we haven't used him yet in any official capacity is, well, it's complicated," Danny replied sheepishly. "Right now, as far as this situation is concerned, he's got nothing we don't have. But if he gets something -"

Wakefield stopped mid-sentence when the phone behind him emitted a warbling beep. He spun and picked it up before the second ring.

"Wakefield," he said sharply. Sandra noted the

change in his tone during the pause. As far as she knew, federal employees were universally trained to answer the phone in a more polite, professional tone. Her own scripted response to a phone - *FBI New Orleans, this is Special Agent Elbee, how may I help you?* - fit closely to the standard government blurb. The NSA must have liked to keep things short and to the point.

"Can you lock it down?" he asked. Yet another pause. "Fine, fine… I understand." Pause again. "Great. Keep me in the loop." Another pause. "Out." Just like that, Wakefield slapped the receiver back down onto the phone and the conversation was over. Elbee sat impatiently with an expectant look on her face, but Danny wheeled back to his computer instead of toward her.

"Do I have to ask?" she prompted him.

"Oscar says someone just posted a video onto YouTube," Danny explained as he called up the popular website and typed in a search string. "He didn't intercept it before it hit the web, so it's out there. Might raise too many suspicions if he purged it now, but he'll try to do better next time. Now that he knows what to look for and from whom, it should be pretty easy." A video played on Wakefield's screen. He maximized the viewing size, then scooted his chair back so that Elbee could see it, too.

A lone figure sat in a totally darkened room. A lone light washed the man - they guessed it was a man - in hard light from above. The figure wore all black: black shirt, black jacket, black gloves; but his face was starkly white, twisted into a sinister smile with rosy cheeks and thin, black, stylized facial hair. It was a mask, obviously enough, one commonly associated with passive-aggressive anti-government extremists.

"Anonymous," Elbee muttered. The Anonymous group was a self-styled cadre of Leftist protesters who saw themselves as the next generation of anti-establishment vigilante crusaders. They routinely posted videos and threatened officials and businesses they saw as corrupt. Their calling card was that they wore the same Guy Fawkes mask as the person in this video.

"I hope I have your attention now, America," a computer-altered voice announced. "If this last week has not woken you up, perhaps you are truly dead inside." The speaker, if the actor in the video was even speaking, remained motionless, seated behind a table or desk that, too, was covered in black. "Let me cut to the point: Some of the people in this country who would call themselves 'leaders' are working very hard to destroy our once-great nation. They are making themselves into kings and queens in the process. We real Americans will no longer tolerate this."

The menacing figure finally moved. He raised his left hand and held a single finger aloft. "Senator Evans was a rich man who made himself richer than he already was in the first place by stealing money from the Katrina Relief Fund that he created." A second finger rose to join the first. "That rich bitch Rogers made herself, her husband, and their businesses exempt from every Socialist program she and her friends in the Communist Congress passed, then raised everyday Americans' taxes to pay for her own personal kingdom." A third finger rose on the figure's upheld hand. "And what kind of judge grants amnesty to thousands of illegal immigrants? To criminals who flood across our borders like dirty locusts swarming our amber waves of grain? Who lets them stay in our country and live off taxpayer-funded programs while they rape and murder our own people? While they steal jobs from our own citizens? One whose loyalties still lay south of the border," the upheld hand closed into a tight fist, "that's who!"

Then, the gloved hand lowered again, but descended below the black table. "The problems of this country all come down to one simple fact," the monotone computer voice continued. "Our nation is being led by a bunch of whores and traitors. And the solution is simple." The speaker's left hand came back above the table, but this time it brought an AR-15 rifle up with it. The speaker held the rifle across his chest with the muzzle pointed downward and the stock in front of his right shoulder. "Death. For all traitors."

A cold hand wrapped its icy fingers around something deep in the pit of Danny's stomach as the video continued. "We the People will no longer allow our elected officials to rape our country and lead it into the toilet. Many Americans will want to join me," the speaker's altered voice continued. "They are welcome to, for we face a grave threat from our domestic enemies. Some folks might want to stand in my way," Though the speaker's head never moved, Wakefield suddenly felt like the masks black, lifeless eyes were somehow focused upon him. "I hope they don't try. Because they will die with the traitors they choose to protect. Patriots - true sons and daughters of liberty - will support what I am doing. The tree of Liberty must, on occasion, be refreshed with the blood of Patriots. America has no kings, and this fight has no innocents."

The speaker placed his rifle down on the table,

reached into his jacket and withdrew a small piece of cloth. He looked down - the first time his head moved during the entire video - as he unfolded the cloth silently. It was a miniature American flag, maybe a little larger than the average adult man's hand. The speaker stretched the flag out and held it before himself upside down with the blue star field oriented toward the lower left corner of the screen. Then, the image faded to black. A second later, the video was over.

Elbee and Wakefield sat in complete silence for moment, their minds swirling with possibilities and implications spawned from what they had just seen.

*   *   *

The eastward drive on Interstate 84 was beautiful beyond explanation. The interstate followed a winding path through the Tetons, whose lush greenery draped peacefully over massive boulders. Sheer edifices in gray and brown stone ripped through the landscape. The interstate ran parallel and adjacent to the Columbia River, which marked the border between Washington and Oregon. With the river on his left and the mid-afternoon sun still high above him, the Patriot heard a news flash about his handiwork as it broke over his truck's radio.

Staccato music was quickly followed by the voice of a woman who tried to sound more confident than he guessed she actually felt. Her account, sold to the public as Breaking News, reiterated Judge Ramierez's death - the car bomb had been the leading headline during each commercial break for hours - and linked it to the video the Patriot had posted online using the unsecured WiFi he found when he grabbed a snack at a McDonald's drive-thru. If the news report was accurate - and no rational human being truly believed the news was, anymore - officials were diligently investigating the attack, yet dramatically stymied at this time by a lack of leads.

The newscaster's double-speak made the Patriot chuckle. Somehow, the liars in the infotainment industry managed to tell the public, day in and day out, that unnamed, nebulous authorities who belonged to omnipotent agencies would somehow protect the public from God-awful boogeymen... all while the fact of the matter was that at this moment nobody was doing anything. Because there was nothing they could do. Not for the immediate future, anyway. Not the police, not the feds, not the media. They were all helpless to do anything except dance to his tune. Because they were all reactors, not instigators. They were counterpunchers, not fighters. They had to act defensively against an unseen enemy who saw that the best defense, as the old saying went, was a good offense.

In his opinion, the Breaking News theme should have been changed from an urgent fanfare to Send in the Clowns. Every account he had heard since his retirement had sounded like it was a chapter read from the Keystone Cops' Playbook. No, he quickly corrected himself, don't get cocky. That's how mistakes are made. Keep leaning forward. Stay on the edge, on the offense. One false step, one wrong move, and his mission would be over before it had truly begun.

CHAPTER 11

"WE NEED TO leverage more assets against this threat," Jonas rubbed his face with enough vigor that it looked to Danny as if his mentor was trying to iron out some of his wrinkles with his own hands. The old Jesuit looked tired, as if he had not slept in the two days since the Olympia car bomb exploded.

"Yes Father," Wakefield agreed. Danny's real father, David Wakefield, lived a quiet and healthy life back in his native Bozeman, Montana. But he had taken to calling his latest boss 'Father' - a moniker born partly in reference to Wiley's religious education and partly in jocular deference to the older man's role as his mentor. Wakefield was a smart enough professional to know when to drop the nickname and when it was safe to use. Most times, Jonas met the title with amusement. Today was not one of those days.

"This whole situation has caught Madame

Director's attention," Jonas continued, "and now occupies a significant part of her time. Which puts her nose firmly in my business until this case is resolved." The older man drummed a staccato rhythm on his desk with his fingertips. One of the universal rules of federal service was that the people at the working level - the ones who actually did stuff - were all but invisible to the senior levels of leadership until something went terribly wrong. During a crisis, however, previously aloof senior executives suddenly became very visible and very interested in their underlings' daily tasks. That was, between televised appearances in which they assured the masses that everything that could be done was being done. Meanwhile, all of the heavy-handed "management" tended to actually interfere with productivity, rather than improve results. Executive meddling. That's what the lower ranks called it. "You of all people know, Danny, that the more time your boss is watching you, the less fun everyone has."

Wakefield nodded silently in the seat opposite his boss. Back in the Marines, the phrase *close to the flagpole* was used to describe one's proximity to senior commands and officials. Conventional wisdom within the ranks purported that such a position held potentially great rewards. One needed only to draw evidence to support that theory from plentiful examples of numerous personnel whose seemingly insignificant contributions and achievements were answered with disproportionately lofty awards. Wakefield's blood pressure rose every time he recalled the story of an Air Force administrative sergeant who spent three months in Afghanistan doing nothing but hiding on base and managing her unit's finances, never once coming in contact with the enemy, only to receive the Bronze Star when she returned home. Danny knew, however, that senior officials often watched their minions with an unforgiving, unblinking eye. At least half of his greatest professional successes had come as the result of actions or behavior that, had his commander or department head been made fully aware of the details, would easily have motivated or compelled them to file charges against him. Indeed, the people Wakefield respected the most - whether back in the Marines or serving with Homeland Security - almost universally held fast to the belief that the freedom of action that came from being ignored by higher authority was usually worth more than the awards and promotions that came from its familiarity.

"And what are Director Dagenhart's orders?" Elbee asked cautiously. Up to this point, she had remained silent in the second seat in front of Dr. Wiley's desk. But, if Cynthia Dagenhart, the Secretary of Homeland Security herself, was aware of the case then surely, she would have provided some sort of guidance or instruction.

"For now, she's staying light handed," Jonas replied. "We're standing up the Crisis Watch to support you two. In return, she gets daily updates on the case and its progression."

"What's the Crisis Watch?" Sandra inquired.

"We've got a secondary watch floor," Wiley explained, "an extra intelligence center here in the building. It serves in a supplementary role. We use it to focus attention on specific, defined problems for a limited period of time. National emergencies and the like. That way the problem can be managed by specialists without drawing too much attention from our normal, more broad-spectrum threat monitoring."

"Kinda like Special Teams in football," she equivocated.

Danny looked at her in disbelief. "I thought you hated sports metaphors."

Jonas winced at the analogy. "That metaphor really only works if your kicker usually works at the concession stand. We're pulling people by onesies-twosies from various other departments and work centers to staff the Crisis Watch around the clock on rotating shifts. By lunch tomorrow, you'll have about two dozen folks - some agents, but mostly analysts - providing you with support."

"We'll need to be able to run it from the field," Wakefield noted. "The reach back will be a great force multiplier, but we cannot be chained to D.C. We need to be free to go wherever the leads take us so that we can eventually get ahead of the threat."

"And by 'we,' he means 'me'," Elbee interjected. Before Wiley could rebuff, she continued. "This case started off as a murder investigation by the Bureau. That makes me the officer in charge. Unless" Sandra raised an eyebrow as if to challenge the old man, "Secretary Dagenhart or FBI Director Robinson have appointed a Senior Special Agent? Or ordered a jurisdictional change?"

Jonas picked an imaginary piece of fuzz off of his tweed jacket as he composed his response. "No, neither of them has. Not yet." He said with a forced calm in his voice. "But I'm gonna level with you, Ms. Elbee: if you want to maintain primacy on this investigation, the FBI needs to kick in some support staff. 'Cause right now, you're the only player from the Bureau on this team, and my people all have jobs that we already pay them for."

So do mine, Elbee looked like she wanted to say. "The FBI and Secret Service are both part of Homeland Security," she pointed. "Has a request for support been sent to the Hoover building yet?"

"I emailed the Station Chief myself earlier, but he hasn't been responded yet," Wiley answered. "But then, it is still Monday morning. Perhaps your buddies would respond faster if the request was repeated by a fellow Bureau member? In person?"

"Yes, sir," Elbee acknowledged. "I'll head over right away."

"Do that, dear," Jonas warned, "because if the Secret Service is going to do all of the heavy lifting, then one of my people will be calling the shots. And you'll be reading about it from New Orleans. It's nothing personal and no strike against you. Just the way things go. Do you have anything further for me? No? Dismissed."

Elbee and Wakefield stood and left Wiley's office. Sandra walked in complete silence until they were fully out of the analysis division. Once the SCIF's vault door closed, however, she shot a glance over her shoulder to her partner. "Well, that was fun."

"Dr. Wiley's a great guy to work for," Danny replied defensively, "but he pulls no punches. He pushes us, but he also knows when to back off."

"Evidently," Sandra fumed as the duet strode to the elevator, "he also knows how to steal my case."

Danny shook his head. "It's not like that Elbee. Not at all. This started as an FBI case, but you heard him. There are a lot of people in this building getting pushed onto it. If the Bureau wants to stay in this game, we've gotta get your bosses to contribute some talent to the team. You know, some players to lend a hand. That's it."

Elbee thought that over for a moment as the elevator descended to the building's underground parking level. "You said, 'we.' Again."

"That's right," Danny affirmed. "You're my partner. And partners get each other's backs. It's your baby. I'd like to you keep it. You do want to keep this case, don't you?"

"Of course," she answered as the elevator doors opened. "What kind of agent hands off an investigation just because it gets hard?"

"Well then, let's rustle up some teammates over at Hoover."

*   *   *

"As we roll into the final hour of the Lonnie Chase program," the solemn voice rolled out of the radio, "I want to focus on the home front. In the last week, we've had two members of Congress - a Representative and a Senator - murdered. We told you about what we thought was the first murder - Senator Duke Evans. And we gave you the update earlier about the leaked report from the National Transportation Safety Bureau in which investigators concluded Linda Rogers' plane was brought down by some sort of explosive device placed inside of both engine compartments. So, now we know that was no accident - as was previously reported by the mainstream media." Lonnie just could not resist pointing out any error made by his competitors on other outlets, even during a somber commentary. "And now, this weekend, a judge - a federal judge! - murdered in front of her own home with a car bomb." The media mogul breathed heavily into his antique microphone to further convey the weight of his mood. "Think about that America, a car bomb. What is this, Iraq? Is this how we treat our officials? Is this what we've come to?"

Yes, the Patriot answered his radio silently in his head. Though he knew the question was rhetorical, he answered it anyway as he listened to the soliloquy. *It really has come to this.* It was not easy to get his hands on large quantities of sufficiently powerful explosives to meet his operational needs. And the Patriot had exhausted his personal stash in the three IEDs - improvised explosive devices - he built for Rogers' plane and Rodriguez's car. So, he sat in Utah, about ten minutes away from a very specific heavy construction company. One that specialized in blasting crevices for highways and tearing down whole buildings with surgically precise explosive charges. One where he knew a specific demolition technician and knew that if he asked the right way, his brother would be able to resupply him with a few pieces of key ordinance... off the books and with no questions asked.

"This is not the America of our fathers," Lonnie's voice continued. "This is not the America of George Washington. I don't care how bad things get; we should always look for the peaceful path to justice! Yes, we want justice. We demand it! But the last thing we as Americans should ever seek is the blood of our fellow countrymen. Choose peace! I beg you - all of you! Do not follow this monster, whoever it is. By now, you've seen his video." Indeed, the fact that the YouTube video of Guy Fawkes had gone viral almost instantly was almost a news story in and of itself. "Millions and millions of views in just two days... Our listeners are not dumb. You know he's recruiting. Don't give in to hate. I beg you. Follow the path of Ghandi, of Martin Luther King, Jr. Follow the path of peace and love, not of hatred and violence. This is not a fight for political control - mark my words! This is a battle for the very soul of America. And it is a battle we cannot afford to lose." The radio personality let his words hang in the air for a beat, then another, letting them sink into his listeners' ears and stroke their hearts.

"Our sponsor this half hour is Goldstein Financial Group..."

*   *   *

Jacob Rousch was called Junior by his family even though his father's name was Leonard. But when your initials were JR, what else could you expect? By the time a Taliban-laid IED blew his left leg and three fingers off, most of his buddies in the Army had taken to calling him Rooster.

Some days the sight of what was left of his twisted and scarred body in the mirror was almost enough to make Jacob want to eat his own pistol. God knew how close he had come, not so long ago. This day though, was a fair day. Junior sat at a desk at the front of the TriState Demolition office sorting invoices and ordering supplies from online vendors while rock music played from his desktop iPod dock. The office was louder than his dad would normally have liked, but quiet enough that Junior could still hear phones and other office noises. When the door chime sounded, he turned the volume down as a courtesy to the unseen customer, then spun his chair around to a face from his past.

"Hey, Rooster," the older man greeted him. Rousche mustered forgotten strength into his good leg and pushed to rise from his chair. "No-no-no, little guy," the Patriot waved in a downward motion, "don't get up. Please." But Rousche would not be deterred. The least he could do for this man was rise from his cushy seat. Honored by the wounded warrior's display, the older man took the younger's hand, pulled him in, and slapped him sharply on the back as he held the other tight. His fraternal display was mirrored simultaneously by the one-legged office worker. It was the kind of greeting commonly shared between combat veterans.

Memories of the last time the pair saw each other flashed through both mens' minds but remained undiscussed. "Boss," Rooster managed after a beat, "what brings you by?"

The Patriot tossed a thumb lazily past his shoulder toward his truck and trailer. The front bumper, which faced the shop's glass front door, lacked a license plate. "A guy from the Unit has family that moved out this way when he didn't make it back," he said with veiled caution. "His widow's about to give birth to his son. We took up a collection, held a couple of fundraisers, and bought everything for the kid's room before the wake, but the admin guys processed everything and shipped all of their stuff out this way before we could get the furniture and stuff for the nursery delivered to their place. So, I'm running it up the road."

Rooster snorted in disgust. "Admin POGs." Rhyming with "vogue", POG - a military acronym equally used to mean People Other than Grunt or Pieces of Garbage - was the name actual warfighters commonly used when referencing personnel in either the S1 division, Administration, or S4 department, Logistics. Another common name for said "lesser" Soldiers, Sailors, Airmen and Marines was Fobbit - in reference to the fact that on those rare occasions that Combat Support Services personnel did actually deploy they spent their entire time huddled in relative safety of the FOB, or Forward Operating Base. The daily life of a Fobbit living under the protection of layered defenses included regular meals, on-base coffee shops, shifts of only eight to ten hours, and Sundays off to enjoy such base amenities as Saddam Hussein's giant pool at Baghdad Palace or the Post Exchange at Kandahar Air Base - a shopping complex that was larger than many malls in the States and even stocked PlayStations for Fobbits to play with in their hootches.

The older man nodded as Rousche reached for a styrofoam cup half-filled with thick, darkened fluid. "I once heard our team intel bubba call it 'Administrative Fratricide'," he told Rooster.

Rousche held the spittoon cup to his bottom lip and dribbled a bit more spit into it. Nobody in the Army seemed to mind the fact that chewing tobacco was more addictive than smoking. Rooster's head bobbed. "Administrative Fratricide," he repeated. "Death by friendly paperwork. I like it. So, which guy? I mean, the guy who didn't make it."

"Sergeant Anderson," the older man answered.

Rooster thought hard for a moment. "I don't think I met him."

The Patriot knew Rooster would not remember Sergeant Anderson - largely because he did not really exist. "Yeah, well, he wasn't with us long." The comment implied the fictional trooper's entire time with the unnamed Unit had occurred since Rooster's discharge. Either way, he knew Rooster would sympathize with his story. Whether they were killed by an enemy bullet or an overdose of pain meds, guys from the Unit always felt the loss of one of their comrades.

"Sorry."

"We all are," the older man gave a somber nod. "Anyway, I heard through the grapevine that you were out in these parts and thought I'd drop by for a favor."

"Name it, Boss," Rooster straightened.

"Mrs. Anderson has some tree stumps that need getting rid of..." he trailed off.

"You want me to send a guy over?" Rooster maneuvered back into his seat and keyed up the company's appointment schedule. "The whole crew's cutting a new throughway for a highway, but I can push Paul off site Wednesday morning for a few hours."

"Actually," the Patriot explained, "I could blow them out myself, but I couldn't pack any ordinance with me when I left Ft. Bragg. You and I both know the trouble that would rain down on me if I drove across state lines with a crate of special issue, military-grade explosives in the back seat of my truck."

Rooster chuckled. "That'd be so friggin' funny, Boss. You know they'd string you up once that dash cam footage made it onto the internet."

"Yeah. Anyway, I don't wanna put you in a spot, but I thought you might have some stuff that you wouldn't miss. Something whose shelf life is about to expire, or some surplus material from a job that never got used?"

"You're asking me to provide explosives to an unlicensed user from out of state?" Rooster responded dryly. Clearly, both men knew that the request was the kind of felony that landed a man in prison for a good, long time.

"Look, man, I don't want any trouble. I just thought, you know, if you had something I could use. Save me the time of digging and cutting the damn things out. But it's no big deal if you can't do anything. I totally understand. Don't sweat it."

Rooster thought it over. A fallen combat veteran's widow needed help, and a fellow vet with whom Rousche had served was asking for it. What could he do? What would he do? "Where's this widow live?"

"Logan. Just up the road." Logan, Utah was, in fact, a short drive north of Salt Lake City. Near the state line. At least that much of his story was true.

"What do you need?" Rooster noncommittally asked.

"Enough stuff to clear two or three stumps. One's kinda big." The older man held his hands in an open circle almost the size of a beach ball. "Again, only if it's no trouble."

Rooster blew out a breath, then relented. He had seen the Boss a few times downrange. He knew the older man was a senior noncommissioned officer, that he belonged to a Unit with no name, no designator, no badges, patches, or rank on their uniforms -

uniforms which were not the general issue togs everyone else in the Army had to wear. He knew Unit Operators employed a vast skill set that often exceeded even his own abilities back when Rooster was on top of his game as a full time EOD technician. And he knew the guys in the Unit would go through hell and back again for each other - or each other's family.

"I do have something that might help," he finally admitted. "I keep a little stash of stuff that's officially been blown. Just for myself. You know, in case zombies come or something."

"Got it tucked in your Bug Out Bag?"

"Yep. Along with my rifle and a dozen mags jacked with M855 rounds." Americans often joked about a zombie apocalypse, but the reality was that the chances of survival during extreme emergencies such as tornados, floods and the like favored those individuals who actually took the time to prepare a perfectly sensible kit with food, first aid, and whatever supplies might be necessary to weather the storm until it passed. And whatever a man felt he needed to keep those around him safe from the unprepared. From the desperate and stupid. From zombies. Rooster, it seemed, was preparing for zombies that wore body armor and needed to be eliminated with extreme prejudice. Just like any true fighter was. "It ain't thermite or C4, but it'll do the job."

"Beggars can't be choosers," the Patriot reminded. "How much'll it cost?"

"Don't sweat it," Rooster replied. "It's already off the books, so it doesn't technically exist anymore. Didn't cost me nothin' and I can always get more."

"Thanks, little guy," the older man responded.

"You're a life saver."

Rooster shook his head. "Just helping a brother out." A beat, and then he raised his right finger in warning. "Just don't get caught with this stuff. 'Cause - if you do - I don't know you."

"We never met," the Patriot assured him. *If I get caught,* he decided long ago, *the only ones getting any answers from me will be the coroner and God Almighty Himself.*

CHAPTER 12

THE INTERNET was abuzz. Blogs, chatrooms, message boards, and social media pages were flooded with posts sharing news, rumors and opinions about the serial killer who targeted government officials. CNN was the first major media outlet to brand the culprit with the name Constitutional Killer - in response to the Guy Fawkes impersonator's use of the signature colonial phrase '*We the People*' during his now-world-famous video. The name caught traction, and soon almost everyone in America was Tweeting and commenting about whether they felt the Constitutional Killer was, in fact, justified in his actions.

MSNBC was quick to report that Michigan resident Jimmy Dale Yates was identified by authorities as the Constitutional Killer and had been arrested for the crimes. Within a few hours, they changed their story to identify him as a person of interest, but he was not actually in custody. By the time the network corrected their reports again to reflect that Yates had only been questioned by the FBI on a matter that may or may not have been related to the Constitutional Killer case, the would-be internet celebrity had already found a vocal, telegenic lawyer who was more than happy to very publicly file a character defamation suit against the news network on her client's behalf. Both Yates and his attorney, one Samantha Andrews, paraded themselves on a whirlwind of news and talk shows across several major networks within two days of MSNBC's *faux pas*. The networks received positive feedback from test markets and pollsters about the lovely young Andrews, a junior associate from the Jaye, Adams and Beckman Law Group in Dearborn whose auburn hair, fair skin and blazing green eyes gave her more the look of a model or beauty pageant contestant than a litigator. And her ability to form a complete, intelligent sentence made her at least four times as smart as any of the bimbos who had competed in the Miss America pageant in the last several years. FOX was the first network to move her chair out from behind the interview desk, pan the camera out into a wider shot, and let the viewers see how the twenty-something filled out a suit whose skirts seemed to get shorter with each subsequent appearance.

All of these goings on were ancillary pieces of data that flashed across a series of giant monitors that covered the main wall at the front of the Crisis Watch floor at the Department of Homeland Security building in Washington, D.C. The video wall - a patchwork of raised screens, each keyed to a different information source and in total picture taller than a man and wider than a two car garage. The watch streamed all information relevant to the Constitutional Killer case to a single location where all of the watch floor analysts could see it in full high definition on those rare occasions when they actually looked up from their computer monitors.

Agent Derek Martin, Wakefield's only real friend from the Analysis Division, dropped by the Crisis Watch from time to time. Elbee had somehow succeeded in begging, borrowing, or stealing fourteen analysts and agents from the FBI during her little sojourn to the J. Edgar Hoover Building, so Dr. Wiley was able to fill out the Crisis Watch without sacrificing any further talent from his own work center. Such being the case, "Little D" - as Wakefield called him - had offered to help whenever he could afford some time away from the caseload Brown dropped almost solely on his desk.

Martin knew that there was a lot of friction between Brown and Wakefield, even if he did not fully understand its root cause. The animosity between those two was a kind of open office secret everybody knew about but nobody discussed. Like how Jenkins was a no-talent hack who managed to keep her workload light by whoring herself around the building. She spends more time under other people's desks, Derek had remarked more than once, than she does at her own.

Derek's intelligent brown eyes danced around the room. From his vantage point along the back wall, he could glance over each analyst's shoulder and read their screens. He already knew everything about the case that they did. Wakefield had quietly slipped Little

D's address into the watch team's internal email distribution list. Everyone on the team used to disseminate raw data, processed information, and finalized reports. Martin was not assigned to the case. He just enjoyed solving puzzles. Underneath an unkept mop of curly brown hair he housed a brain that was insatiably hungry for challenges. The Constitutional Killer case was the kind of mystery his natural curiosity could never have ignored no matter how much extra work Nick gave him. Big D never asked him to help with the analysis, but he happily accepted when Little D offered to keep an eye on things quietly while Wakefield and Elbee flew to Seattle. Besides, when he observed the watch floor analysts' current tasking, Derek could also account for what he did not need to do himself - even accurately enough to anticipate their next step or two in the investigation - and focus his efforts on avenues the other analysts were sure to miss, whether due to lack of manpower, lack of talent, lack of insight, or lack of imagination.

Derek was true rarity in federal service. He possessed an IQ that made garden variety geniuses look like punch drunk chimpanzees. His teachers always said that when he grew up he would cure cancer and the common cold in the same day, then finish the week by building, patenting and marketing flying cars. Unfortunately for the human race as a whole, Derek met a cute Lebanese girl in some random elective he had to take during his junior year at Johns Hopkins. They fell in love, moved into an apartment together, and he took the first job he was offered in the Metro as soon as he graduated with his B.S. in Mathematics. It was the easiest way for him to support Aliyah while she pursued her nursing degree.

The Department of Homeland Security was more than happy to exploit Derek's gifted genius. He was a walking probability engine with an eidetic memory. He could read Moby Dick in less time than most people took to use the bathroom. Unfortunately, he also seemed to be the only person in the Analysis Division who actually did anything - other than Big D, of course - a fact that led to Nick the Dick's unwritten, but no-less-adhered to policy of never letting the two heavy hitters in the shop actually work on the same case at the same time. Still, if he was careful then nobody really noticed when he snuck into the watch floor. He did it a lot while other folks took long lunches or smoke breaks. All he needed to avert their potential suspicion was a clipboard or a file folder and a look of urgency.

A nearby analyst, a short-haired brunette he had never seen before, flipped between open windows on her desktop monitor. The first was a list of all flights in and out of the airports servicing the areas for each murder; the second window was a spreadsheet of flights linking those airports and times between the murders.

"Excuse me," he interrupted her, "but I don't recognize you. Which division are you from?"

The analyst turned her head to meet his attention but kept her chair and body pointed toward her screens. "Dianne Stevenson," she held out her right hand in greeting. She appeared to be in her late twenties, maybe a couple of years older than Derek, with intelligent brown eyes. She wore a light blue blouse and dark slacks; a conservative ensemble that was the opposite of any of Jenkins' office clothes.

This Stevenson chick seemed more interested in working at the office than engaging in social foreplay. "FBI. I'm one of the analysts sent over to help with the investigation."

"Nice to meet you," Derek shook her hand. "What are you working on?"

"Our killer is all over the map," Agent Stevenson explained. "Literally. I'm trying to narrow the possible flights and times he used to travel. Then we can scan the airport security camera footage during those times and look for a face or two that keep popping up. Generate a candidate pool, identify them with facial recognition, then start interviewing suspects until something shakes loose."

"Ah," Derek replied. "Seems like a lot of work."

Agent Stevenson hid most of the pride she felt with her own cleverness. "Well, if that's what it takes to catch our killer…"

Derek pointed at the estimated times of death for each of the murder victims. "You're likely wasting your time, you know. I mean, if catching the killer is actually your goal. He's probably not flying."

"What?" The FBI was shocked, insulted even, at the implication.

"Look at the date and time each victim was probably killed," Derek instructed. "There is enough time between each murder for the killer to have driven. Check the map."

Stevenson pointed to the map projected on one of the screens at the front of the watch floor. "You're talking about driving from Louisiana to California, then to Washington."

"Yep."

"Any of those is a long haul," Stevenson pointed

out. "All of them together is a marathon."

Derek nodded his head in agreement. "But doable. Difficult, but not impossible. Therefore we can't rule it out."

"You think our killer likes to drive?" she asked.

"I don't know," Derek allowed, "but I do think he doesn't want to get caught. And driving on the open road minimizes our chances of picking him up."

Agent Stevenson nodded. "We'd have to analyze days and days of recordings from hundreds, even thousands of traffic cameras along each route. Then, to find him, we'd have to pull from every camera in the country simultaneously. And that's assuming we could identify a common vehicle as a suspect. We just don't have the manpower or computing power to pull it off. The system's just not designed to handle that kind of task."

"Plus, we'd likely generate a metric buttload of false positives at each step along the process," Derek added. "False positives that would grow exponentially the longer it took us." Agent Stevenson set her jaw and hissed in frustration at his assessment. "Don't be hard on yourself. At least you had an original idea. Unfortunately for your theory, our perp appears to be smart enough to understand that freedom equals anonymity equals camouflage. Which presents our killer with more opportunity to move to his next target," Derek concluded. Then an idea struck him. "But, the vehicle thing might not be a bad idea, if you approach it differently." Agent Stevenson's blank expression told Derek that, as usual when dealing with normal people, he was three steps ahead of her. "We ignore the conspiracy theory that Rogers' plane was shot down and assume it was tampered with some time before flight."

"But the flight crew and mechanics all checked out. They were each questioned multiple times and by various agencies."

Obviously, Stevenson still did not get it. *How can we be anywhere near the same pay grade?* Derek thought. *I need a raise.* "Somebody had to have sabotaged it. Which would likely have happened on the ground. The mechanics are the prime suspects. But to rule them out we need to figure out who else had access to the plane. Maybe somebody with faked or stolen credentials snuck into the hangar. Something like that."

"A lot of hangars don't have interior security cameras," Agent Stevenson added.

"So," he pointed to the dot on the map marked as San Francisco, "we pull surveillance footage from the perimeter cameras at the point of origin for the period during which her plane was there and look for anomalies. Out of state plates. Folks lurking or loitering where they shouldn't be. Things like that. Identify the vehicles, track down their owners, check for indicators that any of them might be a viable suspect."

Agent Stevenson seemed to follow his idea and approve. She also appeared comfortable with the plan, with its elegant yet forthright logic. "I'll put in the request. We should be able to start watching video shortly."

"Not 'we'," Derek corrected. "You."

"It was your idea," Agent Stevenson objected, obviously not thrilled about the prospect of watching hours and hours of video in the hope of satisfying somebody else's long shot, hair brained theory.

"Yeah," Derek allowed, "but I don't technically work here. Now, if you'll excuse me, I've got an embezzlement case from Denver that needs my attention." The Secret Service analyst turned on his heel and started for the exit. Two steps from the door, he turned back over his shoulder. "Oh, and Stevenson: you're welcome."

*   *   *

The burned-out wreckage that used to be a sport utility vehicle sat in the center of a hangar leased by the FBI in Seattle. The twisted hulk of charred metal and melted plastic was too massive to be transported to the Bureau's lab downtown, so the local station chief had it relocated here from the Judge Ramierez's driveway.

"Judge drove a Lexus," Wakefield commented, pointing to the scorched grill ornament as he walked between the ghastly wreck and a wall of acrylic paneling a few feet from its nose. Technicians from the local FBI field office had painstakingly recreated a mockup of the area surrounding Judge Ramierez's car when it exploded. In the interests of time and cost, transparent acrylic panels were erected as substitutes for the garage door, entry side of the house, and any other structure within the crime scene. Photos of the original structure were taken at the scene and taped to the acrylic panel representing that object, as well as a clear plastic evidence bag which contained sample materials the forensic technicians gathered from the original substances.

"At least it was a hybrid," Elbee offered.

Danny made a face as if he suddenly smelled

 Daryl E.J. Simmons

something. "Please don't tell me you drive a Prius."

Sandra did not even look at him as she nodded. "Powder blue."

"That's not a car," Danny said with a bad taste in his mouth, "that's a roller skate with air conditioning."

"Not all of us need to compensate for our inadequacies with a testosterone-burning four-by-four that gets three miles to the gallon and has a gun rack in the back."

"It's not a gun rack," Danny said defensively, "it's an emergency kit."

Elbee instantly transformed into a school teacher scolding a willful student. "If more people drove hybrids, we could help salvage what's left of the environment."

"And if more people drove Priuses," Danny practically spat as they resumed their tour of the crime scene reconstruction, "there'd be fewer auto accident survivors. I'm not convinced thinning out the human population is the best way to save the manatees."

Sandra huffed as she stood near a line of black and yellow striped tape strewn along the hangar floor. The taped lines represented where the edges of the driveway and road were back at the original house. All in all, the hangar interior had been transformed into a respectable reconstruction of the crime scene. The building itself afforded the feds some much needed privacy while they conducted their investigation, and the extra space inside the building gave the FBI team plenty of room to set up computers, microscopes, and all manner of equipment that might be necessary to analyze any potential evidence.

Elbee carried a clipboard in her hands. It contained printouts that listed all of the details

185

gathered so far. "CSI says that the blast pattern indicates the explosion was caused by a vehicle-borne improvised explosive device -"

"'*Car bomb*' is still an acceptable, legacy term," Wakefield interjected. "'*VBIED*' is just an acronym some idiot staff officer invented to sound smart and justify their own award."

"The car bomb," she continued, "would have originated..." she looked up, then pointed with the tip of her pen, "here, from behind the left rear wheel." What remained of the wheel was fairly well twisted and flash-corroded from the blast. The tire itself must have been reduced to carbon atoms and ash from the explosion's heat.

Wakefield walked around the vehicle's remains, stopping occasionally to peer inside, or crouch down low to examine the underside. "Makes sense," he remarked. "That's the side with the fuel door, right? So, that's the place to put a car bomb. It's the surest way to make sure the blast hits the fuel tank." He stood upright again. "We've seen this before."

Elbee thought back to an email from the National Transportation Safety Bureau. "The NTSB report said that Rogers' plane was taken down with twin explosive charges against the fuel manifold."

"True, but not what I was talking about." Wakefield's eyes looked squarely at the Lexus, but his mind was thousands of miles away. His attention was focused on something that happened years ago. "We used to see this all of the time when I was in the Marines. Insurgents were strapped for resources. They always are. Rebels only have so much money, and quality explosives are both hard to come by and expensive. So, *Muj* learned a long time ago -"

"Wait," Sandra interrupted. "*Muj?*"

"*Mujahadeen*," Wakefield expanded.

"You mean radicalized Islamic extremists?"

"Islam is radical," Wakefield spit back. "Some folks just follow it more closely than others."

"And you call them '*Muj?*' That term sounds pretty racist and insensitive."

"Look, Elbee," Wakefield kept as calm as he could, but that did not stop his voice from rising just a bit. "You can hold tight to whatever Politically Correct hippie bullshit you want, but don't try to shrink-wrap a pound of crap and label it as hamburger. Alright? I spent most of my adult life in the Middle East watching these barbarians rape and kill each other and everyone around them in the most brutal ways you can imagine. So, yeah - we call 'em *Muj*. Or Fuzzy Muzzy. Or *Hajji*. Or Abu Badguy. Or anything else we want. And we don't apologize for it. Not to those boy raping camel jockeys. Not ever. Because we have that freedom. And if they don't like it and they wanna act all offended then they can get bent."

The hangar was as still as a tomb for a moment. There were a half dozen technicians working on the forensics team, but nobody moved an inch or said a word. Then, from somewhere in the shadows, an unidentified voice yelled, "Hoo-rah!"

"Ooo-rah," Wakefield answered firmly. *Dude must've been in the Army*, he guessed. Then he nodded at Elbee, dropped his voice back to something nearer its normal modulation and added a falsely thick southern drawl. "'Mer-cah," he joked in a fake redneck accent aimed to lighten the suddenly heavy atmosphere.

Everyone else wandered back into whatever task they were doing before Danny's brief sojourn onto his soapbox. Having heard her partner's tirade, Elbee was a little taken back. "I'm sorry," she said quietly. "I see that you have some strong feelings about this subject. I didn't mean to offend you."

Danny waved it off. "Forget about it." *What the hell, Danny?* he chastised himself. *Get a friggin' grip.* "Look, like I was saying: back in Iraq and Afghanistan we saw that the enemy was cheap, evil and ignorant, but not totally stupid. To get the most bang for their buck - no pun intended - they learned to place the device inboard of the wheel nearest the fuel door. The wheel and tire help deflect the blast wave inboard, focusing it on the fuel tank and igniting the gas. The energy from that secondary explosion is what finishes the job. It only takes a fraction of the raw explosive material to create a fireball that burns the victim than it would if you tried to take them out with the actual shock wave from the explosion itself. Especially if you have several gallons of gasoline freely available as a handy accelerant."

Elbee followed his explanation. "We've been operating off the theory that our suspect is a Right-Wing militant. Are you saying you now think we're dealing with a Muslim terrorist?"

Wakefield shook his head. "Nah. *Hajjis* learned it from the Irish Republican Army. Those glorious, drunken bastards perfected the art of the car bomb decades ago during the Trials." He stabbed a finger at her in mock seriousness. "And, before you complain about *that* racial epithet you should remember that my family's Irish, so I can say whatever I want about the bloody Micks. Just like how black people get to use the n-word. It's only racist when *you* say it; when *we* do it, it's poetic."

Sandra could not help but let loose a snicker through her lips. Whatever had crawled up Danny's shorts a minute ago seemed to have passed. "That's all good to know," she said, "but it doesn't help us with the case."

"Maybe it does," Wakefield pointed. "Car bombing a judge is a page straight out of the al Qaeda in Iraq playbook. IRA guys always hit people tied back to the government of England. Likewise, AQI usually car bombed targets associated with the post-2004 Shia government. And our guy copies the tactic to kill a judge." Danny's head rocked back a little with realization. "He's using *Muj* TTTP's - Tactics, Techniques, Tools and Procedures," he amplified for her benefit, "to carry out his killings. Plus, a shooting that could've been a scene in the Godfather. Say, where's that psych profile you gen'ed up last night on our suspect?"

"It's on the share drive," Elbee reminded him. "Saved in a one of the team's folders so that everyone can get to it."

Wakefield's hand darted to his pocket, produced his phone, then punched a series of buttons on the virtual keyboard and he bolted to the hangar door - presumably to step outside and improve the reception on his phone. "I'll be right back."

CHAPTER 13

OUTSIDE THE FBI'S leased hangar in Seattle, Special Agent Wakefield made two phone calls. The first was to set Agent Martin into motion on a task that was too time consuming to occupy Wakefield's attention at the moment, but too close to home for it to be entrusted with a stranger. The second call was a request from their boss, Dr. Wiley.

Because he was on an unsecured mobile phone he had to be discreet, but, if Little D and Father's responses were any indicator, Danny managed to talk around his topics sufficiently to convey his meaning. Special Agent Elbee waited near the hangar door until her partner, further out on the apron, deactivated his cellular phone.

"What was that all about Wakefield?" she drilled.

"Sorry I had to rush out of there," he explained, "but I had an idea."

"Shouldn't you have talked to your partner about it?"

"I'd really like to have," he replied sincerely. Sandra stood there before him, expectantly, while Danny weighed how much he could disclose to his partner without getting either - or both - of them in trouble. *To Hell with it…* he sighed. Rules be damned, it was time to lay his cards on the table. To serve up a dose of that transparent cooperation he had been preaching to his partner. Besides, they could play catch-up with all the paperwork later and make everything right. "You've seen how our killer works. Well, Special Agent Criminal Psychology, tell me what you think about our killer."

Special Agent Elbee did not have to consult her case notes. "We're likely dealing with a man - statistically, most serial killers are male. But he's not some Kazinsky or Dahmer. Our guy doesn't just kill people, he *over*kills them. He strikes his victims with unbridled brutality, which indicates severe anger issues. But he seems to go to some lengths to limit collateral damage - like leaving the prostitute alive. That further suggests that his anger is directed specifically at the individuals he kills. But so far, we have no shared contacts among the victims. Their common denominator is that they're all government officials belonging to the same party. So, our assassin is obviously a Right-Wing radical."

"And where," Wakefield invited, "is the best place to find armed, enthusiastic Conservatives that are also trained killers?"

Elbee thought for a moment. "The military."

"Jackpot." Wakefield motioned his partner to join him for the walk back to the hangar. "Military-grade explosives in Rogers' plane, then again in the judge's car bomb. I bet our guy either is, or more likely was, in the US military."

Sandra did not miss a beat when they burst through the door. "I need you to recheck the residue from Ramierez's car for microdots," she ordered a forensics technician in a lab coat, who obediently moved to a nearby microscope.

"Ma'am," the tech called while peering through her microscope, "we've got 'em."

"Great." Wakefield was surprised by how quickly the tech was able to find the dots.

"Do they match the tags from Roger's plane?" Elbee asked.

"Comparing now... Yes, ma'am. Some of the tags match."

"What do you mean, '*some*'?" she asked.

The technician looked up from his microscope. "The team in Denver actually found a few different types of microdots in the explosive residue around what was left of the Gulfstream's engines and cowling. So did we. Some of these dots match some of those. There are a couple of anomalies from each site, too."

"Each batch of explosives has a unique set of dots, right?" Wakefield clarified.

"Yessir. We only need to find one microdot intact to trace the ordinance back to sale and production."

"And we've got a bunch of different ones?"

"Yessir." The technician's breath mask moved inward, then out again as he thought. "It's like some kid's ball of Play-Dough. You know? There's bits from other colors mixed in with the original. Only instead of individual dye colors, we're dealing with specific batches of C4."

"Be sure to get a copy of your report to the ATF," Elbee ordered. "Speaking of which, where's the result of their trace on the Denver bombs?"

"Should've been back by now, ma'am. The turnaround on a standard trace request can take up to thirty days. Since this is an active investigation I'd've hoped we would get an answer in more like seventy-two hours."

"Typical," Wakefield remarked. *Crimefighting at the speed of government bureaucracy.*

"You still haven't answered my question about your phone call," Elbee probed. "I thought you said partners share everything. So, what gives? You got all pissed at me over the prostitute in New Orleans. Don't hold out on me, Wakefield."

Danny noticed that more than one of the male technicians - and the lone female - looked up after Sandra's remark about a shared prostitute. He suppressed a smile at what he imagined they must have thought when they heard his partner's unintentional *double entendre*, having heard the comment out of context. Then Wakefield grew somber again. When he finally answered, his voice came in a low, hushed tone. "I've got Martin looking into this from another direction."

"I don't understand," Elbee, whether consciously or not, matched his quiet tone.

Danny gestured and the pair walked slowly toward the nearest hangar wall, well out of earshot from the busy FBI technicians. "You remember what you said the other day? About that report - the one where Homeland Security basically said everyone in the military is a potential terrorist?"

Sandra nodded. "If we're right, our killer seems to be validating that assessment."

Danny snorted from his nostrils. "Yeah, well, it turns out that a few years back, when Obama was still president, Homeland Security started keeping a closer track of veterans." Danny made no effort to hide his disdain for what he was saying. It sickened him to think that his own government would hold him and his brothers, after all of their years of service and sacrifice, in such low regard. "Specifically SpecOps guys and anyone with a combat-related PTSD rating. There's a database. I ain't saying it's right. I'm just saying it's there."

"A database of veterans?" Elbee was confused. "Couldn't they just check with Veterans' Affairs?"

"It's not just a roster." Danny's face worked like he had just tasted something he wished he had not eaten. "Names, pictures, phone numbers, addresses - sure. But also copies of their service and medical records, doctors' notes from the Service and the VA... even their private medical stuff pulled out of backdoors in civilian medical systems. They call it Project CANON. And it gets worse." Danny's voice lowered to barely a whisper, forcing Sandra to step even closer as she fought to listen. "It's populated with tracking data and communications intercepts from the NSA. All of which can be queried retroactively if somebody goes off the reservation."

"That could all be helpful," Elbee noted.

"Yeah, well, Homeland started keeping it in case somebody went off the reservation. Or if some SEALs staged a coup or something. Or if someone just plain cracked and started hosing down an office building with an AK or something."

"Just like our guy seems to have," Elbee countered. "Why have I never heard of this before?"

"Officially: because it doesn't exist. The whole thing is strictly need-to-know."

"And unofficially?" she fished.

"Because it's an embarrassment." Danny's voice was starting to rise, seethed in anger. "It's an illegal domestic surveillance operation. No warrants, no probable cause, no intelligence oversight. No Constitution getting in the way of Uncle Sam's prying eyes. It's a gross violation of privacy targeting the men and women who gave the most to this country. The ones who deserve to be treated better."

Realization dawned across Sandra's face. "This is what your boss was talking about with you the other day, wasn't it? The closed-door meeting that I couldn't attend?"

"Consider yourself read into CANON," Danny nodded. Then he drily added, "Congratulations," and traced the papal sign of the blessing in the air between them.

"I understand," Sandra was still calm. "You're offended because you're a vet."

"No, you don't understand," he spat. "I'm offended because I'm an *American*. And in America, we don't treat folks like this. And we sure as Hell don't give the men and women who wore the uniform such a disrespectful treatment." Danny fumed. "Whatever the motivation or method used it's still wrong. Some pinhead, lifetime civilian suggested that vets might come home from the war, see the state of our country, and use our combat skills to set things up the way we thought it should be. *Might*. So, based on a maybe, they just decided to start spying on us. It's a violation of the fundamental tenets of intelligence oversight that date back decades before the war. It's a crime, a high crime that some idiot should've gone to jail for. But instead, the whole thing got turned into policy." He stabbed his index finger into his own heart. "I spent my entire life serving a country that hates and fears me. My own Department is spying on me. Hell, I'm helping."

Sandra remained quiet for a moment. Danny used the time to take a soothing breath. After he cycled his lungs, she found her words. "You're right, Daniel," she said at last. "These are Americans, and they are entitled to certain rights. Maybe even more entitled than most are, given what you have all gone through."

Wakefield hemmed his anger back in again. "Yeah, well, that's all for nothing now," he grumbled. It was surprisingly easy to talk to Sandra. It was probably something to do with her background in psychology. They probably taught folks at shrink school how to just make people want to tell you everything. Wakefield knew that his instructors taught him exactly those types of skills back during interrogation classes and tactical human intelligence school. In contrast, he felt no inclination to give his department-issued crisis counselor so much as the time of day. That tool was, in the agent's opinion, a limp-wristed wimp who Danny suspected spent just as much time crying in his own office as did the agents assigned to see him.

Danny locked his emotions back into their steel box. He was not in the mood for dumping, and he certainly was not going to open himself up to a temporary partner. This case was just about to be wrapped. "Just call me Judas," he sighed.

"Why?" Elbee asked with what appeared to be genuine concern. "What have you done?"

*   *   *

"I'm gonna spend another couple of hours at the office working on this," Derek spoke softly into the phone. "You know, just… stuff. Yes, it's for Daniel." A pause as he listened. "Okay. *Shukrahn, mhboob.*" Another pause. "You, too."

Derek hung up the receiver and returned to his desktop monitor. Aliyah had totally understood when he called to let her know he would miss dinner tonight. It was Tuesday, and he caught her before she had started making the dinner that usually accompanied the second day of the work week. Taco Tuesday was just one of the traditions they held at their little apartment in Alexandria. But he had to stay late tonight so that he could work on his new task after any prying eyes within the division might grow curious about his work. The big wall clock read 17:15HRS. The D.C. streets would be flooded with a tide of government workers freshly released from their various jobs. Of course, Nick Brown and Carrie Jenkins left almost two hours ago. Separately, but at the same time and immediately after a rather lengthy and jovial conversation. *If I bust my ass, maybe I can work an early promotion out of this. Another bump or two in pay and at least I'll have rank over the office slut.* Derek was fairly sure that his "betters" were already a few drinks into happy hour at some Beltway bar.

Dr. Wiley read him into the Special Access Program codenamed CANON earlier that morning. *This database is a sensitive intelligence tool,* Wiley had reminded him, *and intelligence, like any other information, is neither good nor bad. It simply* is.

The CANON server was a treasure trove of information on thousands upon thousands of veterans. He held that image in his mind for a second and compared it to something Big D had told him a while back: About 80 percent of folks in the military were not real fighters. They were logistics monkeys. Mechanics, medics, admin folks… They do not fight, *per se*. They do the stuff that lets other guys fight. And that was stuff that needs to be done, so it was good that somebody did it. Historically, those jobs were filled with women. Out of the whole US military, maybe one trooper in ten is an actual door-kicking trigger puller. Danny's sentiment seemed intuitively wrong when Little D first heard it; but then he recalled a quote by Heraclitus, an ancient Greek philosopher:

'Out of every hundred men, ten should not even be there, eighty are just targets, nine are the real fighters - and we are lucky to have them, for they make the battle. Ah, but the one, one is a warrior, *and he will bring the others back.'*

Martin's suspects fell into Heraclitus' nine percent. They were involved in Special Forces in one capacity or another, whether as Rangers, SEALs, former Marine Special Operations… As he stared at his query results Derek could hardly be surprised by the uniformity or the scope of the results.

Having too broad a field of suspects, Martin knew, was the mathematic equivalent of having no suspects at all. Thus, the need for analysts and detectives to use sound logic and the rules of probability in order to narrow the field to a manageable number of suspects. Derek combed in on the individuals whose CANON profiles matched the parameters Wakefield and Elbee put forth for their suspect.

The next step, Derek narrated in his mind as he regarded his matrix of murder, is to identify zeroes. In this context, the zeroes were all individuals who could not realistically have been at any of the murder scenes. If, for example, Sammy the SEAL was a government contractor confirmed to be at work in Virginia Beach during the murders then he was irrelevant to Martin's investigation. For better or worse, CANON included automated daily updates courtesy of the NSA's broad spectrum domestic surveillance programs - codenamed PRISM - of each of the former operators' location by city and state.

Derek queried all of the location data for his suspect pool and deactivated anyone who had no record of travel to Louisiana, California, or Washington state. Many of the candidates faded away. Then he looked for the exact opposite, for anyone who had been in all three states during the attacks.

There were zero results. Nothing.

A lesser man, driven perhaps by ego, might have been frustrated. But Derek Martin loved solving problems - especially challenging ones. One way or another, he resolved he would figure out the solution to the question that plagued the nation. While Wakefield and Elbee chased their tales flying around the map, he would identify the Constitutional Killer from the relative safety and comfort from Washington D.C. And while he might miss Taco Tuesday, he could grab some ice cream on the way home and celebrate his progress inside his own mind over a nice dessert with Aliyah and stories about her day at nursing school.

*   *   *

Danny looked at the beer in his hand. Disappointment settled onto his face, but he was not sure if he was disgusted with the pale drink warming in his glass, or with the man he was trying so hard not to be. Laughter erupted from the other end of the hotel's bar. Danny turned to see a couple in their mid-twenties still giggling over something. She was a bleach blonde with visible roots that almost matched her black cocktail dress. Danny helped himself to a view of her body, care of the dress' cut - off the shoulder and short enough to showcase a tan that was, unfortunately, tinged with the same orange as her martini. Fake laugh. Fake hair. Fake tan. Fruity drink. *Cute-ish, maybe. But totally not my type.* Her companion, whose back was to Danny, was equally disappointing, but not for romantic reasons. He had an unhealthily thin build to him, upon which hung an untucked gingham shirt and a pair of pants so form fitting that Danny was not sure the lad's feet got sufficient blood flow. A mop of black hair topped his head, and when he turned Danny saw that the young hipster sported the type of beatnik glasses that just screamed "pseudo-intellectual." The glass filled with thick green fluid in the lightweight's hand left no doubt.

Danny's mouth went even more sour. "Hey, barkeep," he slid his unappetizing beer away and pointed to the hipster's algae-colored concoction, "what is that?"

A guy who looked to be easily thirty yet adorned the facial piercings and visible tattoos of a much younger wannabe rockstar, gave him a half-stoned smile. "It's a kale smoothy blended with a shot of Midori. My own original recipe." The hotel bar was neither busy nor loud; when the hipster smiled and raised his glass in Danny's direction, he figured the lad must have heard his question.

Danny looked back at the bartender. "I'll have the opposite of that."

The party girl chortled. The hipster's face fell. The bartender snickered. "Whiskey, neat. Coming right up, sir."

"And a White Russian," a familiar female voice ordered from Danny's blind spot. He turned to see Sandra behind him. At some point during the last few hours, she traded the dark pantsuit from work for a pair of khaki capris and a bright blue blouse worn loose over a form-fitting white tank top. "Mind if I join you?"

"Please do," he pointed at the empty stool to his left. "I thought you'd still be busy with paperwork. Reports to file. Profiles to update. That kind of stuff."

"I'm done for now," she laced her fingers and flexed to stretch the tendons in her hands. "How're things with your people?"

"I dunno. I guess we'll have to wait and see."

"Your drinks," the punkish bartender announced with his delivery. "Enjoy." As Danny took a pull off his whiskey, he glanced past Sandra's shoulder to see the younger blonde eyeing him while her metrosexual counterpart regaled her with some tale from Hipsterville.

"Speaking of '*enjoy*'," Danny's attention returned to his partner as she spoke, "have you had a chance to, ah, *sample the local fare*, yet, Daniel?"

"Sorry, Elbee, but I grabbed a bite right after we

got back from work. But hey, don't let that stop you from ordering. If you're hungry, I mean. I'll get some cheese fries or something so you don't feel like you're eating alone."

"Cheese fries?" Sandra looked shocked. "And from a hotel restaurant at that. How very unadventurous. Whatever happened to experiencing the local culture through indigenous cuisine?"

"Seattle sucks," Danny revisited his whiskey. "It's all twenty bucks for a cup of coffee that tastes like it was filtered with a sweaty sock. And hash-brownies in every bakery. And kale smoothies. I swear, Elbee, when we fly outta here, the total testosterone level in this town'll be cut in half. Hell, aside from me, you're probably the biggest man in this hotel tonight."

"That's horrible," she snickered.

"Not as bad as Mr. Pink Jeans over there."

Sandra fought another giggle. "I think they're salmon. And they are in style this season." She lowered her voice and leaned in. "And I think he heard you."

"I don't care. And if you didn't agree with me then you wouldn't've laughed." Suddenly, Danny became serious. "Not that I'm implying that you're a dude or anything. I mean, you're obviously not."

"Are you so certain?"

"Are you setting me up for a sexual harassment complaint?"

"And why would I do that?"

"You'd have the case back to yourself again."

"Tempting, but no." She took another sip from her cocktail. "Much as I hate to admit it, you've actually been an asset to this investigation."

"Thanks."

"Besides, it's early. I'm still just getting to know my new partner."

"I doubt that very much. I'm really not that complicated. I bet Special Agent Psychology already has me profiled and predicted." Danny consulted his glass again. "I'd rather hear about you. You dodged the question at Black Sam's, but you said you went to school in New Jersey. Did you grow up there?"

"Yeah, in a little suburb upstate."

"So, what was that like?"

"I don't know," Sandra flicked her hair a little and rested her elbow on the bar. "I mean, what's anything like? Quiet, I guess. Dad's an insurance agent. Mom helps around his office every now and again, but she's usually busy taking care of things on the home front. When I was a kid, that meant the usual stuff. Running me to piano lessons, track meets, and such."

"Sounds great," Danny consulted his whiskey again. "So, what made you wanna join the Bureau?"

"I just like to help people," Sandra half-dodged as she revisited her glass of coffee and liquor.

"A noble calling if ever there was one," he toasted. Then he continued with just a hint of disbelief in his eyes. "But I think there's more to it than that."

"What do you mean?"

"Don't be coy," Danny sniffed. "You know better than I do that people do stuff for a reason. Action always follows motivation. So, take yourself out of the equation for a second. Why does anyone become a cop?"

"Like I said," Sandra sat up again. She was rigid. Defensive. "To help people."

"Or?"

Sandra bit her lower lip for a moment, then

sighed. "Other than that," she relented, "some people go into law enforcement because they feel like they have something to prove. Some because they love having power over other people. Some see themselves as crusaders fighting for an idealized form of justice. Or they can be motivated by an overworked feeling of victimization."

Danny's eyes probed her, explored her. "And which one of those are you?"

Sandra spun her glass between her fingers for a moment and tried to peer through the bottom. "How drunk do I have to get you to turn off your Interrogator Mode?"

"I'm sorry," he rapped his left fist softly against the bar between them, twice. "Not trying to pry. Just getting to know my partner better. That's all. Didn't mean to touch a nerve."

Sandra caught his hand with hers. "You didn't," she started. "I mean, it's just not..." She released his hand just as quickly as she had seized it just a second ago, then pulled back and huffed. Her shoulders sagged a little under the weight of a memory. "Okay. I guess it goes back to something from college." Danny waited in attentive silence for her to continue. "It was my sophomore year. My roommate Angie and I were pretty close. We were in the same sorority, had some of the same classes, went out together a lot. Anyway, she was dating this guy. Jake. Things seemed totally normal between them." She took a longer, slower pull from her tumbler. "One night, Angie came back from a party at Jake's fraternity - I'd stayed behind to work on a mid-term paper - and she was just a mess. She spent almost an hour in the bathroom, crying in the shower. I figured she and Jake had had a fight or something, but when I went to talk to her about it, she told me that Jake and two of his frat brothers had raped her at the party." Danny bit back a curse so that she could continue her story but did nothing to hide the wince from his face.

"I tried to help her through it. Angie filed a complaint, but by the time I talked her into completing a rape kit with the authorities there was too little evidence to go on. Nobody else at the party saw or heard anything, and everybody in Jake's fraternity vouched for each other. And during the course of the investigation, some folks - even some of our own sorority sisters - said if anything really did happen then Angie should at the least have known what was coming. 'What did you expect to happen at a frat party?' 'People who lie with dogs...' and all that. So in the end it was Angie's word against nobody's. She was a wreck emotionally. Her reputation at the school was tarnished. Eventually, she dropped out. Last I heard, she'd moved back in with her folks."

"That's a tough thing to deal with," Danny consoled, "for her and for you, I'm sure."

"Yeah, well, I guess the wrongness of it all was just too much for me," Sandra fumed. "I mean, somebody should've been able to make it right. You know? And I guess that's what made me decide to try to make things right," she shrugged, "for all of the other Angies out there. The ones whose stories are lost in the shuffle. Victims whose voices don't always get heard. People who just need a hand."

Touched, Danny raised his glass in a belated toast. "Well, like I said: that's a damn noble calling you have there, Special Agent Elbee." They each drained what little was left of their respective drinks. Danny signaled the bartender for another round. "And," he looked Sandra squarely in the eye, "quite the heart, I might add."

"Thank you."

"Seriously," he continued. "My dad was a cop. I met a lot of his 'mates before he retired, and I can tell you've got the chops for the gig."

"I appreciate that, Daniel. I really do." The bartender dropped off a fresh pair of drinks before the duo. "You know, it isn't easy. Being a woman and an agent."

"Really?"

"I get the feeling that some of the guys I work with don't take me seriously. They don't see me as an equal."

"And are you their equal?"

"What do you mean?" she stiffened. "How can you even ask a question like that? Of course I am!"

"Really?" Danny kept his voice soft. Appeasing. "Do you have the time in service they do?"

"Well," she hemmed, "not all of them, no."

"How about your case clearance rate?" he continued. "Do you process the same number of perps that they do?"

Sandra's head bobbled back and forth. "More or less, yes. I'd say my caseload is about average. But," she brightened with newfound pride, "the percentage of convictions obtained from my cases is a lot higher than most other agents."

"There you go," Danny decided not to ask about appeals. Or to suggest that it might be easier to convict a suspect on drug charges than, say, racketeering, extortion, money laundering, murder, or various other types of cases that her colleagues might have investigated. This was one of those moments when partners needed to show solidarity.

Sandra seemed less-than-convinced by his concession. "I've busted my butt on this case," she continued. Danny knew that her argument was with somebody else, but whoever that person was, they were not present to hear her gripes. So, like a good partner, he just nodded in utter agreement as she continued to tell him what he already knew. "I've built profiles. Reviewed evidence. Assembled a team. Chased leads. Coordinated techs at different FBI labs across the country…"

"You've done everything humanly possible," he acknowledged truthfully.

"I've used every resource."

"Yep."

"Tapped different departments."

"Don't I know it."

"So why can't I catch this bastard?"

Danny drove his finger into the top of the bar. Had the furniture been made of lesser stuff, the digit might have penetrated. But it was not. And it did not. It only bounced. Once. Twice. "You know, Elbee," he announced with stoic resolve, "some guys are just uncatchable."

"I don't believe it," she shook her head.

"No, I mean it. Most criminals are idiots. If they were a little bit smarter, they wouldn't need to be crooks, would they? And if they were really, really smart then we'd never catch 'em. I mean, the system's rigged in our favor - and don't get me wrong here, 'cause I believe in the system. But the average mope has a few seconds, maybe a couple of minutes to pull off his caper. Most don't even plan ahead, and those that do don't know how to properly plan. And even if he brings his absolute A-game, the average mope just has to make do as best as his little mope brain can with what little he's got going for him. And what do we get? We get months - years, sometimes - to build a case against him. We have lots of money to spend on tools to tear his work to pieces and folks to analyze it on the microscopic level. Hell, these days we're even on the scene before the mope is half the time, what with video surveillance, online monitoring and all of that jazz. But sometimes despite everything we do, some dirtbag every now and again is bound to just plain get away with it. Maybe he's a garden variety mope charged with selling bootlegged videos on the street. Maybe he's a Mopeasaurus Rex who's running a prostitution ring out of a kindergarten classroom. Whoever it is and whatever he's done, the only way to survive in this game is to know that every once in a while you're going to lose."

Sandra seemed to have forgotten about her drink. "Are you trying to tell me that you think we can't get this guy? That our suspect is untouchable? That we should just throw in the towel?"

"Oh, Hell no," Danny looked genuinely offended at the proposition. "We're gonna nail this guy. He's good, but he ain't that good. You'll see."

CHAPTER 14

THOUGH HE technically worked in a more law enforcement centered role at the Secret Service, Daniel Wakefield conducted himself in many ways as if he still served in the Intelligence Community. To that end, he often thought that if anyone ever bothered to ask on some future day, Daniel Wakefield would have offered up the opinion that the single most useful tool employed by the intelligence community during the first half of the twenty-first century was the video teleconference, or VTC for short.

The Constitutional Killer was all over the map. To follow leads and pursue their quarry, Danny and his partner needed to be mobile. So, Wakefield and Wiley established a protocol: Special Agents Elbee and Wakefield were free to travel anywhere in the continental United States that their investigation might lead them, so long as they dialed up the Crisis Watch at the Department of Homeland Security in Washington every Monday, Wednesday, and Friday at ten o'clock sharp Eastern time from the nearest secure VTC suite. In practice, this required the agents to drop by the nearest FBI field office at least three mornings each week to collaborate and receive updated tasking.

And so it came to be that Wednesday morning the main screen on the Crisis Watch floor switched to a larger-than-life projection of the Special Agents. Right on schedule. The attendees muted their already quiet conversations. Those few who continued with incidental tasks even managed to type in a whisper.

"Good morning D.C.," Wakefield spoke from a blandly decorated conference room in Seattle. "How do you read me?"

"We read you five-by-five," Dr. Wiley replied from the watch floor. It was a throwback military term which meant that both audio and video feeds were clear. "How are we?"

"Good audio, good video, sir," Special Agent Elbee answered.

Dr. Wiley wore his customary tweed jacket, accessorized with an amused expression and his scroll pipe. "I see from your notes that we've got a lead on the explosives used in the last two attacks."

"Yes, sir," Elbee replied. "The ATF confirmed that all three devices used native C4 as the main charge. There were traces from at least three different batches, with ordinance shipments which were delivered to the Army over a five-year period."

"So," Jonas twiddled his pipe, "we're definitely dealing with an American."

"Most likely. Yes, sir," Sandra continued. "Someone with steady access to plastic explosives, which allowed him to skim a little bit every now and again."

"Remember that SEAL a few years back, sir?" Wakefield interjected. "The one who was busted selling AK's and stuff that he brought back off target from missions? Well, he also had more than 500 pounds of C4 and a few cases of grenades that he logged as ordinance spent on missions and during training."

"Does our stuff link back to him?" Brown asked from his boss's shoulder.

"No," Danny shook his head. "Just using that case as an example of how easy it would be for a good guy with a bad idea to take some stuff home and amass his own private stash."

"How do we know our killer isn't just some redneck who bought ordinance from a dirty trooper?" Nick pressed. "The way I remember it, that frogman was black marketing AK-47s online."

"I believe the PC Police prefer when we use the term *'Parallel Market'*," Danny corrected. "And we don't know for sure. But the simplest answer is that someone who routinely played with plastique snuck a little home every now and again for personal use."

"*Lex parsimoniae*," Dr. Wiley nodded. Beside him Nick nodded knowingly, though in truth Wakefield knew that Nick the Dick had no more idea what Jonas had just said than the analysts on the Crisis Watch whose faces pantomimed their confusion. The rule of *lex parsimoniae*, Latin for *'the law of simplicity'* and commonly known as Occam's Razor, was the idea that in any given scenario with multiple potential solutions the simplest solution was most likely to be the correct one. Silently, Danny figured that Little D would explain it to Nick later in terms their supervisor could understand when there weren't any witnesses. Small words. No Latin.

"Alright," Jonas assented, "what do we know about the plastique?"

Elbee did not have to look at her notes to answer. "All of the C4 was delivered to fulfill longstanding contracts originally secured through official requisitions channels. Some from each of several different purchases. None of it was from special order or anything. And it was all delivered to the same place: Fort Bragg, North Carolina."

"JSOC," Nick grumbled. The United States Joint Special Operations Command was comprised of highly trained war fighters who conducted highly classified, highly dangerous missions around the globe. "The idea of some guy out there targeting government officials is scary enough. If a pipe hitter from JSOC has decided to use his skills against American targets then we've got a nightmare on our hands."

Everyone on both sides of the video conversation took a moment to absorb the implications of what could happen if one of America's most elite troopers really did become disgruntled and turn against his former masters. Eventually, Dr. Wiley broke the silence. "You know, there's an old saying: *It is a great tragedy to push a man who truly loves his country to the point where he no longer cares.*' Our leadership treats our soldiers and vets like dog crap. When you think of it from a certain point-of-view, I'm surprised something like this hasn't happened before. While we're sorting this mess out, I challenge each of you to examine your own attitudes toward our troopers and do a better job of appreciating them. Of showing them the respect and courtesy they deserve. 'Cause you never know when you might make the difference in a guy's life and keep him from becoming completely unhinged." A wave of sober nods passed around the watch floor.

"Sir," Danny hid his discomfort as he took his turn. "As per our conversation yesterday, I've got Agent Martin tasked on whipping up some candidates." CANON was a Special Access Program, and not everyone in the Crisis Watch had been granted SAP clearance, so Wakefield and Wiley could not talk about it, even though it was pertinent to the current discussion. Nick made a face that either meant he was curious, or he had just passed gas. Danny chose the former to be the most likely. *Lex parsimoniae.*

"Without getting into any details," Jonas warned, "how's that coming along?"

"He's got a loose pool right now. We're gonna flag anyone who links back to JSOC during the time period in question. Should narrow it down to a workable field. In the meantime, I'm going to copy his data over to an old friend of mine working out at Ft. Meade. See what he can come up with." Though Oscar was not his colleague's real name, Daniel felt uncomfortable saying it over the video feed - secured or not. And as a rule, he tried to avoid any mention to Oscar's employer, the NSA, in conversation.

Closer to the back of the watch floor, Derek made a noncommittal sound. "There are lots of potentials, but I haven't found anybody who just screams, I'm running off the reservation to go kill Congressmen." Nick's expression told Danny that as soon as the VTC was over he was going to have a direct conversation with his junior-most analyst about who, exactly, controlled his tasking. Nick Brown had a firm but unpublished policy to keep Wakefield and Martin from working on the same project at the same time. If they did team up then it was likely nothing else got done in the division.

"Keep on it," Dr. Wiley ordered, "because this is exactly what we need. There's no pattern to this guy's movements and his M.O. keeps changing." Criminals of limited skill or attention tended to stick to the same *modus operandi* - the same methodology - for their crimes. While it tended to give the crooks a sense of confidence in their nefarious actions, it also tended to provide law enforcement with the means to eventually catch the bad guys, and often provided investigators with the tools to link separate incidents to repeat offenders. The Constitutional Killer, unfortunately, had not struck in the same manner twice. This added yet another layer of difficulty to the team tasked with taking him down. "The only consistency so far seems to be his penchant for killing Liberal Democrats. People he disagrees with politically. And that spells bad news for anyone who votes the wrong way or believes something other than what he likes."

"Sir," Elbee chimed in, "it may be more than that. I believe our killer is motivated by a deeply seated sense of betrayal. Look at his videos and the note he left at the first scene. Special Agent Wakefield and I believe that our killer sees himself as a crusader. A deliverer of higher justice that supersedes the letter of the law. He's not just attacking people he disagrees with. He's executing people that he identifies as traitors."

"I dig it," Dr. Wiley declared. "Keep running with it, Elbee. Make something happen. And Wakefield: don't be afraid to use any of your connections with MARSOC to find out if they know anything."

If that doesn't get Nick the Dick's goat then nothing will. "Yes, sir."

"Anything else?" Dr. Wiley invited.

"Sir," Elbee again. "I received a report from Agent Stevenson. She's spent the last few days checking security camera footage at airports to see if we could find our killer flying between cities."

"Who's Stevenson?" he asked the watch floor *en masse.* A woman with short, dark hair raised her hand and stood at her desk from the back row. "Well, did it work?"

"Um, sir?" It looked like Agent Stevenson's nerves threatened to overwhelm her. Speaking to someone of such a senior grade was intimidating enough for most agents. More than one analyst had completely broken down when they were unexpectedly called on the carpet in front of a crowd. Stevenson's hands worked nervously as she wrestled with whether it was better to give her superior the answer he wanted or the truth. As Wakefield watched through the camera, he theorized that if he gave her a set of knitting needles she could have made him a sweater by now with those fidgeting hands. "Uh, not exactly, sir. I mean, nothing yet, sir."

"How do you figure a guy is flying across the United States on commercial carriers with guns and explosives?" Wiley asked.

"Um, well, um, maybe he's…"

"'*I don't know'* is still a viable answer," the old Jesuit directed.

"Yes, sir. I mean, I don't know. Sir." Stevenson flushed with embarrassment.

"And that, dear, is your lesson for the day." Danny had often heard Father describe being an analyst as working in a trade. Jonas felt that their unique profession was, in many ways, a lot like being a plumber. It was composed of equal parts art, science, and talent refined through a constant process of trial and error. And under Jonas Wiley's leadership an analyst's education never ended. The older man addressed his agents as a body again. "Well, there haven't been any reports of anyone else getting killed in the last few days. Do we have any other good news?"

Elbee cleared her throat. "Sir, the Bureau is starting to hear sympathetic whispers around the nation. Posts on social media and blogs that seem to approve of what the Constitutional Killer is doing. He's actually starting to amass a cult-like following among fringe Right-wingers. Tea Party folk and the like."

"The media has already done a good enough job trying to marry our serial killer to the Tea Party," Dr. Wiley shook his head. "Any time something like this happens, reporters try to hang it on hardcore Conservatives. Tea Party. Oath Keepers. Three Percenters. I'm hesitant to drink the Kool-Aide on that one just yet. We'll wait and see who the guy ends up being before we try to blindly fish for him from among the ranks of Libertarian voters."

"You don't think the Constitutional Killer is a Tea Party guy?" Sandra asked. Most of the people who worked around Dr. Wiley lacked the courage to openly question him. It was not because he punished such behavior, because he did not. It was more out of simple deference to his seniority combined with too much selfish pride on their own individual parts to admit that they themselves did not, in fact, know everything. And it seemed most times that Father did.

"I think, Special Agent Elbee, that one should never trust any individual who makes a living in front of a camera. Actors, reporters and the like are all paid to get our attention. They tend to do that by exaggeration, supposition, and outright fabrication. And the good ones do it while wearing the guise of sincerity. Never forget that their first job is to sell us something - themselves, advertising time, an agenda, whatever. Actually getting the story right and presenting the truth comes in a distant second at best, and usually third or fourth place."

"Yes sir," she conceded.

"Alright folks. If there isn't anything else, then get back to rowing."

*　　　*　　　*

It only took the Patriot about five seconds to place the shape charge on Judge Ramierez's car back in Seattle. Unfortunately, the device - not much bigger than a large soup can - had used up the last of his personal cache of C4. One of the other guys from the Unit had shown him how to stretch the Army's seemingly limited supply of plastique back when he was new to the team. The practice was perfectly justified. If they used all of their ordinance up too quickly on the mission, it seemed to follow that they would always need just a little bit more later to finish the job. It became a pretty normal occurrence in the field to take a pinch here or a pat there, maybe one block out of twenty, and keep it in reserve. Just in case. *Better to have and not need,* the old adage went, *then to need and not have.* It was a simple enough matter to sneak the plastic explosives home, especially after routine training missions Stateside. The Patriot did not know one guy from the Unit that did not keep a stash of 'daddy's special Play-Doh' tucked away somewhere in their house. In a jar in the garage, in a freezer bag tucked away under the stairs, or something like that. Unlike nitroglycerine, C4 was perfectly stable all by itself. He had taken to molding his into penetrating shape charges after he saw firsthand how effectively bad actors from Hizballah had fielded them against US forces in the war. And after his family was killed, there was no need for him to worry about who might accidentally stumble upon them while looking for hot dogs.

Fortunately for him, the party favors Rooster gave him could be quite useful toward his future plans - if they worked. And there was only one way to know for sure if they did.

The Patriot looked at the gift that the one-legged bomb tech had unwittingly donated to The Cause: a coil of about fifty feet of homemade detonation cord assembled from sealed intravenous tubing stuffed with some sort of kitchen-recipe powder, plus a second cord identical to it in every way except that it was only about ten feet long; a fistful of blasting caps that were due for disposal and had allegedly already been used on some job site clearing boulders; and three steel pipes - two about as long as his forearm, the third about the size of a candy bar - with wax-sealed caps and waterproof fuses pulled from some higher grade commercial fireworks. All very useful for removing tree stumps - or bigger problems - from a person's life.

He seized a nearby rock - limestone, he guessed - about the size of a small watermelon and wrapped the short length of improvised det cord around it. Then he marched into the northern Arizona desert with his test bundle and the small pipe bomb. He was in the middle of nowhere. There was nobody else around as far as the eye could see. Once he was a safe distance away from the truck he would detonate each device in turn and evaluate the results. Their performance this afternoon would help him plan his next engagement. He hoped he was about to take the next step on the path to liberating his own country.

CHAPTER 15

BY THE CLOSE of business Monday night, it became apparent to Elbee that their continued presence in Seattle contributed nothing more to the investigation. So, she and Wakefield caught the red-eye back to Washington D.C. The flight was uneventful and allowed them each to catch a nap. After the usual ground-side logistics, both enjoyed a good night's sleep - Sandra in her hotel room with a Nissan Leaf parked outside, and Daniel back at his apartment with his guitar on the couch next to him and half a bottle of Jameson on the coffee table.

After a morning of chasing their own tails, Danny and Sandra grabbed lunch on the road to Quantico. The headquarters for the United States Federal Bureau of Investigation was only about an hour drive away with agreeable traffic. Elbee drove her fuel-efficient rental car and Wakefield filled the transit time with idle, meaningless chatter mixed with the occasional barb about his partner's misfortune in her quest to score a more sporty rental vehicle. Once they met up with Elbee's new support team at a round table meeting in the FBI's SCIF conference room though, Daniel was all business.

Martin's continued analysis of the CANON data back at DHS HQ had generated too many leads for just one or two people to sort through. The job itself was simple enough and given enough time it was perfectly doable. But the longer they spent chasing the killer, the more opportunities he had to pile up more victims. Danny knew that he and his partner were up against the proverbial clock. It was only a matter of time before their killer struck again. They needed a force multiplier to get ahead in this game. Backed by the authority that came from a written order by Dr. Wiley, Danny dropped this new task order on his sister agency's specially picked crew like it was a bomb.

"What's PRIMER?" one of the FBI junior analysts asked.

Senior Special Agent Justus McConnell, Elbee's chief and Wiley's mirror on this side of the Beltway, perked up and fielded the question for Wakefield. "It's a database maintained by the FBI. In theory it stores the ballistic signature of every gun sold in the country for the last fifty years or so."

"That sounds handy. How come I've never heard of it before?" the analyst, Agent Burns, continued. Wakefield could tell by the surprised looks and hushed gasps from around the conference table that most of the federal agents were shocked by the implications of PRIMER's existence. He had expected as much. He had only learned about it when Father read him into the program the day he and Elbee flew in to D.C. from New Orleans. All these days later the mere thought of PRIMER's existence threatened to make bile boil into Danny's mouth. "And if it's an FBI SAP program, why's the Secret Service reading us in?"

"First off, it's a DHS thing. Not exclusively FBI. Secondly, it's all very need-to-know," Wakefield explained. Within the military and other government entities, a clearance did not give the holder open access to everything classified… not even everything at that particular holder's level of classification. Even though most FBI analysts held Top Secret clearances - better by far than the Secret clearances issued to most Agents and Special Agents - information was still separated and doled out piecemeal to minimize the risk of a catastrophic breach of security. "The PRIMER program is compartmentalized, and even with an SCI clearance, you still need to demonstrate a serious justification to use it. Or even be told about its existence."

"A tool like that could really help solve a lot of cases," Burns persisted. "I'd say we've got a need."

SSA McConnel shook his head. "Imagine what would happen Burns, if somebody from the Bureau eventually leaked its existence. It'd be like CARNIVORE all over again."

The FBI's CARNIVORE program was a famous example of both violating citizen's privacy and simultaneously a breach of internal security. The covert tool was first defeated, then made publicly known, by the very hackers it was originally conceived to monitor. It even appeared as a drive-by talking point in a couple of Hollywood blockbusters. This publicity, in turn, brought scrutiny from American citizens and some members of Congress who raised concerns the program might violate the people's right to privacy. CARNIVORE was reportedly suspended by then-President Clinton's second inauguration. But in reality the program was repaired and activated by the turn of the millennium.

Wakefield interjected, "Also, because it's incomplete. PRIMER was started decades ago, but never really got the traction its authors hoped it would." He swept the room with his eyes. "How many of you own a gun? Not your service weapon, but a privately purchased firearm." McConnell, and few of the FBI analysts raised a hand to shoulder height in hesitant admission. "Right. Remember when you bought it, there was a single spent shell casing in a little envelope somewhere in the case?" Most of the same heads nodded.

Burns, again. "I thought that was to show the buyer that gun had been function checked. You know, a live fire demo to make sure it worked."

"That's what most consumers assume," Wakefield explained. "That's even what most licensed dealers think it's for. But what the manufacturers don't tell anyone is that they are required by the ATF to discreetly collect that bullet and brass from that test. They submit the projectile and images of the spent casing back to the ATF along with the gun's serial number. From there, the bullet's ballistic signature is recorded and catalogued, as are the case's markings. The theory was that we'd be able to match any bullet or any spent casing recovered from a crime scene back to the gun that shot it, and therefore the owner."

"Hold on," another agent interrupted. "Everyone knows that we can link the scratches on a bullet to a gun's rifling - but the casing?"

"The distance from the precise center that the firing pin strikes a round is the same every time," Elbee explained. "So are the scratches and other tool markings on the inside of the chamber. Just like the rifling that gives a projectile its distinct ballistic fingerprint, these marks are also variable from one gun to the next. You and Wakefield here might both have the same model of Sig Sauer and shoot ammo from the same manufacturer, but the dimple on the primer made by the firing pin will be measurably different on your casings than his. As will the chamber marks. Measurable that is, with the nanometer resolution of instrumentation, which can not only measure the radian distance on the primer's dimple, but on a good sample we can sometimes also pick up the negative impression made by the firing pin itself."

"We're dealing with variances measured at the microscopic range," Danny cautioned. "And since casings can tumble when they fall, there's no way to know which way the brass was oriented in the chamber. So the direction in which that pin has drifted from center is impossible to determine on scene. Likewise, it's hard to get a brass sample that isn't scratched in some way if it hits hard ground like concrete or gravel. All of that introduces a bunch of variables that prevent this data from ever being submissible in court - which in turn, makes PRIMER a purely investigative tool for narrowing possibilities. It cannot provide a positive ID on a suspect."

"It still sounds to me like this PRIMER database

is a tool that could help us solve a lot of crimes," Burns persisted.

"The program isn't without its flaws," McConnell explained further. "First, for obvious reasons it only covers guns sold after it was implemented. And even then, it assumes the gun's owner never sells it again. Once that chain of custody is broken, it becomes almost impossible to trace the gun."

"Wouldn't mandatory gun registration fix that?" Burns asked. Wakefield mentally noted that Burns had not previously self-identified as a private gun owner. *Mandatory gun registration?* Danny thought. *Why not just wear a fluorescent jacket with 'Vote Democrat' stitched on the back?*

"Not at all," Elbee countered. "People could still lie and say they don't have any guns. Deny private purchases or claim they sold or gave away their own guns."

"Or," Danny resumed, "you could just swap the barrel out and change the ballistic signature of your gun. Even if there was a law requiring every barrel to be checked, a decent machinist could turn out fresh pipes under the radar. What're we gonna do - register every lathe in America? Plus, there is still the very real possibility that two different guns shooting the same caliber can measure in with depressions of the same radial distance, depth, and diameter, just made at different angles - a difference that gets lost by the fact that the spent casing tumbles when it falls. We wouldn't be able to distinguish between the two. It's a statistical long shot, but it's still a potentially misleading false positive. Finally, as McConnell alluded to a minute ago, collecting this data basically constitutes a warrantless search. We can't just assume a gun owner is probably going to shoot someone else just because he or she bought a gun any more than we can automatically assume that everyone who buys a car is going to be a drunk driver. A lot of Americans out there would see this a violation of their Constitutional Rights. Of preemptively treating them as a suspect of a crime that may or may not ever happen without demonstrable probable cause."

"So, if PRIMER doesn't work," Burns pressed, "why are we checking it?"

"Special Agent Wakefield and I have a pending appointment," Sandra leaned forward in her seat, "but after we leave, the SSO is also going to brief you into a program called CANON. Due to the sensitive nature of this information, it is absolutely imperative that you regard it as strictly informational and non-incriminating all by itself. But we need you to take the information from each shell casing we have recovered from this case - as well as any others that might turn up in the unfortunate event that our killer strikes again - and cross reference them with data from PRIMER and CANON. It's a long shot and requires a lot of manpower, but you never know where a break might come from on a case like this."

"How big of a field are we trying to narrow?" Burns eyed her suspiciously.

"Best guess? There are about three hundred million guns in the US," Danny offered deadpan. "Give or take. You'll be cross-referencing possible matches whose owners pop as significantly interesting in CANON. You'll be turning a big haystack into a smaller haystack."

"We're exhausting every resource or potential lead on this one," Elbee added. "We might get a hit that lines up with someone we were already looking at for other reasons. It's not conclusive, but the PRIMER data can help shape our decisions. Focus our attention somewhere that might pan out. So, if anyone else has any other ideas, I'd love to hear them. No? Great." Finished, she gestured to McConnell, handing the floor back to the FBI's in-house boss and signaled Danny that they were finished.

On his way out of the briefing room, Wakefield theorized that Burns and a few other holdouts would likely waste a good half-hour of the day bellyaching about the task at hand, PRIMER, and the cryptic maze that compartmentalized all Special Access Programs before starting to do any actual work. As they cleared the door, Special Agent Elbee stepped nearer to her partner's side so that she could speak quietly while they walked.

"That's a lot of work to hand out to a bunch of conscripts," Elbee commented.

"I don't expect them to get it all done tonight," Wakefield conceded, "but they can at least start data mining. Besides, under the circumstances, I don't think any of us will be kicking off in the middle of the day until this case is settled."

Sandra nodded. Despite the fact that they were supposed to be pursuing a high-profile serial murderer, most of the people who had been in that room just two minutes ago had likely planned to start their weekend within the next hour. Some were probably peeved by the fact that they had to stick around the office for a briefing that started after lunch.

"Daniel," she started, "I'm sorry I didn't tell you about PRIMER myself. I only learned about it the week we met. I wasn't trying to withhold information from my partner. Just following my orders. You know how it works."

Wakefield considered her apology. She seemed sincere enough. "Let me ask you something, Elbee. Would you have told a stranger on the street?"

"Of course not," she protested.

"Then you shouldn't've told me, either."

"But you told me about CANON," she countered.

"Not initially," he reminded her. "Only when it became pertinent to the investigation. Look, I know I busted your hump about holding out on me with the hooker in the beginning, but we've gotta accept that just because we're partners on this case doesn't mean we're not each gonna know something else in our career or lives that the other doesn't hear about. Compartmentalization is there because it works," he declared. "And I gotta tell you, this PRIMER business has tasted like a turd sandwich since the moment Father told me about it."

"You don't think it's a potentially valuable tool?"

Danny shook his head. "I think it comes at too high a price. And I'm not just talking about the money involved with separate servers, administrivia and all of that nonsense Elbee. I'm talking about how our government has just up and decided to treat every American citizen with suspicion. Little things like due process, probable cause, innocent until proven guilty... It just seems like those things have disappeared. You know? They've gone the way of the dodo. Every now and again we hear about another government program designed solely to monitor non-criminal activity by law abiding citizens. Broad spectrum domestic collection by the NSA. PRIMER. CANON. And who knows what other dirty little deeds are being done to us by our own people?" he seethed. His jaw was clenched. His teeth ground against each other hard enough that they threatened to shatter. His fists balled with barely contained fury. The feeling of betrayal burned like acid through his arms. It ran like a river of fire down his legs and twisted his toes into knots.

For a moment neither of them said anything. But as they walked in silence, Danny's heartbeat slowly returned to its normal rhythm. The ringing in his ears subsided a bit. Fury still clouded the corners of his vision when Sandra touched one of his steely arms and leaned in closer. "Thank you for your trust, Daniel," she said in a near-whisper. "I hope I can live up to it."

"Speaking of trust," Wakefield fought to keep the growl out of his voice, "we've got one more stop to make before we call it a day." He looked at her more seriously than she had ever seen him. "And Elbee, it should go without saying, but you can never tell anyone about where we're about to go."

CHAPTER 16

THE SUMMER SUN had just begun to set on a rolling field filled with row after row of vines strewn across taught wires. Attendants quickly moved amongst the trellised plants, checking the leafy clusters for problems. Danny slowed his Jeep to a crawl to minimize the cloud of dust he kicked up as he drove.

"This doesn't look like Ft. Meade." Sandra cast him a dubious look. "I thought you said we were visiting your NSA pal."

"Oscar doesn't like when you talk about his employer," Danny advised. "But, yes, we are. He's got a little place behind the distillery." With a nod of his head, he indicated the building on the far end of the dirt road.

"And why couldn't we just meet him at -" Sandra caught herself, "at his office?"

"Because he's home now."

"And you know this because…?"

"Checked my phone when we got back to the Jeep. I had a fresh text. It came in while we were inside at Quantico." Danny guided them through a curve in the dirt road, which was actually a two-mile-long private driveway and brought the Jeep to a smooth stop between a colonial-style farmhouse and an oversized barn that looked like it had been converted to a retail space. He shut the engine off and gestured to the compound around them with grandiose élan. "Welcome to northern Maryland's finest winery."

They walked from the truck through the cluster of buildings that comprised the vintner's estate. Danny watched as Sandra's eyes swept the old, white farmhouse and the rustic sales center on opposite sides of the parking apron - which was empty, but for Danny's Jeep. A woman in her late forties peeked at them through a window in the barn, nodded at him in recognition and waived as they passed.

"This place is beautiful," Sandra remarked. "I didn't know they made wine out here in the Mid-Atlantic area."

"Puts some of the swill I've had from California and France to shame. You really should try it. We'll grab a couple of bottles on the way out." A few score paces carried them behind another building which Danny knew to contain the massive vats in which the grapes fermented in their juices until they transformed into their prized nectar. "This place wins awards all of the time. I'm no wine snob, but they make some tasty stuff here."

"Does your buddy have something against living in the city like a normal person?"

"That might be an understatement." Danny led her around the big barn to a plain utility building on its blind side. "Oscar's big on privacy." He continued to guide them to the small building. It was little more than a gray steel shed and could not have measured more than a dozen feet on each side. Sandra stopped short.

"Please don't tell me your friend lives in a garden shed," she glared at him. "I've seen this movie. This is the part where the blonde girl gets kidnapped."

"Relax," Danny smiled. "Just follow me."

"Alright," she wore her incredulous face again for the first time in days, "but if I see any rope or duct tape, I'm shooting the guy holding it."

"Huh. I figured you as the non-violent type," he admitted.

"I am against violence, but I'm re-evaluating that policy as we speak."

Danny walked up to the door and pressed a buzzer. A moment later, the door clicked with the telltale sound of a cycling electronic lock. He held the door open for Sandra, then let it swing shut on its own after they entered. Given the warm, wet summer air outside, the inside of the shed was remarkably cool. Danny knew that it was fed conditioned air from a vent in the floor. "Shoes, please," Danny matched his own actions to his words as he kicked his own shoes off and tucked them aside. "Oscar can be a bit of a neat freak. Keep your gun if you like, but you might wanna hang your sport coat on the wall." Danny relieved himself of his own blue suit jacket, but left his department-issued Sig in its brown leather shoulder holster. Sandra looked like she was still trying to figure out the meticulously clean shed, which was completely empty on the inside except for several pairs of shoes tucked against one wall and a number of coat hooks anchored a little lower than chest height. "Excuse me," Danny said as he pointed to the floor under her feet, "but I need to get the door."

*   *   *

The shed's trapdoor serviced a stairwell that was steep enough to qualify as a ladder. Luckily, it came equipped with handrails. "Mind your shins," Danny warned as he descended the tight tunnel backwards, "it took me a few visits to learn to not kick the stairs on my way down." The stairwell ended on a solid concrete pad that led into a tunnel-like room well below ground.

"Evening, Chumly," a squat man greeted them with a smile at the base of the ladder. He waived at Danny casually, then presented a set of stubby fingers to Sandra. "Special Agent Elbee, I presume?"

"Nice to meet you," Sandra smiled politely as she shook the little man's hand. Danny could tell that she fought hard to contain her surprise at their host's stature. At 4'9" tall, Oscar just barely qualified as an honest to goodness, real life dwarf. There was simply not enough distance between his barrel chest and stumpy legs for his waistline to do anything at all, but he was far from fat. At least, he would have been far from fat if his frame was somehow stretched to that of someone more keeping with the baseline norm of human proportion. As it was, he looked almost like a caricature of a man or a comedic character that had just walked off the movie screen.

"A pleasure," Oscar grinned. He could obviously

tell that Sandra was struggling on whether to say anything. Or what exactly could be said without raising an offense. "Please," he beckoned them deeper into his hovel, "have a seat. Make yourselves comfortable. Can I get you something to drink?"

"Surprise me," Danny answered as he availed himself of the nearby couch, which was set along the edge of the long, tubular shaped room. Like his counterparts in high fantasy, Oscar's home was a series of underground tunnels - though in his case it was a collection of carefully buried storm shelters and such rather than a hole in a mountain or under a tree.

"And you, miss Agent ma'am? A glass of the local berry, perhaps?"

"That would be lovely. And please, call me Sandra." She perched herself atop a full-sized bar stool with a fully cushioned leather seat back - obviously designed for Oscar's more long-legged guests.

"As you wish," their host waddled over to a wine rack set into another wall. He produced a bottle from the rack - built to accommodate his unique stature - and held it up for their approval. "Here we go," he announced in triumph. "Dandelion wine. Last year's vintage. Sprightly without being cloy. Perfect for a light summer's eve."

Sandra cupped her hand over her mouth to catch her snicker at Oscar's use of the word '*sprite*.'

"You're in a good mood tonight," Danny challenged. Then he turned sideways to his partner. "We don't just call him Oscar because he's Muppet-sized. He's usually the angriest man you'll ever meet."

Sandra looked over at their smiling host in obvious doubt.

"Hey, Wakefield," Oscar's eyes flared, but his smile remained fixed, "bite me."

Sandra laughed out loud. "So, what's your real name?"

"Don't you say it!" the bronze-haired man warned Danny.

When he saw Sandra's quizzical expression, Danny knowingly smiled. "If you say his name three times, he disappears."

"Everybody's got jokes," Oscar rolled his eyes. "Keep it up Wakefield. And don't mind the pubes you find floating in your glass in a minute. Nothing you haven't tasted before." He smiled at his fairer guest. "Not that you have anything to worry about, Sandra. Your wine will be clean. No, the truth is much more cruel than some crappy fairy tale. My parents thought it would be funny to give their son a girl's name. People who do that ought to be kicked repeatedly in their crotch in the public square. If I can ever muster the stomach to visit the circle of hell that I call my childhood home again, I think I'll just start junk-punching relatives. Which leads me to this," he smiled as he handed her a freshly poured glass, "I have a special gift for you."

"You really should work on your segues Oscar." Danny offered from the couch.

"A gift? Really?" Sandra acted like she did not hear her partner. "And what would that be?"

"A suspect." He gave Danny his know-it-all grin. "Yep. Doin' your job for you chumly. Again. Now, ain't that a shot to the ball sack?"

Danny checked his wine glass carefully after Oscar handed it to him. "Really?"

"Yep." The stout spook reached into a leather

satchel on the kitchen counter and produced a large, manilla envelope sealed with industrial strength packing tape, which he handed to Sandra. "I did some things I can't tell you about to come up with this but suffice it to say that you are lucky to have a man of my singular brilliance throwing you a bone from time to time."

"Thank you," Sandra replied as she ripped open the envelope. "That sounds like a lot of work." Inside the envelope was a darkened brown, heavy duty file folder.

"It's a lot more work when you don't have the kind of tools I have at my disposal," Oscar beamed. "Not to mention my unparalleled talent. Honestly, I don't know how the world got along without me. I'm hungry. You want a bite?"

"You bet," Danny answered. "Need a hand?"

"Nonsense," Oscar waived for him to sit down, "I'm just gonna carve up some cheese. Then I'm going to rub my Johnson all over yours while your partner and I eat the clean stuff."

"If the pants are coming down," Danny shot back, "can I get in on the action? I've been wanting a picture of you holding my junk. Those little hands of yours would make me look like the white Wilt Chamberlin." Danny turned back to his partner. "Not that I'm - well, I mean. Never mind." Sandra sat with wide eyes and a jaw hung in utter disbelief. She appeared to be so shocked by the jocular exchange that she had completely forgotten the folder in her hands. "Seriously, though," he asked Oscar, "that does remind me of something. Do you still have some of that deer sausage?" Then he turned back to his partner. "Oscar and I bagged a couple of bucks this last fall. He makes this amazing deer sausage…"

"I don't mean to sound ungrateful," Sandra resumed in a more-than-slightly irritated voice, "but why did we have to drive out into the middle of Maryland to get this information? Couldn't we have picked this up earlier this afternoon at your -" Danny waived at her, a reminder of his warning from earlier. "I mean, you know."

"Yeah, I know," Oscar grumbled. "Look, first off, not to sound like a total douche-cicle, but you don't have sufficient clearance to visit me at work. Hell, the president doesn't have sufficient clearance to come into my office without an escort. Prometheus comes down from Olympus. You understand what I'm saying here? Which means I've gotta go to the Situation Room every time there's a…" the miniature misogynist stopped short. "Nevermind. So anyway, this way's easier. Besides," he looked up at the ceiling, but his expression indicated his focus was miles above it, "I'd prefer it if none of my people ever found out that I actually gave you this. You never know who knows. You know? And if you guys monkey this up then God only knows who'd be coming around to pour a bucket of Hateraide all over my head."

"More like spilling it off the counter," Danny fired back. "Which is about the same height for you." He turned to Elbee. "Oscar spends his days staring at monitors full of highly sensitive information until he goes screen-blind and crosseyed, but it's not just the need to unplug that drives him to live underground in a storm shelter."

"Hey!" Oscar aimed an angry index finger at his friend as if it was a snub-nosed revolver. "It ain't paranoia if people really are spying on you!"

"Are people really spying on you?" Sandra inquired in a clinical tone. Danny could tell she was feeling Oscar out. Trying to determine whether he was sane enough that she could trust the information he provided them.

"Of course they are! The government has people spying on everyone! And ours isn't the only government out there. You know who spent the most money spying on America last year? Friggin' Canada! I mean, if you can't trust the Canadians then who can you trust, eh? They're pretty much the most benign and harmless nation in the friggin' industrial world. And don't even get me started on corporate espionage, hackers, and stoner computer science majors. Everyone's got spies these days. If they didn't, I wouldn't have a job! What do you think I do for a living?"

"Dig jewels out of the depths of Moria?" Danny guessed.

Oscar swapped his index finger for another digit, which he offered to Danny in its place. Then he turned back to his cheese block and wire knife. "Besides, this place is, like, fifteen hundred square feet of pure awesome. It sure beats the Hell outta his little generic apartment in town. I get three times the square footage per dollar out here. Plus, a peace and quiet that you can't get in the city. And a lease that includes a generous supply of the local berry. Oh, and if the weekend's hooker is ugly, I just feign ignorance and let her think the people from the main house ordered her."

"What?"

"There's a hidden camera trained on the door," Danny explained. "He checks the video feed before he pops the lock."

"Not what I meant, Daniel."

Oscar brought a plate loaded with sliced cheese, crackers, and a few slices from a length of sausage into the room's open seating area. "Look, there's nothing wrong with wanting some privacy," he offered, "and I admit that Wakefield might not've been half wrong with the crack about me being a little misanthropic."

"Stalin was a little misanthropic," Danny ventured. "You can be downright mean."

"But even the little man has needs," Oscar ignored his friend as he continued. "You know what I mean? It's like the man said: just because I choose to avoid the emotional baggage doesn't mean that I choose to avoid the act. And my way holds no guilt. No strings. But I sure as hell ain't scoring at a bar, club, or whatever cattle den you normals use as a meeting place these days. Not when all of you gals would rather go home with some muscly meathead who uses the top of my head as a drink stand. Like Chuckles over there." Danny gave a deadpan nod, as if to confess his previous sins. "I live by five simple rules," Oscar ticked a count on his stubby little fingers as he continued. "Never trust." Finger. "Especially a woman." Finger. "Especially if she's interested." Finger. "Especially in me."

Sandra looked at his diminutive thumb, still tucked against his palm. "And rule number five?"

The jaded man flashed a smile. "Always keep something in reserve. Leverage. Against my enemies, my friends, my boss - everyone. It's all just part of having an escape route. A prepackaged alibi. A backup plan to your backup plan. Some form of foolproof exit strategy. An out of some kind that nobody would ever suspect." Sandra seemed to consider Oscar's life philosophy for a moment, then opened the file folder he had given her. "Lucky for you it's the end of the month," Oscar made no attempt to hide the pride from his voice. "Your boy switches phones every few weeks, but I caught his new handset that he just activated the other day. That should give us a window to act. And when I say, 'us' I mean you clowns that actually do field work." The bitter analyst rolled his eyes in disgust. "Freaking amateurs. Anyway, I took the liberty of putting together a brief history, biography, and pattern-of-life analysis on him. It's all in there. I would've included a copy of his service and medical records, but I don't wanna waste my time doing Derek's work for him."

"Did you talk to Little D?" Danny asked.

"Why would I do that?" Oscar sounded offended by the question. "I mean, don't get me wrong, Martin seems like a good guy and all - at least, for a normie - but I'm pretty sure that desert flower of his has ties to Hizballah. No way am I lettin' myself get pinged on those guys' radar."

Danny started to defend Derek and Aliyah, but Sandra was a flurry of activity as she flipped through pages within the folder. She pulled her phone and waived him down all at the same time. "I'll call the field office and have them put some assets on this guy right away." She looked up at her partner with her thumb poised over her phone. "We'd better book a flight out to El Paso."

"Your phone won't work down here," Oscar interrupted, "and you can catch the red-eye outta Dulles. But I'll understand if you two need to get going. Since you only got a sip of the wine, please feel free to take the bottle. I have plenty."

CHAPTER 17

"I HAD OSCAR forward his findings to the Intelligence Fusion Center in Austin," Danny stuffed his phone back into his pocket. The two agents flashed their badges as they rushed past the security checkpoint at the Dulles concourse. Danny always had a travel bag packed. Just in case. Based on how short Sandra's trip into and out of her hotel had been when they stopped to grab her luggage, it seemed to him as though his partner was similarly mobile. Danny was impressed.

"How is it that you and Oscar can phone each other, but my cell doesn't work in his - what was that, a top secret missile silo or something?"

"I wouldn't put it past him," Danny chuckled. "He spliced a land line off the main house. When he's out and about, though, he uses a cellphone."

"Just like everyone else?" Sandra seemed

surprised. "Isn't he afraid Big Brother might be listening?"

"He says he's maintaining appearances so that they don't know that he knows."

Sandra checked her watch and picked up her already quick pace. "Door closes in six minutes."

Danny followed suit but his voice still held casual disdain. "Relax, Elbee. They're not gonna leave until we're onboard. That's the beauty of being a federal agent with an official ticket. The plane flies for us tonight."

"You wanna bet they won't leave without us?" she challenged.

Small rubber wheels rumbled behind the agents as they scurried down the concourse's length. They arrived one minute after the gate was scheduled to close. A ticket agent and flight attendant stood by the open portal with impatient expressions on their faces.

Sandra's phone buzzed while they crossed the gantry to the plane. "Austin IFC confirms they're coordinating assets," she scrolled along the email on her screen. Contrary to public knowledge, airline regulations regarding the use of cellular phones on airplanes were somewhat flexible for the right people. And a pair of federal agents with emergency tickets on a mostly empty plane definitely qualified as the right people. Sandra made her way down the aisle, scanning the seat row markings.

"I'm sure anywhere's fine," Daniel offered as he stuffed his rolling case into a nearby overhead bin. "I bet they'd like to push off as soon as possible."

"Here we are," Sandra spied a set of seats. "G-3 and 4."

Danny flopped down into an aisle seat a few rows

ahead of her. "Whatever. The front third of the cabin is totally empty."

"I'm sorry, sir," a flight attendant appeared right next to him, "but we'll have to ask you to find your ticketed seat, please."

He looked up at a blonde a few years older than himself. "Seriously?" The woman nodded humorlessly. A part of himself made Daniel want to find out what a good look at his badge would do to the officious woman's demeanor, but he shifted to the seat on his boarding pass anyway. *Pick your fights*, he reminded himself.

Sandra flipped through the file folder containing Oscar's synopsis. "So, tell me how your buddy was able to come up with this guy."

"Well, we can't talk about the mechanics of it here," Danny explained as the plane taxied out to the flight line. Then he lowered his voice to a discreet volume. "As a matter of fact, it's probably best if you put that away. We don't want any of the other passengers to see something they're not supposed to see." At his prompt, Sandra closed the folder and tucked it back into her carry on. "As a matter of fact," he continued, "you might want to not ask about the technical side of some of that stuff. Ever. Suffice it to say that he's given us what we need to get what we need to finally bag our guy."

Sandra leaned forward as if she could get the plane to taxi faster through sheer willpower. "I just hope we get there before he makes his next move."

Danny settled into his seat for the flight. "Me too Elbee. Me too."

CHAPTER 18

THE FULL MOON washed the Texas desert in a blue-silver glow. Just a few miles outside of El Paso, the city lights were a distant memory. The world was dim enough that a person could easily see by the night's natural light. Full lunar illumination, as it was called. Purple-black cacti and sage brushes were clearly visible against the paler, dusty ground. The sky was a dark curtain gilded with stars like jewels, treasures normally unseen by residents trapped in their suburban prisons.

Nighttime freed all manner of creatures to scurry and scamper through the open countryside. Without the sun blazing overhead, the desert was robbed of its punishing heat. The night air was still dry, but cool. A gentle breeze tickled some of the lighter bushes.

The Patriot took another sip from a small rubber hose that led to a bladder strapped to his back that was filled with water. Memories of snowfall in Iraq and the ground frozen solid played in the back of his mind. He remained completely still but for his lips working on the straw's flexible, self-sealing bit. The human eye's ability to see at night, he was trained, was based on movement. As long as he stayed fairly still while he was prone, any passersby would not likely be able to distinguish him from the rest of the terrain. He was just another rock in another shadow cast by the bright full moon.

In the distance a silhouette moved. The Patriot smoothly adjusted his head so that his cheek found a familiar spot on his rifle's stock. His scope's big 50mm objective lens let in plenty of light as it magnified the image in front of him. A shroud on the device's front side - the objective lens - kept light from gleaming off the scope. His support hand cradled the rifle's stock, held it tightly against his shoulder. He used this left hand to steer his rifle from its back end, panning slowly until he saw the suspicious shape picking its way across the borderland. His dominant arm was relaxed, his firing hand remained limp. Nothing moved on that side of his body but his trigger finger. Just like he was trained.

The shadow out in front of him turned out to be more than a dozen figures picking their way through the open country. The bottoms of the figures opened and closed like scissors. *The inverted V is a shape not found in nature*, his teachers taught him in survival school. *But it's a dead giveaway of where your legs are. And bodies ride on top of legs.* The figures walked in a cluster. They made their way through the desert night along a track that was an almost perfectly straight line. It was likely that at least some of them were familiar with this patch of earth. They moved like they knew exactly where they were and exactly how to get to their intended destination.

With his drinking tube still in his mouth, the Patriot used the marks on his crosshairs to measure the shadows' height. He mentally plugged this data into a series of familiar calculations. Practiced ratios produced numbered solutions in head. He estimated the shadows were just a touch under 350 yards out from his position. They walked in a generally northward direction. Every step carried them a few feet closer to him. A few more feet away from the Mexican border - miles behind them on this fair summer night. At this range the negligible breeze would have no real effect on the 168-grain boat tailed hollow point bullets jacked into his AR-10.

As he watched the dark figures grow larger in his scope, the Patriot noted that the same two shadows maintained flanking positions around the main herd. Every once in a while, one of them would turn enough to one side or another to reveal a short weapon. Was it a club? A shotgun? He could not tell for sure, but he bet it was a shotgun. That would make sense. A club was of little use against desert wildlife and far less intimidating to the people being herded through the outback. He thought he could make out the brim of a cowboy hat atop the lead shadow as his head glanced to and fro, up and down.

Somewhere in the night a coyote yelped. Its "yip-yip-yip" meant that it had probably found its dinner - maybe a desert hare or some such critter. The Patriot's senses grew more acute. He was no stranger to the act of staring down his scope at a man-shaped target in the dead of night. It was a little odd however, for him to do so without the buzz of radio chatter in his ear. But now he did not need some command element telling him what to do.

The Patriot knew what the right thing to do was. Sneaking across the border under cover of darkness was not the right thing to do. Boatloads of people came into the United States legally every year. Illegal immigrants like these *vatos* broke the law from the get-go just by coming into the country this way. It was not a good way to start a relationship between a prospective citizen and their intended destination. A lot of the trespassers were rapists, murderers, drug dealers and cartel enforcers who saw America as an open field in which they could play their hurtful games. None of those crimes were the right thing to do - not back in Mexico, and certainly not here in America. Most of the rest of the illegals were like ants at a picnic. The low wages they got north of the Rio Grande were far better than the pittance they were paid down south. And a growing number of them greedily gobbled up the spoils of Social Security, unemployment, and medical benefits that were originally intended for the hard-working Americans who actually paid into the system. Mooching off of a system built to protect real Americans was not the right thing to do.

The right thing to do would be to build a wall. Two walls, really. A pair of matched, thirty-foot-tall walls topped with broken glass. One on the north side of the Rio Grande and the other about twenty or thirty yards north of that running parallel to the first. With row after row of concertina wire around the base. And then a mine field that extended for at least 100 feet north of the second wall. Then, like the comedian said, station the National Guard and any red-blooded American who wanted to volunteer within about a half-mile north of that perimeter with a rifle and a spotlight pointed south and orders to shoot on sight anyone or anything coming north. The right thing to do would be for America's leaders and her citizens to stop the tide of illegals and terrorists entering their country from unsecured borders. To stop treating the issue of illegal immigration as a source for votes and start treating it like the national security threat it really was. That would be the right thing to do.

The lead shadow - the one with the cowboy hat - closed to three hundred yards. That was the distance at which the Patriot had confirmed the zero on his AR-10 earlier in the day. He flicked the safety on his .308 over to FIRE, exhaled slowly, and pressed the trigger with a smooth, even motion. Although suppressed, the cold bore shot thundered into the night. One of the shadows crumpled. Most of the rest fluttered in confusion. Panic. Cowboy and the flankers crouched, motionless but for their heads, which scanned the horizon for the shot's point of origin. The Patriot centered his crosshairs just below the hat's wide brim. Exhale. *Thoom!* Down went the hat. *Thoom!* Down went a shadow. *Thoom!* Flanker down. He pressed the trigger with each natural pause in his respiration. Thumb! Tango down. Breath. *Thoom!* Tango down. He did not worry about repositioning to conceal his location. The night did that for him. *Thoom!* Tango down. Suddenly, the fish seemed to figure out their barrel was all in their own imagination. A half dozen or so shadows scattered into the night, bolted in different directions by ones and twos. He skipped the one running due north - straight toward him - for a second and traversed right. He led the runner a step. *Thoom!* Tango down. Left. Lead. Breath. *Thoom!* Tango down. Further left. Pushed the crosshairs a little more. Breath. *Thoom!* Tango down.

The shadow he had skipped a moment ago had closed to almost fifty yards. The Patriot switched his rifle back to SAFE, drew his Glock 17 and quickly screwed on his homemade suppressor. Thirty yards. He could see it more clearly now. Moonlight painted a woman in tones of silver and blue. She cradled a bundle in front of her as she ran blindly, unknowingly, straight toward him. A backpack bounced from her shoulders with each desperate step. Fifteen yards. The Patriot jumped up from his prone position like a jack-in-the-box from some horror movie. The woman screamed and fell to her knees maybe a half-dozen paces in front of him. Her wails were punctuated by rapid fire Spanish.

"*Por favor... por favor... por favor no me mates... estoy embarazada!*"

He closed the final few yards between them with his muzzle pointed squarely at her chest. Right above the woman's bulging belly. "You speak English?" He spoke in a growl that masked the sound of his natural voice.

"*Lo siento. No se.*"

The Patriot shopped short of an expanding puddle under the woman's knees that he prayed to God was only urine. "There's no room at the inn. You get it? You got a choice. Go back home now or you and your baby die right here." At point blank range he raised the suppressor and pointed the gun straight at her forehead. "I'll do you quick. Dead before you even hit the ground. You won't feel it. That's as much mercy as we've got for you up here tonight."

"*Por favor, señor. No se. Lo siento. Solo quiero mi niño...*"

"Shut. Up!" he yelled. She clamped her mouth closed with both hands to muffle another wail. She may not have spoken a lick of English, but the *chica* seemed to understand him perfectly well. In his experience, the Glock usually made a great translator. "Go back to Mexico," he pointed back south, "and stay there until you learn English! *Comprende?*" Sparkling tears glistened in the moonlight as they cascaded down her face. "I said: Take your anchor baby to the back of the line!" The terrified woman nodded up and down in understanding. Slowly at first, then gaining speed, she got up from the damp, dusty ground. Without another word she turned south and waddled into the night running as fast as her belly, flip-flops, and stifled cries allowed.

The Patriot scanned the area. The other border bandits - if any survived - had disappeared. He waited until he could no longer see the woman, then pressed a button to illuminate the dial on his watch. *Coming up on oh-two-thirty.* The sun would be up in a few hours and there was still work to do before exfiltration. He unscrewed the suppressor from his pistol and got busy.

*   *   *

Corporal Wakefield picked his way through the dusty rubble that used to be a city block. A week ago, these buildings were people's homes. What was left of the structures now sat mostly empty, save for the rubble strewn about from collapsed ceilings and blown out walls. Some meager furnishings remained. Things that the residents could not carry out with them. Splintered furniture. Larger rugs. Occasionally he saw a body among the ruins, but as the daylong battles turned into weeks of sustained fighting and what had started to look like it would become a months-long campaign, the macabre discoveries had become rarer.

Wild dogs ran in packs along the streets and alleyways at night. No doubt they feasted on whatever meat they could find mixed in with the mortar. But perhaps the people had finally gotten wise. Maybe the noncombatant indigenous holdouts had gotten smart and left town until things simmered down. There came a point after the Marines laid fire to your town when anyone who stuck around was just assumed to be an enemy combatant. And they were treated as such. The practice seemed callous right up until report after report came in about platoons that routinely took fire from 13-year-old lads who sniped at patrols from rooftops with Dragunov rifles.

Wakefield and his partner, Lance Corporal Casper, were careful to stay out of the direct sunlight as they picked their way through the house's upper floor. The shade did little to alleviate the desert's oppressive heat - it was 128°F under shady cover. After the third day in a row where the temperature on the street was over 140°F, they had stopped keeping track of the numbers in direct sunlight. Stepping into the light did, however, make a fellow more visible from outside the building. Especially when - as was the case in this building - that spotlight fell from a hole in the roof that looked like it was made by dropping a Volkswagen through it. Fortunately, the shared wall between this level of this particular house and the adjoining one that faced the opposite side of the block was little more than a memory. Not a good situation for the homeowners, but since another wall in that hootch was also blown out, Wakefield and his partner could cut across the block faster and under cover than if they had walked around it. Casper had found the little cut-between when he was on patrol a few days ago and suggested they use it today.

The Marines' silent footfalls fell amongst the debris strewn across the room as an explosion echoed from the other side of town. Small arms fire cracked in the distance like popping corn, then died down. Then rose and died down again. Corporal Wakefield, privileged by his rank, cradled an M40-A3 whose original black and green body was transformed by a can of cheap spray paint to match his dusty tan surroundings. Carter kept his own spray-painted M4 at a loosely held low-ready while he checked their backs from just a step or two behind his senior.

The latest reports indicated that a group of *hajjis* that belonged to al Qaeda in Iraq were holed up somewhere in this neighborhood. The group - maybe a half dozen, maybe two dozen - were supposedly responsible for a number of US casualties across the city. The powers-that-be wanted Fallujah pacified before New Year's though, and that would not happen until resistance cells like this one were silenced. Thus, teams of Recon Marines like Wakefield and Casper sneaked through the town, scouted locations and movements, and supported the main action elements when the Big Green Weenie pushed through a sector.

It was a hell of a job for just two guys. And only one of them was old enough to buy beer back in the States.

Another explosion thundered. It seemed to come from everywhere. Wakefield felt it in his chest as much as he heard it. Chunks of rock flew through the air in defiance of gravity - an irresistible force which in turn, punished the Marine by pulling him through the floor that was just under his boots a second ago. The blinding midday sunlight faded to black as Wakefield fell. His screams were met with a mouthful of dust. Fire washed through his body as something in his left knee snapped with an impact with the ground deep beneath him.

*   *   *

Danny awoke in almost complete darkness. He did not know how long he had been unconscious or the situation around him. Years of instinct made up for his semi-delirious state. His hand immediately found his pistol, even while his mind tried to orient himself.

A half ton of concrete pinned his left knee to the ground - but it yielded to his efforts as he pushed against it. Much to his surprise, the chunk of debris that crushed his knee was actually quite soft. Plush, even. And the chalky dust that covered everything in Iraq flew off him like a sheet as he struggled to his feet. But the suddenly soft ground gave too much and made it impossible to stand. He fell back to his knees.

The spinning world around Wakefield resolved itself into a dimly lit hotel room. He caught his breath, fought to steady a heart that beat like a drum solo in his chest. The ringing in his ears subsided a bit as the air conditioner turned itself on. The hundreds of pounds of debris that had injured his knees years ago became the pillow to which he had clung in his fitful sleep, easily removed, and set aside.

He sat up, rubbed his face, and took a calming breath. He was not Corporal Wakefield, United States Marine Corps, anymore. Nor was he Sergeant, or even Staff Sergeant Wakefield. He was a Special Agent with the Secret Service. He was not in Fallujah or some one-goat village in Afghanistan. He was in - he checked the signage on his hotel desk - El Paso. The pistol in his hand was not the M9 the Corps issued him as a sidearm, but a much more preferable Sig Sauer P-230 courtesy of the Department of Homeland Security.

Danny's mind rebounded from the dream. He found himself once more in time and space. He was safe. He was good. And there was no way in hell that he would go back to sleep this night.

His left hand groped across the room's nightstand through the darkness. The light-up face on his watch told him that it was just a few minutes after oh-five hundred. *Oh well,* he thought, *might as well head down to the hotel's gym and get in a workout.*

It had only been a couple of hours since he and his partner landed, but time in the desert had brought back the dreams. The memories. The dusty night reminded him too much of another life. Another time. And his mind never paid him the mercy of dreaming about the fun he had enjoyed with his friends. No, his traitorous subconscious had decided to revisit the worst of times from the worst of places. Again. It was an all-too-familiar pattern.

God only knew what thoughts would fight their way to the surface of his mind after a few daylight hours out here.

As Danny stuffed his pistol back into his suitcase and found some suitable shorts for exercise, his hand found a small pill bottle. He was not ready for the light, but he did not need to turn on the lamp to know that the bottle was brown. Or that it contained a fistful of Ambien, which the doctors at the VA handed out like breath mints to combat veterans who had troubles sleeping. But it was only Monday night. Wednesday night was Ambien night. If he took the drug a few nights before schedule, then Danny might have to worry he had a problem.

Danny grabbed his room's pass card and padded his way to the door. A hard workout this morning, a hard day's work, and a hard night with a bottle. That was what he needed. Maybe that would help him sleep for more than four hours next time.

*   *   *

Drums thundered in his ears. The hotel's tiny fitness room was flooded with wailing guitars and lyrics that were more screamed than sung. A wall of sound isolated Danny from the rest of the universe as he forced the machine's bar up again and again with a huff. Beads of sweat dotted his face. Soaked his shirt. Throbbing muscles burned the nightmares out of his system. At the other end of the machine's cable a stack of iron plates rose into the air. For an added degree of difficulty Danny kept his legs out straight as a pine board hung off the far end of the bench while he worked the gym's neglected weight machine. He slowly lowered the bar to his chest, breathed in, then puffed the weight back into the air. This was exactly what he needed. A nice, hard workout would clear his head. As he lowered the bar again, Danny wondered how long he would have to keep going before his sweat evaporated, condensed on the enclosed room's ceiling, and then start to fall again. If it could get the memories of Fallujah out of his head, Wakefield swore he would make it rain like the Amazon in this room.

Something moved in his peripheral vision. Danny held the bar aloft and spared a glance to the side. Dressed in black yoga pants, a teal running top, and matched sneakers, Sandra maneuvered around him to the treadmill tucked into the corner opposite from the weight machine. The two pieces of equipment were the spartan room's only features, save a sad little yoga mat rolled up in another corner.

Danny lowered his feet and the bar slowly, then plucked the buds out of his ears. "S'up?"

Sandra fiddled with her own headphones, plugged into her phone. "Morning," she nodded back. "Here I thought I hit it pretty early. Looks like you've been at it a while."

"I'm an early riser." Danny used the truth as a good excuse to not talk about his nightmares. Six days a week Danny woke in the wee hours. It was the surest way to cram a workout into the day. "Please tell me you got some sleep last night."

"A little cat nap. Yeah."

"Well, I'll leave you to it then. I was just wrapping up. Physical fitness is part of the job, you know."

Elbee mounted the treadmill and punched a few

buttons. Danny had started his session with a run, so he sympathized with her lack of choices in the selection menu. Still, Sandra chose one and, seemingly satisfied, began her jog. "Looks like you've exceeded your job requirements," she joked. She kept her headphones in her hand and cast a meaningful look at Danny's naked feet. "Isn't wearing shoes part of the job, too?"

"I prefer to exercise barefoot."

"Ick," she scrunched her face. "Please tell me you didn't run barefoot this thing, Daniel."

Wakefield pointed at a dispenser mounted to the wall next to the door. "Don't worry, Elbee. I wiped it off."

"Speaking of wiping things off after you've used them," Sandra cast him a meaningful glance, "I thought I saw you trying to score with the hotel barmaid on my way to my room last night. How'd that go?"

"I wasn't trying to pick her up," he defended. "I was just getting a drink."

"She was pretty giggly for a girl who was only serving booze," Sandra charged.

"That's 'cause I told her my bear joke while I finished my drink."

"Your bear joke?" Elbee raised an eyebrow in intrigue. "How's that go?"

Danny smiled. "Well enough to get me a second whiskey on the house." He got up, grabbed another disinfectant towel from the dispenser, and wiped the bench he had just used. "I'm gonna go get cleaned up. Breakfast at eight-thirty?"

"I'll be there." Sandra popped in her earbuds and started up her music. Danny tried not to notice her evaluative gaze as he padded out of the hotel's fitness center, though he was just a bit curious as to whether it was in response to his late-night habits or her glimpse at his post-workout physique, usually hidden within his work attire. *Was she judging me,* he wondered, *or checking me out?*

CHAPTER 19

HITTING THE MEXICANS was a good idea, the Patriot decided. He hoped that people on both sides of the boarder got his message. The Patriot had no problem at all with immigration, so long as American laws were followed by people coming into the country and enforced by officials. Beyond the principle, though, the illegals he caught sneaking into America had provided him with some much-needed resources. Most of the Mexicans themselves had nothing of value on them aside from several kilos of cocaine in each of their backpacks - which he scattered onto the desert ground. But he found a sawed-off shotgun, a couple of cheap revolvers, a *bona fide* AK-47 - the fully auto kind made in Russia, as opposed to the semi-auto clones you could buy at almost any gun shop in the States - and a little ammo scattered among the escorts. He also recovered a fat wad of cash from the lifeless body of the coyote - a slang title for people who funneled illegals across the US/Mexican border - surreptitiously leading his charges through the sagebrush.

The Patriot had to operate on cash as much as possible. Credit cards and checks left a trail that was traceable from anywhere. And the accounts themselves could be frozen with the click of a mouse. So long as he stuck to currency he was harder to follow. Harder to track. Harder to shut down.

He seriously thought about keeping the dope and reselling it. He was not surprised to find that the illegals were laden drugs. He remembered a briefing note from a while back saying that people paid upwards of $10,000 each to be smuggled from Mexico into the United States. Most folks trying to sneak into the country simply did not have that kind of cash laying around, so it was fairly common for them to be used to carry drugs. The poor saps themselves were called 'mules' by people in the business. They smuggled loads of dope up to America on behalf of the drug cartels. The same cartels who also controlled the lion's share of human trafficking across the Rio Grande. He'd counted twenty kilos of cocaine from the eight mules. If that was high quality powder, then it was easily worth twenty grand per kilo. Four hundred thousand dollars, just from one small group of illegal aliens out of untold hoards that crossed each night. He could have taken it into El Paso and offloaded it within two hours for a fraction of that amount.

It was quite a tempting idea. It was a lot of cash to watch float away in the desert breeze. But it was the right thing to do. He would just have to live cheaply and hold close to the area until he could find more operational funds. As much as the Patriot would have liked the idea of camping out in the desert for a week or two and harvest more coyotes, he was pretty sure that there would be a host of cartel enforcers and federal agents swarming all over this area as soon as those bodies from last night were found. Besides, he would never have been able to look his wife and kid in the eye again if he dirtied his righteous cause with drug money. And a part of him held out hope that after this world was done with him, he would see them again in the next one.

The Patriot tried not to think about how many of the people that were surely about to comb through this desert were both cartel mooks and law enforcement at the same time. The idea of a Zeta with an American badge made The Patriot want to set up a hide and send a .308 Winchester instant message to the traitor. He knew a few had to be out there. Nonetheless, he decided to head up the dusty highway with a sense of satisfaction and a truckload of justice.

*   *   *

There was just something right - something fundamentally American - about a gun show. Normal people gathered around to appreciate little marvels of engineering, share innovations, address issues of individual and community safety, and partake in the beautiful intercourse of capitalism all in one place. What can I get for you? How much does it cost? How much is this worth? What are you willing to pay for it? At a gun show, shopping became like the hunt for a new lover. Negotiations were a dance as intimate and regulated as any courtship. Sometimes they were more rewarding, too.

Letters printed across the back of some redneck's t-shirt attracted his brown eyes. *If guns kill people, how does anyone get out of a gun show alive?* The Patriot allowed himself a grin. It was the kind of logical argument that he knew drove Liberals absolutely insane. He had to suppress the urge to find one in his size, though. The trick to staying hidden in public was to not draw attention to himself. Bland clothes and a face that could be anybody's - that was his style now.

The Patriot was not in the market for a new gun, either. Not exactly. He could make due with what he had hidden away in his little trailer. Besides, he really did not want to appear on the radar so close to where he had just performed an operation. There was a myth about gun shows that dealers tried to use them to get around background checks for their prospective customers. That story was a lie purposefully spread by Liberals with an agenda and only believed by people who were completely ignorant and totally gullible. While some states allowed private citizens to sell their own guns much like they sold their own cars, no dealer in his or her right mind anywhere in the Union would risk the loss of their license and years of jail time just to transfer a new firearm to some random schmuck on the street.

But the Patriot did have a mental shopping list of things other than guns that could make his job a lot easier. And thanks to the guns he brought back from the bodies in the desert - weapons which were, he was confident, were obtained by their previous owners without a proper background check - he also had a little bit of capital to spend. Because even if a dealer would never sell a gun without a background check, most vendors would not pass up the opportunity to buy a piece from an attendee if the price was right. So he took his time as he wandered through aisle after aisle, each packed with vendors selling handguns, rifles, shotguns, gear, knives…

A collection of local cops checked all guns coming into the building to make sure that they were unloaded, but the sheer volume of guns coming in and out of the fairground made it impossible for any law enforcement agent to consider trying to check serial numbers. An armed man at a gun show was as common and invisible as a pack of gum at a candy store. He did not have to worry about being seen here. His truck was just one of an innumerable mass in the parking lot, many of which had trailers hitched to them just like his. He was safely anonymous among the swarming crowd. And though he usually avoided large groups of people these days, he felt much more at ease in the crowded arena than he usually did in even a nearly-empty shopping mall.

Gun show patrons mostly treated each other with a certain level of courtesy that had become harder to find in the regular day-to-day world. These folk reflected the old saying, *A well-armed society is a polite society.* They also illustrated how foolish the notion of a "gun free zone" was. According to the laws on the books, schools were gun free zones. Most malls and movie theaters were gun free zones. Military bases and recruiting stations were gun free zones. And that was where all mass shootings seemed to happen. *Then again,* he reminded himself, *if gun laws worked then Detroit, Los Angeles and Washington D.C. would be the safest cities in America.*

He meandered past booths brimming with AR-

15s and clones of the ubiquitous AK-47, the most common firearm on Earth. One vendor in particular caught his eye. He saddled up to a set of tables that displayed ammunition like a buffet. His attention quickly fixated on one section in particular which offered up a variety of 12-gauge shotgun shells, some of which produced some rather novel but potentially useful effects. It did not take long before a cowboy wearing a flannel shirt and a ten-dollar smile saddled up opposite him.

"Lookin' fer anything in particular?" the wiry dude asked him from the business side of the table.

"Just seeing what'cha got," he answered.

"Help yerself," the long rancher said smoothly. "This here is our own line." He pointed to the label on the ammo boxes which depicted a cartoon of a redneck with coveralls, a flaming red flannel shirt, and a hayseed stuck in his mouth. "Uncle Jim's. Made with Pride in the U. S. of A. My pappy and uncle started this company."

"What're these?" the Patriot held up a box for examination.

"We call that the Putty-Him Down," the skinny salesman smiled. " 'Stead o' a lead slug it launches a wad o' Funny Putty into the target. It's soft, so all o' that energy just smashes inta' whatever it hits like a gol' dern truck. Took the old bucket from pappy's busted up tractor out to a field and tested it. Them there rounds ripped through three-quarter inch steel like it wuz paper."

The Patriot smiled at the novel idea, then grabbed another box and read the description on the label. "Wax and birdshot?"

"You got good taste, pard'ner. That right there's

m'pride n'joy." The salesman pulled one of the shells out of the box and held it up on display. "We pour number-four shot into a mold with molten wax, then load it into the shell case once it's dried. Flies solid then pulverizes on contact. That there'll rip a hog in half when it hits."

The Patriot marveled at the wonder that was the 12-gauge shotgun. This firearm was more like a miniature canon than a more conventional firearm. It used a smooth bore whose size allowed for massive payloads that could be customized in nearly endless ways. Aside from the traditional loads of birdshot, buckshot or solid slugs, a fellow could easily find shells that launched clusters of barbed needles, rubber balls, bean bags, burning phosphorous... The list went on and on. And the 12-gauge itself was so common that virtually everyone in America seemed to have one. Or at least they should, anyway. *Folks should just include them as part of their house,* he thought, *like a garage door opener or refrigerator.*

"How much?"

"Fifteen bucks per box on awl speciality 12-gauge." The cowboy grinned wide enough that his dimples almost touched the brim of his white Stetson on opposite sides of his face. "That there's a special price fer the show."

"Gimme four boxes of the putty slugs plus a box each of dragons' breath, shredder, and the wax shot."

"Awl'raht," the salesman stuffed the order into a flimsy plastic bag. "That'll be one oh five, pard'ner."

The Patriot pulled one of his newly acquired revolvers out of his pocket. Like all other guns in the arena, it had a brightly colored zip tie fastened through the action and trigger guard to show that the security guards at the door had properly confirmed that it was unloaded and to prevent anyone from putting any ammunition into it. "Will you take this in trade?"

"Six shooter, eh? Lemme take a look, 'ere." The cowboy carefully examined the pistol. "Smith & Wesson Model Ten." He eyed the Patriot suspiciously. "Huh. No offense, but you kind'a struck me as more o'a sem-eye-auto kind'a guy."

"That was my old man's service revolver from when he was with the Chicago PD."

"Ah see," the salesman flipped the gun around. "Look, it looks nice an' clean, but ah can't swing a dead cat 'round here without hittin' an old thirty-eight. Ah'll take half off for the wheel gun. Round it down to fifty bucks. Best ah can do, pard'ner."

The Patriot sighed heavily. He spent two hours swabbing that dead Mexican's pistol in the back of his trailer during a driving break. There was nothing special about it, but it was now very, very clean and in perfect working order. It was easily worth a hundred dollars cash. And if the cowboys were selling the ammo for a hundred dollars, they had to be making at least twenty five. "What if I toss in his buddy, too?" He dug a nickel plated snub-nosed revolver out of his other pocket and placed it on the counter next to the other gun. "But this .357 has been with me for a long time and it's still worth a mint. You gotta toss in some more boot to even it up."

The cowboy salesman looked at the shorter, more powerful pistol with much more approval. "Now that is a nice little Model 686." He chewed on a thought for a moment. "Tell you what, pard'ner, ah've been in the mood for a new pocket rocket, so grab a stack of buckshot an' ah'll call it even." The Patriot knew that the guns he pilfered from the Mexican smugglers had a higher street value and much higher new cost than what he was about to get out of them, but he also knew that they were not new. And the dealer had to make a buck when he sold them. He added a short stack of buckshot - five boxes - to his bag and walked away. Under the circumstances, it was as good a deal as he was likely to find. And really, it was not like it actually cost him anything. In exchange for two free guns that he did not particularly care for he had gained a bundle of ammunition that could be very useful indeed. *All in all,* he concluded, *I'll count that as fair enough.*

*   *   *

"Hey, Elbee. Check this out." At the FBI field office in El Paso, Wakefield turned the monitor at his borrowed workstation so that his partner could see the image of a man clad in black. The figure stood before a black background and wore a Guy Fawkes mask. Once he knew that Sandra was paying attention, Danny clicked on his mouse and restarted the video.

"Take heart, America," the anonymous figure announced. His voice was once again scrambled. "I am still out here. I am still doing the job that your so-called protectors fail to do."

"Did this make it onto the web?" Elbee inquired.

With another mouse click, Danny paused the playback. "Oscar caught it the first time it posted this morning and stopped it from getting out. But it was successfully uploaded to the 'net just a few minutes ago. Our killer certainly is persistent." He resumed playback with another mouse click.

"Actually," the digitally altered voice behind the equally anonymous mask continued, "I've been spending some time keeping the homeland safe from varmints and predators. Coyote hunting. It's not as hard as some people claim. All you have to do is get out from behind your desk. See the outdoors. If you look around, you can see the flea-bitten pests all over the place. Scavenging. Scrounging. Like any rancher or farmer, I can do this job easily. Just stay out of my way. Or join me. Drive the unwanted mongrels off of your land. It is your right. It is your duty. Fight for your freedoms. Fight to take back our once-great nation. Fight to defend our Constitution and our country against all threats. Foreign and domestic." The video ended as abruptly as it began.

"I thought Oscar was able to screen these things and keep them from going public."

"He's one guy with a lot of masters," Danny countered. "And a dude's gotta take a bathroom break sometime. We're happy to have his help, but Oscar's got a lot on his plate. That said, he was able to trace the IP address to a McDonald's right here in El Paso."

"Just like he said," Sandra nodded. "Though I have a hard time believing our serial killer is a fry cook."

"True," Danny nodded. "But think about it. What is El Paso famous for?"

"Illegal immigration," she answered. "I don't think he could send a clearer message that he finds our current immigration policy lacking."

"I think he's telling us who his latest victims are," Danny added. "And where."

"Coyotes," she nodded. Then louder, she called out to the rest of the agents around the open workroom. "Has there been any word on anyone moving against any VIPs from Texas?" Nobody answered. She rose to her feet and projected her voice off the room's far walls. "Anyone hurt or missing? Senators? Congressmen? Judges?"

"Nothing yet," Danny shook his head and answered on behalf of Elbee's lethargic peers. "The House is in session today. Should be easy enough to account for their delegates."

Elbee nodded in agreement. "Get on it. I'll call the senators' offices. Oh, and you! What's your name? Yeah, you. All the people on your row need to track down and roll call every federal judge in the state. Right now, please. And the state senate and representatives."

Danny already had a phone in his hand. "I'll have somebody send an alert to all the federal offices in state, too. Just as a precaution."

"Do it," she ordered as she spun around to her desktop to look up some phone numbers. "And remind every law enforcement agency in the area that a threat has been made against Mexican smugglers and undocumented migrants. See if anything pops up on that end."

CHAPTER 20

"GOOD MORNING, America. Lonnie Chase here bringing you the Thursday morning edition of the Lonnie Chase show. Let's get right to it. Over the week a number of American citizens - the official count is a few dozen, but we're told by sources closer to the story that the real number is more like several hundred - took to the deserts of the southwestern United States. These everyday folks told the media that they were motivated by the story earlier this week of some dead immigrants found just a few miles outside of El Paso. You'll remember that nine Mexicans were found gunned down in the open desert."

The voice of Kyp, Lonnie's cohost, chimed in. "Yeah, and didn't ICE release a presser yesterday that one of the dead guys was a well-known coyote? That's the term people use for a guy who specializes in smuggling people - illegal immigrants, drug dealers and such - from Mexico into the US?"

"Yes they did," Factcheck Fred affirmed. "Not that you would know that if you listened to the mainstream media. The major networks either ignored the story or they are completely out of the loop."

"They buried it," Kyp asserted. "That's what they did. The Liberal-controlled media outlets don't want to tell you anything about who these people really are. They don't wanna talk about the revolving door of Immigrations and Customs Enforcement agents catching and deporting illegal immigrants, only to catch the same illegals crossing again later. Or not catch them. I'm not sure which is worse, really."

"They also neglect to address how many Americans every year are the victims of crimes committed by illegal aliens," Factcheck Fred added. "I mean, we'll have those numbers for you in this afternoon's edition of Factcheck Fred's Finds, but none of the big networks that can be identified by a random jumble of letters will tell you anything like that."

Paid subscribers could see Lonnie lean into his microphone on the Chase Camera. "The other networks won't tell you anything that doesn't fit with their contrived, artificial, totally fictionalized Progressive agenda. Which is why we've sent a team of investigative reporters to do the job the news agencies refuse to do anymore. And what we've been hearing so far is nothing short of extraordinary."

"And what makes it so extraordinary," Kyp chimed in, "is the fact that we're just talking about ordinary citizens."

"That's right," Lonnie resumed. "Ordinary folks are grabbing their guns, their binoculars and their flashlights. They're heading down to Texas, to Arizona, to New Mexico, to Baja California… They're going down there themselves - sometimes in small groups, sometimes all by themselves - and they're setting up watch. They're patrolling the open desert of the American southwest in trucks, on four-wheelers. They're bringing their own horses from Oklahoma and Tennessee - or they're renting them. One of our guys on the ground - and I'm convinced we're the only media outlet out there today who still fields real investigative journalists to bring you the truth, rather than a bunch of talking heads who recite the party line - discovered that total strangers are coming up to Texas ranchers and renting their horses. Or buying them outright! It's amazing, I tell you. Absolutely amazing. But don't just take my word for it," he challenged his unseen audience. "Go online. Go and see the videos they're posting themselves. Go to your favorite social media network and see their pictures. Hear their stories. And share them. 'Cause we've gotta get the word out. It's up to us to force the mainstream media to start doing their jobs. Because the choice is for them to either step up to the plate or become completely irrelevant."

Factcheck Fred circled the program back to the point before his boss got carried even further away on his tangent. "So, what they're doing, it looks like, is they're out combing the desert looking for folks that they suspect have crossed into this country illegally. And then they're calling ICE, they're calling the Border Patrol agents to come out and arrest them."

"So, what you're saying here is that Joe the

Plumber is out there doing Immigration and Customs Enforcement's job for them," Kyp stabbed.

"Not *for* them," Lonnie corrected. "*With* them. With them. And it's amazing. There's a report of a group of twelve men on horseback - contractors, truck drivers and the like - who encircled a group of almost forty people and held them until Border Patrol could come out and take possession. All forty were Mexican nationals. Thirteen of them had backpacks full of cocaine. I'm not talking about a little bag of weed here and there, but multiple kilos of cocaine each. And once Border Patrol took the bad guys away, the good guys went right back into the desert and found another batch. Then another."

"But, I mean, this is basically a militia movement," Kyp insisted, "isn't it?"

"I'm not sure what label we should put on this," Factcheck Fred fumbled, "but according to what we've been able to gather, about nine hundred people were intercepted by everyday American citizens just since this story broke. Nine hundred in three days. Now, granted, that's an area from Brownsville to Baja. But still, that's a huge deal. A video goes viral, a bunch of folks are moved into action, and this is what we get."

"My personal favorite," Kyp added, "was the report out of McAllen State Park. Did you hear this?"

"I heard it," Lonnie nodded.

"Four Americans - call them militia, call them patriots, call them the neighborhood watch, call them whatever - four Americans approached some suspicious characters that they watched walk up from the banks of the Rio Grande and asked if they had any ID. Not one of the suspects spoke a lick of English.

Things escalated and a shootout broke out. One of the Americans was seriously wounded. I hear he's in a local hospital listed in critical condition. Anyway, at the end of the firefight, the four suspects are dead on the ground. Texas Rangers arrive on the scene and find almost two hundred brass casings scattered around - a mix of rounds fired from both sides."

"And which of the Mexican nationals was an innocent woman who dreamed that her anchor baby could be born in a decent hospital?" Factcheck Fred interrupted.

"Evidently we're not supposed to say *'anchor baby'* anymore. And, none. But one of the dead guys was a Mexican male, Jose Rosalez-Chavez, who has been arrested four times by US officials ferrying drugs or people into America. Oh, and this information came to us by way of the Mexican Federal Police - the ones who aren't working for one cartel or another."

"And, what was his job for the Zetas?" Lonnie begged. "Was he working to improve working conditions for the Zeta union? Was he pursuing a dream of livable wages and quality health insurance for the women and children who process the cartel's cocaine? Maybe a fifteen-dollar per hour minimum wage for all crack whores?"

"Uh, no," Kyp answered. "Not this particular guy. This was the Jose Rosalez-Chavez who was a trigger man for the Zeta drug network who has killed, conservatively, at least twenty-seven people for his narco bosses."

"You mean he was not just another of these Dreamers we've heard about?" Lonnie asked.

"I think his dreams involved stuffing people into old tires and lighting them on fire," Factcheck Fred offered. "I think that's the kind of social justice he subscribed to."

"Oh, it gets better," Kyp resumed. "Two of the other dead guys. Guess where they came from?"

"Mexico?" Lonnie offered.

"Guatemala?" Factcheck Fred played along.

"One was from Syria and the other from Yemen." Kyp corrected. "Now, what do we know about the people from those countries? Other than the fact that they love shawarma."

"That they don't usually live in Mexico," Fred answered in perfect deadpan.

"That they are predominantly Sunni," Lonnie answered more soberly.

"Yes. The same flavor of Islam that brought us such cultural gems as al Qaeda and ISIS." Kyp declared.

"And don't forget the Muslim Brotherhood," Fred reminded. "You know, for those of us who prefer the oldies."

"I am more of an oldies guy," Lonnie offered wistfully. "Buddy Holly. Beach Boys. Muslim Brotherhood. You know what they say: Whether it's terrorism or rock n'roll, there's no school like the old school."

"My point," Kyp resumed, "is that there's more to the issue of border security than many people realize. It's not just about leeches crawling into our country and draining our resources with social security fraud, voter fraud, unemployment fraud, etc. By leaving the border open we leave the door open for bad people to come into our country and do bad things to our citizens. Whether they're serial rapists, hitmen for a cartel, or Islamic terrorists sneaking into our country so that they can conduct the next 9/11, it really doesn't matter. They're crossing the border and our leaders are doing nothing. There's no action from the White House. There's no action from Capitol Hill. And by turning a blind eye to the problem, or by politicizing it, our national leaders are actually doing a great disservice to our citizens."

"I wanna keep talking about this," Lonnie put in. "I think this is an important issue and I want to give it a voice. Because you know none of the other networks are gonna touch this thing with a ten-foot pole. But first, we need to take a break. I wanna talk to you about my friends over at Goldstein Financial Group…"

*   *   *

"Turn it off," a man wearing green fatigues and a blue jacket with *Border Patrol* stenciled across the back in blazing letters. "I can't stand that guy."

"Dude's got a point," Danny offered as he obediently switched off the radio. He and Elbee were inside a trailer on the Texas/New Mexico state line that doubled as a mobile command post for Border Patrol agents. "But at least we managed to keep a lid on the helicopter story."

"Yeah, for now," the man scoffed.

Danny glanced at the shiny railroad tracks on the officer's collars. "Where are we with that anyway, Captain Sanchez?"

Raul Sanchez was an American citizen by birth. He held his job with the US Border Patrol as a sacred duty to the country he loved. He treated his duties with the utmost care and diligence. But most of the illegals he dealt with on a daily basis treated him with the highest level of hostility. They called him *Capitan Traidor*, a traitor to his own people. "That, my friend, is a time bomb waiting to go off in my ass."

Elbee shook her head. "We're making a mistake. We need to break the story ourselves so that we control the narrative. Once we establish the tone of the dialogue-"

"There is no 'we' here, boss lady," Captain Sanchez interrupted. "Some *gringos* see a chopper fly north from the border and flash a light at it. That's a felony. The only good news is that it wasn't one of ours."

"And the bad news is that the chopper opened fire on the civilians on the ground," Danny offered.

"No, brother," Sanchez corrected, "the bad news is that one of the guys on the ground had armor piercing rounds in his rifle and he returned fire. Shot the bird down. And since the chopper happens to belong to the Mexican Army that's an act of war."

"Bird was ten miles north of the border," Danny pointed. "Violating sovereign airspace is an act of aggression. The Mexicans committed the first act of war."

"Oh, yeah," Raul nodded sarcastically, "the Ministry of Defense is going to totally understand. They'll just do the honorable thing and own up to it. There's no way this'll turn into an international *joder cluster*."

"So, what do we do?" Elbee asked.

"Again, with the 'we'..." Sanchez's bushy mustache danced atop his lip while he literally chewed in thought. "Okay, I got it. You go back to D.C. Send your boy Captain America here to talk it out with the

Mexicans. Let me know how that works out. In the meantime, I'll go home and get shot in a drive-by or shivved at the grocery store when some sleeper sells me out. Everybody good with that?"

Special Agent Elbee bristled at the officer's macabre humor. "One of my analysts believes that one or more of these attacks in the last few days might have been carried out by my suspect," she said dryly. "I'd like to talk to the men you're holding from the helicopter incident."

Sanchez nodded. "Of course. We're holding them in isolation at the county jail until my boy calls me from the hospital where we MEDEVAC'd the Mexican aircrew. Gotta know if we're charging those *gringos* with assault or murder." Raul winced comically. "I only like to do a collar's paperwork once. I'm funny that way."

The Special Agents dismissed themselves and allowed Captain Sanchez to get back to work. Danny drove the Ford Escape they picked up at the El Paso airport days ago. As the desert highway passed across his windows, he was silently thankful for the air-conditioned cabin. He spent a lot of time in the desert as a Marine, but the Hummvees and MRAPs they used back in the Corps were like giant ovens on wheels. "Nice to see the captain's in good spirits," Danny commented, "all things considered."

"You know that the Mexicans have gotta know their bird went down on US soil," Elbee declared. "You think maybe our suspect is trying to start a war?"

"I dunno," Danny admitted. "I mean, it's pretty common knowledge that the Mexicans conduct incursions into US airspace all the time."

"According to the *Federales* they're doing the same thing we are: watching the border for illegal activity," Sandra reiterated from a report they had read earlier.

"That's what the Mexicans say in their reports. And even though we all know that's a load of crap, everyone on our side of the river who wants to kiss up to the Mexican government just smiles goes along with the story."

"You don't think they're patrolling the border?" Elbee challenged.

Wakefield hesitated, then finally answered. "I did a training bit down along the river early on in the Corps," he recalled. "Spent a few weeks doing pretty standard recon stuff. Cross country mobility through the outback. Nighttime movement and night vision training. Report suspicious activity to the rear - which in this case was Border Patrol. Anyway, during the eighteen days we spent in the field we saw eight military helos fly from beyond the horizon to the south to well past the horizon to the north. We were never more than five clicks from the border, so those choppers had to've come from Mexico. Our intel bubba called 'em *saltamontes.* Grasshoppers. Little short flights from staging areas just on their side of the river the Mexicans use to drop narcotics and bad actors off here in the States."

"What'd you do?" Sandra's tone made it evident that she had previously been unaware of the problem's historic frequency.

"Not a damn thing," Danny hissed and shook his head, "though it wasn't for a lack of motivation. After the first couple of contact reports some of the guys started getting itchy trigger fingers. Word came down the pipe that under no circumstances were we to engage those helos. But I gotta tell ya, Elbee, there was more than one time that I sat there cradling my rifle, looking at one of those birds in my crosshairs and thought that with just a little tickle of my right finger I could give those flyboys a reason to think twice before busting up our airspace again."

"You heard Captain Sanchez earlier, Daniel. He said that one of the guys in custody was previously in the Army. He did a tour in Afghanistan. Maybe he had an experience like yours in the service and couldn't resist the temptation."

"Maybe," Danny shrugged. "Can't say as I blame him, really."

"What's that supposed to mean?"

"Just sayin' that there's a lot of folks that don't see what our killer is doing as a crime, *per se*."

"I'm going to pretend I didn't hear you say that." Elbee shook her head in disgust. "Let's just focus on this shooter Captain Sanchez told us about."

"You think he's our guy?"

"Why not? Look, Daniel. It all fits. Military training. Combat experience. The use of small arms with specialized ammunition. Emotionally aligned with a Right-wing cause. This guy fits our profile perfectly."

"You're right, Elbee. He does."

"You don't sound convinced," Sandra probed. "You don't think he's our suspect?"

"I think Oscar gave us a suspect," he reminded her. "That tip put us right here in the middle of a boiling pot of stew."

"So this is all a coincidence?" she challenged him. "Oscar is never wrong? Just go with the Secret Squirrel, evidence be damned?"

"I dunno. There's two million combat vets in our nation, Elbee. Most of them lean Right politically. Most of them shoot guns and a lot of guys like ammo that comes in all sorts of whimsical flavors."

"Most of them aren't out there killing congressmen," she countered.

"It's good that they aren't," he warned, "'cause there's nothing we'd be able to do about it if they'd did."

"Is it that you don't think we could stop some disgruntled vets," she challenged, "or that you are one yourself?"

"There's more than two million combat vets in our country right now, Elbee," he shot back. "Two million combat hardened, experienced warriors. Some of us have spent our whole adult lives fighting. That's the biggest fighting force our civilization has ever seen. We're having problems with one guy who doesn't like where the country's headed. Can you imagine what would happen if a whole bunch of vets just picked up their guns and said, 'enough'? You've got no prayer against that."

"The police and DHS could mobilize," she countered. "Call in the National Guard -"

"You don't get it." He shook his head. "We are the police. The ones that aren't all fat retards, anyway. And the National Guard? How many of those clowns do you think wouldn't side with us? Eh? And if you think the conventional military folks are just gonna turn their guns on their brothers and former teammates - whether they agree with the rebels or not - then you're delusional. The first time some idiot lieutenant gives the order to kick in a red-blooded American's door in the dead of night, his own men'll shoot him themselves." Danny allowed himself a sarcastic giggle.

Sandra shrank a little in her seat. "You're sounding more and more like this guy every minute." She cautiously eyed him from her side of the truck. "If you want off this case, Daniel, just say the word. No hard feelings."

"I've got a job to do, Elbee. And I know my duty."

"Do you?"

Danny gripped the steering wheel harder than usual. "Make no mistake about it, Elbee. I'll bleed on the flag to keep the stripes red. This guy's breaking the law. He's killing Americans. We don't just let that happen. This ain't Colombia, or Turkey, or some other country run by hoodlums, warlords, or tyrants. I just think we should be focusing on the lead that Oscar gave us."

"We'll follow your magical intelligence hunch after we do some real, honest criminal investigation. If it's still necessary."

"It probably will be," he sang.

"If you think this is a waste of time then why are we out here?" she demanded.

Danny grimaced. "Look, you may be right. Right? I'm keeping an open mind. This dude may be our suspect. But let's not let our wishes interfere with our judgement. Okay? You're my partner and I've got your back. You think this guy smells, and that's why we're gonna go check him out. But let the real evidence lead us down a conclusive road. Don't marry an assessment based on circumstantial evidence."

"I know the difference between deductive and inductive reasoning Daniel," she assured him. "This is not my first case." She stared out her window at the open desert for a heartbeat. "And I'm not going to take it easy on this guy just because you're soft on vets."

"What?" Danny made no effort to hide his hurt feelings. "I'm not soft on vets."

"You don't think you make excuses for your own kind?" she asked.

"My own kind? Gimme a break Elbee."

"Do you deny that you feel a sense of camaraderie with other veterans?" she accused.

"With some other vets, yeah. But I'd never let it interfere with my duty." Wakefield shook his head and huffed. "Soft on vets," he pouted. "I'm not soft on vets."

"I'll understand if you don't want to sit in while I interview the suspect," Sandra offered.

"Interviews are for jobs. It's still okay to call it an interrogation."

"The FBI prefers the term 'interview.' It's less confrontational."

"Less confrontational? Now who's being soft on vets?" Danny countered mockingly. He turned at their exit and proceeded toward the county jail. "Who in their right mind sits in a tiny room with a conspicuous mirror in it right after being arrested, sees two feds walk in, and doesn't think it's an interrogation when they start asking questions?" He shook his head. "Besides, there's no way I'm going soft on this dude. The guy was in the Army. If he was a real man he'd've made it into the Corps."

CHAPTER 21

"I TOOK AN OATH to defend my country from all enemies. Foreign and domestic." The man's voice was even. Calm. He spoke in clear, matter-of-fact phrases. His face was flat. Blank. Neutral. He sat back easily in his seat. His hands rested on his chair's arms as if the shackles around his wrists were a fashion accessory rather than a restraint.

"Alright, Corporal Lenner, let's take it from the top again," Sandra flipped through her interview notes.

"It's just Mr. Lenner, Special Agent Elbee," he politely corrected her. "But you can call me Boyd. If you like."

Danny sat silently beside his partner in what was often called the Number Two seat. He brought no notepad, no pen, nothing at all into the cold, gray interrogation room. His eyes were fixed on the man before him. His penetrating stare probed every movement, every tic, every breath that the detainee made. He scrutinized the words the subject used. The way he turned a phrase when he responded to a question about this, as compared with how he answered to that. A thousand data points ticked through Wakefield's mind. They flashed in his vision like some robot's heads up display, each one linked to related information that he either already knew or had gathered just by observing the subject. Some of those data points were flags, indicators of what future questions needed to be asked. Others helped him predict likely answers to questions they had not yet given. They clued him in to gaps in the subject's story. Overlapping, repetitive language that indicated he had rehearsed his answer. Any change in posture that might clue Danny and his partner in on a possible lie, a prepared diatribe, an uncomfortable subject. Based upon the last forty minutes Danny guessed that the subject was just being coy; that he offered the pretty blonde FBI agent a clumsy, thinly veiled flirtation. It could have been a ploy to establish a rapport, to get his interrogator to emotionally invest in her subject in such a way that she might like him. Might go easy on him. Might even become his advocate. The tactic was one of a dozen defensive strategies taught at SERE - Survival, Evasion, Resistance, and Escape - school. Lima Syndrome, they called it. It was the reverse of its more famous cousin, Stockholm Syndrome, but in Lima the captor grew sympathetic with the captive instead of the other way around. It was possible that Boyd Lenner was trying to take control of his interrogation, to gain sympathy from his audience in the hopes that it would buy him an easier time - if not outright release.

Or it could have been because he was a normal guy. Danny had to admit that Sandra was hot in a way that had nothing to do with the desert. This was an undeniable fact that could not be hidden by conservative clothing and minimal cosmetics. Either way, Special Agent Sandra Elbee did not take the bait. She was an ice queen. "Fine, Mr. Lenner. You live in Waco, correct?"

"No ma'am," he corrected. "I grew up in Waco. Now I live in Gardendale."

"Oh, that's right," she pretended to correct her notes. "And you've lived there ever since you left the Army in - when was that again?"

"I was Honorably Discharged on thirteen October, twenty-fourteen."

"And how long were you in the Army?"

"Five years."

"And what was your job in the Army?"

"Infantry, ma'am."

"And what did you do in the infantry, exactly?"

Boyd smiled dryly. "Mostly got shot at. Occasionally we got to shoot back."

"And you were personally injured during your time in the Army?"

"Yes ma'am. Just as I said earlier."

"That's right," Elbee touched her notes with her pen, "And you said earlier that you didn't feel particularly inclined to discuss the details of your injuries."

Lenner sat for a moment in silence. "Was that a question ma'am?"

Another invisible flag flew up in Wakefield's vision. That last comment - the question about the question - told Wakefield that the man chained to the chair on the other side of the table had a plan. An agenda. And no matter how ill advised, ill-conceived or poorly executed, when a criminal's head was full of stupid thoughts it usually complicated matters for law enforcement.

"Here's a question for you, Lenner," Wakefield offered, "why'd you do it?"

Boyd's eyes shifted from Elbee. Danny could tell that the wiry veteran was sizing him up. He could see the gears moving behind the suspect's eyes. "You were in, weren't you?" A beat. "Yeah, I can tell. We can usually tell just by looking, can't we? Who served. Who didn't. She didn't. It shows. She's too pretty, even for the Air Force. But you - you've got the stink on you."

"The stink?" Sandra enquired. "What stink?"

"The smell of battle," Lenner explained. "It clings to you, you know. Long after the smoke clears and you come home. It doesn't shower off. It's something you wear for the rest of your days. It gets into you. Deeper than your pores. The eyes that've seen what we've seen. Hands that have done what we had to do. It's in your bones. No offense, Miss Federal Agent Lady, but he's got it. And you don't." He turned back to Danny. "So, what were you?"

"This ain't about me," Wakefield held firmly, "and it ain't about the war. You shot down a helicopter."

"I defended my 'mates and my countrymen against an aerial incursion by an armed, hostile foreign force," Lenner countered. "As far as I'm concerned, I'm just a soldier keeping his oath. You know? To defend the Constitution of the United States against all enemies. Foreign and domestic."

"Did you and your buddies plan for this?" Danny pressed. "Is that why you were packing steel-cored ammo? So that you could be sure to punch through the chopper's fuselage?"

"I always carry a little bit of that," Boyd answered. "Just in case."

"And what about your companions?" Sandra continued. "Was this whole thing their idea? Who came up with the plan?"

"There was no plan ma'am. Just some Americans riding through the American countryside enjoying the free air. And doing our patriotic duty when we found ourselves in the right place at the right time to do the right thing. And no, we didn't discuss shooting down the helo. But nobody tried to stop me either."

"You didn't think that was an American bird?" Danny asked.

"*Gringos* don't fly Hueys much these days," Lenner explained. "Especially with door gunners in place over American soil. And it was flying out of the south. Pretty obvious where it came from. And what they were doing. Running drugs or some such up from Mexico. They do it all the time."

Elbee flipped through the loose papers that she had tucked into one of the pockets in her leather portfolio. Behind a few pages she found a sheet topped with ornate letterhead. "I have here a message from the Mexican Ministry of Defense. According to the MoD, there is a bilateral agreement on file between them and the DoD to conduct cross-border security flights - by and from either side. You were in their declared Area of Operations."

Boyd Allan Lenner tried to hide a look of panic as

he suddenly realized that he might not have all of the information he needed to make a sound decision.

"Congratulations Boyd," Wakefield mocked, "you just shot down a friendly. That's not just a felony either. Since that's a military asset from a partner force conducting a sanctioned mission in a unified AO, they're protected by law the same as US Forces. We can charge you with fratricide and treason." The previously cool veteran began to shake and stammer unintelligibly, but there were no clever words for how he felt. For the first time since the interrogation started, Lenner was off balance. "And since you were in the Army, that means more than just a few years at Leavenworth. It's a capital offense. You get the chair." *Now*, Danny thought, *is the time to strike*.

"Is that why you shot Senator Evans?" Elbee pounced coldly as if she had heard Wakefield's mental cue. "Was that just another case of you doing your patriotic duty?"

Behind his rough mask Danny smiled inwardly, pleased with his partner's timing. She really did know how to play the game. Her competence was a comfort. Her display at the table had started with a somewhat subtle 'Good Cop/Bad Cop' routine. When they first saw Lenner through the room's two-way mirror, they had agreed that he would expect some sort of tactic on their part. And everyone in the world knew about 'Good Cop/Bad Cop.' But Elbee seamlessly followed Wakefield's lead when he shifted midway through the interrogation to the 'We Know All' approach. Danny was pleasantly surprised when Sandra swung for the fences.

"Who? The guy from the news? That wasn't me."

"Oh, really?" Elbee did not seem convinced in the

least. *Either that*, Danny judged, *or she missed her calling as an actress. No matter.* It was time to step up the pressure. And as long as the subject was busy thinking about other things Wakefield knew that it would be harder for the subject to play his game. Harder for Lenner to lie.

"C'mon Lenner," Wakefield goaded, "it's time to own it man. Here's your chance to tell us about how the country's gone to the crapper."

"Well, I mean, it has."

"And you just wanna make things better," Elbee continued where her partner left off.

"Yeah."

"You're not a bad guy," Sandra shifted her track again, instantly becoming Boyd's Best Friend in the Booth. "We totally get that. You were just doing what you thought was right."

"Tell you what Lenner," Danny leaned in, "if you come clean right now, make it easy on everybody, then we'll recommend a light sentence. We own you for last night - gun, ballistics, witnesses, the whole nine yards. A turnip could get a conviction on this. The District Attorney doesn't even have to try. You give up the rest of what you've been up to, and we'll call it done. But if you keep stonewalling us - well son, you know how it goes. The harder we have to work for it, the harder the hammer falls on you."

"Okay, okay, okay," Boyd held his hands up in surrender. "Look, I admit, I shot that chopper down. But we thought they were running drugs or something. Honest. You've gotta believe me."

"What else?" Elbee raised her eyebrows.

"Fine. We might've had a little too much to drink," Lenner continued. "But we were on horses.

It's not like we were driving cars or anything."

"She means Louisiana," Wakefield pointed.

"I told you. I've never been to Louisiana."

"Suit yourself Boyd." Sandra slammed her leather notepad closed. Danny recognized his cue, and both agents left the interrogation room.

*　　　*　　　*

Fate, it seemed, had chosen to give the Patriot a gift. Two gifts, really. More and more Americans had followed his example, accepted his invitation and, in the last few days, had chosen to follow his lead. To take matters into their own hands. To do the job their government had failed to do for them. Just like the founding fathers had done when their own government back in London failed them one time too many. That was good news in itself. Then the news anchors all announced that two enemies of the state had decided to meet and discuss the situation. Obviously, the whole affair was a publicity stunt designed by the media hogs to jointly ease the mounting public tension and garner a little camera time pursuant to the upcoming election cycle. Either way, it was a small surprise that two senior senators would hold a public meeting on the last working day before the Fourth of July weekend.

And they were coming to him.

Twenty-four hours ago, the Patriot had assumed that he would have to hit the road again to strike against his next objective. But now a pair of names from fairly high up on his target list were on their way to his area. *How very fortunate for me - and for the nation.*

*   *   *

"You don't think Lenner's our guy?" Sandra asked as the truck's air conditioner fought to cool the cabin air heated by the southwestern summer sun. It was her turn to drive. Her eyes stared straight over the steering wheel while she consulted her partner.

"You do?" Danny worked his tie loose in the passenger seat to relieve himself of some excess heat. "He's not the guy Oscar gave us," he started. "Accepting that and allowing for the possibility that Oscar could possibly be wrong, I'm not sure he's the one." Sandra drew a breath to protest, but he cut her off. "Look, Elbee, I don't wanna oversell our assumptions, but my gut tells me that whoever the Constitutional Killer ends up being he won't be coy about it."

"You think our guy'll own up to his misdeeds under questioning?"

"I don't think the real Constitutional Killer thinks he's got anything to be ashamed of," he opined. "I don't think he'll hide behind denials."

"Oh," she gasped mockingly, "so now you're the psychologist?"

"I'm just not convinced Lenner's the Constitutional Killer."

"Well, the last time I checked, I'm the one who studies how people's brains work, and you're the guy who just splatters them against the wall. And I'm also the lead investigator on this case. And I say Lenner's our best lead."

"If that's how you wanna play it," he shrugged in resignation. "I just wanna make sure we catch the right guy. You know, so that the real killer doesn't assassinate any more politicians. But hey, if you're dead set on pinning this on some random guy -"

"Lenner isn't some random guy!" she rolled her eyes while she drove. "He's guilty of a fistful of felonies just from his confession today. And that's just what he's told us so far. Who knows what else we can get him to cop to under pressure?"

"Oh, well, if that's how you want this to go then just gimme a bucket of water, a towel, and a roll of duct tape. In ten minutes or less, I'll have him confessing to the JFK assassination."

Sandra was disgusted by the idea of her partner's casual offer to waterboard a suspect. "That's barbaric!"

"Oh, no," Danny's voice ran up and down its register, "it's only barbaric when you don't find it professionally expedient or politically convenient. But when it works for you then it suddenly becomes a deniable, necessary evil. Doesn't it? You're just like all the rest. You think any random soldier is disposable, so long as he serves your purpose. Like a good little tool. 'Cause that's what random people are to folks like you. Just tools."

"I hardly…" Elbee's voice caught in her throat at the accusation. "Random…" Another catch. "Random? Daniel, don't you see? He's random. That's his pattern!"

"The Constitutional Killer's pattern is that he's random?" Danny thought about it for a second. "I don't think so."

"He's all over the map."

"So, he's mobile."

"His victims come from all over the place," she insisted.

"But they do share one thing in common, Elbee."

"They're all Democrats."

Danny shook his head. "They're all Progressives," he corrected. "Look at their stances. Their votes, views, and speeches. This guy's going after anyone that he thinks is attacking what he sees our country being about."

"That's half the country, Daniel."

"Is it?" he challenged her. "I mean, really, Elbee. We can split hairs over the details, but do you really think that half - or even a lot - of regular Americans are really so different from this guy? Massive majorities in this country vote to support the Constitution Elbee. On everything from gay marriage to Second Amendment issues, we mostly agree with each other - at least in broad terms. It's our politicians and their agendas that make everything complicated."

"I'm not sure you and I agree on much, Daniel."

The Secret Service agent smiled. "We come from different places. We do different things. We see the world differently Elbee, but we both love justice. We both serve the law. And we both want what's best for our people. That's a start. There's a lot of room to maneuver there. A lot of room for folks to meet."

Sandra thought about what he said. Then she drew in an inspired breath. "He's anonymous."

"No, we've been down that road-"

"Not anonymous, the person or group," she corrected. "He's anonymous. As in he's an everyman. Our killer isn't making it hard to find his victims, just to pin down his identity. Right?"

"Right. So long as we don't know who he is he's able to operate. To kill again. In the service we called it Freedom of Movement." Danny bit his lip. "I like it. And it keeps him perfectly asymmetric."

"It fits everything. Think about it, Daniel. Up to now his victims have all represented things that every man and woman in the country would identify as problems. Duke Evans was a corrupt official. Linda Rogers was a hardline idealist of the opposite political spectrum. He painted Rodriguez as a judicial activist. In his little web broadcasts, he's presenting himself to the public just another brave soldier hiding behind the same sense of duty shared by everyone in uniform. No offense."

"None taken. I dig what you're giving off here." Wakefield used his time freed from the wheel to sift through his own folder. "Okay. Lenner's a loser and a dirtbag. Fine. We let the D.A. sort him out. But I want to go over the bit from Oscar again with you and just hear me out." He flipped to the appropriate page on his lap. "Master Sergeant Thomas J. Phillips, US Army, Retired. We both read Phillips' bio; Lenner sure as hell ain't the same guy using an alias. Speaking of reading," he began surfing through page after page from his notes, "am I missing something here? I've got nothing on this MoU you mentioned to Lenner."

Sandra smiled behind her sunglasses. "There is no MoU. I made it up. I thought you'd pick up on that, Mr. Interrogator."

"Well played," he grinned and tuned the radio. "So, what's our next move?"

"Still no word from Captain Sanchez. Let's head over to the crash site and hit up the local techs for their forensic data. I want to send it back to Hudson's team for review and further analysis. Just in case something comes back. Maybe Lenner and Phillips are connected somehow. There's a lot of vets out there, but you guys tend to live in small circles."

"Good thinking. You want Hudson, not the local team?"

"She's good at what she does," Elbee nodded. "She's been on the case from the start. And I want a single set of eyes combing over all the data." The blonde federal agent smiled wryly again. "Besides, I get the feeling she'd love an excuse to VTC with a certain Secret Service agent."

"What? Really?"

"You seem surprised."

"Well, I mean, I didn't think she was into me."

"Oh, please Daniel. You didn't notice the way she fawns over you? Hanging on your every word? Laughing at your stupid jokes?"

"Hey! My jokes aren't stupid."

"Whatever." Sandra exited for a connecting highway that would take them deeper into the desert. "You should hook up with her if we get back to New Orleans."

"You think so?" he fished.

"Why not?" she countered. "Unless she's not your type."

"My type?" he rebuffed. "Elbee, you don't know me too well after all. For the sake of your psychological profile on me, let me clarify: my type is, officially, a pretty broad category."

"I don't just up and profile everyone I meet, Daniel," she protested. Sandra seemed genuinely offended by the insinuation. For a moment anyway. Then she smirked. "It figures though," she shook her head, "I shouldn't be surprised. You're just another man-whore."

"Whoa, whoa, whoa," Danny held his hands up

defensively, as if her words were punches thrown in the truck's close cabin. "I'm a healthy, single man. I like women. There's nothing wrong with that."

"I thought you were Catholic."

"And I know you're not," he rebuffed. "Besides, you know the old saying: Good Catholics go to Heaven, and the bad ones go everywhere."

Sandra shook her head and laughed in mockery. "Let me ask you a question, Daniel. Just how low is the bar with you? With women, I mean."

"Why? Are you trying to see if you'd clear it?"

"In your dreams," she laughed.

Wakefield's brain processed the inquiry behind his sunglasses. "Well, I guess I'm just like any other guy. Obviously, there's a standard, and then there's an ideal. But there's lots of different things that can make a woman attractive."

"Aside from the obvious two?" Sandra challenged. "And Hudson's 'things' aren't that big."

"Okay, first off, size isn't that big a deal. And - at the risk of sounding like a pig - hers are plenty perky. I mean, that's not the point. The point is, she's fine. I mean, they're fine. I mean - you know what I mean. So just don't. And secondly, there's more to attraction than numbers. It's about qualities, not quantities. What kind of person she is, not her score on some contrived and meaningless scale. I'd've thought you of all people would understand that. And," his voice assumed a holier-than-thou tone as he tilted his head so that he could literally looked down his nose at her, "quite frankly, I'm more than just a little offended that you'd objectify a woman like that."

"Gimme a break Daniel. You're the one staring at every chick's rack."

"I am not," he protested at first, then admitted with a smirk, "but I am checking for concealed weapons."

"You're a pig."

"Hey! If you don't want us to look, don't put them out there on display."

"Oh, I'm gonna slap the stupid right outta your face, Daniel."

"What are you mad about?" he maintained. "You started this whole conversation. And I said that wasn't all there was to it."

"Fine. Like what?"

"Brains. Personality -"

"That's what you say when you're describing fat chicks," she accused.

"Okay, Hudson's totally not a fatty. Not that I was looking. 'Cause that could be misconstrued as sexual harassment. Which is totally unprofessional and I would never do it." Suddenly it was Danny's turn to smile wryly. "Besides, bigger girls do try harder. Them and nerdy chicks. They always bring their A-game into the bedroom."

"That's awful!" This time, Sandra did backhand him in the shoulder. "You really are a pig."

Wakefield saw the fight was hopeless and shifted his attention back to the truck's radio. He finally found the station for which he had been looking.

"... you just tuning in, the Associated Press is reporting that a man in southeastern New Mexico shot down a Mexican Army helicopter flying over US soil last night. According to the story that just posted on the 'net, Boyd Allan Lenner, an Army veteran, used a high-powered rifle to bring down the bird, which was allegedly..."

Sandra reached over and stabbed the radio's power button. "So much for our media blackout," she hissed. "Was it too much to ask for? Just one freaking day without the press on this shoot-down?"

"Evidently," Danny nodded.

"You're still a pig, though," she chided.

"Well then we might as well hurry up and get to the site before too many flies gather 'round the barbecue. Besides, what's the point of having that FBI badge if you don't use it to get out of a speeding ticket every now and then?"

CHAPTER 22

"I THINK YOU'RE RIGHT," Jonas' face agreed from the video screen. "It sounds like another Dry Hole."

"Those are the worst kind," Nick joked from his boss' shoulder. Several of the watch floor analysts snickered at the innuendo. A few others fought the urge to join in on the jocular mood. 'Dry Hole' was operational slang for a mission which ended without the primary suspect being arrested or killed, but most people also knew it could also describe problematic coitus.

"Speaking of which," the department head resumed, "everybody needs to lube up and get ready to grab your ankles. Because that Yates guy - you remember him Special Agent Elbee? - Yeah, his lawyer dropped paperwork today at the 19th District Courthouse. They're filing a suit under the Federal

Tort Claims Act claiming that when the DoJ nabbed him for questioning in this case without what they say is sufficient probable cause, they violated Yates' civil rights and damaged his private property."

"Great," Danny grumbled. "Our litigious society strikes again."

"Oh, it gets better," Wiley's face beamed, but everyone on both sides of the camera knew he was being sarcastic. "They listed every agent, analyst, and administrator who's touched this investigation as an offending party. Some nonsense about 'contributory negligence' or whatnot. It's all legalese to me. I can speak six languages including Greek and Latin, but I swear these lawyers just make up words sometimes. Bottom line here: guess who's being sued? By name?" Danny's eyes closed tightly as he braced for another sudden onset headache. Jonas sang out the news like a game show announcer. "That's right, kids. You guys!"

"But" Elbee stammered, "we were just doing our jobs. Investigating leads."

"Oh, I know," Jonas offered sympathetically, "and for what it's worth, you can believe that I think you did the right thing. You can believe it, but of course, I'm not going to actually say that you did the right thing because if it comes down to my job on the line, you'd best believe that I'll throw you both under the bus in a heartbeat. But hey, those are the breaks. Water and blame, kids. They both flow downhill."

Nick's eyes were positively ecstatic as they locked onto Danny through the video teleconference monitor. "I'd be willing to testify under oath that he and I both gave you a direct order to leave Mr. Yates alone unless you had specific evidence implicating him in a felony and official authorization, including a signed warrant, prior to contact."

"I was totally there," Special Agent Jenkins chimed in from the second row, right behind Brown's shoulder. "That's how it went down."

"Of course, you know all about how things go down in the office, Carrie," Danny retorted. "You're usually going down under one desk or another." A wave of catcalls sounded from the crowd sitting around the D.C. watch floor.

"Jesus, Daniel," Sandra hissed through clenched teeth. Her voice was probably too quiet for the microphone on their side to pick up her admonition.

Dr. Wiley waived his hands in a downward motion. "Alright, alright... Simmer down, now." He returned his attention to the video wall. "Seriously, though. I wouldn't sweat it too much. You two are among dozens of named individuals and a handful of agencies that fall under the combined DHS/DoJ umbrella. It's all likely a ploy by Yates and his lawyer to garner attention. This probably won't go anywhere. These sorts of cases rarely do. Worst case scenario: the DoJ settles out of court for an undisclosed sum of money under terms of strict confidentiality. Which, of course, Yates will completely violate when he tries to parlay all of this into a book deal or something. Personally, I doubt it'll even get that far."

"Roger that," Danny nodded. "In the meantime?"

"In the meantime," Nick the Dick pushed in, "Jenkins has a theory I think we should all hear." Danny cycled a slow breath as his marginally competent coworker flipped through some working papers in a file folder that she had previously held out of view.

"I've been analyzing the open-source reporting on your case," she started.

I watched the news, Danny translated in his head.

"And most of the reporting related to the Constitutional Killer can been characterized as moderate or understandably critical," the fake redhead continued.

I like to say things that make me sound smarter than I really am...

"One outlet in particular seems overly sympathetic to the killer."

... because it hides my insecurities.

"When we take into consideration the fact that an insurgency requires covert support as well as overt support in order to operate successfully..."

I clear less than one tenth of the number of cases either Wakefield or Martin handle...

"... it seems that we need to consider the possibility..."

... but I still manage to stray into their lanes whenever I need some face time with the boss or a bullet for my evaluation, rather than take care of my own investigations...

"... that the Lonnie Chase network is somehow directly involved with the Constitutional Killer in some way."

... because I am a glory-mongering bitch.

"This relationship may extend past providing merely emotional or vocal support for the suspect," Jenkins assessed, completely unaware of Danny's inner dialogue, "and may include actual financial contribution or logistics support."

"'May' is a big universe," Sandra pointed. "Do you have any evidence that supports this assessment?"

"Not exactly," Jenkins dodged, "but it just makes

sense. It's totally logical."

"Logical," Danny repeated. "You keep using that word, but I don't think it means what you think it means."

"Let's try to keep an open mind here," Nick insisted.

"On a scale of pure probability," Dr. Wiley asked the faux redhead as she stood next to him, "what chance would you assign to your assessment being correct?"

"Very likely," Carrie insisted.

"There's a big gaping chasm that separates 'may' from 'very likely'," Wakefield countered.

"What percentage?" Father repeated.

Jenkins's eyes moved under the cover of her red mop as she struggled to find the right number. "I'd say between 75 and 80 percent likely."

"You can't be serious," Danny shook his head. "Sir, she's pulling that completely out of her -"

"Chase's corporate headquarters are in Plano," Jenkins cut in. "Texas is a convenient launching point for all of the killer's appearances so far."

"Texas is a big place," Sandra countered, "and our working theory right now is that the killer is mobile. Staying in motels or living out of an R/V or something. Not taking day trips from a centralized location. Until some new evidence gives us reason to believe otherwise, we'll stick with what we're doing."

"But you can't just discount my theory," Jenkins protested like a child throwing a tantrum.

"'Can't' is just 'won't' wrapped in a lie," Wakefield warned her.

"You need to open your mind to the possibility -" Nick jumped to his protege's defense.

"Why is she even here?" Danny's sense of humor had just about reached its limits. He turned to his partner. "Did you invite her into your investigation?" Sandra shook her head. "I know I didn't put her on the team. Hey Jenkins, who asked you to come monkey up our case?"

"I did," Nick the Dick answered.

"And who asked you to get involved in my investigation?" Sandra reposted. "With all due respect," she added without too much sincerity, "things will go a lot more smoothly if we can keep the Task Force free of outside interference." Rebuffed, Jenkins' face turned a bright crimson that was made even more visible by her cheaply dyed burgundy locks.

Dr. Wiley assumed control of the conversation once more. "There's a disconcerting number of reports coming in from the Border Patrol and FBI in the Southwest region about dead bodies found in the open," Jonas pointed. "Some of this might be us finally paying attention to a preexisting problem. Crossing the open desert like that can be treacherous. And some might be the work of the cartels. But is there any reason to suspect that our guy could also be responsible for some of it?"

"Given the context of the killer's last video," Sandra nodded, "I'd say that is likely. Yes, sir."

"What's the percentage on that?" Nick the Dick demanded. Danny and Sandra ignored him.

Dr. Wiley's eyes locked onto Wakefield's image on the big screen. "Your suspect's last message seemed to encourage exactly that kind of vigilantism. You mentioned a theory, Miss Elbee, in one of your assessments. You said that in your expert opinion this guy isn't just a garden variety psychopath. Please elaborate for the audience."

Sandra laid down her pen and lined up her argument. "Certainly, sir. As you all know, a typical serial killer operates toward a goal. In a typical case, the suspect's victims aren't just linked - they're usually steps, like a path toward his ultimate objective. Our role in law enforcement is usually to discover that motivation and head the suspect off before he reaches it."

"And?"

"Sir," she resumed, "we think that the Constitutional Killer is wholly atypical of serial killers. And not just because of his obvious skill set. We don't think the killer is working his way toward a particular objective, *per se,* but toward a desired end state."

Danny leaned toward the microphone on their end. "Emphasis on the 'state,' sir. We think the Constitutional Killer isn't so much killing his way up the food chain as he is crossing names off a shopping list."

"And what gets your name on the list?" Nick challenged him.

"Being un-American," Danny answered. "Or, more specifically, leading the country away from what our suspect thinks the Founding Fathers had in mind."

"If that's the case," Jonas thought aloud, "then he might be less concerned about his body count than some sort of idealistic goal to change domestic policy."

"Yes, sir. Special Agent Wakefield and I came to that same conclusion while discussing the case the other day. At this time, I believe it to be the theory most supported by the evidence we have in hand. It also fits the profile of our most likely suspects."

"And just how did you two find this Phillips guy?" Nick inquired.

"His name came up during the course of my investigation," Sandra dodged, "the details of which I am not inclined to share with outside personnel at this time."

"Well," Dr. Wiley challenged, "at the risk of sounding meddlesome, I have some task guidance for the both of you."

"We welcome your insight, sir," Sandra invited, as though she had any choice in the matter.

"Then you'll be happy to hear what we have next." Jonas looked around the watch floor. "Everyone who doesn't have Level 5 clearance: Get out. If you don't know what that is or whether you do or not, this means you." Almost everyone on the DHS HQ watch floor logged off of their workstations and vacated the premises. There were just a few murmurs, but no real protest. Danny was more than slightly tickled to watch Nick the Dick lead the exodus. At the faint sound of the SCIF's heavy vault door closing, Dr. Wiley gestured off screen. "Santa's little helper has brought you an early Christmas present." A familiar, diminutive man in a box-patterned shirt waddled into the camera's view.

"Oscar," Danny beamed. "Good to see you."

Oscar's face did not echo the sentiment, but at least he kept from audibly growling. "We're tracking your primary suspect's device," he announced without preamble. "As of last reporting, it was headed west along Interstate 10. He should be in Phoenix by lunch."

Danny racked his brain for a moment. "Other than the obvious - federal buildings, the usual characters, blah blah blah - is there anything special about Phoenix?"

"Jack McQueen and Chip MacDougal are having a meeting there tomorrow," Jonas announced. Anyone with any knowledge of American politics knew those names. Jack McQueen, the senior senator from Arizona, looked to be one of the frontrunners in the upcoming Republican Primary and by many estimates only a stone's throw away from becoming President. Chip MacDougal, a Blue Dog Democrat from neighboring Nevada, was his peer in age as well as years of service. "It's your typical political dog-and-pony show. A show of bipartisanship before the Fourth of July weekend to show that they can work across the aisle. Makes them both stronger in the polls." Dr. Wiley scratched his chin. "Thing is, though, a lot of folks'er complaining that McQueen's too moderate. Calling him a RINO and all that. And, well, Chip MacDougal's just about as Progressive as they come."

"We assess the conference is his next target," Oscar offered. "At least, we would assess that, if we were at all involved in this. Which we aren't. Especially if that assessment is wrong."

"The Senate Minority Leader and a potential future President of the United States in the same place at the same time. It's as ripe a target as the Constitutional Killer could hope for. And Phillips is headed straight for it."

"We're on our way," Elbee declared as she reached to deactivate the camera on their end.

"I don't wanna spook this guy," Wiley continued.

"Not if you can avoid it. The Senate just contracted Bywater Security Group for the event. They'll be McQueen and MacDougal's PSD in Phoenix."

"Bywater?" Elbee asked.

"A top-dollar company based in Virginia Beach that employs former SEALs as security contractors, advisors and trainers," Jonas explained.

"I know who they are," Sandra countered. "They're the mercenary thugs who shot a bunch of civilians in Iraq, right?"

"If by 'bunch' you mean four," Oscar corrected her, "and by 'civilians' you mean -"

"You know what I mean. But if the senators want personal security detachments for their appearance then why use contractors? Why not use the police? Or the Secret Service?"

"Obviously they don't think regular law enforcement is up to the job," Danny offered. "Government officials like these guys always have an inflated opinion of themselves. I remember one time when I was in the Corps, the Vice President came out to Baghdad on a visit. The guy spent millions of taxpayer dollars to have a team of a dozen or so Bywater mercenaries escort him through the combat zone. In the VP's estimate, his normal Secret Service contingent and fifty thousand US military personnel on the ground at the time was an insufficient force to ensure his personal safety." He blew out a puff of air in disgust.

"Yeah," Dr. Wiley ordered, "well, I sent word that you'd be meeting up with the senators' entourage. As far as anyone knows, we're all just trying to score some *wastah* with the bigwigs so that they don't indict us all for the Yates fiasco. Because of the outside players involved and the possibility of leaks, we haven't said anything about a direct threat. Keep our suspicions on the down-low. Integrate yourselves into the local chain of command and coordinate security for the event. If Phillips is there, you're heroes. If not, try not to look like complete taints."

"Sir," a voice sounded from the back of the watch floor, "we may have an 'in' with Phillips." Jonas and Oscar turned to the back of the room, where Derek Martin still sat logged onto somebody's terminal.

"Lay it on me," Wiley ushered.

"It seems that we've identified Phillips as a suspect," he summarized, "but lack the probable cause that usually leads us to him. What if we backfill it?" Derek took the quartet's silence as a sign that they - like so many people - needed him to explain things to them. So he drew a deep breath. "This morning's report from Quantico just came in - I'm sure nobody has had time to read it yet - and one of our people was able to use the PRIMER database to match up at least some of the casings from the New Orleans crime scene to a gun bought at a gun store in Mesa, Arizona. It was bought by a guy who was active duty at the time of purchase. His CANON profile indicates he probably knew Phillips - who could have bought it from him at any time."

"It's flimsy and inadmissible," Wiley stroked his chin.

"Sir," Derek said defensively, "the linkages are two sigmas beyond the statistical norm. Surely-"

"It'll never fly on its own," Jonas cut in with an emphatic shake of his head. "Elbee, can you turn it into something that gives you an excuse to zero in on him?"

Sandra thought for a moment. "I don't think so, Sir. Not without using the classified data."

"My people will disappear me if you do that," Oscar grumbled. "Please don't mistake that objection as encouragement."

"You'll just have to do this the old fashioned way," Jonas advised. "And that means catching him in the act. I don't want anyone throwing this out on a technicality. Or throwing any of us in jail."

"Yes, Father," Danny signed off.

CHAPTER 23

WAKEFIELD AND ELBEE caught a lucky break and just barely made the next shuttle flight from El Paso to Phoenix before the doors closed. It was a quick hop in a little puddle jumper, but it shaved a few hours from their transit time when compared to driving from Texas to Arizona. And they both agreed that the sooner they caught up with the senators, the more likely they were to get ahead of their quarry. Their plane had barely attained cruising altitude when Danny's phone vibrated.

"Isn't that supposed to be turned off in flight?" Sandra's eyes were full of judgement and scorn.

"We're on duty," Danny reminded her while he reached into his pocket. "And the airline doesn't care - as long as you pay a little more." His eyes flashed as he pressed the green virtual button on his screen. "Which Uncle Sam did." Danny's attention turned into the phone - held out between the two of them. He keyed it for speaker phone. The passenger cabin was sparsely populated, and those folks who were scattered around all isolated themselves within their own little worlds with headphones. "What's up, Little D?"

"Nothing work-related, buddy," the phone's disembodied voice responded. "But Aliyah wanted to know if you'd still be joining us for fireworks over the river this weekend."

"Assume yes," Danny replied. "If I'm in town then I'm still on. If not, there's nothing I can do."

"And will you be bringing anyone?" Derek coyly asked.

"I dunno."

"Elbee," Derek offered, "do you have plans?"

"I didn't know I was invited," Sandra answered in surprise.

"I'm sure Aliyah would love to meet *akh akbar Daniyal*'s new partner."

Sandra shot her partner a sideways glance. "Big brother," Danny translated.

"Sure," she smiled, "I'd love to come. Thanks."

"Great," Derek chimed, "and hey, Big D, grab some decent tequila while you're out there."

"This close to the border, I might be able to score some good *mezcal*," Danny offered.

"No worms," Little D countered, "you know that grosses Aliyah out."

"I'll double check the bottle," he assured.

"Excellent! Well, I'll let you go."

"Hey," Danny interjected before his friend could hang up, "text us the contact info for somebody responsible for this security goat rope so that we can link up with them when we get there."

"Will do," Derek acknowledged.

"Okay. See you on the other side," Danny signed off.

The two agents rode in silence for a moment, then Sandra turned to her partner. "Your boss is trying to shoplift my case."

"I'm not surprised," he shook his head. "Not in the least. There's a reason we call him 'Nick the Dick.' He'll do anything to make himself look better than he is. Or more important than he really is." Danny's mind recalled his supervisor's laundry list of indiscretions and unprofessional sleights. The flight to Phoenix was not long enough to recite them aloud. "Don't sweat it. We play this right and the whole thing's over in a day or two. Nothing left but the paperwork."

"I hope so," Sandra sighed. "So, fireworks on the river? What's that all about?"

"Big display over the Potomac every Fourth of July in D.C." he explained. "You can see it from Derek and Aliyah's balcony. They've got a little apartment in town. We typically get together each year for our own little private Star Spangled Spectacular. Beer, apple pie, the whole shebang."

"Sounds nice."

"Her folks came here from Lebanon," he continued. "Aliyah got naturalized in college. Nursing school. She really loves to celebrate her adoptive nation."

"That's cute." Sandra looked at him quizzically, "So, does she drink, too, or are you guys just that insensitive to her culture?"

Danny shook his head. "It's a popular myth that

alcohol consumption is *harram* throughout the entire Middle East," he lectured. "There are plenty of countries where attitudes about a lot of things are much more secular than you might imagine. Especially around the Mediterranean. When I was in Bahrain, for example, we used to get a kick outta watching all of the Saudi tourists driving across the border for the weekend. Some Audi or Lexus would pull over, the women would get out of the back seat of their car, take off their headscarves, and then hop up to the front seats and drive their husbands and brothers around while they were on our side. And you'd see other cars on their way back pull over, the women jump out, wrap up, and get back into the back seat so that their men could resume in their so-called 'rightful place' before anyone in their own country saw them breaking the rules. Stuff like that varies from one country to the next."

"I didn't know that," Sandra admitted. "I thought all Arabs were forbidden from drinking."

"Hardly," Danny chuckled. "Generally, Muzzies forbid booze. But not all Arabs are good Muslims. Or even Muslims at all. There's this moonshine they drink in Lebanon called *arak*. It looks like watered down skim milk and tastes like rubbing alcohol." Wakefield's face puckered at the memory of his last glass of iced *arak*. "Drinking that stuff is like getting tear gassed. Every time I do it, I swear it'll be the last."

Elbee's eyebrow shot up. "You get tear gassed a lot?"

"Not for the fun of it," he answered. "But you know how it goes. Occupational hazard."

"I've been in the FBI for six years Daniel," she retorted, "and I've never been tear gassed."

"Huh," Danny mused as he closed his eyes and relaxed into his seat. "I guess one of us is doing it wrong." He popped his own headphones into his ears and turned on the Lonnie Chase Program, which was being rebroadcast on one of the in-flight entertainment channels.

*   *   *

"And did you see this new report from ICE?" Kyp asked. "This just came out yesterday. The one where a woman told Immigrations and Customs Enforcement agents that she was in Texas the other night with a group of people and a ghost killed them all?"

"All but her, you mean," Factcheck Fred pointed.

"Well obviously all but her," Kyp conceded. "I mean, dead people don't usually talk to the authorities."

"Not usually," Fred joked.

"Where was this?" Lonnie asked.

"She ran into a hospital in El Paso and told them that a ghost appeared in the middle of the night and shot all of her friends," Kyp explained.

"And this shooing was in their house or something?" Lonnie baited. He knew the real answer.

"Uh, not exactly," Kyp hedged. "I mean, if by 'in their house' you mean 'sneaking through the desert after illegally crossing the border in the dead of night,' then yeah."

"In the dead of night," Fred chuckled. "That's great. Nice pun-manship."

"So, then, the cops arrested her, right?" Lonnie came back. "I mean, since she was breaking the law by coming into the country illegally - and she admitted to that - they put her on a bus and shipped her back to Mexico, right?"

"Uh, no."

"And why not?" Lonnie begged. "She was breaking the law. Did they let her stay so that she could be a material witness to a crime?"

"Actually," Kyp half sang, "they let her stay because she gave birth right there in the hospital to a baby boy. So now they have to let her remain in our country to raise her kid, the instant US citizen."

"That's two new Democrat voters right there," Factcheck Fred offered. "But don't call the kid an 'anchor baby' or someone will get offended."

"Actually," Kyp offered, "you can fairly well bet that the dead folks will vote Democrat, too. Most dead folks do."

"When we get back from the break I wanna talk about this some more," Lonnie said. "But first: our sponsor this half hour is Goldstein Financial Group…"

*   *   *

An aggressive drumbeat thundered in Wakefield's ears. It dulled the thud that accompanied his fists impacting their heavy target again and again.

An hour ago, Bywater's team leader - a guy by the name of Isaac "Woody" Franklin, whose shirts all fit him as if they had come from the little boy's clothing department instead of the men's - assured the agents that his men had the entire security situation well in hand. He explained their operational plan to Elbee over dinner and drinks at some hole-in-the-wall

Mexican joint, completely unaware that her male counterpart was also at the table.

Danny was no fan of contractors. *Let the troops do the soldiering, the cops do the policing, and if you aren't one of them then just go home.* That was what he always said. As soon as Woody finished outlining his plan, the agents left the mercenaries and checked into their own hotel.

Now, the former Marine's left hand felt like a dumbbell as he lifted it up to protect his head from an anticipated punch to his face. Danny drove another right cross into the hotel gym's heavy bag. Every blow hit like a hammer trying to knock the stuffing out of the seldom-used bag's backside. He quickly retracted his right hand, then doubled back and delivered an uppercut which would have bent a steel girder. The bag folded, then sprung back to its elongated form. Danny followed it up with a left hook that turned into an elbow strike to an imaginary face.

Sweat poured down from his head and showered his body with saltwater. Thursday night was ladies' night at Black Sam's, so when Danny was in D.C., he ducked into the dojo for fight night with the guys. It was the same crowd each week, more-or-less, but the men all came from different fighting backgrounds, so there was a good mix of different styles represented each session. Danny tried not to fight the same guy twice in a row. It helped him to focus on the fight and not the fighter. To test his skills - born on the schoolyard and honed by the Marines - and keep them sharp. Being out of town on a Thursday forced Danny to miss fight night every now and again - but it also forced him to miss his weekly anger management sessions. In his mind, the positives outweighed the negatives.

Danny closed with the swaying bag, seized it in a clinch, and held his head tightly against his target. He drove his right knee into it where a normal man's abdomen would be with enough force to cause serious internal injuries to just about any adult. Then again. And again. His sweat made the bag slippery, which only encouraged him to ratchet his arms tighter and squeeze harder. The force from another knee strike popped one of his headphones out of his ear, but he ignored it and delivered two more. Then he pushed off the bag and reset himself in a boxer's stance just a step away, left foot forward, ready to go another round with his simulated opponent.

"Ahem," a familiar voice sounded from behind him. Danny spun to see his partner standing just inside the gym door, leaned against the foggy, full-wall mirror.

"Elbee," he pulled out the other earbud and breathed heavily. "S'up?"

"You weren't at the bar," she noted as she read the front of the black t-shirt plastered to his chest. The slogan I AM COMFORTABLE WITH VIOLENCE looked like it had been painted onto his pecs in photo negative by an epileptic tattoo artist. Danny could tell by her expression that Sandra tried to hide her contempt for the sentiment. Curiosity - or concern - drove one of Sandra's eyebrows up toward her hairline. "Is everything okay?"

"You bet." His voice was light despite the panting.

Sandra's eyes jumped to the heavy bag, then back to his. "Guy owe you money?"

Danny snatched up his nearby water bottle and shook his head side to side. "Talked smack about my mom." He grimaced. "But he's Canadian. Whaddaya expect?"

"Aaah," she nodded in mock understanding. "The trash-talking Canadians strike again." She gave the bag an inquisitive look. "Think we should bring him in for questioning?"

"Nah," Danny half spat, "we'll just let him stew in a puddle of his own puke and blood for a while. Standard procedure."

"Can't argue with procedure," she surrendered. Her face grew more serious. "Look, Daniel, we've got a big day tomorrow. Don't burn yourself out."

"Don't worry, Elbee," he anticipated where this conversation was going. "I've got plenty." She remained fixed against the wall, neither her body nor her mind moved by his words. "Seriously. Three things you just don't do the night before the game: whiskey, women, or wear yourself out."

"I hate sports metaphors."

"Well, you can guarantee that Woody and his bearded boy band are doing - and thinking - pretty much the same thing in their hotel right now."

Sandra drew herself up to her full height and crossed her arms. "Is there anything about tomorrow's plan that you think we need to change?"

Danny took a long pull from his water bottle before he answered. "I'm sure we'll be fine."

"If you think we need to do anything -"

"Can it," he said bluntly. "I don't mean you. The meeting. Cancel the whole thing. Move it. Lock out the press and the public. Keep it from becoming a circus."

"We can't," she shook her head. "The senators would never agree to it."

"Your case, your call," he shrugged. "Why are we friggin' here, Elbee?"

Sandra looked puzzled at her partner's question. Maybe she thought he was delirious from hydration. "You heard Dr. Wiley. We're here to make sure nothing happens to the senators tomorrow."

"That's the problem," he hissed. "I thought our duty was to catch a killer."

"Which we will do tomorrow if he shows up."

Wakefield sniffed. "You know, Elbee? Action is faster than reaction. In a situation like this. In life. Events are driven by actors, not reactors."

"What are you trying to say, Daniel?"

"I'm trying to say that sooner or later you're gonna have to make a decision. Which is more important to you: protect the senators or catch the bad guy? 'Cause at the end of the day we can probably do one, but not both. It's your case, Elbee. It's your call."

"Now, if you have any concerns about Franklin or his plan -"

Danny shook his head. "If the use of hair products and a penchant for wearing designer sunglasses after sunset is any indicator of combat proficiency, those Bywater guys must be world class fighters. It's hardly their first rodeo. I'm sure they know what they're doing. But that doesn't change what I said. Right here, right now, we can only do one of two things. Serve or protect."

Sandra shook her head. "It's our duty to do both, Daniel."

Wakefield huffed the last of the bad air out of his lungs. "Well, I'm not sure that's possible this time. Look, Elbee, this isn't a cut on you, me, or anyone.

This guy's just too friggin' good. This isn't a garden variety, textbook serial killer here. Phillips is too perfect. He's perfectly asymmetrical. He's calling the shots. He's prepared - whatever his next step is, he's ready. He's been in the driver's seat from the beginning."

"What happened to Mr. 'Oh, we're gonna get this guy?' Where's your commitment now, Daniel?"

"Oh, I'm committed."

"I don't think so," she countered. "I think you're addicted. To the chase. I don't think you want the case to really end. I think a part of you is still stuck in the Marines. Oh, you put up a good front with your supposed quest for the quiet life in the anonymous shadows of a back-office desk job. But I think your mind is still stuck in hunting mode. I think you're addicted to the thrill of the chase, Daniel. And that hunting Phillips is more important to you than actually catching him."

"You're way off the mark here, Elbee. I know my duty."

"Fine," she glared for a moment. The two agents stood there in silence for a moment. "Well, then," she turned for the door, "be sure to get a good night's sleep."

Danny downed another swig of water, then popped his headphones back into his sweat-soaked ears and drank in the dark dirge.

I'm good, I'm fine.
This life, divine.
No hate. No shame.
No one, to blame…

CHAPTER 24

MANY OF THE PEOPLE who streamed into the Phoenix Convention Center took a moment to thank the boys in blue on their way inside. Their attitude was a welcome break from the cluster of self-victimized protestors a couple of blocks away who rallied around misspelled signs and misinformed chants of perceived police brutality. A contingent of officers from the Phoenix Police Department comprised the bulk of the event's security. There were two officers posted street-side at each corner of the building. Eight more officers maintained checkpoints and roving patrols inside the 6000 square foot hall. Sixteen noses sniffed the air for trouble. Thirty-two eyes watched for signs of trouble. And citizens who arrived in ones and twos became a few hundred, then grew to almost a thousand people gathered into the center's main hall to hear their elected representatives speak.

In the Green Room, Senators Jack McQueen, the senior Republican from Arizona, and Chip MacDougal, an equally elder statesman from Nevada and the leader of the Senate's Democrat minority, exchanged off-color jokes over rich cups of Colombian roast. A half dozen short haired men in dark suits - all of whom looked like they just leapt off the pages of various fitness magazines - were strategically arranged around the room. Two more stood outside the door wearing stern expressions, earpiece radios, and designer sunglasses that were perfectly identical to their six brothers' gear. Sandra glanced at one of the private security contractors, then back to her partner.

"Hey, Wakefield," Sandra smiled, "you were in the service. Why aren't you cut like these guys?"

"Because unlike these Former Action Guys, I actually worked for a living." Danny made no attempt to hush his voice. "Like we used to say in the Corps: SEAL stands for Sleep, Eat, and Lift." Out of the corner of his eye he saw that one of the meatheads almost smirked.

Sandra lowered her voice until it became little more than a whisper. "Maybe they should've changed it to Sex, Eat, and Lift," she teased while sizing up that same bodyguard, whom Wakefield mentally dubbed Laughing Boy. Laughing Boy saw her undress him with her eyes, which prompted him to jerk his eyebrow up and pucker his lips for a fraction of a second.

Danny's eyebrows furrowed. "I thought you didn't like to mix business and pleasure."

"I don't," the blonde federal agent grinned, "but then again, I don't work with these guys."

"Easy, Elbee," Wakefield warned, "most of these shaven gorillas come away from Coronado with the clap. And being Sailors, if one of them gets it, they all have it."

"So, Special Agent Elbee," Senator McQueen called from his seat, "how are our security precautions today?"

Sandra snapped back to the situation at hand. "As thorough as can be expected, Senator. We have two dozen men in and around the building doing everything they can to keep things safe for everyone."

"I talked to Cindy Dagenhart just the other day," MacDougal commented. "She told me you were heading the Constitutional Killer case. How's that coming along?"

Elbee straightened at the name Senator MacDougal had just dropped. Cynthia Dagenhart was the Director of the Department of Homeland Security. Her bosses' boss's boss's boss. The fact that the senator casually mentioned a happenstance meeting with a Cabinet member as if he had just commented on a sandwich reminded Sandra of Dr. Wiley's orders, relayed through Agent Martin. *A little face time...* Chip MacDougal was not just another potential target, she reminded herself. He was the Senate minority leader. Killer or no killer, one wrong move today could spell the end of her career. "We're confident in the direction our investigation is going," she answered with her most professional face.

"Was there a specific threat against us?" he pressed. "Is that why you're here?"

"Nothing specific, Senator," she shook her head. "But given the optics of the situation, Homeland Security wanted to maintain an official presence on the ground. Special Agent Wakefield and I were in the area anyway, so our bosses flexed us here for a day or two."

"Like we told your mercs," Danny chimed in, "this is all precautionary. With the killer's last presumed location in this region our people saw the potential for trouble."

"So, the Constitutional Killer was behind the desert murders?"

"At this time we believe he was responsible for some, yes."

MacDougal casually stabbed a finger at McQueen. "I told you so, Jack."

"That's an assessment, Chip. Some analyst's wild-assed guess. Not actual confirmed evidence." The Republican from the state of Arizona looked at them in apology. "No offense, Agents. I'm sure you and your people are working hard on this one," he turned back to his host, "but I'm not paying out on just an assessment."

"Bullshit Jack," MacDougal scoffed. "You owe me a bottle of scotch. One that's truly eighteen years old, too. Not like that -" the older gentleman stopped himself as he caught a glimpse of Elbee out of the corner of his eye and cleared his throat meaningfully, "- I mean, ah, you remember. Anyway. Pay up. Don't be a sore loser."

Danny turned to his watch in a desperate bid to keep his mind from connecting the terms 'elder Senator,' 'eighteen year old,' and 'sore' in myriad meaningful combinations.

"No proof, no booze," Jack McQueen held.

"If you didn't believe the killer was around, you wouldn't've hired the muscle," his congressional counterpart reposted. "Face it, Jack. Money never lies. The danger is real."

"Fine, fine…"

A knock sounded from the door. Two raps spaced exactly one second apart. One of the private security contractors next to the door reached over blindly and answered with a single knock of his own. "Gentlemen," he announced in a calm, firm voice, "two minutes to show time." The senators stood from their modest circular table and turned to their respective aids. Each of the congressmen received whispered reminders or assurances from their handlers. Blue and red ties were straightened. Invisible bits of dust were brushed off their expensive wool suit jackets. An alert went out over the radio frequency that the guards, local police and federal agents used for the event.

"So far so good," Elbee remarked.

"The day's not done," Wakefield cautioned her. "They do their jobs. We do ours. Just stick to the plan. These Bywater Security guys know their tradecraft. The gorillas will escort the principals and maintain formation according to their SOPs. Local cops maintain the perimeter. We provide oversight, move freely, and if anyone tangos up we intercept them while the principals bug out."

*   *   *

Senator MacDougal made his introductory remarks, then surrendered the camera to his longtime friend and colleague from the neighboring state. Jack McQueen, a veteran of the previous generation's war, stood confidently as he began a speech filled with patriotic resolve, bipartisan principles and overtures that called for national unity. Fifty seconds into the Republican senator's yarn a voice buzzed on the radio.

"Two-Adam-Thirty-two. Suspicious package. Southeast corner." Elbee's eyes locked with Wakefield's as they roved around the edge of the seated crowd. Neither of them knew precisely who 2A-32 was, but the 2A prefix belonged to the PPD officers outside. For this event, the Bywater contractors used the radio designators Spartan-01 through Spartan-08, plus Delta-01 and Delta-02 for the two drivers who waited at armored Suburbans in the parking garage caddy-corner to the convention center. As federal agents, Elbee and Wakefield had chosen the callsigns Eagle-01 and Eagle-02, respectively. This was somebody's idea of a simple, clean communications plan.

"Copy that, Thirty-two," Elbee spoke calmly into her mic. "Standby all players."

"Thirty-two, Eagle Two," Wakefield asked, "can you safely ascertain the nature of the object from your position? Over." The Constitutional Killer case was Elbee's case, so she was in charge on the scene. But Danny had years of combat experience and far more training dealing with situations like this than his FBI partner. *Any clue…* he thought to himself.

"Eagle Two, Two Adam Thirty-two. I see an unattended black bag next to a trash bin. It wasn't there a few minutes ago." Elbee's eyes went wide as the same obvious thought went through her mind as everyone else on the team: the bag could very well contain an Improvised Explosive Device.

The location for the town hall meeting had been announced in advance, but the Phoenix Convention

Center was actually comprised of three buildings. A massive building at the southeast corner of 3rd Street and Monroe; the smaller building at the southwest corner of the same intersection; and an even smaller adjoining building to the south of that. In the interest of security, the fact that the senators would hold court in the mid-sized facility was not disclosed until people actually arrived at the event.

And the suspected IED was smack in the middle of all three buildings. Right where - if it was powerful enough - it could not miss if it exploded.

"Romeo, Romeo," Sandra quietly spoke into her mic. Romeo was the pre-arranged brevity code that ordered the senators' immediate evacuation from the convention center and withdrawal to a pre-designated safe location. "All personnel, I repeat. Romeo. Execute."

A series of acknowledgements sounded over the radio as a pair of Bywater contractors briskly took the stage - one from either side. Each seized their designated dignitary by the arms and shoulders and scurried back to the wings. The crowd stirred in their seats while Elbee and Wakefield quickly and quietly slipped out the nearest exit. Before the door was fully closed, the agents broke into a dead run.

"Two Adam Thirty-two to all stations," the cop's voice came back onto the radio. "I'm going to check out the bag."

"Negative, Three-Two," Wakefield barked as the agents joined the Bywater team at the stage's rear service door - which was manned by a uniformed PPD officer. "Secure the area and keep bystanders away until EOD arrives. Over." Danny bit back a curse as the agents, in tandem with eight pipe hitters with their Sigs all drawn, escorted the senators through the convention center's corridors. The lack of on-site Explosives Ordinance Disposal technicians was a critical vulnerability in their plan that he had mentioned from the beginning. But EOD personnel were a rare commodity. Just like in the Corps, most law enforcement agencies simply did not have enough qualified technicians to preemptively cover most operational desires. It was simply a case of too little talent spread too thinly across a large playing field. And it often led to good men putting themselves into unnecessary danger by treading where they were neither qualified nor prepared. Just like 2A-32 seemed ready to do.

"Spartan Zero-One to all stations," one of the Bywater contractors barked into his mic, "exiting building zero-one. Northwest corner. Ten Falcons plus both packages. Execute." A split second later the team burst through the convention center's most northwesterly door. A few paces away, the two PPD officers who had been monitoring the intersection of 2nd and Monroe Streets were already on guard, their guns drawn as their eyes scanned the area for surprises. "Moving to building zero-six!" the contractor yelled. On cue, the PPD officers rushed into the intersection and immediately brought all traffic to a halt. As soon as the sound of barking tires ended, the Bywater team pushed the senators through the intersection and straight for the parking garage located diagonally across the street.

"All stations," the radio buzzed, "Two Adam Thirty-two. There's nothing in the bag but a pot. Like a pressure cooker or something. But there's nothing in it. It's empty."

"Goddammit, Three-Two!" Wakefield hissed. Though he did not transmit his curse over the radio, the team members around him clearly received his message. The Boston Marathon bombing of 2013, law enforcement agencies had become especially leery of pressure cookers - which were used by terrorists as the containers for a set of IEDs that killed so many innocents on what was supposed to be a beautiful spring day.

"All stations, Eagle One," Sandra ordered, "maintain ready and threat scan. Be on the lookout for anything suspicious. Over." She cut her mic and cast Danny a sideways glance as the group stepped into the parking garage. "Looks our guy rope-a-doped us again," she grumbled.

Nobody doubted for a second that the Constitutional Killer was behind this tactical boondoggle. The question that buzzed in the back of Wakefield's mind, though, was, *If the IED was the feint, where's the hook?* The security detail continued to move to safety at a quick shuffle.

Two hurried steps inside the garage, a thunderous explosion rang out from the convention center's southeast corner. Exactly where 2A-32 had reported the dummy IED. Exactly where the officer had said he was standing a few seconds ago.

The security detail all flinched, ducking down instinctively at the sound of the blast. "Avalanche!" someone yelled on the radio net. Avalanche. It was a legacy brevity code from the war. It meant that a boobytrap had been found. The codeword was usually immediately followed by everyone in the area diving for cover or out of the building they occupied. It certainly prompted everyone in the senators' security detail to drop low to the ground. To their credit, the Bywater operators were the first gophers to pop their heads back up and resume pulling the principals along their track. The first of the Suburbans, driven by Delta One, was parked safely in the garage only a few yards away and within clear line of sight. *Delta Two is upstairs,* Danny reminded himself. Elbee and Wakefield, a few steps behind the main contingent, fought to catch back up with the others.

"Break!" Spartan One shouted. At once, the cluster of guards divided into two smaller teams of four men. Each fire team moved in a new direction with a senator at its nucleus. "Spartan One moving to Delta One with Alpha," he transmitted.

"Spartan Five moving to Delta Two with Bravo," Laughing Boy announced.

Wakefield waived his partner toward the nearest group. "Go with MacDougal!" he yelled. "I've got McQueen!" He matched actions to words, sparing only the merest glance to ensure his partner followed his lead.

Each of the senators traveled in an armored SUV. To minimize risk to the principals, the security team had pre-parked the senators' vehicles on separate floors within the garage. Spartans 01 through 04 rushed Chip MacDougal across the ground floor with Special Agent Elbee in tow. The rest of the Bywater crew and Wakefield spirited Jack McQueen up to the far end of the second level ramp where his truck awaited.

"Spartan One at Delta One. Loading the package now. Standby." Danny had previously been nervous about how clear radio transmissions would be within the parking garage. Fortunately it seemed that particular concern was irrelevant.

His academic worry was replaced with utter dread as a massive *BOOM!* erupted from the garage's ground level. Concussive waves rang against concrete and steel as they overtook Wakefield's team. Time stood still. The universe was silent, then muffled. When sound finally came back to his world, it washed over Wakefield like an ocean wave hitting a beach.

"I say again," Sandra's voice called over the cracking radio, "Victor One, Delta One and Spartan Two. All Tango Uniform. Over." *Torn Up.* A military euphemism for "destroyed," typically used when operational urgency precluded the use of emotional words like killed or dead. Vehicle One, its driver, and another of the Bywater guards had just been killed by the Constitutional Killer's real attack - which Wakefield assumed was a car bomb of some sort.

"Eagle One?" Danny demanded. "What's your status? Over."

"I'm okay," the radio cracked again. Or was she coughing? Danny could not tell. "We need a medic down here, stat! I'm sending the package and one Falcon to you. Over."

"Roger that," Danny growled. *Why does Sandra need a medic?* he asked himself. But the answer to that question, he knew, would have to wait. In no time at all, one of the pipe hitters emerged from the ground floor. The ripped and ragged remains of his suit were covered in dust. A few splatters of red were sprinkled on his shirt. He ran up the garage's ramp at the best speed that Senator MacDougal seemed to be able to manage. *What about the other two Bywater guards?* Danny signaled Laughing Boy to hold short for a moment so that his teammate and charge could join them. Once the half dozen became a gang of eight, they made for the last armored truck as quickly as possible. The driver was already inside the second Suburban and had the engine running, ready to go.

"Secure the area!" Laughing boy ordered. His teammates fanned out. Each swept an area for threats. Senator MacDougal's babysitter stooped low and checked the black Suburban's undercarriage for surprises. Laughing Boy circled the vehicle with Senator McQueen so that the two could load from the truck's far side. "I've got Bravo!" he yelled. "Get Bravo into the back!" The battle-damaged contractor complied while the rest of their teammates maintained their vigil. "Spartan Zero-Five to all stations. At Delta Two. Commencing EXFIL." *Exfiltration* was a word the military had adopted a long time ago. It was faster and sounded much more professional than the phrase "bat out of hell," but the idea was the same.

As soon as the back doors were shut the Suburban launched into motion. Tires squealed at the far end of the parking level where the truck made its quick turn down the exit ramp. Danny was about to take what was left of the Bywater team downstairs to Elbee's last known position when a quick pair of flashes lit the truck's interior, accompanied by the appearance of a spiderweb pattern on the driver's window. Then a third flash.

"On me!" Danny ordered as he ran up to the black Suburban. The Bywater contractors followed suit in a loose formation with two hitters on each side of the lane, weapons drawn and ready as they approached. The driver darted from the truck a split second before another light, much larger this time, filled the SUV's cabin with a sustained, rolling orange-yellow glow.

"Holy -" Danny managed. He bolted to the open driver's side door and hit the button to release the rear locks, then rushed to the door behind him and checked on the occupants. Wisps of smoke carried the smell of burnt hair mixed with cooked flesh and melted plastic through the passenger compartment - which itself was covered with burn marks and a fine layer of soot. Danny fought a wave of bile that threatened to leap out of his mouth.

"All stations, Eagle Two. We need containment on the Convention Center parking garage. Now! And push all available medical personnel to the second floor, stat!"

Then Jack McQueen's eyes snapped open.

Danny yelped in surprise, then plucked the knife clipped to his trouser pocket and cut the senator's seat belt. As gently as speed allowed, he lowered McQueen to the pavement and found an erratic pulse deep beneath raw flesh and charred clothing. Out of the corner of his eye he saw a pair of Bywater contractors jogging up to his position. "Get the other one! Now!" The duo followed their instructions.

"He's conscious," one contractor announced as they carried Senator MacDougal over and laid him next to his colleague.

Mother of God... Danny thought as he keyed his mic. "This is Eagle Two. I need medics on the ramp between the second and third floor of the parking garage. Stat!"

"Just as soon as we've -" a PPD officer started.

"Belay that!" Danny barked. "Command priority override." He checked MacDougal's neck, too. Again, an uneven pulse vibrated under crispy skin. "I need every ambulance you can find in this building, now!

We have men down and in critical condition! Including both senators!" Danny turned to the contractors, all focused on rendering what combat care they could to their charges under the less-than-ideal circumstances. "Treat for shock," he ordered, "and keep on them 'til help arrives. I'm going after the driver." One of the Bywater operators absently waived a bloodied hand in his general direction in dismissal as each of the men knelt next to their charges and administered tactical first aid.

Danny ran around the blind corner with his weapon at the low ready, then sprinted down the exit ramp. "All stations," he announced into his mic, "be on the lookout for a male on foot trying to exit the garage. Do not let anyone out. Repeat. Nobody leaves this building unless they've been checked by me or Eagle One." *God, Elbee,* he thought about two thirds of the way to the ground floor, *please be okay.*

A dozen yards ahead of him, a pair of PPD officers tried to stop a lone black male as he tried to walk away from the garage exit. The man looked disheveled and confused, like he was in shock. Then one of the officers placed his left hand on the pedestrian's right shoulder to corral him back into the building. The black man seized the officer's hand, cranked hard on the wrist to lock the officer's arm and reached around behind the cop with his inside hand - all the while using the surprised officer as a shield between himself and the second cop's drawn pistol. The trapped patrolman winced at a punch to his lower back - beneath his protective vest. Then his face twisted in horror as his assailant pulled the officer's own gun and snapped two shots into his partner's chest. A third shot punched into the cop's back at point blank range. As the blue shirted men fell, the black man knelt down on one knee. He took careful aim and fired a single round up the ramp at Danny, who had been lining up his own shot. Danny instinctively dodged left, then came up to see the back of the suspect's shoes as he fled the scene.

"Contact!" Danny radioed as he gave pursuit. "Two men down, first floor exit onto Van Buren! Send medics! Suspect fleeing on foot," he narrated as he turned, "headed north on First Street from Van Buren. Black male. Athletic build. Black pants and a wife beater. Eagle Two is on foot. Send back-up!" Danny pushed his legs harder and sucked down as much oxygen as he could move. "Suspect is armed and dangerous."

Danny spied his suspect to his left as the agent crossed Polk Street a block north of the garage. The black man had opened up his lead though and was already headed onto Central Street. Danny used his radio to update the rest of the team, whom he hoped were in the process of setting up a net to contain their swiftly fleeing target. Danny found new speed as he rounded onto Central -

- and the wind fell completely out of his sails at the sight of nearly two hundred college students, mostly black. Most of them held signs that protested the various alleged police abuses around the country.

Phoenix Police Department cruisers were two blocks out in each direction and closing as quickly as they could. The protestors, apparently unmoved by the commotion just a few blocks away, grew quite agitated at the sight of a black brother being chased by a white guy whose face just exuded "cop stink." And Danny saw that they became even more animated in the face of an even greater police presence as his PPD backup converged on their location. The mild rumblings of a college demonstration grew into a furor as a growing number of young black people saw themselves at the center of their own civil rights war. *Can't get caught in the middle of a race riot,* Danny sighed with resignation. Rather than provoke his own lynching, he broke off his pursuit of the suspect. A part of Danny's mind wished religious services in America held as much zeal as political rallies, even as he surrendered to the conclusion that there was no way he would catch his suspect today.

*　　*　　*

Danny spat and swore. *Some days, you just can't win.* Then Special Agent Wakefield holstered his sidearm and cued his mic again. "Eagle One, Eagle Two. SITREP. Over." The microsecond between racing heartbeats stretched into a weeklong moment of silence as he waited for a situational report.

"Eagle Two," a man's voice answered, "Spartan Zero-Seven. Advise you return to Victor One ASAP."

In spite of everything that had just happened, utter dread crept into Danny's chest for the first time today. He made it back to the parking garage at his best possible speed. When he entered the lower level once more, all of his efforts were rewarded with a vision of complete and utter carnage. For a moment, he was no longer in Phoenix. He was back in Fallujah.

Danny's eyes saw the smoking remains of Senator MacDougal's truck even while his mind wondered why the Senator was in Iraq. From the wreckage, it looked like the blast originated from somewhere near the Suburban's front passengers' side. Delta One, whose name Wakefield never knew, sat slumped and smoldering in the driver's seat. One of the men from the fire team had his gun out as he scanned the surrounding area in each direction, this way then that, for any new threats. A couple of paces away from the rear driver's side wheel Sandra Elbee knelt on the ground. The massive hulk of a Bywater Security operator was stretched out at her feet.

"I could use a hand here!" Sandra called. A pair of gorillas, freshly arrived, rushed to her aid. Danny saw that Sandra was pushing down hard on the operator's left femoral pressure point with her own left knee while her right hand was buried up to the last knuckle in a tear in the left side of the large man's neck. He recognized both actions as desperate bids to arrest major hemorrhages and prevent the bleeding patient from succumbing to hypovolemic shock.

Sirens sounded everywhere. Some of the PPD and PFD trucks were still blocks away. *Closer still,* Danny mused, than the Iraqi Police. *I wonder which one will arrive first…*

One of the Bywater operators dug a half-burnt, rugged plastic case with the remains of a giant red cross emblazoned upon it out of the back of the ruined Suburban and heaved it to the ground next to his buddy. He produced a tourniquet from within the trauma kit, slipped it up his fallen comrade's leg, and ratcheted it tight to cut off the blood flow better than Elbee's knee could. The other gorilla dropped to his knees on the opposite side of her, checked the undamaged side of his teammate's neck for a pulse, then called for another buddy and began counting chest compressions out loud. The third contractor assumed his position near the injured man's head and periodically breathed into his 'mates mouth to oxygenate his lungs. Nearby, one of the Bywater guys knelt to monitor Senators MacDougal and McQueen, who were stretched out on the pavement but in remarkably good shape for a pair of men who mere moments ago were on fire. The remaining operators stood back-to-back near what used to be the front of the Suburban, a few paces away, their guns ready to burn down anything other than an ambulance that might try to approach the scene.

There was nothing Danny could do to assist with the trauma care that his teammates already provided. So Corporal Wakefield stepped out of his flashback, and Special Agent Wakefield took up position with the contractors and maintained security on the scene until the medics arrived.

CHAPTER 25

"ALRIGHT," Nick Brown's deep voice commanded. "Let's go over it again. Just to make sure we're all on the same page here."

Danny ran the tip of his finger up and down the water bottle on the table before him. A cool bead of condensation gathered on his fingertip. He was no stranger to After Action Reports, but he did not like the fact that Nick sat in on this particular debriefing. Their personal conflicts aside, Wakefield was none too keen on the idea of having the split-second decisions he and Elbee made on the scene and during a crisis questioned by some Monday morning quarterback. His position within the Department's chain-of-command notwithstanding, when it came to managing a tactical level, heat of the moment crisis, Danny put no stock in the opinion of a fifty-year-old drunken adolescent whose own definition of 'combat' included riding in a submarine while it played hide-and-go-seek with the Russian Navy. But Wakefield held his tongue, blew out his breath, sat back in his chair and accepted his fate. At least for the temporary and foreseeable future, the DHS HQ Analysis Division's SCIF conference room was his home.

Whether she sensed her partner's frustration or simply assumed responsibility as the Special Agent in Charge on the scene during the incident, Elbee leaned forward, backed her slides up to the beginning for what felt like the hundredth time, and reiterated her account of the day's carnage. As he had for the entirety of the debriefing session up to this point, Danny stayed his tongue. Whatever Elbee said was the way things were. If her story was that the Constitutional Killer had ridden down the street on the back of a pink elephant, he would keep his mouth shut and nod. If compelled to offer his own testimony then Danny could offer the opinion that it might have been an Indian elephant, but that he was certainly no expert. This was one of those moments when partners needed to show solidarity.

"Forensic analysis of the site combined with analysis of the statements from multiple PPD witnesses present during the incident indicates that the device Officer Michaels reported as a dummy IED was, in fact, paired with an actual bomb, which we assess was detonated remotely."

"What kind of remote?" Brown asked. "Radio? Cell phone? Command wire?"

"Those details are still forthcoming," Elbee answered, "but are also immaterial within the context of this AAR. Of course, once we find out more, we'll provide updated reporting and chase down any leads."

"So, you discounted the threat from the pressure cooker when you thought it was a dummy device," Nick charged.

"No," she corrected. "Special Agent Wakefield ordered caution. Unfortunately, Officer Michaels felt compelled to disregard that order. To his own demise, I'm afraid." Michaels was the one on the radio that Wakefield had known only as 2A-32. He was the officer who - bravely or foolishly, depending upon one's perspective - discovered the IED. Fortunately for everyone else on the scene, he was also the only one within its blast radius when the device exploded. The police officer had been the day's first casualty, but far from its last. "At this time, it appears that there was a functioning device somewhere near the fake IED. That's what killed Officer Michaels. And by the time it blew we were well into exfiltrating both senators," Elbee resumed. "All according to the pre-agreed operational plan." She clicked a remote which advanced her slide on the main screen as she continued. "The group split into two fire teams, again according to plan, and moved each of the principals to their respective vehicles. Which were - as planned - waiting at an area that was preselected for its balance of safe distance versus proximity for convenience. My team was in the process of loading Senator MacDougal when our vehicle was caught in the blast of a second IED. Forensics technicians indicate the device was placed inside the wheel well of the nearest car. The driver checks out clean. Little old lady. No priors."

Jonas thumbed his oversized pipe. "And that's when you pushed MacDougal to the other vehicle."

"Yes, sir," Elbee did not flinch, but Wakefield knew from his own personal experience that the memory of the microsecond in which that bomb exploded played itself over and over again in her mind. "Davidson was killed instantly by the blast. As team leader, he was getting into the front seat. So, he was the closest. Wade, the guy to my right, was struck by debris. I rendered first aid as best as I could. Johnson stayed behind to cover me."

Wiley stabbed the pipe's bit straight at her chest. "Your actions on target saved that guy's life, Elbee. Make no mistake about that."

"I did what I could," she shrugged, "but the credit really goes to the guys who helped me after Wakefield got the rest of the team back to my position."

"Before we get to that," Nick interjected, "let's talk about the part where Special Agent Wakefield loaded the principals - a pair of senior US senators - into a vehicle driven by a serial killer." He stabbed his fat finger at his subordinate in accusation. "The very same serial killer that you were supposed to be chasing. 'Cause that's a pretty big turd to swallow."

Danny's face grew red. "You'd think that maybe one of the Bywater guys would've noticed that their own driver had mysteriously changed into a dude who wasn't on their team," he protested.

"We didn't find the real Delta Two - Avery Winters - until a PPD officer found his body under an enclosed stairwell during the after-action sweep of the garage," Sandra countered.

The SCIF conference room's fifth occupant, a muscular man in his mid-thirties, cleared his throat. "In all fairness to your agents, sir, Davidson never brought either of our drivers to the Op Brief. So, neither of them had ever seen Winters before. And when I saw the picture that Special Agent Elbee showed me-"

"That would be the picture of the guy who eluded Wakefield after he shot two PPD officers?" Nick insisted.

Sandra clicked her remote a few times to cue up an image not contained within her original slides. The conference room's main screen showed a single, frozen frame. "Indeed. We pulled this from one of the Convention Center's security cameras. The guy's moving around a bit, so it's a little blurry. Combined with the street camera's fairly low resolution, it's hard to get a clear picture of the suspect's face. Nonetheless, if we roll the video," Sandra matched her words to action with a click of her mouse, "we can see how he overpowered both officers and, utilizing a significant head start, ducked into a crowd of locals. PPD were unable to re-establish contact with him because of the mob. Officers don't know for sure what exactly those protesters were doing before the incident, but as soon as the uniforms showed up things got pretty heated. PPD had to back off in order to prevent further escalation."

"So, the beat cop probably figured this mope was some guy who was just freaking out on the scene during the attack," Nick paraphrased.

Elbee nodded. "Just like anyone easily would."

"And that assumption nearly got him, and his partner killed." Wiley announced.

"Both shots penetrated his vest," Elbee nodded. "But at that range, that's no surprise, really. He suffered a collapsed lung, but the doctors were able to fix it. They say he'll pull through. Corporal

Sappington's vest stopped both rounds that were fired at him," she added. "He's got a few cracked ribs, but he's already back on his feet."

"That's not all," the Bywater representative pointed at the assailant's picture on the big screen. "Look at him. I mean, just look at the guy. Compare him to the poor, fat cops who're getting their asses handed to them. He's not huge, but he's lean. Cut."

"Athletic build," Elbee nodded. "Really athletic, too. Not just 'not fat'…"

Wakefield squinted at the image as though he could improve its clarity by sheer force of will. "What're you thinking Tom? Ranger?"

"He's about that size," the contractor nodded. "Most of the Team guys are pretty stacked." Danny figured he would have to explain to his partner later that 'Team Guys' was military slang for Navy SEALs. "Especially the East Coast guys," Tom continued. "I mean, snipers are usually smaller… but yeah, I could see him in the 75th. And, not to speak ill of the dead, but in the heat of the moment I can kinda see why if Rick wasn't paying attention this guy might be able to pass for Avery. At least for a minute or two."

Nobody in the room dared label the fallen former SEAL - Rick Travis, Spartan Zero Five - who could not tell one black man from another, as a racist. Nobody felt inclined to attack the character of a man who was not alive to defend himself. No one dared utter the phrase a lot of black guys look the same. The statement was crude and racially charged. Also, given the grave circumstances nobody was in a particularly humorous mood. But the fact remained that under stress, people's perceptions became skewed, and the human mind had a habit - sometimes terrible, sometimes helpful - of filling in visual blanks with memories and assumptions. Especially during times of heightened stress. That was why five different witnesses to the same crime could provide five different accounts of the event. And that was how an experienced, well-paid, highly trained operator could, in the heat of an emergency, jump into a vehicle and assume its driver was someone other than who he actually was.

"Sir," Wakefield continued, "this pretty much cinches it as Phillips." He punched a key and showed side-by-side pictures of the beefy black man from the Phoenix attack and Master Sergeant Phillips' service photo. "I'll admit I didn't get as close to him as I wanted…"

"Who's this guy?" Nick demanded. "Why are we just now finding out about him?"

"*We* aren't," Jonas corrected his deputy. "*You* are." He returned his attention to Danny. "There's no shame in losing a footrace to a Ranger son," Wily offered. "And I gotta tell you Danny Boy, that if you - a white fed - chased an African American male suspect into a crowd of Black Lives Matter protesters," the older man's face twisted and skewed, "we'd've been scraping pieces of you up off the street." Danny would not have offered such a plea as his own defense. But he was not about to turn down a lifeline, either. Especially when such an out was being offered by one of the people with whose very ire he was trying desperately to avoid today.

"You can try to put lipstick on this pig all you want," Nick the Dick maintained, "but at the end of the day the fact remains that Wakefield handed a killer his intended targets and watched as they drove away.

Then he let the killer escape."

"Thanks, Nick," Danny spat, "I forgot that part."

"Gentlemen," Dr. Wiley held a cautionary hand up to cool tempers around the room. "I think that's just about the worst interpretation of the events as they played out."

"It's what the press is already starting to say," Nick pointed. "And they're only gonna get uglier."

Dr. Wiley gave Nick a look that Danny's real father always called *'the hairy eyeball.'* "Then it's our responsibility to correct that narrative. Because it's a gigantic disservice to the men and women on the ground." He drove his finger into the briefing table. "And it's damned disrespectful to the fallen heroes."

Nick backed down, but only a little. "It's still a pretty big screw up Wakefield. You can't seriously expect us to just overlook that fact."

Sandra glared daggers at her partner's intermediate supervisor. She still had not resolved the issue from earlier where Nick the Dick seemed to have taken it upon himself to start making decisions about how her case was handled. And now he sat at the head of the table like he was in charge of events in which he had no hand. "We're also not overlooking the fact that it was Wakefield who caught everyone's mistake. And who recovered the senators. And who facilitated lifesaving medical care that they needed on the scene by ensuring a secure environment until back-up arrived. And gave the most successful pursuit of the suspect on scene that day - even when compared with an entire squad of police officers with vehicles and radios to coordinate their efforts. Without Wakefield's quick thinking we'd have two more bodies in the morgue. Instead, we have two

Senators who walked out of the burn ward at Johns Hopkins with relatively minor injuries. And - might I add - a sense of gratitude toward this Task Force for all that we did to save them."

"As congressmen," Dr. Wiley quipped, "you can bet that they're getting the very best of medical care available. Good thing they don't have to slum it in the civilian healthcare system with the plebes." Bemused by his own dark humor, Father chewed on his pipe for a long moment.

"They wouldn't've needed medical attention in the first place if anyone had taken even a moment to confirm the driver was, in fact, one of the Bywater guys." Nick seemed like a dog with a bone. He just did not seem to be willing let go of this opportunity to tear into his least favorite lackey.

Danny held his jaw firmly in place. Blood rushed into his ears, filled his head with a ringing sound. His left hand unconsciously clenched into a fist at Nick's goading words. But it was not his own voice that responded to Nick's latest criticism.

"I really don't think," Tom Franklin bristled, "that you're the least bit qualified to question how me and my boys do our jobs."

Danny noted that the Bywater leader's retort did not include the customary courtesy of so much as a *with all due respect.* His own response leapt to mind as well, but no matter what he wanted to do, what he wanted to say, it would only add fuel to an existing fire. And Wakefield really did not need the extra heat. Nick's personal beef with him had worked its way into yet another workplace matter, just as the agent had predicted it would. He and his partner had already agreed that the best course of action was to just let her handle the debriefing. He and Sandra had gone over the events dozens of times in the last two days. And it was her case. *Just let Elbee handle this one*, he told himself as he took a calming breath. *And if Franklin wants to draw some fire too, so be it.*

"Let's not lose focus here," Wiley cut in. "This is a debriefing and After Action Report, not a disciplinary review," he cast a sideways glance at Nick, "which, frankly, I see no need for." He let his unspoken order, *drop it*, hang in the air for a heartbeat. "Sorry, Special Agent Elbee. Please continue."

"Thank you, sir." Sandra cued up another slide. "FBI forensics techs were able to recover the slugs that killed Mr. Travis." The screen displayed a pair of twisted blobs. "They didn't show up on x-ray, but an examination of the wound cavities revealed a pair of synthetic globs. Funny Putty, to be exact. The medical examiner was able to detect it during a physical examination of the wound cavity because it burns differently than flesh. There are eccentric types of shotgun ammunition that specifically use this kind of material. Back at the FBI forensics lab in New Orleans, Hudson recreated the scenario and found the putty ripped through plate armor like it wasn't even there."

"That'll be why his vest failed," Tom chimed in. "The armor we wear should normally be able to take a round or two from a twelve-gauge, even at close range."

Danny's face and body betrayed nothing. He could have been a cast statue for all the others could tell. But inwardly he could not help but begrudgingly admire the Constitutional Killer just a bit. His passion. His commitment to a cause with which many people

- Danny included - could emotionally identify. The way he chose his targets. The tactics and hardware he used. *He's got style, but the bastard's still going down.*

"As for the senators themselves," Elbee continued, "our team found glass fragments in the floorboards which - combined with the burn damage - indicates that after he shot Travis, the killer tossed a Molotov cocktail into the back of the truck and walked away."

Nick shook his head and wiped his face in disgust. "Can't imagine a worse way to go than be burned to death."

"Maybe," Sandra offered, "but it's also not a very efficient way to kill somebody. Given our killer's previous history of using utterly ruthless and brutally efficient tactics, I'd say that this was about more than just killing the senators. He was also trying to make a statement."

"There's no chance in hell of tracing a Molotov back to its maker," Jonas pointed out as he scraped out his pipe's cup.

"That is correct, sir," Elbee picked up, "But we were able to trace the conventional ordinance back to a demolition company in Utah. One that employs a guy close enough to our profile that if he isn't the Constitutional Killer, it's likely he has a deep personal connection with him. At the bare minimum, he most likely supplied the ordinance that was used in this attack. So at least he knows our guy. He can confirm whether it's Phillips or somebody else. Might also be able to provide us with more actionable intelligence."

"I assume we're picking this demo tech up?" Father asked.

Sandra glanced up at the clock. "FBI Direct

Action teams in Utah are striking three suspected bed down locations right now. Nick intercepted us on our way to the watch floor so that we could conduct Command and Control from there during the operation. He escorted us here for this meeting instead. At this point, I assume the op has been executed. Of course, we'd like to get back to it as soon as possible. Sir."

Dr. Wiley rapped his pipe on the table as if trying to dislodge some unseen debris. "Alright. I think we're done with you, Mr. Franklin. Thank you for your time." The Bywater contractor nodded, stood, and left the conference room. Special Agent Carrie Jenkins met him at the conference room door with blouse straining at its buttons and an accommodating smile on her face. She quickly made small talk with the pipe hitter as she escorted him out of the SCIF. Once he was sure the civilian was out of earshot, Jonas continued. "Now, just to put all of our cards on the table: Yesterday I reviewed the operational plan you put together before the event. I don't know how much of it was your brainchild and how much of it came from those Bywater guys, but between the bunch of you I can't see any internal flaws in the plan itself. Based on what I'm hearing from you two and the other reports, it sounds like you stuck to a good plan as best as you could and improvised when appropriate. And though you're no doubt gonna take some heat for anything and everything that happened that day, when things got really squirrelly, I think you made all of the right decisions. The threat assessment - which you Nick, didn't totally buy; so, don't pretend to sit in informed judgment now - was spot on. You guys did everything you could in the field and at the end of the day you saved those two senators from a determined, prepared, trained killer despite everything that was working against you. So long as the doctors do their part, we've got two living senators instead of two more dead ones. I'll count that as a small win for our side."

One of the knots between Danny's shoulder blades loosened just a little bit. Then Nick spoke again. "Can somebody please explain to me why we don't just act on the intel from your NSA source?"

"Up to this point we couldn't," Danny rebuffed. "The info is forbidden fruit. It was gathered via a domestic surveillance program that is in direct violation of Intelligence Oversight directives. One operated by, among others, a contact of mine at Ft. Meade."

"Executive Order 12333, signed into effect by then-President Reagan," Sandra reminded them all, "clearly and explicitly forbids the use of American intelligence assets on US soil or against US persons. In the strictest interpretation, we can't even hear about this sort of stuff unless the proper authorities designate an individual as an enemy combatant. Our hands are tied by our own laws."

"It's the fruit of the poisoned tree," Dr. Wiley nodded in understanding. "Any evidence gathered from illegal, illicit, or unauthorized activity is completely inadmissible. *Ist verboten.* And so is any follow-on information gathered there from."

"You've gotta be friggin' kidding me," Nick grumbled. "Surely there are exceptions. Some sort of waiver or something."

"In America," Danny put a little starch in his voice, "people's civil rights are sovereign. At least, they're supposed to be. We don't just waive them because we find them inconvenient."

"What my partner means," Sandra interjected a little more coolly, "is that there is a mountain of legal precedents that would have to be overcome. At the Justice Department we see cases tossed out all of the time over just these sorts of technicalities. Sometimes even small ones. This isn't an esoteric guideline tucked into an obscure rulebook here. This doctrine is foundational to our entire system of jurisprudence. We could build an airtight case against this guy, but if it's based on some forbidden piece of NSA data that should never be fair game then we'll have spent a lot of time and resources just to watch our killer walk away free."

"That's true," Dr. Wiley conceded. "I've seen it before. But now that you've seen him directly -"

"- we have already issued an APB and BOLO," Elbee finished for him. "Someone, somewhere, is gonna see Phillips and call him in. It's just a matter of time now."

Danny cleared his throat. It was the first time he offered an unsolicited comment to his superiors all day. "We're also pursuing him via other means. Problem is, sir, that he's a ghost. This guy's a widower. Wife and kid ate it in an auto accident a little over a year ago. No ties to the immediate family. A couple of weeks after the funeral, he up and sells his house, liquidates almost everything, pays off his debts and drives off. Family never sees him. His Army pension and VA compensation are paid into an account in some distant relative's name, then automatically allotted and transferred to Phillips via money wire."

"I saw that in a movie once," Nick commented.

"Given that he's just become the chief suspect in a murder investigation, we've put together an official request to cut off Phillips' pension," Danny continued "A federal judge is reviewing it."

"You think you'll get him by squeezing his pocketbook," Father reiterated. "And since we're the Department of Treasury, defunding this guy is firmly in our mission set." The older man leaned back in his chair and brushed some invisible lint off his tweed jacket. "Good thinking. But that doesn't change the fact that we have a big mess on our hands. A domestic terrorist just ran a Batman gambit on you guys. The bodies are piling up too high to see over. The press is having a hay day with all of this. And the higher-ups are so far up my ass right now that when I scratch my own balls Director Dagenhart gets tickled in the ribs. I don't see the need to keep you any longer, so get back to work. And for God's sake, when I see you again, please tell me you have somebody in chains. Somebody significant. Anything else? No? Then good hunting."

*   *   *

By the time they finally reached the watch floor, Danny and Sandra were greeted by a wall of video monitors that showed teams of heavily armed, ill-tempered federal agents swarming around and through two residences and a small construction office in Utah. Screens around the perimeter were littered with talking heads as news anchors raced to break the story.

"Report," Elbee called as she strode up to her workstation at the watch floor commander's desk.

"Jackpot," Agent Stevenson, who sat in as her substitute, answered. "Agents have the suspect in custody and are en route to the detention facility. Teams are still conducting on-site exploitation of each of the scenes. Ordinance and demolition materials have been recovered from the commercial location and one of the residences, as well as firearms. Multiple personnel from all scenes have been temporarily detained for questioning."

"It's the bomb tech," Agent Martin amplified from the sideline. "None of the individuals on target match Phillips' description."

Sandra hissed as she bit back a curse.

"Us being here wouldn't've changed the outcome," Danny reminded her. "These are professionals. They'll do their jobs so that we can do ours."

"It's still a slap in the face," she replied, "getting pulled out of the command chair during my own operation." Back in control of her own investigation, Special Agent Elbee stood in silent stillness for a moment. Her eyes danced across the monitors on the wall and the screens on the desks around her as she took in as much information as possible as quickly as she could. And Wakefield stood right by her side the whole time. After a moment, she found her voice again. It was just a whisper, for her partner's ears only. "They're gonna take this case away from me. Aren't they, Daniel?"

"Not today," he assured her. "You got a big win, back in Phoenix. It doesn't feel like it now, but you did good. And today? Today, we moved the ball forward a little bit."

"I hate sports metaphors."

"It's a small victory." Danny turned away from the monitors and looked into Sandra's deep, blue eyes. "But the game continues. And you did something else, too. You stuck up for your partner. Thanks for that."

"That's what partners are for," Sandra turned back to the wall of data as it poured into the room. "What did Dr. Wiley mean by a *Batman gambit*?"

"It's a term from the world of games and strategy," Danny explained. "In the beginning, when you first learn something, you learn mechanics. We call them rules. Novices try to figure out how to work within those rules. Amateurs try to devise winning strategies. Adepts learn to recognize other players' strategies and counter them. Some more advanced players explore the outer limits of a system in order to come up with new schemes in the hopes that the idea's novelty might throw their opponent off track.

"But then there's the guys who are scary good at a game. Whether it's football, chess, wrestling, or warfare… It really doesn't matter. Those guys are able to anticipate their opponents' actions before an encounter. Then they devise a plan that actually encourages their adversary to do exactly what should help that other guy win the fight - but that adversary's own plan is actually part of the original player's ultimate strategy. He's the quarterback who wants to be blitzed because he's already got two linemen running full tilt toward his own position where the other team can't see them. The chess master who makes it look like his queen is vulnerable so that you create his hole when you strike at her and hand the other guy your king. The whole time you think you're winning you're actually playing his game for him. And when it works, you don't even know that you've killed yourself until the death blow falls.

"Our killer is more than just a guy who's pissed off at the government. There's plenty of those out there." Danny pointed to the watch floor's outer wall as if through a window that did not exist. "Hell, thanks to the last few weeks they're starting to take to the streets. You saw the reports this morning. There are copycats popping up all over the country. As good as the Constitutional Killer is, he's more than a motivated murderer. He knows our playbook. He's got it memorized. He knows how to exploit it. And he's going to continue to do so until we stop him."

EPILOGUE

"WE'VE ONLY GOT a couple of minutes before we have to take a break," Lonnie segued, "but I just wanna touch base on this real quick. I got a call from our legal team this morning just before the show started, and it turns out that the Department of Homeland Security has launched a criminal probe on this show alleging that we are somehow connected to the Constitutional Killer."

"Which totally makes sense," Factcheck Fred deadpanned, "if you look at things from their perspective. Which is with your head planted firmly up your own butt."

"At least from that point of view, the methane fumes give everything a lovely, greenish hue," Kyp offered.

"According to the feds," Lonnie continued, "and this is a direct quote from the affidavit submitted to the US Attorney's office, *'the cast and officers of the Lonnie Chase Program are suspected of lending aid and comfort to a domestic terrorist…'* End quote."

"Which, of course, is completely false," Factcheck Fred reminded the audience. "But that demonstrable fact will not stop certain federal agencies from raping us now."

"No, it won't."

"You know, that begs the question," Kyp surmised, "and I guess we'll have to discuss this after the break. But, if the feds are gonna treat innocent citizens like criminals without any demonstration of probable cause, what's to stop us from just acting like criminals?"

"If you're gonna get punched anyway then why not hit back?" Fred paraphrased.

"We'll talk about that more on the other side," Lonnie cut in. "But first, a word from our sponsor - which, this half-hour, is Goldstein Financial Group…"

The Patriot listened to the radio as he crossed the open road. Of course, the highway was mostly empty. It was mid-day on a Monday afternoon right after the Fourth of July weekend. Most people were at work. Most of the vehicles on the interstate were driven by working men delivering their goods to the people across this land who needed them. In a way, that made those truck drivers just like him.

The Patriot's long haul crossed from one broadcast area to the next and then another, but all of the voices on the radio carried the same conversation. Across state lines and time zones everyone in the nation seemed to be talking about the same thing. The speakers' accents might vary from time to time, but the talking points never changed.

According to a frequently repeated headline it looked like both of the senators from the other day's operation were going to pull through. A moment's thought brought the Patriot to the conclusion that whether his targets lived or died did not matter. The lesson was the same. The shock value of his actions and their effect on the country were unchanged either way. In other news, sympathizers around the nation had begun to voice their own displeasure with the conduct of their own representatives. A few other patriots had even started taking matters into their own hands too. People across America had started to rise up and tell their government that they would no longer tolerate gross incompetence from their so-called leaders. Just like him. The talking heads kept telling the story of a popular model breaking up with her athlete boyfriend, but the stations were still bombarded with calls and emails about anti-government protests which had started to crop up at a courthouse here and a federal building there. They network hype focused on America's sweetheart and her new movie, but it was hard to hide the fact that more and more demonstrators carried signs at the Washington Mall just outside of the Capitol building in D.C., while fewer and fewer lined up at the shopping mall box office for another recycled script. And all the networks went to great lengths to avoid talking about the wide scale referendum that a number of voters had started to demand.

The American people had started to wake up. The black man smiled as he recalled the old joke while he drove:

What do you call a dozen congressmen drowned at the bottom of the pool?

A good start. That's what.

A road sign indicated a rest stop ahead. There was still more than a hundred miles of highway between the Patriot and St. Louis. He decided to pull in for a short rest. There was still much work to be done, but perhaps by morning there would be more soldiers to help him carry the fight.

NOTES

"Ambien" is a registered trademark of Sanofi-Aventus. All rights reserved.

"Armani" is a registered trademark of Giorgio Armani S.p.A. All rights reserved.

"Batman" was created by Bob Kane and Bill Finger and is a registered trademark of D.C. Comics. All rights reserved.

"BMW," and "535i" are registered trademarks of Bayerische Motoren Werke AG. All rights reserved.

"Butterball" is a registered trademark of Butterball LLC, a subsidiary of Seaboard Corporation. All rights reserved.

"Chevy," "Cherolet," "Camero," and "Suburban" are registered trademarks of General Motors Company. All rights reserved.

"Fender" and "Stratocaster" are registered trademarks of Fender Musical Instruments Corporation. All rights reserved.

"Ford," "Focus," and "Mustang" are registered trademarks of the Ford Motor Company. All rights reserved.

"Glock" and "Glock 17" are registered trademarks of Glock Ges.m.b.H. All rights reserved.

"Gucci" is a registered trademark of Gucci Group, a subsidiary of Kering. All rights reserved.

"Gulfstream" and "G280" are registered trademarks of Gulfstream Aerospace Corporation. All rights reserved.

"Jag" is a registered trademark of Jaguar Land Rover, a subsidiary of Tata Motors. All rights reserved.

"Jeep," and "Rubicon" are registered trademarks of FCA US LLC, a wholly owned subsidiary of Fiat Chrysler Automobiles. All rights reserved.

"iPhone" is a registered trademark of Apple, Inc. All rights reserved.

"Jameson" is a registered trademark of John Jameson & Son Limited, a subsidiary of Penrod Ricard. All rights reserved.

"Kel-Tec," are registered trademarks of Kel-Tec CNC Industries Incorporated. All rights reserved.

"Mazda" and "Mazda 6" are registered trademarks of Mazda Motor Corporation. All rights reserved.

"McDonald's" is a registered trademark of McDonald's. All rights reserved.

"Mercedes" is a registered trademark of Mercedes-Benz, a division of Daimler AG. All rights reserved.

"Nissan" and "Leaf" are registered trademarks of Nissan Motor Company, Ltd. All rights reserved.

"Oreo" is a registered trademark of Nabisco, a division of Mondelēz International. All rights reserved.

"Prada" is a registered trademark of Prada S.p.A. All rights reserved.

"Sig," "Sig Sauer," "Sig Arms," and "P-230" are registered trademarks of Sig Sauer, a division of Swiss Arms. All rights reserved.

"Smith and Wesson," "Smith & Wesson," "S&W," "Model 686," "Model Ten," and "Model 10" are registered trademarks of Smith & Wesson. All rights reserved.

"Taurus" is a registered trademark of Forjas Taurus S.A. All rights reserved.

"Toyota," "Prius," and "Camry" are registered trademarks of Toyota Motor Corporation. All rights reserved.

RECOMMENDED PLAYLIST

I was raised as a musician. I find music in everything, and everything in music. It is my escape. It is my inspiration. And when my words fail me, it is my voice. The following songs capture the mood within some of the various scenes in this book. Think of them as a soundtrack to enhance your reading experience. They certainly helped me.

"Desire" - Meg Myers. *Make a Shadow.*
"Louisiana Bayou" - Dave Matthews Band. *Stand Up.*
"Ain't No Rest for the Wicked" - Cage the Elephant. *Cage the Elephant.*
"Queen Gorgo" - Junkie XL. *300: Rise of an Empire (Original Motion Picture Soundtrack.)*
"Only God Knows Why" - Kid Rock. *Devil Without a Cause.*
"Uprising" - Muse. *The Resistance.*
"Blue on Black" - Kenny Wayne Shepherd. *Trouble is…*
"45 (Acoustic Version)" - Shinedown. *Leave a Whisper.*
"Hater" - Korn. *Hater - Single.*
"Bourne Vivaldi" - The Piano Guys. *Bourne Vivaldi - Single.*
"Wolf Uprising" - Immediate Music. *Nu Epiq.*
"Getting Away with Murder" - Papa Roach. *Getting Away with Murder.*

- DEJS

ABOUT THE AUTHOR...

DARYL E.J. SIMMONS is a distinguished former naval intelligence analyst and decorated veteran whose career includes multiple combat deployments embedded with Special Operations elements. He has hunted terrorists and drug traffickers on five continents. Mr. Simmons is an esteemed expert on international relations. He has served as the policy advisor to American and Allied leaders on complex issues including global security, counterterrorism, counternarcotics, and counter-human trafficking.

A graduate of the University of Tulsa, Mr. Simmons serves as a trainer and consultant for various agencies and organizations. When he is not writing, he counsels with other vets and enjoys public speaking.

Mr. Simmons is a recognized and unapologetic Conservative thought leader. You can find his podcast, the Daily Dose of Daryl, through FortySix News Oklahoma, Red River TV, and Project 46 Media (ProjectFortySix.com) websites as well as the panoply of social media platforms.

And now, an excerpt from "Land of the Free," the action-packed sequel to "Oath Keeper" by Daryl E.J. Simmons. Coming soon!

It was always darkest just before the dawn. That was the old saying. *Whoever says that,* Danny thought, *clearly sleeps in.* The sun was still low, nestled under its covers on the eastern horizon, but pre-dawn light painted the West Virginia countryside in tones of muted bronze mixed with gray. Leaves rustled under leather and nylon boots as an FBI tactical team bounded through the broken tree cover and approached the old farmhouse from its blindspots.

Danny slipped out from behind an oak tree and shuffled as quietly as haste would allow. Blue jeans and a brown leather jacket worn over light body armor made him stand out from the tactical team's olive drab uniforms and heavy, black assault gear. As did his personal AR-15, splashed with bits of desert tan and drab green here and there, unlike the FBI team's department-issued, all-black guns. *Poor guys,* he had thought as they kitted up an hour ago, *can't even get their department to spring for suppressors.* He carried his tool at the low ready while the FBI pipe hitters covered his movement. He assumed the point position in the stack with his muzzle - capped with a can he found years ago at an online clearance sale - and signaled the fire team at his back to follow him.

The best intelligence on Earth reported that this old house in rural West Virginia was the last place Thomas Phillips, the Constitutional Killer, had been located. The information was barely a day old. Midway up the length of the house's longest exterior wall, Danny signaled breachers that he knew were prepositioned without so much as a glance.

A pair of operators - each one at least thirty pounds heavier than anyone else on the team and both as solid as brick walls - burst from their hiding spot. They hefted a massive battering ram between the two of them and made for the kitchen door at a dead run. At the last possible second, the feds swung their steel pipe and drove it through the wooden portal - now barely a foot in front of Danny. The cheap door put up about the same resistance as so much tissue paper. In a well-practiced maneuver, the breachers dropped their ram and fell bodily to the floor, drawing their guns on the way down. Wakefield, no stranger to kicking in doors, followed them in smoothly with his rifle shouldered. "DHS! Down! Down! *Down!*" he ordered the people he assumed were inside as his team made entry.

Danny cleared the door in a flash and bolted for the far side of the kitchen. *Penetrate and exploit,* his sergeants had taught him. He checked corners for threats as he moved, knowing that the man one step behind him would do the same. He just met these guys a few hours ago and could not remember all of their names to save his soul, but he knew that everyone on this team had his back and they knew he had theirs. That was all it took to be a part of the team this morning.

Something - or someone - upstairs fell to the floor with a hard thud. A woman's voice screamed. Danny held his shoulder tight against the wall and yelled "Set!" as the next man in the stack - *was it Collins?* - bounded past him with the rest of the stack. The breachers scrambled back to their feet and assumed control of the room. *Set,* he heard ProbablyCollins yell from the next choke point. That would be the end of the hall, if the floor plan they had for this place was at all right.

"Moving!" Danny bounded past an assaulter who held a firing position at some random doorway - *utility room, maybe?* - while that officer's battle buddy cleared whatever was on the other side. He grabbed JustGonnaCallHimCollins' shoulder hard to let him know he was ready just as FBI officer keyed his radio and ordered the second element of the assault team to breach the door on the far side of the room into which he was already looking.

Wakefield learned a long time ago - and not too long after joining the Corps - that only idiots and fools breached a building from its main entrance. *The direct route is always mined,* his NCO's had taught him. People had a habit of watching their front doors, of preparing to greet folks - or resist the uninvited - there. They also had a habit of running out the back when they spotted trouble. Hence, Danny's long-standing preference for coming in exactly where the bad guys would likely try to come out.

The second fire team's entrance ripped the front door out of its jamb. If the splintered chunks of debris flying through the air were any indication, the door was apparently designed to open outward, but the FBI's insistence was stronger than wood. In the time it took for the door, hinges, and parts of the casing to fall into separate piles, Danny prayed that the second unit would remember his instructions to not throw a flash bang into the room before entry. Four more olive-and-black figures rushed in with guns drawn and took up firing positions within the living room and staircase. They barely stopped moving when somebody called out *Set!*

Definitely Collins yelled "Stairs! Moving!" and bolted up to the second floor. That was where the bedrooms were supposed to be. Danny held onto the back of the assaulter's armor carrier and stayed barely a half step behind him, watching their six. "Door left!" You're Collins Now turned so hard to port at the top of the stairs that he practically doubled back on himself. His maneuver forced Danny to spin back into the point position and sweep the rest of the hall for threats. Collins braced himself at the ready position next to the thin wooden railing with his M4 carbine - the assault rifle cousin of Wakefield's civilian rifle - trained on the door.

"Set!" Danny yelled. A third fire team washed up the stairs and flooded down the hallway in front of him. *Ready,* somebody called from behind a face shield. *They've got the hallway,* Danny confirmed. Danny spun around, lined his rifle up with Collins', and squeezed the assaulter's shoulder again. A microsecond later, a black boot kicked the white door open and the duet charged into the bedroom. "DHS! Hands in the air!"

Backlit by the window, it was hard to tell in the dimly lit bedroom whether the man who stood before them was brown skinned, black, or white. He could have been nineteen. Or ninety. The 12-gauge shotgun held across his hip and pointed at the officers eliminated any time they might have had to ask him any personal questions. Adrenaline dilated Danny's perception of time as the shotgun erupted with thunder and knocked Collins backwards. He fell hard into Danny, who watched the FBI agent's muzzle fall downward at an impossibly slow pace that violated the norms of gravity. But the forces of psychology and the laws of physics are bitter rivals, and when reality snapped back, it did so by answering the surreal slow motion with a moment of time-lapse where everything sped by at an accelerated rate.

When Danny's temporal equilibrium was restored, the shotgun was on the carpet. The backlit suspect was falling from his knees the rest of the way to the floor. The window that had been behind the suspect was marked with two telltale spiderwebs from bullets that exited the shooter and passed through the glass. Danny's right index finger still pressed his custom trigger to the rear. His left hand held fast to the carry handle built into the back of Collins' vest and bore his wingman's dead weight.

Not again, Wakefield prayed as he fought to control himself, his rifle, and his teammate's body. *Please, God. Not again…*

Made in the USA
Monee, IL
19 March 2023

29771067R00215